LOOI
WIN

MW00986269

**A steamy jungle, an ancient curse, a deadly secret—
one big sweaty mess!**

**From the award-winning author of the Deadwood
Mystery Series comes *Look What the Wind Blew In*, the
first book in the Dig Site Mystery series.**

"Intelligent and witty characters, a baby javelina, and an exotic
mystery set in an archeology dig among Maya ruins—don't
miss this entertaining adventure!"
~**Pamela Beason**, Author of the Summer Westin Mysteries
& the Neema Mysteries

"Ann Charles delivers yet another action-packed, page-
turning adventure filled with mystery, romance, and quirky
characters that will leave you on the edge of your seat! If you
are a fan of the Deadwood Mystery Series you'll love *Look
What The Wind Blew In*!"
~**Joleen James**, Author of *Cowboy, I'm Yours*

"Ann Charles' talent, wit, and the pure pleasure of her voice
earn her a place among the master storytellers. The pages of
Look What the Wind Blew In couldn't turn fast enough."
~**Gerri Russell**, Bestselling Author of *Flirting with Felicity*

"Non-stop action ... steamy and entertaining mystery with
ancient curses, deadly secrets, and heated passion."
~**Chanticleer Book Reviews**

Also by Ann Charles

Deadwood Mystery Series
Nearly Departed in Deadwood (Book 1)
Optical Delusions in Deadwood (Book 2)
Dead Case in Deadwood (Book 3)
Better Off Dead in Deadwood (Book 4)
An Ex to Grind in Deadwood (Book 5)

Short Stories from the Deadwood Mystery Series
Deadwood Shorts: Seeing Trouble
Deadwood Shorts: Boot Points

Jackrabbit Junction Mystery Series
Dance of the Winnebagos (Book 1)
Jackrabbit Junction Jitters (Book 2)
The Great Jackalope Stampede (Book 3)

Goldwash Mystery Series (a future series)
The Old Man's Back in Town (Short Story)

Coming Next from Ann Charles

Deadwood Mystery Series
Meanwhile, Back in Deadwood (Book 6)

Jackrabbit Junction Mystery Series
The Rowdy Coyote Rumble (Book 4)

Dear Reader,

A long, long time ago in a college far, far away, I took a class called History of Mexico. My major was Spanish and I was fascinated with all things south of the United States border—language, art, food, and culture to name a few. Oh, and margaritas, iced or blended, I wasn't picky. But I digress … in that history class, I learned about the Maya. I read about their famous cities, such as Tulum and Chichen Itza, and I viewed artists' renditions of their grandeur-filled past as well as current day photographs. I soaked up stories about what their lives may have been like, the day-to-day challenges, the rituals, the architecture, and the sacrifices.

During that class I met Dr. Angélica García, the heroine in *Look What the Wind Blew In*. I was looking out the window at the blowing snow, wondering what it would be like to be an archaeologist at one of those amazing sites.

From the moment Angélica stepped into my daydreams, she was giving orders to her crew and searching through Maya ruins, determined to find key pieces of history. One hundred percent alpha-female, she needed someone to show her softer side—hence, her father, Dr. Juan García, joined her in my thoughts. Next came the need for a hero who'd give her a run for her money, an outsider she couldn't control. A photojournalist maybe, working for a renowned magazine, going by the name of Wayne.

Thus, *Look What the Wind Blew In* was born.

I wrote the first draft while I was in my twenties. It was the second book I'd written at the start of my career. Needless to say, I was still learning how to write a good book (and still am) and it showed in that first draft. My critique partners would agree, because they hated my hero, Wayne.

It's never good when your readers cringe at the sound of your hero's name.

I set this story aside and wrote another book, improving my skills. Then I returned to Angélica's story, excited to try once again to bring her story to life. When I started this second version, my critique partners made me promise to shove Wayne into a closet in my brain and throw away the key. So, Wayne went away, and Quint Parker showed up for hero auditions. He won the role hands down, and I rewrote the story. This next draft was nominated as a finalist in the Romance Writers of America Golden Heart national contest, but it didn't win with the final judges nor several of the literary agents to whom I submitted it after the contest. The time was not right for Angélica and Quint's story … not yet.

Putting the book aside to be fine-tuned again after I'd honed my skills some more, I wrote *Dance of the Winnebagos* and *Jackrabbit Junction Jitters*. Then I returned to Angélica, took another swipe at this story, and sent it off to the agent I'd signed with in the meantime. It fell through the cracks somehow, temporarily forgotten as I wrote *Nearly Departed in Deadwood* and launched my publishing career with the Deadwood Mystery Series starring Violet Parker, Quint's younger sister.

Now, many MANY moons after I sat in that classroom looking out at the snow, it's time to share this story with you. I have spent several months working on it, revising yet again. Finally, I feel like it's the story I have always dreamed about, full of mystery, adventure, humor, suspense, and romance with just a sprinkle of paranormal.

And so, I present to you the first book in a new Dig Site Mystery series: *Look What the Wind Blew In*. Hold onto your Panama hat, because we're venturing deep into the Yucatán jungle for some fun … and murder.

Ann Charles

www.anncharles.com

For Jacquie Rogers, Wendy Delaney, Sherry Walker, the best Just-This-Side-of-Deranged critique group a girl could have. Fourth time is a charm, right?

For Kathy Thomas and all of those long walks when we talked about what would happen next to Angélica and Rover.

For "Wayne Coleman" who never made it past the first draft and whose name I've been banned from ever using again as a hero in a book.

Acknowledgements

I could write a book the size of *War and Peace* full of Acknowledgements alone. However, to save your eyesight, I'll try to keep it a little shorter.

A big, wet-nosed sloppy Thank You to all of the following brilliant people:

My critique partners, first-draft and second-draft readers, second-tier editors, and all of you kick-ass beta readers. Without you, I'd have scrambled eggs all over my face.

My husband, kids, and ornery cat, who each take turns giving me hugs, kisses, purrs, and Coke Slurpees when I'm worried about a transition scene, a publishing deadline, or a herd of javelinas in my yard.

Mimi "The Grammar Chick" (my editor), and Marguerite Phipps (consulting editor), who use their magic wands to turn my story pumpkins into beautiful sparkling carriages.

My older brother, C.S. Kunkle (cover artist and illustrator) for sharing his talent and letting me watch *Humanoids from the Deep* when I was way too young; and his wife, Stephanie, for helping to pick out illustrations and drinking way too much Whiskey Slush with me.

The band Queen for their seven-minute-long version of "Somebody to Love."

Sharon Benton (cover graphic artist) for loving wine, an essential component in our working relationship—ha!

Wendy Gildersleeve for helping me shoot for the moon and laughing with me when I fall on my ass in the process.

My superstar, on-the-ground publicists and promoters— my mom and brother (Margo Taylor and Dave Taylor), my aunt (Judy Routt), and my sister (Laura Rensberger). I'm so lucky you're related to me and have to be nice to me!

Jim McKay (played by Gregory Peck) for riding Ol' Thunder in *The Big Country*.

Diane Garland for her amazing spreadsheets and

strawberry flavored Kit Kats from the Far East.

Jacquie Rogers, Wendy Delaney, Amber Scott, Gerri Russell, and Joleen James for agreeing to be buried with me in my Egyptian tomb when I die so my trusted fellow scribes are with me in the next life.

My family and friends who have finally accepted that they're stuck with me. Period.

My online friends (Facebook, Twitter, Instagram, Pinterest, and more) who publicly support my bouts of insomnia-induced schizophrenia.

My fellow Purple Door Saloon buddies on Facebook, where everybody knows my name and curses it regularly.

My brother, Clint Taylor, for blowing through all of his money on video games during an Iowa bus stop. Clint, you still owe me for sharing my French fries in Chicago!

Look What the Wind Blew In

Copyright © 2015 by Ann Charles

All rights reserved. Except as permitted under the U.S. Copyright Act of 1976, no part of this publication may be reproduced, distributed, or transmitted in any form or by any means now known or hereafter invented, or stored in a database or retrieval system, without the prior written permission of the author, Ann Charles.

This book is a work of fiction. Names, characters, places, and incidents are the product of the author's imagination or are used fictitiously. Any resemblance to actual persons, living or dead, business establishments, events, or locales is coincidental.

Cover Art by C.S. Kunkle (www.charlesskunkle.com)
Cover Design by Sharon Benton (www.q42designs.com)
Editing by the "Grammar Chick" (www.grammarchick.com)
Formatting by Biddles ebooks

Print ISBN-13: 978-1-940364-23-0
E-book ISBN-13: 978-1-940364-22-3

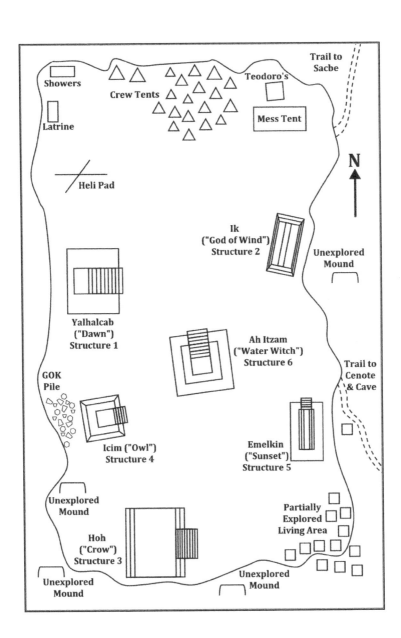

LOOK WHAT THE WIND BLEW IN

ANN CHARLES

ILLUSTRATED BY C.S. KUNKLE

North Richland Hills Public Library

Author's Note

The following is what I chose to follow for this book:

The adjective "Mayan" is used in reference to the language or languages; "Maya" is used as a noun or adjective when referring to people, places, culture, etc., whether singular or plural.

(Source: http://archaeology.about.com/od/mameterms/a/Maya-or-Mayan.htm)

To learn more about some of the words at the beginning of each chapter, I recommend browsing the internet. There are so many wonderful Maya resources out there to explore.

Chapter One

Mal Viento: An evil wind that can cause sickness or death.

I t's a curse."

Angélica García frowned at her father over the beam of her flashlight, wondering if the heat had fried his brain. "It's not a curse, Dad."

"Go over it again, *gatita*. And this time, use plain, old English." Juan García reached out and gently tweaked the tip of her nose. "Not all of us speak Mayan in our sleep."

Angélica wiped away the sweat trailing down her cheek. She tilted the flashlight beam slightly away from the temple wall, grazing the surface so the shadows added depth to the blocks of Maya glyphs.

She pointed at the first set. "This shows *Yum Cimil*, the Lord of Death. It says he rode in on the wind with a traveler." She moved to the next. "Here, the king is performing a sacrificial ceremony, offering his blood for the lives of his people. And in this one, *Yum Cimil* has turned his back on the king's sacrifice and is devouring the village."

"What about that last set?" Juan asked.

"It shows the Lord of Death crouching inside a temple. It

says he 'waits.'"

"Waits for what?"

"It doesn't show."

"Sounds like a curse to me."

Angélica aimed the flashlight at her father.

He stared back at her, all traces of his usual grin absent. His silver-haired sideburns glistened with sweat.

She shook her head. He couldn't be serious. "You're losing it." She pointed the beam back at the first glyph set. "Look here. The Lord of Death rode in on the wind with the traveler. That means the proof we need is at this site. I just have to find it." She skimmed her fingers over the warm chiseled stone and smiled at him. "I knew Mom was right."

"I still think it's a curse," he said, mopping his brow with a handkerchief. "You shouldn't have read it aloud."

She growled in her throat. After almost four decades of digging in tombs and temples throughout the Yucatán Peninsula, northern Guatemala, and Belize, how could he still believe in curses? "Be serious, Dad. That Lord of Death Waiting glyph is just the Maya equivalent of a ghost story."

He lifted his eyebrows. "What makes you so certain it's not a curse?"

Angélica scrubbed her hand down her face. She couldn't believe they were even having this discussion.

"Listen, child," Juan started.

"I'm almost thirty-five now, Dad."

"Maybe so, but I've been on this earth—in temples just like this one—a lot longer than you have. It's time you …"

She crossed her arms over her chest, bracing herself for the usual I'm-your-father speech.

He paused, glancing down at her arms then back up into her face. "And now you're giving me *that* look," he snorted. "I don't know why I try to tell you anything. You never listen anyway. One of these days you're going to learn that I'm almost always right."

"*Almost* being the key word there." Her grin took the sting out of her words.

Juan chuckled, patting her on the head. "You're getting more and more like your mother every day."

Tilting her head, she batted her eyelashes several times. "You mean intelligent and beautiful?"

"Mouthy and obstinate." He pointed at the carvings on the wall. "Whether you like it or not, this curse could mean trouble."

Angélica heard a nervous-sounding groan from the shadows behind her father. She shined the flashlight over Juan's shoulder into the wide eyes of Esteban, a nineteen-year-old Maya boy from a nearby village who had worked for her off and on over the last few years. He must have finished recording the artifacts in the other chamber and slipped into the room without her hearing him.

"Shit," she said under her breath. The last thing she needed right now were rumors spreading through camp that an ancient curse had come back to life. She turned back to Juan. "Dad, it's not a curse." Clearing her throat, she glanced pointedly toward her Maya crewmember. "It's merely an artist showing a grim vision of the future."

"Call it what it is, *gatita*. It's a curse warning whoever sees it that death is waiting for its next meal," Juan argued.

Esteban visibly shivered. "Are we its next meal?"

This was going from not good to really, really bad in seconds. "Can we talk about this back in my tent? *Alone?*"

Juan stared at the glyphs and rubbed the back of his neck. "If only Marianne were here."

"If Mom were here, she'd say you always were more superstitious than logical." Angélica grabbed her father's arm. It was going to take physical persuasion to get him to leave the temple.

She herded Juan and Esteban back toward the exit, a hole in the wall just big enough for them to squeeze through. "I may not be able to interpret glyphs as well as Mom could, but I can decipher the gist of what they're showing. I'm positive this is not a curse." She stared into Esteban's eyes as she delivered that last line.

"How can you be so certain? You know as well as I do that odd things happen when you're rooting around in the past." Juan grunted as he lowered onto the hard-packed dirt floor and eased headfirst through the hole.

Esteban slid through next. After his feet disappeared from view, Angélica squatted and peered through the hole. "Tell me," she coughed on some temple dust, "how can a piece of rock over a thousand years old contain a force released simply by verbalizing the hieroglyphic inscription chiseled there by a human?"

Without waiting for an answer, she snaked through the hole. Esteban lent her a hand on the other side.

Juan took the flashlight from her as she brushed the dust off her tank top and khaki pants. He led them through a narrow passageway. "Maybe I am too superstitious for my own good." He looked back at Angélica. "But bad things have happened at this site." His tone sounded ominous.

Resisting the urge to roll her eyes, she stole the flashlight out of her father's hand and walked past him. It wasn't the time, let alone the place, for this argument.

Angélica reached the ladder and climbed to the main level. Juan followed, and then Esteban.

After he stepped off the ladder, Esteban's gaze darted around the pitch-black corners of the room. "What bad things, Dr. García?" the boy asked, his voice a whisper.

She shot her dad a now-look-what-you've-done glare.

Juan shrugged. "Several things, actually."

"Please, Dad. Don't start with that whole 'something stole my maps of the Temple of the Water Witch, filled my notebooks with gibberish scrawls, and left a sacrificed wild turkey outside of my tent' crap again."

Juan took the flashlight back from her. "Well, Miss Skeptic, all of that did happen." He started down the passage that would lead them outside. "But I'm not talking about those incidents," he said over his shoulder.

"What then?" Angélica followed him.

"I'm talking about Dr. Hughes."

She puffed her cheeks with a sigh. "Here we go again."

"He's been missing for twenty years now, you know. And the last time anyone saw him was at this very site."

"Maybe Death ate him," Esteban spoke from behind her, sounding like an extra from a Boris Karloff film.

"My point exactly," Juan said.

She wrinkled her nose at her father's back. "Honestly, you sound like a pair of delusional paranoids."

Juan stopped several feet inside the entrance, waiting for Angélica to reach his side. Esteban pushed past both of them, his shirt soaking wet and smelling like he'd sweated through his deodorant hours ago. She watched him go, noting his rush to escape the temple's thick shadows.

"All I'm saying, *gatita*, is that maybe you should think twice before being so quick to rule out this cu—"

"Dr. García!" Esteban cried.

A high-pitched scream cut through the heavy air.

Angélica and her father raced to where Esteban stood frozen in the temple opening.

She gasped at the sight in front of her. Tree limbs smacked against each other, debris tumbled across the ground, tents buckled and ripped free of their stakes.

Dust particles stung her cheeks as she stepped out into the strong gusts. She shielded her face, frowning. Where had this windstorm come from? An hour ago, the air had been still and thick enough to drink. She looked up at the sky. And why weren't there any clouds?

Angélica turned to her father in time to see Esteban lean closer and yell something to Juan over the cacophony of the thrashing jungle. Juan nodded in agreement.

"What?" Angélica moved closer to her father. "What did he say?"

"*Mal viento*," Juan hollered and grabbed Angélica's arm,

dragging her back into the safety of the temple and out of the howling tempest. "He says the evil winds have come."

"Evil winds?" Angélica squeezed the bridge of her nose. "Must you insist upon scaring the hell out of my crew?"

Esteban screamed in pain from somewhere outside.

Angélica's heart stopped for a second.

"I told you it was a curse." Juan pushed past her toward the entrance.

"Dammit!" Following on his heels, she leaned into the gale, dodging a flying tree limb. "It's not a curse!"

Chapter Two

**Xtabay: A bewitching woman or female demon with a
frigid touch and a lethal embrace.**

A week and a half later …

Holy shit it was hot.

A face melting, sweltering version of Hell kind of hot.

Quint Parker lifted his Panama hat and fanned himself
with it, staring across the dirt parking lot at the rippling waves
rising under the sun's blasts. Chickens would lay hard boiled
eggs in this heat.

He grimaced as a drop of sweat trailed down his spine.
Damn. The good ol' steamy Yucatán Peninsula. Two decades
ago he'd sworn never to return, yet here he stood … dripping.
Coming down to this jungle again was crazy for more reasons
than the miserable temperatures.

Jamming his hat back on, he looked around for his escort
to Dr. García's dig site. The only sign of life was a round, well-
wrinkled Maya woman tugging a rusted Radio Flyer wagon
across the parking lot. Strapped to the wagon was a large cage
jam-packed with live chickens, their beaks poking through the
wire mesh here and there. The wagon wheels squeak-squeaked
under the weight of its load.

Speaking of chickens … Quint snorted. Was this today's

lunch special at the village's only hotel? Maybe he should rescue one and ship it home to his niece. Her pet chicken ruled the roost, which made his sister growl and grumble.

He checked the time. His ride was a half-hour late. A drop of sweat splattered onto the face of his watch. He blew out a breath, frustrated with more than this stifling pit stop that had liquefied his deodorant five minutes after he had put it on. His shirt was ringed with sweat, his jeans damp at the waistline. So much for giving a good first impression to the highly esteemed archaeology professor from the University of Arizona.

He leaned back against the stucco-covered wall of the *tienda*, the only grocery store around for miles and miles of thick forest. Unscrewing the lid of the water he'd bought inside, he watched as a brown chicken feather escaped the cage, caught sail in a light breeze, and floated toward the grassy plaza on the other side of the parking lot.

What would Dr. Juan García be like in person? Quint sipped some lukewarm water, pondering. So far he'd only spoken to Dr. García on the phone. Their conversations had been short, polite, professional. But he'd read plenty about the professor and his work on this particular site and learned even more about his accomplishments, including his many accolades and grants awarded over the years.

A movement near his boots drew Quint's gaze. A gecko zipped in front of him, zigzagging across the parking lot toward the Poultry Express wagon. He capped his water.

From out of nowhere, a wind whipped up, swaying tree limbs as it grew in strength, churning closer. Dust eddied across the dirt lot, coating the chickens and Maya woman in a layer of powder.

He grimaced on her behalf.

Instead of ebbing, the wind intensified, sucking up more dirt into a whirling dance. In the midst of the sudden squall, the Radio Flyer tipped over. The cage of chickens crashed to the ground and the door popped open.

For a moment, there was only the whistle of the wind in

Quint's ears, then an uproar of squawking filled the air.

Dirt swirled faster, the vortex doubling in size. It reminded him of the dust devils he'd seen a few months ago in the Nevada desert while writing a piece on the old ghost town of Goldwash.

The whirlwind surrounded the Maya woman and her freed flock. Feathers filled the air.

The distinct rumble of a diesel engine made Quint's chest tighten. A tour bus turned into the parking lot. The driver was looking down at something, not paying attention, the bus moving too fast toward the cloud of dirt.

Quint pushed away from the stucco wall. "Hey!" he yelled, stepping out into the late morning sunshine waving his arms. The bus driver didn't look up, didn't veer, didn't even slow.

"Hey! Stop!" Quint tried again, and then raced into the churning dust cloud. He had seconds to drag the Maya woman out of the way before the dust devil and loose chickens became the least of her problems. Dirt peppered his face and arms. He stepped on one chicken and stumbled over another. Inside the whistling, swirling mix of dust and feathers, he found the old lady. She was clutching two chickens to her chest while she searched the ground for more.

He grabbed her arm, trying to pull her toward safety, but she slapped at his hand, pushing him away.

The screech of brakes and grating sound of tires sliding over the hardpan made him cringe; the blare of a horn nearly blasted his heart out of his chest cavity. He reached for the woman, dodging out of the way right before a huge chrome grill shoved into the thick cloud. The Maya woman screamed next to his ear; her chickens squawked and fluttered out of the way.

Crap! That had been a close one. Too close.

Over the bedlam, Quint heard the shouts of the bus driver. He was leaning out the window, shaking his fist.

"*Lo siento*," he apologized to the driver, trying to smooth things over now that a fatality had been avoided. He coughed from the dust and the pungent odor of burning brake pads.

Another gust of wind blew Quint's hat off, sending it tumbling, rolling out of the dusty chaos. With one last check on the chicken lady, who was busy stuffing hens back into the cage, he jogged after his hat.

Escaping from the swirling dust devil's clutches, he found his hat resting against the back tire of a tandem bicycle. Standing next to the handle bars was a man probably in his mid-sixties, wearing a straw hat, a green sweat-soaked T-shirt, blue jeans, and leather sandals. His heavy eyelids and large earlobes gave away his Maya heritage.

The cyclist held a piece of cardboard with a name scrawled on it—Quint's name.

"Howdy," he shouted to the bike rider over the rattle of the bus engine. Quint bent and grabbed his hat, brushing off the dust. He slammed it on his head and nodded at the sign. "That's me."

The man's forehead wrinkled. "*Señor* Parker?"

Nodding, he held out his hand. "Call me Quint."

The biker gave him a thorough onceover. Then he crossed himself as Catholics tended to do, muttered something undecipherable under his breath, and spit over his left shoulder.

Quint cocked his head to the side. That was a new ending to the centuries old ritual.

The bike rider grasped his outstretched hand and gave it two hard shakes. "Teodoro Cruz," he said, squinting up at Quint. Then in a blink, he smiled coat-hanger wide.

Quint smiled back, glad to see a friendly face after staring down a bug-splattered bus grill.

"We go now?" Teodoro asked.

"I'm ready when you are." The sooner he made it to the dig site, the sooner he could get started on his reason for returning to this overgrown, godforsaken sweat lodge. "Let me grab my backpack." He walked over to the store's stucco wall and collected his things.

Teodoro took Quint's pack from him and secured the bulky bag to the metal shelf over the back tire.

Meanwhile, Quint tried to swipe the dust from his clothes, smearing it across the sweat-soaked cotton. He gave up on his clothes and shook the dust from his hair. Every nook and cranny of his skin felt gritty, damn it. When he looked up, Teodoro waited on the bike's front seat. He motioned for Quint to take the seat behind him.

With a chuckle, Quint climbed on. He hadn't figured his first trip to the dig site would be by two-seater bike. Hell, nothing had gone as planned since he'd agreed to take this trip to the Yucatán to solve a twenty-year-old mystery.

As Teodoro steered past the bus, Quint squirmed on the rock-hard seat while he pedaled. He'd had rougher rides in his line of work, but sitting too long on this bike was going to impair his ability to have kids someday.

"Do you usually take a bike to and from the dig site?" he asked.

Teodoro glanced back. "Curse got our motorcycle."

He stopped squirming. "Did you say *curse*?"

"*Sí.*"

No shit? This must be his lucky day. Not for the first time since he'd stepped off the plane, he wondered if he should turn around and fly back to the States.

Teodoro steered them onto the raised white *sacbe*.

Quint remembered the limestone-coated, ancient Maya roadway from the last time he had been at the dig site. As he peddled along behind Teodoro into the shadow-filled jungle, several other memories surfaced, including Dr. Hughes' love of solving puzzles from the past.

And who could forget that son of a bitch, Jared Steel?

* * *

Angélica waited for the last of her crew to leave the mess tent after lunch before facing off with her father. "Dad, I swear," she shook her spoon at him, "if I hear one more word about this stupid, damned nonexistent curse, I'm throwing you in the nearest *cenote*."

"It's not my fault. You're the one who read that glyph."

She tossed her spoon onto the table. "Well, the least you could do is support me on dispelling all of this superstitious bullshit, especially in front of my men."

"You need to stop swearing so much, *gatita*. You're beginning to sound like your mother."

"Quit trying to change the subject."

"Fine. You don't believe in the curse." Juan picked up her spoon and used it to scrape the remains of her lunch onto his plate. "But your crew does. If you want to quell all of the whispers and fears, you need to come up with a believable explanation for what happened to Francisco, Lorenzo, and Rafael."

"What? They got sick."

"You know it's more than that. It's not normal for three young men to come down with severe stomachaches at the same time. And don't blame María's cooking either, because we all shared the same meal."

"It was a twenty-four-hour flu. Period. End of story."

He lifted his coffee, glancing over her head at the entrance to the mess tent. "You don't find it odd that all three were working in the *Ik* Temple?"

That was the third time in the last few minutes that she'd noticed him looking at the entrance. Angélica checked behind her and found it empty.

She focused back on her father. "No, I do not find it odd. Just because they were working in a temple named after the god of wind does not mean their sudden illness has anything to do with some kind of superstitious jinx."

He sipped from his cup, frowning at her over the rim. "A destructive wind did blow after you read that curse."

"It's not a curse, Dad." She pinched the bridge of her nose. How many times did she have to say it for crissake?

Lowering his cup to the table, he shrugged. "Okay." He didn't sound convinced though. "So you're going to stick with the notion that the Temple of the Crow caving in on Fernando and Alonso was just an accident, too?"

"Of course."

"They could have been killed."

Angélica held up her hand, counting off on her fingers. "First of all, only a small section of the ceiling crumbled. Second, they merely suffered a few scratches and bruises. Third, you yourself told me at the end of last year's dig that we might need to shore up the ceiling in that part of the temple."

"No, the chamber to which I was referring is not the same one that came down on them."

She stood and stretched her arms upward, thanking this whole curse sham for several new knots in her back. "It's an old structure, Dad. Don't you think it's inevitable something that ancient would periodically succumb to the effects of gravity?"

Juan brushed crumbs from the table as he rose. "Sure. But how do you explain Diego being shoved into the *cenote* this morning while collecting water for María?"

"He slipped."

"Your crew happens to think he was pushed by *Xtabay*."

Her crew also believed in malevolent gods and the evil eye. It was no surprise they blamed *Xtabay* rather than something rational.

"And what do you think?" she asked.

"I don't know. Diego swears he felt her hands on his back, and he's not usually one for tall tales." Juan carried their plates to the counter that divided the kitchen from the eating area. "I know you think this is all a bunch of delusory nonsense, and maybe you're right, but you have to admit that ever since we found that curse, things keep happening that are hard to explain."

"Not that hard." She joined him at the counter.

"Maybe not in your logical left brain, but your men don't

always think like scientists." His brow wrinkled, his brown eyes serious. "You need to keep that in mind when calming them down after the next incident."

"There isn't going to be another incident."

"You can't control everything, Angélica."

María slid through a side tent flap at that moment, putting an end to the curse debate. She nodded at Angélica and her father. Angélica waved back, complimenting her in Mayan on the beautiful, handmade white *huipil* dress she was wearing. With her round face looking more flushed than usual, María thanked her and then gathered up their dishes and waddled into the kitchen.

Angélica stared after her, realizing she hadn't seen Teodoro at all during lunch, and María's husband made it a priority to make it to every meal.

"I like how María still wears traditional Maya clothing," Juan said. "It makes her cooking taste more authentic."

She turned back to her father. "Have you seen Teodoro?"

Juan looked all around, avoiding her gaze. "No, nope, I … I sure haven't. Not for a while. He must be busy doing uh … something else." He nodded as if agreeing with himself and then made a beeline for the exit.

Please, she wasn't born yesterday.

"Dad." She caught up with him out in the hot sunshine, grabbing his sleeve. "Where's Teodoro?"

"He's probably out gathering more herbs to make another one of his foul potions. You should really rein him in on using those horrible tasting, eye-watering pastes on poor, injured men." He was still avoiding her.

A pair of jays chased each other across the sunburned landscape, flying from the tree-cresting top of the gray-streaked Temple of the Water Witch to the single-story *Ik* Temple in front of her. The birds' noisy calls pierced the air, interrupting them for a moment.

"Dad, just answer my quest …" The sound of twigs snapping in the jungle to the side of the mess tent made her look around. Teodoro stepped out of the thick bushes edging the trail to the *sacbe*.

"There he is," Juan said from behind her.

The brush shivered again and a stranger stepped out, following in Teodoro's wake. He was tall, dirt-streaked, and uninvited.

Angélica took in the stranger's wide shoulders and confident gaze. She'd dealt with enough machismo-filled, cocks of the walk in her time to know trouble when it came strutting up to her front door.

"Dad, who's that?" she spoke under her breath.

"Uh, yeah. Sweetheart, I forgot to mention something about this year's dig."

Teodoro pointed at Juan and then he darted into the mess tent. Without hesitation, the stranger headed their way.

Angélica growled. "What have you done?"

"You must be Dr. García," the stranger said to Juan, sliding a frowning glance her way. He lowered his backpack to the ground and held out his hand toward her dad. "It's nice to finally meet you in person."

Juan looked down at Angélica, wincing visibly at whatever he saw on her face. Then his lips curled into a smile and he shook the newcomer's hand. "Glad to have you here, Mr. Parker."

"Please, call me Quint."

Angélica's left eyelid began to twitch. He couldn't have. He just couldn't have. "Dad." It was more of an accusation than question.

"Angélica, this is Quint Parker." Juan ignored her glare. "He's a photojournalist who's going to write a piece about what goes on behind the scenes at our dig site."

What? No. Absolutely not. No way in hell. Heat crept up her neck and singed her cheeks. She was going to pay Teodoro to torture her father with one of his shaman cures—the one using leeches would be a good start.

Juan gestured toward Angélica. "Quint, this is my

daughter, Dr. Angélica García."

How could he have done this to her? This year of all years?

Quint's grin faltered. "Your daughter?"

"And please, call me Juan. My daughter is the only 'Dr. García' on this site. I hope the ride in wasn't too grueling. Our motorcycle refuses to start, so we had to rely on backup transportation."

"The ride was … interesting," their visitor said, his smile returning. "It's been a while since I've eaten that many bugs in one sitting."

In no mood for polite conversation, Angélica grabbed Juan's arm. "Could you excuse us for a moment, Mr. Parker?"

"Sure. I'll just stand here and watch for passing snakes."

Swell, a comedian. Her dad was going to love this guy.

Angélica towed her father a small distance from Quint, and then shot Juan a scorching look. "Why didn't you tell me about this *before* he showed up?"

Juan held her gaze. "Because I know you."

"Humph!" Then he should have known better. "And just who is he supposed to follow around while he's here?"

"The both of us."

"Really?"

Juan nodded. "But mainly you."

"Ahhh!" Angélica threw her hands up in frustration. "Just as I suspected." Her father had lost his mind.

"Well, since you're the one with the crew, he'll gain more insight into what we do here from you."

"Dad, I don't have the time—"

"I know, darling," Juan said, waving at Teodoro as he passed them on the way to the latrine.

"Or the energy—"

"Yes, *gatita*." He squeezed her shoulder.

"Or the patience—"

"Of course not."

"To take care of this … this …" Words escaped her

sparking brain.

"Photojournalist," Quint supplied from behind her.

"Thank you, Mr. Parker," she snapped without taking her eyes from her father. "To take care of a photojournalist right now. Especially with all of the other little problems we've been having lately." Not including this damned curse bullshit.

Juan smiled. "I agree with you completely."

"Great." She blew out a sigh of relief. He'd come back to his senses. "Then what's your solution?" They should probably offer to feed Mr. Parker first and then have Teodoro haul him to the village.

Placing his hands on her cheeks, Juan leaned forward and kissed her forehead. "Play nice."

He stepped back and said to Quint, "I'll catch up with you after my daughter gets you settled."

"Dad!" She jammed her hands on her hips when he turned to leave. "Don't you walk away!"

Her father winked at her and did just that, whistling as he left.

* * *

Quint watched Juan stroll toward a small, crumbling temple, leaving his daughter standing there spitting and sputtering.

Angélica García.

In the flesh.

Damn.

He'd almost fallen over when Juan had introduced her. Jared Steel's ex-wife was one of the last people he'd expected to run into down here.

That old newspaper photo had been deceptive. She didn't look anything like the cold bitch he'd imagined her to be. On the contrary, she was fiery. He risked a peek down over her shirt, settling on where her khaki pants rode low on her hips. Curvier, too. The black and white picture didn't do her justice, especially when it came to the flames of red in her hair.

His focus returned to her face and ran into her hard green gaze.

She waved him over to where she stood glaring at him.

He cringed, wishing he were wearing a cup—just in case she starting swinging.

"Mr. Parker." The calm tone in her voice surprised him.

"Quint," he reiterated. How had he missed that she was an archaeologist, too? He'd been too fixed on her father and his long association with Steel, maybe.

Her lips were pressed tight when she held out her hand, her expression schooled. "It's nice to meet you, Quint."

Figuring there was some anger smoldering beneath the surface, he cautiously shook her hand. She had a firm grip with rough calluses dotting her palm. A hard worker, too. Another misconception about Steel's ex-wife crumbled.

"I apologize for being a surprise, Dr. García."

She pulled her hand free. "That you were. My father has a habit of …" she sighed. "Well, let's just say he keeps my life exciting."

Quint stood there for a few seconds, his eyes locked with hers, not sure if she expected him to head back to the village or set up camp. Trying to break the standoff, he motioned toward his dirt-stained shirt. "You wouldn't happen to have a place where I could clean up and change, would you?"

She glanced down his front, her forehead wrinkling as if she'd just noticed how much of a mess he was. "What'd you do? Fall off the bike?"

He didn't want to make a big deal of the old woman and him almost becoming bug splatter on the bus grill, so he kept it short. "I rescued some chickens."

Her grin was the spitting image of her father's. The softening of her features made him do a double take. She needed to smile more often.

"Grab that." She pointed at his backpack sitting next to him on the ground. "I'll show you where you can park yourself for however long you plan to stay with us. You can take the afternoon to settle in and acclimate."

In other words, she was going to let him stick around, but she didn't want to deal with him at the moment. That was fine with him. He needed a break to figure out how to keep Dr. Angélica García from interfering with his reason for returning to this hellhole.

He hoisted his pack and followed her lead, debating whether to ask if she knew of Dr. Hughes. No, better to bide his time, step carefully. Her rigid spine and no-nonsense gait made it clear that she wasn't in the mood for questions.

After leading him past several tents, including a large green one, she opened the flap of a weathered gray tent.

"You can bunk in here for now." She stood aside and waited for him to enter.

He slipped past her. The smell of sun-baked canvas greeted him as he looked around his new home, taking in the stack of waterlogged boxes in the corner, the jumble of smashed and dented electronic equipment on the wooden desk, and the pile of thick books on the canvas floor next to a cot strewn with notebooks. He fanned himself with his hat. A sauna would be refreshing in comparison.

Angélica stepped in behind him and zipped closed a piece of fine mesh across the opening. She glanced around the tent. "Sorry about how cramped it is right now," she said, lifting off what looked like a mangled satellite phone base from the desk and dropping it onto the tent floor. A laptop broken into two pieces followed it, along with a tangled nest of cables. "A tree fell on our communications tent last week. We've been storing the salvaged remains in here along with our other supplies. I'll have someone remove this stuff after supper."

He opened his mouth to ask if the so-called "curse" had taken out their electronics, too, but then reconsidered, figuring she might take a bite out of his hide in response.

The satellite phone being disabled was unfortunate, since Quint couldn't get any cell phone service here under the thick canopy of trees. He'd left his own satellite phone at home because Juan had written that they already had one on the dig site. Maybe if he climbed to the top of one of the temples, he could get a signal. He needed a way to contact folks in the States in case he found something down here. For now, he'd have to rely on the backup plan—using the hotel in the village as a base for incoming and outgoing packages and messages.

"Don't worry about it." Quint dropped his backpack onto the floor next to the desk.

"Supper's at seven. We eat in the mess tent, which is what we were standing next to when we met."

"Great." Right now the idea of eating in this heat made him nauseated. He'd have to be careful about heat stroke these first few days and drink lots of water.

He eyed the cot jammed against one side of the tent. Switching from the freezing Canadian Rockies to the sweltering Yucatán jungle in less than a week was taking its toll. He rubbed the back of his neck, feeling every one of his thirty-eight years.

Later, he could ask Juan García and his daughter more about the curse Teodoro had mentioned and somehow convince them to share what they knew about the history of this place.

Angélica must have seen him staring at the cot, because she collected the mound of battered notebooks off the top of it and dropped them onto the floor over by the boxes. "If you need anything, find Teodoro. His place is behind the mess tent. He can show you where the latrine is located." She glanced at his shirt, "And the showers, too."

"A shower would be fantastic."

"Yeah, well keep in mind this isn't a Hilton Hotel."

"Darn. I suppose a visit to the spa for a massage is out of the question," he joked.

The only thing he needed right now was that cot. And some time to regroup and modify his plan of attack. There was also a certain newspaper picture he wanted to check out again.

She nodded and unzipped the mesh flap. "Be sure to zip this closed after I leave or the mosquitoes will drain your blood in an hour."

"Got it." Some things hadn't changed in twenty years.

"I'm sorry to play bad hostess and skip out on you," she paused to zip the flap closed behind her before he had a chance to do it, "but I need to go find my father and string him high up in the nearest tree canopy for the spider monkeys to have their way with him."

Quint listened to the fading crunch of her footfalls in the dead grass as she marched away. When the coast was clear, he closed the main tent flap for total privacy and reached for his backpack. Unzipping the top of it, he sorted through several shirts and pairs of socks before finding the blue plastic file holder; his old friend, Jeff Hughes, had given it to him when they had met for drinks last month back home in Rapid City. He dropped onto the cot and unwound the string securing the cover.

He sorted through photos of Jared Steel that Jeff's mother had hired a private detective to take before she'd died last year, double checking to see if Angélica was in any of them. She wasn't.

Setting them aside, he fingered through the handful of yellowing newspaper articles about Jared Steel, his mind flitting back in time to that last summer here at the dig site with Dr. Hughes as it had many, many times before. Was there some clue he'd missed? Something he'd overlooked before flying back home and never seeing Jeff's dad again?

He flipped past the magazine article covering Steel's latest accomplishments in the archaeology community and an older university newspaper article with a picture of Steel kissing the hand of a good-looking brunette. Mrs. Hughes was amazingly thorough in her detective skills. He wasn't surprised, really, when he thought back to the way she'd always been able to sniff out any trouble Jeff and he had gotten into back in junior high. Jeff used to say his mom didn't have eyes in the back of her head; she had spyglasses.

"Ah ha," he whispered, finding the newspaper photo from over a decade ago that he'd been thinking about since seeing Dr. Angélica García in the flesh.

Easing onto his back, he stared at the princess in the photo. With her frosty smile and poised demeanor, Quint had assumed she'd fit perfectly into Jared Steel's high society life. Steel stood behind her in the engagement photo, acting the loving fiancé, flaunting his trademark smirk. The same smirk Quint had wanted to put his fist through twenty years ago.

His focus drifted back to the photo of Angélica in her high-collared shirt, her perfectly coiffed hairdo, her flawless skin. So different. He thought of how animated she'd been with her father when Quint had introduced himself. The sweat lining her brow and ringing her neck, the way strands of her hair escaped her braid and stuck out like live wires, her heated cheeks. So much more vibrant. She was not the porcelain doll he'd imagined.

Tracing the outline of Angélica's face, he chewed on his lower lip. Should he tell the Garcías he'd been here before, back when it was mostly jungle with a couple of temples rising out of the brush? That he'd known Dr. Hughes and his family since childhood? That his reason for coming to this dig site had nothing to do with an article about the site and everything to do with a promise made to Jeff Hughes after his mother's funeral?

He covered Jared Steel's image with his thumb and focused on Angélica with her over-glossed smile. "Can I trust you, Dr. García?"

Chapter Three

Dzulob: Foreigners or outsiders.

Later that evening, after crashing on his cot for a couple of hours and then scrubbing off a layer of dust under a short camp-style shower, Quint headed for the mess tent. At the entrance, small buckets with burning citronella candles stood guard, flickering in the twilight. Male voices rumbled on the other side of the thick canvas. His thoughts replayed a similar moment from twenty years ago, triggering a twang of melancholy that fueled the anger smoldering inside of him. Dr. Hughes should still be around, damn it, cracking his corny jokes and filling Quint's head with more stories about Maya life long ago.

Shaking off the past, he stepped through the tent flaps. He scanned the sea of heads, locking onto Angélica and Juan. They sat at a picnic table against the far wall.

As he squeezed between tables, brushing past sweat-soaked backs, several heads turned. He nodded at a few of the men at first, but after receiving no greeting in return, he gave up on making any new best friends forever. He dropped onto the bench next to Juan. A spicy scent filled the humid air, making his mouth water.

Juan greeted him with a shoulder bump. "Boy, am I glad to see you. My daughter's been picking on me about my dining room etiquette since I dug in."

"A lot of good it's doing," Angélica said as Juan picked up his meat-filled tortilla, dripped orange sauce all over his fingers, and bit a chunk out of the wrap. As he chewed, he smirked across the table at her.

She shook her head. "You need a keeper."

"Why do you think I had you?"

"I was an accident, remember?"

"No, spilling my drink down the front of your mother's dress on our first date was an accident. You were an adorable bundle of surprise with Marianne's lovely hair color and my striking good looks."

Angélica laughed. "Good thing I got Mom's unpretentiousness along with her hair." She cut a bite-sized piece of her much thinner tortilla. "Hungry, Mr. Parker?" she asked before sticking the morsel into her mouth.

"Quint," he corrected, his stomach rumbling. "I could eat a horse."

She swallowed. "That's too bad. We have no horse here. Teodoro has a donkey, but we need him since the motorcycle is out of commission." She surveyed the room. "Teodoro," she called above the murmur of conversation. "Will you please ask María to make up a plate of food for Mr. Parker?"

"I can get my own plate." He started to stand, but Teodoro was already at the kitchen counter.

"You will not," she told him, her tone leaving no room for argument. "Tonight you're our guest." She tapped the shoulder of the man sitting to her left. "Fernando, this is Quint Parker. He's going to write an article about the dig site. Quint, meet Fernando, my foreman."

Fernando nodded at him before taking a sip of his coffee. Judging from the lines fanning from Fernando's eyes and the gray at his temples, Quint guessed him to be a half a decade his senior.

When he looked back at the boss lady, he found himself the bull's eye of her focus.

"As of tomorrow," she said, "you're one of the crew, and that involves a couple of rules."

Ah, crap. Here we go. He knew the drill—smile and nod as she explained how this was her territory, her crew, and her dig, blah, blah, blah. Then thank her dutifully after she explained where, when, and how often he could eat, breathe, and use the latrine. No problem, he'd play along. He had no choice, really. He'd do whatever it took to buy the time he needed to find the answers he and Jeff Hughes were looking for down here.

Teodoro placed a tin plate laden with a thick, meaty-looking burrito wrapped in a homemade tortilla in front of Quint. The smell alone had him drooling like his nephew back when the kid had been teething. "Thanks. What is this?"

"It's called a *panucho*," Angélica said. "It's a tortilla typically stuffed with black beans and topped with onion, tomatoes, *chile*, and sometimes egg. María, our cook, has her own versions of it with various meats, which she super-sizes for the men. It includes what we call her 'special sauce,' which is orange and delicious and very top secret. I wouldn't advise asking her about it."

"She'll threaten you with a cleaver and chase you out of the kitchen," Juan warned.

"She does that only to you, Dad."

Using both hands, Quint lifted the *panucho* toward his mouth, his teeth all ready to tear into it. At that moment, he didn't give a rat's ass about the heat, the lack of modern plumbing, or the bossy woman eyeing him from across the table. He just wanted a moment alone with his food.

Angélica cleared her throat.

He hesitated, his jaw open and ready to chomp.

Juan leaned over. "Don't give her an inch, boy." His tone was full of mirth. "Trust me, I know my daughter. She takes after the bulldozer we have back home on our ranch. A real chip off the old diesel."

"Dad, that is a blatant misrepresentation of one of my better character traits."

"I knew there was something wrong with her early on when she asked me to read the dictionary to her at bedtime."

"And *that* is another." She turned to Quint. "It was a book on Mayan language and symbolism that my mother treasured and often studied aloud with me in the room."

"A dictionary." Juan stuck to his guns.

Glancing back and forth between father and daughter, Quint lowered the wrap to his plate and picked up his fork. His mother would have patted his head, but it wasn't good manners that won him over. It was his goal to get on Angélica's good side so she'd spill all she knew about Dr. Hughes.

"You'll rue this day, Quint," Juan said, his grin wide.

"You're going to rue this day, Dad, after I have Teodoro move your tent next to the latrines," she joked with her father. But then her expression sobered and she hit Quint with both barrels. "As I was saying, there are rules here. We eat breakfast at six, lunch at one, and supper at seven. From two to three, you can take a *siesta* if you'd like, and I suggest you do. We work long, hard hours because the dig season is so short. After supper, the rest of the evening is yours to do with as you please."

"Gotcha." He chewed the *panucho*, swallowing a groan of appreciation for María's mouth-watering food, and stuck another forkful in his mouth. Hard work wasn't new to him. Neither were strong-minded women. He'd gotten his hands messy with both in the past.

Juan finished his meal and wiped his fingers on his napkin. "Warn him about the *cenote*."

Angélica stabbed the last piece of her tortilla. "Do you know what a *cenote* is, Quint?"

"A sinkhole in the limestone, usually full of water, considered sacred by the Maya people," he shot back.

She nodded, appearing impressed. "You know your Maya terminology."

"I read it in a guidebook on the plane ride down here," he lied. Way back when, he and a couple of Dr. Hughes' crew used to sneak swims in the big *cenote* about a hundred yards from the site until they were caught and lectured thoroughly on the dangers lurking under the water.

He struggled with cutting through the tortilla for a moment before giving up, picking it up, and taking a bite.

"That's more like it!" Juan clapped him on the back.

"You dripped sauce on your shirt, Mr. Parker." She pointed her fork at her father's chest. "You, too. Now you're twins."

"It'll wash out," Juan said, dabbing his napkin on the orange stains.

"Not María's special sauce. It's potent." She piled her napkin and fork on her plate and then watched Quint take another bite, her forehead wrinkling. "Everyone has been ordered to stay away from the *cenote* unless instructed otherwise. If you are asked to go, take someone with you. We had an accident this morning," she said in a louder voice, addressing all who'd turned in their seats at her words. "We don't need any more."

Quint made a mental note to find out later what had happened at the *cenote*. "Got it. What else?"

"Don't be nosing around in any of the temples. I'll take you on a tour of each so there's no need for you to explore on your own."

He'd bet his sister's favorite purple boots Angélica wanted to keep him out of those temples for some reason other than his safety.

"Don't go into the jungle alone. You're unfamiliar with the surroundings and it's very easy to get turned around."

"Plus there are venomous snakes, hairy spiders, and huge Paca jungle rats," Juan added.

Quint knew all about those nasty critters. They were part

of why he'd sworn never to return to this dreadful place.

"Your time will be divided between my father, Fernando, and me," Angélica continued.

Quint wondered how many years Fernando had worked with her, and how much he knew about the history of the site.

"You're free to talk to other members of the crew, but don't try to get them to take you any place that's off-limits, or you'll be sent back to the village, backpack in hand."

Her stern expression emphasized her point. He needed to step carefully. He didn't need Angélica as an adversary.

"I'm responsible for every person here," she continued. "Any accidents or problems need to be brought to my attention immediately. Teodoro is our resident healer, so if you get bit by a snake and need immediate attention, he's the person to see."

"He's good with toothaches, too," Juan added.

Teodoro was apparently a real jack of all trades.

"In the States, the freedom of speech allows the press many excesses. But this is Mexican soil, and since I work for the Mexican government, I have the authority to limit your freedom. So, I'll let you know what you can and can't take pictures of around here."

Ah ha! That's why she ruled over the men instead of Juan. The University of Arizona wasn't paying for all of this, Mexico's National Institute of Anthropology and History was. Quint measured her with a stare. With dirt smudged from her temple to her jawline and a petite nose sprinkled with freckles, she didn't look like a lead archaeologist. Then again, neither had Dr. Hughes.

"Do you have any questions?" she asked.

Quint lowered his cup to the table, weighing all she'd divulged. "Do you send anyone into the village on a regular basis? I left a forwarding address at the hotel, and I need someone to check for mail."

"You're having mail shipped to the hotel?" Her green eyes narrowed, suspicion lurking there. "How long do you plan on sticking around, Mr. Parker?"

"As long as it takes to get all I need for the article." And then some. He doubted he'd get to the bottom of Dr. Hughes' disappearance in a couple of days.

Her jaw tightened. She didn't seem to like his answer. "How about we take it one day at a time and see how everything works out?"

"With us?" he deliberately misunderstood, flirting with a wink, testing those waters.

"With you," she snapped, slamming the door on his attempt to charm her. Gathering her father's and Quint's plates, she stacked them on top of hers. "Teodoro goes to the village on Tuesdays. I'll have him check for mail then." She stood with the plates in hand. "Anything else?"

There was something he'd been curious about all afternoon. "What's this I hear about a curse?"

The hum of conversation throughout the tent ceased.

Quint scanned the room, shifting in his seat under the weight of all of the stares focused on him. What? Had he opened Pandora's box?

Angélica frowned at her dad. "What did you tell him?"

Juan held up his hands. "It wasn't me, I swear." His eyes sparkling with excitement, he turned to Quint. "We found some glyphs that read like a curse and—"

"We found some glyphs that tell a story from the past," Angélica spoke over him loud and clear, as if giving an announcement at a podium. "And some people have jumped to the conclusion that it sounds like a curse. However, I'm sure you all will soon realize that it's not a curse." She peered around the room, her hard expression hammering her point home. "Just a few mishaps."

The sound of silverware scraping across tin plates and the rumbling of voices started up again as if on cue, but Quint could feel the tension still in the air. Maybe he could get Angélica to show him these curse glyphs, find out what the big deal was about.

"Time will tell." Juan's voice was low, meant for only those at their table.

"Yes, it will," Angélica challenged back, and then leaned over the table and kissed her father on the cheek. "Now, if you'll excuse me, I'm going back to my tent to look up a few things." Carrying their dirty plates, she negotiated through the other tables while bidding her crew "goodnight," set the plates on the counter, and left the tent.

This was it, Quint's opportunity to catch Angélica alone and see what she knew about the site's past. "Excuse me," he said to her father and Fernando and then rushed after her. "Dr. García," he called, catching sight of her white shirt in the shadowy darkness outside the tent. She held still as he jogged up to her. "Can I ask you something?"

"That depends."

"On what?"

"Your question." She crossed her arms, waiting.

Sheesh, porcupines were less prickly. He formed his sentences carefully, trying not to be too obvious. "I like to begin an article with a little history of the location I'm covering. Give the readers some background, you know." He paused to see if she'd allow him to continue or shut him down before he got out of the gate.

A cricket chirped in the grass. She remained silent.

Crossing his fingers behind his back, he continued. "What was the first thing to be excavated at this site?"

"I don't know. I wasn't working here at that time." Her tone said that was it. End of story. Goodnight. "I'll see you at breakfast, Mr. Parker." She took off toward her tent, the beam of her flashlight bouncing with each step.

If she thought she could get away that easily, she didn't know with whom she was messing. He hadn't made it this far in his career by giving up when faced with a brick wall—or a closed-lipped, hard-headed female. Determined to get some answers, he fell in step beside her. "So, was it your father who first began the work here?"

"No." She picked up her pace. "My dad and mom took over eight years ago."

"Do you know when the first excavation took place?" When she didn't answer, he added, "Even an estimate?"

She halted in front of a large tent, her eyes sparkling in the light of the half-moon. A small breeze rustled the trees behind her, sounding like distant applause. Quint held his ground, waiting.

"It was thirty years ago." She finally caved. "From the pictures I've seen of the early site, it was so hidden by the surrounding jungle that all temples except the Temple of the Water Witch—the tall one over there," she pointed to his left, "were unrecognizable as they stand today."

Quint followed the direction of her finger, imagining what the site must have looked like in the beginning. Dr. Hughes must have spent that first season when Quint and Jeff were still in elementary school with a machete in one hand and matches in the other.

"Thirty years of work." He tested her knowledge.

"Make that eighteen years of work. This site was occupied for ten years, and then went untouched for twelve years until my parents took over."

"I see." That answer confirmed a note Mrs. Hughes had scrawled on the back of a picture of Juan from the University of Arizona Alumni magazine. So far, everything checked out with what he already knew. "Why the break in time?"

"There was a change of caretakers."

"Do you know who was working here before your parents?" There, he'd asked. Enough dancing around it.

She looked up at the moonlit sky for several heartbeats as if waiting for the answer to flash across it. "Dr. Henry Hughes." She unzipped the tent flap. "I'll see you tomorrow morning at six," she called out, stepping inside and zipping the tent closed in his face.

Well, all right then. That was it from the bossier of the two Dr. Garcías for tonight, apparently. Shaking his head at what he was up against with her, Quint headed back to the mess tent and Angélica's much friendlier father. Why couldn't Juan be in charge here? Why did it have to be her, with her watchful eyes and tight lips?

His fingers were crossed that Juan felt like being more of a chatterbox than his daughter, or Quint would be stuck down here until the rains started and the dig season closed for the year.

* * *

The next morning dawned hot and muggy. He rolled out of the cot and stretched, his back protesting the current sleeping conditions.

He slipped on a clean pair of khakis. As much as he hated wearing pants in this heat, he'd learned long ago from Dr. Hughes about the chiggers down here and how they liked to crawl up inside pant legs. Dr. Hughes always stuffed his pants inside his boots—something he'd learned in the service.

"Damn you, Henry Hughes," he said, frowning at his stubble-covered jaw in a small mirror hanging on the wall over the cot. "Where did you go?"

Last night had been a bust. Juan and Fernando had both been gone when Quint had returned to the mess tent, so he'd given up and returned to his tent to go through more of the documents Mrs. Hughes had left behind after her death.

He hadn't found anything revealing, only more useless drivel about Steel. He'd gone to bed feeling defeated, but while tossing and turning in the night, he'd come up with a new plan of attack. At first he'd considered using good old fashioned charm, but Angélica had quickly put the kibosh on his attempt at light flirting last night during supper.

Instead of charm, he decided to try to earn her trust through hard work and following her rules over the next few days. Then he'd start asking questions about her education, her experiences, her theories. In his travels he'd learned something about people—most liked to talk about themselves, share their adventures in life. Listening had always opened doors for him, especially with women. And underneath her no-nonsense, professional exterior, Dr. Angélica García was very much a female.

He swiped at a bead of sweat rolling down from his temple. Christ, just getting dressed made him leak. "Stupid humidity." He tugged his T-shirt over his head, finger-combed his hair, and tied his hiking boots. Twenty years ago, he'd grouched plenty about working in the heat. Dr. Hughes had always chuckled at him, told him to suck it up and take it like a man.

He unzipped his tent and stepped out, looking across the site at the early morning haze blanketing the temples. Without a doubt, he knew this was going to be a long hard day. He had a gut feeling Angélica would make sure of it, pushing him to prove his merit and not be a burden to the rest of her crew. There was no way in hell he'd let her win a battle of wills.

A warm, sticky breeze fluttered across his face, leaving another layer of sweat in its wake.

He cursed. Today's weather report: increasingly humid with recurring blasts of wither-his-balls-to-raisins heat. His deodorant would be vapor by nine, his clothes soaked through by ten.

It was time to suck it up and take it like a man.

But first there was an enticing smell coming from the mess tent that he needed to investigate.

The sound of flatware clanging on tin plates greeted him inside the tent flaps. The hum of conversation was quieter this morning, more like a series of grunts with a few low murmurs between bites. Angélica and her father sat across from each other at the same table as the night before, only Juan's back was to the exit today. Fernando was there as well this morning, holding down the bench beside Juan.

Quint saluted Angélica's wary stare and then followed one of her crew members up to the counter. Minutes later, he joined her and set his plate on the table next to her breakfast remains. Eyeing the stack of tortillas covering a steaming mound of eggs and peppers soaked in the same orange sauce from his *panucho* last night, he licked his chops.

"Good morning." He greeted one and all and picked up his fork. "Who left the heat on overnight?" he asked, stealing one of Dr. Hughes' favorite corny lines. "This place is cooking."

Juan grinned. "I like this guy already," he told his daughter. "We should invite him to our ranch sometime."

Angélica handed Quint a napkin. "You're late," she started in on him right off.

"Yes, but only fashionably." He glanced around. Everyone else at the table was finishing up or done and working on their coffee.

After a loud yawn, Juan said, "Cut him some slack, *gatita*. He's probably jetlagged yet."

"He came to see how a dig site works." She wrapped her hands around her coffee mug, strangling it. "At my dig site, we don't have time to sleep in. There's too much work to be done before the rainy season hits."

She would make a great drill instructor. Quint could picture her striding through the tents at the break of dawn, blowing on a bugle. Ignoring the temptation to provoke her with a smartass comeback, he stayed true to his trust-building plan. "I'll eat fast."

Digging in, he listened as she, her father, and Fernando made plans for the day.

In the midst of detailing which crew she wanted working with Fernando, Angélica stopped mid-sentence.

Then she gasped.

Quint paused in his rush to clear his plate. He glanced her way. Her eyes were wide in surprise. As he watched, her cheeks flared bright red.

"What in the hell is he doing here?" She spoke low through clenched teeth.

Quint followed her line of sight and nearly choked on his mouthful of eggs when he saw who stood just inside the entrance.

Jared Steel.

The pompous asshole.

What was he doing down here?

A drop of sweat rolled down Quint's back as he watched Jared make his way toward them through the crowd of stares.

Dressed in a crisp, cream linen shirt and tan khakis, Steel looked fresh from one of the fancy Tiki bars over in Cancun. The asshole held his chin high, acting as if he owned the joint. Charm oozed from the over-polished smile he aimed at his ex-wife as he approached their table.

Quint swallowed the bile that had crawled up his throat at the sight of Dr. Hughes' old grad student. Some things in this wretched place never changed—not the heat, not the bugs, and apparently not the vermin.

"Hello, darling," Jared winked down at Angélica. "Mind if I join you for breakfast?"

She shoved to her feet, bumping Quint's shoulder in her haste. If looks could blast someone to smithereens, Jared would be a pile of smoking ashes.

"Mexico's full." Her upper lip wrinkled like one of Pancho Villa's banditos. "Go home, Jared."

Hot damn! Quint bit back a cheer from her corner of the ring. The gloves were off and she'd already finished with her warm up. There would be no hiding her frustrations behind a professional veneer today.

"Dr. Steel," Juan interrupted the Mexican standoff, smiling so wide it was a wonder his ears didn't pop off. He extended his hand, shooting his daughter a warning glance. "What a surprise to see you down here."

More like a kick to the gut. Quint pushed his plate away. This quick trip to the Yucatán was turning into a thorny journey back in time.

Steel shook Juan's hand. "A good surprise, I hope."

Angélica grunted. Or maybe that was a swear word pushed out between locked jaws.

Quint seconded her response. Steel's appearance smashed his backup plan flat. It was only a matter of minutes until the jackass blew Quint's cover and filled everyone in about his history at this site. As pissed as Angélica was thanks to this morning's surprise visitor, she would have Quint's head on a pike for playing twenty questions with her last night. At the least, she'd send him packing by noon.

"A wonderful surprise." Juan was still playing referee. "We're thrilled you took the time out of your busy schedule to pay us a visit." Juan scooted over to make room for Steel between himself and Fernando.

Quint sipped his coffee, glaring over the rim of the cup at Steel as he settled onto the opposite bench seat. Why had Mrs. Hughes been so fascinated with the arrogant dickhead?

"So, Dr. Steel." Juan gestured at his daughter to sit back down. "Is this just a quick check-in visit on your way to one of the university's other sites to the south of us?"

"Actually, it's my final stop before heading home. I saved the best for last."

"Don't get comfy. You're not staying long." Angélica was still standing looking ready to pounce.

Jared tsk-tsked his ex-wife. "I thought I'd stay and help out until the dig season is over."

"You thought wrong," she bit out.

"Your father mentioned you were short-staffed this year due to lack of funding."

"We're fine. Go home."

"Angélica," Juan chastised.

"Absolutely not," she told her father. "We already have one visitor. Two's a crowd."

"Do you find the idea of me working here with your father for a month so appalling?" Steel reached for her hand.

She pulled away before he could catch her. "Incredibly."

"You didn't used to feel that way about spending time

with me, darling."

"What do you want, Jared?" She crossed her arms over her chest. "Why are you really down here with the lowly commoners?" She emphasized the last part as if referencing something he'd said before.

Steel frowned up at her. "Fine, if you want to skip the niceties, I'll play along." He looked at Juan. "The university wanted me to come down and personally oversee your work. The decision on whether to continue your funding for this research project will be based on my findings."

The smile Juan had been sporting slipped. "What? You're kidding. You mean all of the paperwork I turned in on the scientific importance of Maya architectural styles and know-how that we catalogued down here wasn't enough?"

Quint lowered his cup to the table, an epiphany hitting him. So that was why Juan had invited Quint to come down even though he had known it would piss off his daughter. This article in a well-known and respected national publication could very likely improve the chances of Juan receiving continued funding.

"The thing is," Angélica said, "I don't remember the university petitioning for additional archeologists to be allowed at the dig site this year."

Steel shrugged. "They must have overlooked it."

She leaned forward, both fists on the table. "Overlooked my ass, Jared. You know damned well you need permission from the Mexican government to have another archeologist at this site. I put that clause in the university's contract myself to control who could work down here and how often. If you think you can start sniffing around on these premises without my permission, you'd better be prepared to deal with the *federales*."

"Maybe you should discuss this with your father." Jared's tone warned.

"Maybe you should go to—"

"Angélica!" Juan interrupted, all stern and fatherly. "Let's finish our breakfast and go back to your tent to discuss this."

She didn't move except to blink. And grind her molars.

"In private," Juan added. "Please, *gatita*. Sit down."

Quint couldn't take his eyes off of Angélica. There was something about a woman who could spit fire that made a man sit up straight and pay attention.

Several hushed seconds passed before she settled back onto the bench seat next to him. But those green eyes remained locked on her ex-husband. It didn't take a fortune teller to see a butt-kicking in Steel's future if he didn't remove himself from her dig site sooner rather than later.

"Thank you, Juan." Steel smiled in the face of Angélica's lack of love. "Now what does an archaeologist have to do to get a cup of coffee around here?"

Juan motioned to María, who had been watching the showdown from the counter next to Teodoro. She waddled into the kitchen.

"Good to see you again, Fernando," Steel said. "How are the wife and kids?"

Fernando looked at Angélica. At her nod, he answered, "They are well."

"Glad to hear it." Steel thanked Teodoro for the coffee he placed in front of him. Then, for the first time since he'd entered the tent, he spared Quint a dismissive look. "I see you have several new faces since I was here last."

Quint's shoulders tensed, waiting for the anvil to fall out of the sky.

Gathering up dishes from around the table, Angélica scoffed, "It *has* been over four years, Jared, since you last graced us with your presence."

Juan beamed at Quint like he was his favorite student. "We're fortunate to have a renowned photojournalist interested in our work this season. He's going to write an article on the work we're doing. Dr. Steel, I'd like to introduce you to—"

"Quint Parker," Steel finished for him.

Juan cocked his head to the side. "How do you …"

"I met Mr. Parker years ago. At this very site as a matter of fact." Steel lifted his cup to Quint in a mock toast. The jerk's smug expression made Quint want to throw the last dregs of his coffee in Steel's face.

Angélica paused in the midst of standing. He could feel her gaze boring into him. He peeked at her from the corner of his eye. Wrinkled brow, flared nostrils, death rays shooting from her peepers. Yep, he was dog shit now. It'd only be a matter of time until she scraped him off the bottom of her shoe.

"How long has it been, Quint?" Steel asked. "Almost two decades since we worked at this dig site with Dr. Hughes?"

Wincing, he tossed back the last of his coffee and held tight to the cup, waiting for Angélica to jump on his back and pummel the crap out of him.

"Isn't that what you told me last evening, Quint?" She picked up her mug and put it on top of the stack of plates she held. "You know, when you walked me to my tent?"

Quint nodded cautiously, wondering what game she was playing now. He guessed it was something to do with appearing in the know in front of Steel and the rest of her crew who were eavesdropping.

"Have some breakfast, Jared. But don't unpack your bag just yet." She cast her father a weighted stare. "Dad, I need to talk to you." With a nod at her foreman, she left the table, dropping her load of dishes onto the counter.

"Excuse us, please." Juan followed her out.

Quint watched them go, unsure if he should stay in the mess tent or go pack his stuff to head home. One look at Steel's smug expression and he knew one thing for certain—this dig site wasn't big enough for the two of them.

* * *

"We have a problem," Juan said, zipping the tent's mesh

flap closed behind him.

Angélica paced the floor. No, they had a category five hurricane about to make landfall at her dig site. "Did you know he was coming?"

"Last I heard, my request for continued funding was out of his hands." Pushing several books aside, he sat down on the corner of her desk. "He assured me he would do his best but made no guarantees."

"Do you really think they sent him down here to monitor your work?" Why Jared? Why now? She didn't need him nosing around. There was too much at stake.

"I wouldn't put it past the board to send him. They've cut funding left and right this year. Money is tight, and the state doesn't have any extra in their budget to help."

A snort sounded from under her cot, reminding her of the tortilla she'd stuffed in her pocket earlier. She squatted next to the cot. "Come here, Rover. I brought your breakfast."

The pudgy, reddish-brown baby javelina scrambled out.

"I can't believe you're keeping that overgrown rat in here, *gatita.*"

Rover snarfed the tortilla in one grunt. Angélica stroked the wiry hair on his head. "You're not a rat, are you? You're just a baby *jabalí.*" She used the Spanish name for javelina because it sounded cuter.

"Where did I go wrong with you, child? You know how destructive the herds of javelinas can be on our ranch. Not to mention how much they reek." He made a pinched face at Rover. "There's a reason they call them skunk pigs, you know."

"For one thing, his scent gland isn't active yet, so he doesn't stink. For another, javelinas make good pets if you start domesticating them young."

"He's a wild animal, *gatita.*"

"If you'd have just let me have a dog—"

"Don't start with that again. You know we weren't home long enough between your mother's and my digs to have pets."

"I know, I know. And Mom had allergies."

"And, yes, there were her allergies to consider. She hated breaking out in hives. What with her auburn hair and those red bumps, she said they made her look like Raggedy Ann." He smiled wistfully for a moment and then sobered, looking haggard around the edges. "What're we gonna do about Jared?"

"I don't know. Teodoro doesn't have enough codeine to make the jerk tolerable for a day or two, let alone a month."

Her father scoffed in agreement.

Straightening her makeshift splint on Rover's leg, she sighed. "I'd like to send him on his way back to Arizona, but I have a feeling you're going to do your best to talk me out of it."

Rover nuzzled her forearm with his cool snout, grunting softly. She scratched his head and smiled in spite of the fact that her ex-husband was about one thousand miles too close at the moment.

"I need that funding, Angélica. Without it, I won't be able to come back here next year."

"I know that, but I don't want him around right now." She tightened the knots holding the splint to Rover's leg. "Or your photojournalist either, for that matter." The bastard had tried to put one over on her already and he hadn't even been here twenty-four hours.

"Quint's article could bring some much needed additional funding for me. Besides, he's harmless. He just wants to follow you around and take pictures and notes."

"Quint is not harmless." She sank to the floor and lifted Rover onto her lap. "And he's not down here just to take pictures and notes."

"What then?"

"I haven't figured that out, but I'll have some answers before he follows me anywhere." He'd better cough up the truth or he'd find himself writing that article from wherever the hell he'd come from back in the States.

"I had no idea he'd been here before."

"That makes two of us."

She'd wanted to hit Quint upside the head with a tin plate back in the mess tent. Lord, what a fool she'd been last night, coming within a breath of telling him about the letter she'd received two years ago from Dr. Hughes' wife.

She blamed the moonlight and his citrus-scented cologne for her near slip. Hell, she was probably just low on vitamin C. It was simply a case of lust or scurvy. Quint was lucky she hadn't taken a bite out of him.

As much as that idea tickled her funny bone, she knew better. Or rather, she knew *herself* better. Ever since being burned by Jared's golden boy looks over a decade ago, she'd turned to the dark side. The tall, rugged, dark-haired sort of temptation Quint offered was her Achilles heel. Smelling like a mix of mandarin orange, jasmine, and musk he had offered her a heady dessert. Fortunately, common sense had prevailed, as it usually did.

"Well, whatever his reason for being here," her father said, "I highly doubt it will interfere with what we're trying to accomplish."

She stroked Rover's back. "How can you be so certain?"

"I may not know his personal history very well, but I did do some investigating and made some calls when it comes to his résumé."

"And?"

"He's no slouch in his field."

She shrugged. "I still think we should keep our lips sealed about Mom's theory."

"Of course. Although, if we find the evidence—"

"You mean *when* we find it."

He crossed his ankles. "You're that sure it's here?"

"Positive." Well, mostly, she thought, but he didn't need to hear about her doubts, not with so much working against them this year. "I read through all of Mom's notes again before the season started, including the list of items at the other site that led her to the glyph. The key here is the glyph we found that shows *Yum Cimil* riding in on the wind with the traveler."

"You mean the curse."

"No curse." She set Rover down in the mound of towels he was using for a bed and got to her feet. "A clue." One she knew would lead her to the proof they needed.

"It could be both."

"Dad," she started with a growl, then noticed the twinkling in his brown eyes.

"What do we do about Jared?" he asked again.

"Sacrifice him in the *cenote*. We can tell the crew his death will satisfy the curse's creator, and then everyone will stop jumping at shadows and get back to work."

Juan laughed. The sound of it made Angélica smile, easing some of her frustration. She picked up her leather pouch that held her tools. "If Jared stays, he sticks with you and does what he says he's down here to do."

"So, we work on finding the proof after everyone goes to bed?"

"Exactly." This was going to make her long days even longer, but she had no choice. She didn't want her father to lose funding. She needed his help and loved having him at her side during the dig season.

"No matter what, we can't let Jared find out what we're up to," she told her dad as she strapped on her tool pouch. "You could lose your funding."

Maybe even his job.

"And Quint?" Juan asked

As far as she was concerned, Mr. Photojournalist could go into the *cenote*, too. "Leave him to me."

Not knowing how well Quint was associated with Jared, she needed to tiptoe around both men. They could be old pals, reunited again to give her an even bigger headache than the curse.

She patted Rover on the head. His light snores continued without interruption. He wasn't a morning *jabalí*.

"Okay, we have a plan." Juan stood and dusted off the seat of his pants. He sneezed and then sneezed again. "*Gatita*, you need a maid in here. Why don't you dust occasionally?" He eyeballed the pile of clothes she'd thrown in the corner on the tent floor. "This place is a sty." He pointed at Rover. "You even have the pig to prove it."

"He's not a pig."

"He's got hooves, so that's close enough."

She stuck her tongue out at him. "I've been too busy to clean lately." Or sleep. Unzipping the mesh flap, she motioned for her father to lead the way. "Remember, mum's the word." She grabbed her straw sunhat from a hook on the main support pole.

"Uh, Angélica …" Juan called in through the tent flap.

"Especially around Quint," she added as she stepped out into the morning sunshine and ran smack into the blasted photojournalist.

Hells bells! She stumbled back a couple of steps, regaining her balance and handle on the situation.

She leveled her chin at him. "Hello, Mr. Parker." There was no time like the present to set him straight on how his time here would be spent going forward, and how she felt about lies and likewise, deceit.

"It seems you and I need to discuss your future at this site," she told him. "And *your* past."

Chapter Four

H-men: Traditional Maya priest-curer; a shaman.

Years ago while working on a job up near Kodiak, Alaska, for an outdoor magazine, Quint had stepped out of his tent in the middle of the night to take a piss and had found himself nose-to-nose with a grizzly bear. Luckily, the bear had been equally surprised and had left Quint's face intact before dashing off into the dark.

Quint wasn't sure Angélica would be as kind as the grizzly had been, especially with her expression now mirroring Mr. Hyde's on a bad hair day. He needed to figure out how to get Dr. Jekyll to come back and quick.

Several questions flew through his mind as he stared into her squint. What did she not want her dad to tell him? Was it about Dr. Hughes? About something they'd found in one of the temples? Something to do with Steel? Quint's curiosity was sniffing the air, but he was smart enough to keep his trap shut. Convincing her not to kick him off the dig site took priority over everything else right then.

"See you at lunch, Dad." Angélica dismissed her father without taking her eyes off of Quint.

He dove right in. "Dr. García, we need to talk."

She scoffed, "Ya think?"

"Let me start with: *I'm sorry.*"

Her expression remained granite-like, not crumbling even a smidgen at the edges. "Before I decide whether to accept your apology, Mr. Parker, would you care to explain what you were trying to accomplish last night?"

"Are you going to kick me off the dig site?" He didn't feel like wasting his breath if all was for naught.

"That depends on your explanation."

A new rash of sweat formed on his upper lip. "I wanted to see how much you knew about the history of this place." That was mostly true.

"Why didn't you ask me?"

"I was trying to be clever." He aimed for a little levity.

"Turns out you were just being an ass."

He deserved that. "I'm sorry."

"You already said that." She crossed her arms over her chest. "Why are you really here?"

"To write an article about the site Dr. Hughes put so much blood, sweat, and tears into—a sort of tribute."

One auburn eyebrow lifted in response.

"He was a good man, taking me under his wing when I was rebelling against my father's rule," he continued truthfully. "I thought it'd be a fitting way to thank him for his part in straightening me out, helping me to find my way when I was too young and stupid to realize I was lost."

"What's your plan of attack?"

"What do you mean?" He was tiptoeing here and didn't want to misread her question and step on a land mine.

"Well, knowing that you were here with Dr. Hughes twenty years ago makes me wonder if this will be some kind of comparison of how he ran the site back then to how I'm running it now. A measurement of his successes versus mine, maybe? Or were you thinking about incorporating my parents and their efforts?"

"No, not a comparison. More along the lines of noting how things have changed—methods of finding artifacts, site geography, ideas on structural architecture. Things like that." He was winging it, his fingers crossed that it sounded plausible. "I'd only mention your parents in a brief history, if at all. Although your father has some interesting theories that I'd like to talk to him about and consider including." Before she got her shoulders all hunched about that last line, he added, "In a favorable light only, of course."

She cocked her head to the side, studying him. "When were you going to tell me the truth about your history here?"

"After I'd found out what you knew about the site. I thought that you might be more open if you didn't know I'd been here before."

"Was I?"

It was his turn to scoff. "Hell, no."

"Good." Her gaze darted past him, her nostrils flaring. She swore under her breath.

"Am I staying or going, Dr. García?" Quint asked, looking around to see what had her attention.

Steel was coming their way across the plaza.

She focused back on Quint. "My father has faith in you and thinks you could be beneficial to his future. Because of that you can stay."

"Thank you." He held out his hand to shake on it. "I appreciate the second chance."

"No more games." She looked at his open palm, hesitating, and then clasped his hand. "Trust me when I say that you do not want to get on my bad side." To his surprise, she pulled him down to her level. When she spoke, her voice was low and sinister. "I may be known for digging up bones in this jungle, but I can bury them here as easily, too."

Quint blinked in surprise. When he pulled his hand back, he saw the twinkle of amusement in her green eyes. She had a wicked sense of humor. He liked that in a woman. His gaze slid down, stalling on her lips. Firm but lush. He liked them, too.

Steel's voice sliced through his contemplation of the fun he could have with the witty doctor and those lips of hers. "Angélica, I need to talk to you." He pushed his expensive sunglasses up on his head, blatantly avoiding looking in Quint's direction as he drew near. "Darling, couldn't you find something more appropriate to wear in front of your crew?"

Angélica glanced down at her yellow T-shirt, wiping some dirt and what looked like hairbrush bristles from her chest.

Quint considered offering her his help. He was pretty sure he'd do a more thorough job of removing every single bristle.

"What I wear is none of your business, Jared." She touched Quint's forearm, drawing his gaze back northward. "I need to talk to María. Meet me outside the supply tent in ten minutes."

"Will do." Quint wanted to grab his camera from his tent and a bottle of water.

With a nod at both of them, she strode off toward the mess tent.

"What about me?" Steel called after her.

She turned, walking backwards a few steps. "You're not my problem. Dad's waiting for you in the Sunset Temple." She spun back around and left Quint alone with Steel, both of them watching her go.

"Lovely, isn't she?" Steel asked.

"I hadn't noticed," he lied without missing a beat. "I've been too busy taking orders from her since I arrived."

"Then continue not noticing." Jared hadn't changed in twenty years, still trying to rule where he had no authority. "And keep your hands to yourself."

Fuck off, Steel. "When it comes to Angélica, what I do with my *hands* should be the least of your concern." Quint hoped she never caught wind of his boast, or she'd have him buried up to his neck next to a red ant hill.

"Dr. Steel!" Juan's voice echoed across the plaza, interrupting their tête-à-tête. "Dr. Steel, please come with me.

I could use your expertise."

Expertise? That should feed Steel's ego … for the moment anyway.

"Looks like you need to go." Quint resisted the urge to use his boot to help Steel on his way.

"What are you doing here, Parker?"

Quint hid his hostility behind a cheesy smile. "I might ask you the same thing, Dr. Steel."

* * *

A short time later, Angélica led Mr. Big-time Photojournalist to the crumbling limestone steps outside the Temple of the Crow where Esteban waited for them while smoking a cigarette.

She paused at the base of the steps, noticing the worried pinch of Esteban's face as he stared over at the Temple of the Water Witch. The boy had been wound tight since the night he'd fractured his arm, and trying to convince him that no curse existed was a waste of breath.

"Esteban, this is Mr. Parker. He's going to work with us today and take some pictures."

"Call me Quint." He pointed at the sling wrapped around Esteban's right arm. "What happened?"

"*Mal viento*," Esteban whispered, his gaze darting across to the other temple as he inhaled more nicotine.

Quint turned to Angélica. "An evil wind?"

"He fell down some steps," she explained, wondering how much Spanish Quint understood.

Before Esteban could spur more questions with his paranoia, she told him to catch up when he finished his cigarette and motioned for Quint to follow her. She outpaced him to the top, much more accustomed to the heat than he. She waited inside the dim passageway leading to the heart of the temple while her eyes adjusted.

Quint caught up to her, fanning his sweat-soaked shirt.

"Jesus, it's hot." He leaned against the wall, breathing hard.

If he was this hot already, he'd be melting by noon. She pulled out the extra water she'd brought along for him and held it out to him. "Take a drink."

He looked down at the bottle. "Thanks, but I brought my own."

"You'll need more, take it."

He smirked at the bottle but did as told. "Has anyone ever told you that you're a tad bossy?"

"My father may have mentioned it in passing once or twice." She watched him tip the bottle back and swallow several gulps, his Adam's apple bobbing under the dark stubble shadowing his neck. Her gaze drifted down to the front of his shirt, noticing the contours underneath the cotton fabric sticking to him.

She turned away, picking at a loose stone on the opposite wall. It had been a while since she'd thought about a male as anything other than another body to help her achieve her goals for a dig season. If she were going to succeed this year in finding the proof she needed, she'd better keep it that way.

Quint capped the bottle. "I thought you said at breakfast that we'd be working with Alonso today."

"Change of plans. Fernando needs him." She flicked on her flashlight and led the way deeper into the temple. "Watch your head." Quint was about six inches too tall to stand up straight in the tunnel. The ancient Maya people were mostly Angélica's size or shorter. They hadn't built these temples for someone of his height or shoulder width.

"Any questions before we get started?" She checked the floor for fresh rat or mouse scat.

"Do you ever work after supper?"

Yes, she did. Alone. Almost every night. But only her father knew about that.

"No. I'm not sure if you remember, but these temples soak up the heat throughout the day. By suppertime, it'll feel like a sauna in here."

The sound of footfalls drew close, followed by the smell of cigarette smoke.

"*¿Listo?*" She checked to see if Esteban was ready to get started.

At his nod, she led them further down the passageway, checking behind her every few feet to make sure Quint and Esteban were following without trouble.

Where the tunnel forked, she glanced at Quint. "That daylight you see up ahead on the right is the main hall. I'll take you there this afternoon."

"It's a date." He took another swig from the bottle she'd given him.

Did he always flirt on a job? Or was she being oversensitive and making something out of nothing like Harriet in Jane Austen's *Emma*? It had been a while since she'd slept with a man. Maybe her radar was rusty.

Moving on, she headed down the cramped corridor on her left. A short way into it, she stopped. "Hold up a minute." She shined the light on the ceiling and walls, and then studied the hard-packed dirt floor. "Okay, it's clear."

"Of what?" Quint's breath warmed her damp neck.

"Mice, rats, snakes, and bats." She stepped over a large chunk of limestone that had fallen from the ceiling last month, antsy to put more space between them.

Quint followed. "Are you looking for tracks?"

"Yes, along with waste and food remains." She waited until Esteban had made it past the stone before moving on.

"What do you do if you see a sign?" His tone had a slight edge to it.

"Step carefully."

She chuckled at the litany of swear words he grumbled about the jungle and its many wonderful dangers. Quint Parker might be a hindrance, but she found herself smiling more during their trek through the dark temple than she had since the damned curse had shown up.

The corridor opened into a small, rectangular room.

Angélica grabbed two LED flashlights from the far side of the chamber. "Quint and I are taking the tunnel to Sub Chamber F," she told Esteban, handing him one of the lights, and then motioned to the fresco-covered wall behind her. "You stay here and continue charting."

Esteban pulled a drawing pad from his pack.

"If you finish with this before lunch," she continued, "you can take over where Alonso left off yesterday charting the other tunnel."

He nodded, his gaze darting from one shadow-filled corner to the next.

She squeezed his shoulder reassuringly and then handed the other light to Quint. At his wrinkled brow, she motioned for him to follow, trekking through a narrow archway into a separate room. She crossed the stone floor and slid sideways through a wide fissure in the far wall.

He peered into the thick crack after her, holding back. "You've got to be kidding me. You call this a tunnel?"

"I call this claustrophobic." She slid deeper into the tunnel. In her line of work, she couldn't afford to get fidgety in tight places. "Come on, it's only like this for about ten feet."

"Then what?"

She looked back at him. "Then we crawl."

His eyes widened in alarm. "There's no way in hell you are getting me in that tiny crack. I'll wait out here, see if Esteban needs some help."

No, he wouldn't. Esteban would fill Quint's head with tales about *Xtabay* and curses. Besides, she really wanted him to see what was down this particular rabbit hole.

"Don't tell me you're afraid," she taunted. "Not a big, strong, brave photojournalist like you? I thought you ate adventure for breakfast every morning."

"That was in my twenties. Adventure gives me heartburn now. I prefer breathing on a regular basis to risking life and limb every other day."

"Come on, Parker. Don't be a wuss about this."

"You can call me all of the names you want, but I'm not going to get stuck and possibly crushed in a temple wall today. It's not on my agenda."

"You won't get crushed, trust me. Maybe just pinched a little with a scrape here and there." She held out her hand. "Take my hand. I'll keep you safe."

He shined his flashlight in her eyes. "Being nice to me now, Dr. García, will not lure me into that snake hole."

She squinted in the brightness. "I've been nice to you since you got here." She hadn't sent him back to the village like she'd originally wanted to, had she? Not even after the game he'd played last night.

"Not nice enough to get me in there."

"Take my hand, Quint." She spoke soothingly this time, trying a different tactic.

He frowned, lowering the beam of light. "Why do we even need to go in there?"

"Because there's something I want you to see. Something that will 'wow' you."

"Really?" His gaze strayed down over her profile, stalling on her hips. "It's been a while since I've been 'wowed.'"

That made two of them. How long was he talking? Was there a wanna-be Mrs. Parker back in the States pining for him? She'd noticed the lack of a ring or tan line, but that didn't mean he was unattached. Maybe she could figure out a way to hint at …

What in the hell are you doing?!

Shit.

Double shit.

This couldn't happen. Not now. Not here. Not with Jared on site. And certainly not with her father's future at stake. She needed to diffuse the situation somehow.

Making a show of rolling her eyes, she tried to jest about what had passed between them. "Parker, did you really just go *there?*"

"Hey, I can't help it that my mind would rather go *there*

than inside this crack where I could get squished flat."

"You won't get squished." She slid closer to him, stretching her hand out further. "Come on."

After a few more seconds of hesitation, he took her hand, his palm slick with sweat. He slid sideways inside the fissure with her.

"Before we do this," he said, dragging anchor until she stopped, "I want to apologize for what I insinuated a moment ago. You being an attractive woman doesn't give me license to be crude. My mother would have flicked my ear for not being a gentleman. I blame testosterone."

He thought she was attractive? Even in this heat when she was constantly covered in sweat and dirt and grime? Even without a hint of makeup and her deodorant struggling to keep up? Sheesh. He must not have been 'wowed' in a *really* long time.

Appreciating his apology, she joked, "I thought I told you to leave your testosterone back in your tent." She tugged him onward.

"No, you ordered me to leave my smart ass comebacks behind," he whispered, as if afraid his voice might bring down the walls. He licked his lips. "Are you sure there aren't any snakes in here?"

"Mostly."

His grip on her hand tightened. "You're not being very comforting."

"I'm already holding your hand, Parker. What more do you need? Your binkie?"

"How come you got to bring your smart ass comebacks along but I didn't?"

"Because I'm in charge."

"Hmmm. Normally I like it when a woman's in charge."

Did he? A flurry of pulse-racing images flew through her head until she squelched them.

They slid along in silence for a short time, the end in sight.

"Ever thought of widening this?" he asked.

"Dad isn't confident the surrounding structure could handle that kind of activity."

He cursed. "I appreciate your honesty while I'm sardined by this 'surrounding structure.'"

She chuckled. When he growled in response, her chuckles grew into giggles.

"I am so going to pay you back for this, Angélica."

The tunnel widened at the bottom and narrowed to a slit at the top. Pulling free of his grip, she dropped to her hands and knees and crawled through the remaining few feet, ordering him to follow. He obeyed, cursing again.

She took the flashlight from Quint as he scrambled out of the crevice, helping him to his feet.

Holding up the light for him to see the walls encircling them, she smiled with pride. "What do you think?" The sight before her still made her heart quicken.

"That I should never let you talk me into squeezing through cracks again."

She patted his back. "I'll make it up to you later."

"Yes, you will." He wiped the sweat from his face with the bottom of his shirt, giving her a glance at his bare stomach.

Turning away, she made a point of searching the floor with the beam of light until she was sure he'd lowered his shirt. When she looked back at him, he was studying the walls with a perplexed expression.

"What is this place?" He ran his hand over one of the hundreds of glyphs surrounding them.

"A tomb."

He moved over to the grave-sized hole she'd excavated last week. "Are there other tombs in this temple?"

"Nope. The Temple of the Crow was not made for burial tomb purposes." She handed the flashlight back.

He took it. "You're contradicting yourself."

No, she was having fun with him, adding some excitement to her show-and-tell presentation. "This isn't the Temple of the Crow."

He frowned. "Now you're losing me."

"That crack we just slid through was the outer wall to a temple built centuries before the Temple of the Crow."

"You mean they built over the top of this one?"

"Yes." She pulled a trowel and paintbrush out of her tool pouch and handed the paintbrush to him.

"Are there other temples inside of this one?"

"I doubt it. This temple isn't big enough to encompass another. The Temple of the Water Witch is another story."

He fanned the brush. "How many are under that one?"

"So far two, maybe three. But don't even think about nosing around in there without me."

"I won't."

"I mean it, Quint." She emphasized her feelings with a pointed glare. "These temples are dangerous."

"Isn't that sweet?" His hazel eyes crinkled in jest. "You being so concerned about me and all."

"Yeah, well I don't need an injured photojournalist messing up my dig season schedule." She shot him a quick grin to take the sting out of the truth.

"Ah, shucks. I bet you say that to all of the photojournalists who sweat their asses off with you inside of these death traps."

"Nope. Just the ones who need their hands held while squeezing through dark tunnels."

His laughter filled the small burial chamber. "You know what, Dr. García? I like you."

"Splendid." She hid the flame set alight by his words behind a shield of sarcasm. "I'll be sure to write your name over and over in my diary tonight, dotting the *i* in 'Quint' with a little heart."

His teeth looked even whiter with his beard stubble darkening his cheeks and chin. The shadows added an aspect of ruggedness to his face that made her stomach do loop-de-loops. "I had no idea you'd be so clever, Angélica."

The way he phrased that gave her pause. "What do you

mean you had no idea?"

He looked down at the brush in his hands, fiddling with it. "It's just that from the moment I arrived you've been so serious. I thought maybe you were always like that. Serious, I mean."

No, he'd meant something else, but Angélica could tell he wasn't going to cough it up at the moment. She decided to let it go, but her guard stepped back into place, quelling their banter. "Do you have any other questions about this sub chamber?"

"Yes." He seemed anxious to return to the past. "Why did they build over the top of the old temples?"

She dropped her tool pouch on the mound of dirt next to the shallow hole. "There are several theories around regarding the subject. Lack of space, easier than knocking down the old one, a desire not to disturb the dead buried in the older temples." She stepped into the hole, glancing across the floor at him.

"So what exactly are you and your father trying to accomplish here?" He extracted a small digital camera from his back pocket, taking several pictures.

"That's too broad of a question."

He looked over at her, his eyes soft and glittering in the low light. "Okay, what are you doing here?"

Finishing what her mother started. "I work for the Mexican government." She picked up her trowel and carefully dug in the dark soil at the bottom of the hole.

"Have you always?"

"No. I used to work for the same university as Dad a long time ago."

He pocketed his camera and moved closer, his khakis rustling as he squatted next to the hole. "Why did you leave?"

Jared's face popped into her head, followed by a chest burning flash of irritation as usual. "It wasn't working out."

"Did it have anything to do with Dr. Steel?"

She stopped and stared up at him, not liking the direction

this was going. "How about we stick to the past?"

He gave her a lopsided smile. "I thought I was."

"Your job is to ask about what we do here at the site." She mopped the sweat from her brow with her forearm. "Not about my personal history."

"Curiosity got the best of me. Sorry."

"Apology accepted. Now get busy brushing off those glyphs on that wall over there. We need to make impressions of them when we're done in the other chamber."

Quint brushed in silence for a while as she dug.

"You know," he said, interrupting her fantasy of telling Jared off for using her father to worm his way onto her dig site and then shipping the lying bastard out of there. "I bet readers would love to learn more about how a young woman from the States wound up running a Maya dig site."

"I'm not that young."

"Young-ish then."

"Exploit someone else's life, Parker. Mine's off limits."

"What about your mom?"

"Hers is, too."

"Even off the record?"

"Definitely." She didn't trust a journalist ever to be truly off the record.

"Did you know Dr. Hughes?"

She blinked in surprise. That had come out of nowhere. "He was before my time."

"Did your father know him?"

She stopped digging. "Aren't you supposed to be taking pictures of things in here for that article?"

He shrugged. "I already took a few. The lighting isn't the best."

"What about notes? Don't journalists carry around a pad of paper? Where are your notes?"

He tapped his head. "I keep them up here."

Fine! Climbing out of the hole, she dusted off her pants. "Take this," she grabbed his hand and slapped the trowel into his palm.

"What am I doing with it?"

"Experiencing the joy of digging firsthand. And while you dig, I'll explain the Mexican government's process for finding, naming, documenting, excavating, and profiting from archaeological ruins."

"Then what?" he asked, gripping the trowel.

"Lunch."

His gaze narrowed. "Are you going out of your way to vex me, or does it come naturally to you?"

Angélica smiled. "Dig."

* * *

Later that afternoon, Quint leaned against the passage wall in the outer Temple of the Crow. After working in the heat and humidity all morning and then swimming through it again following lunch and a quick *siesta*, he felt like he'd been wrung out and hung up to drip—there was no way he'd dry in this sauna.

"We're not going back in that tomb are we?" He didn't even bother wiping away the sweat rolling down from his temple. More would follow as soon as he sopped it up.

Angélica shook her head. "It's too hot in there now. As the day goes on, we work our way from inner chambers to outer ones."

"Thank the Maya gods for that. I had visions of you shoehorning me back through that damned crevice."

"Listen, I may be bossy, but I'm not a slave driver. We're not building Egyptian pyramids here." She sipped from her bottle of water while frowning at him. "If you have a heat stroke where I can't pull you out quick, we're in trouble."

Eyeing her up and down, he considered her words. He couldn't see her dragging him out of anywhere, although she was no lightweight.

She packed away her water bottle. "When you're ready, I'll

show you the main hall I told you about earlier. Esteban can catch up with us when he's finished outside with his cigarette."

Quint pushed away from the wall, careful not to split open his skull on the low ceiling. He trailed behind her, admiring the view of her backside. He might be hotter than hell, but he wasn't dead. Not yet anyway.

She'd tucked the sleeves of her T-shirt under her bra straps, leaving the curves of her shoulders bare. Sweat glistened on her skin, dotting the back of her top. Not once today had she complained about the heat or even slowed down. He was starting to doubt she was human.

"Here we are," she whispered a minute later and led him by the arm. She tiptoed into a large open chamber, pulling him along behind her, shushing him with her index finger to her lips. He nodded, pretending to zip his lips. When they stilled, she released her hold on him.

A rustling sound echoed through the room, mixed with an assortment of hoarse, grating-like rattles, clicks, and coos. So this was why it was named the Temple of the Crow.

He stepped gingerly through the bird droppings, peering up at the high ceiling. Thick shadows swallowed the light where steep vaults came together. The birds must have built their nests on the flat, square capitals that connected each of the limestone columns running the length of the room to the vaulted ceiling. Across the vast chamber, a platform rose two feet above the rest of the floor.

Slivers of light pierced through thin apertures in the walls, adding a sacred air to the room. He peered across the room in the half-light, trying to make sense of the decorative carvings covering the low wall of the platform.

A brief fluttering overhead brought his attention back to the tall columns. At the base of each, faded and chipped paintings wrapped around the limestone. He'd need his other camera to really capture the hallowed feel of the chamber, maybe enhancing the colors with a tobacco filter, sharpening with a polarizer.

In the empty spaces between each column, a three-foot statue stood guard. Some of the statues had crumbled, but the majority remained intact, complete with impressive detail work emphasized by the room's deep shadows.

For now, he'd take some quick shots.

As he pulled his camera from his pocket, Angélica caught his hand. She pointed at the ceiling.

"I know," he mouthed back. He already had his shutter set to silent mode on his camera.

She pulled him down so she could whisper close to his ear. "It's a corbel-vaulted ceiling."

Her words tickled over his skin, the heat of her breath making him sweat for an entirely different reason. He tried to focus on the task at hand, to rein in his growing attraction for Steel's ex-wife. He did not need to think about her trailing her tongue along his outer ear.

"What's that?" he whispered back in her ear, inhaling the sweet lemony-orange fragrance of her shampoo. The smell blended with her coconut-scented sunblock. Pour some wine and a little brandy on her skin and she'd probably taste like sangria. The thought alone made his pulse jackhammer.

"A characteristic of the Classic Maya Period," she whispered, but he didn't give a flying fuck about ceilings, crows, or Jared Steel at that moment.

He stared down at her face, wondering what it would feel like to kiss those lips, but then he doused the fantasy. She'd probably kill him if she knew he was even pondering touching her, and then she'd hang him from the corbel-vaulted ceiling as an example for any other males who forgot she was The Boss.

She went up on her toes again. "Ask Dad about it later," she breathed. She must have mistaken his silent look for incomprehension. He was lucky she couldn't read minds as well as she could Maya glyphs.

Holding up his camera, he showed her the flash button, making a point of turning it off.

She nodded.

He wanted to try a shot with the afternoon sunlight streaming in. Squatting to get a better angle, he leaned against a column to steady his shot. As he pushed the shutter release, something slammed into him from behind, knocking him into one of the crumbling statues. His camera flew out of his hands.

The ceiling exploded. Squawking and screeching, the crows whirled and darted out through the window slits.

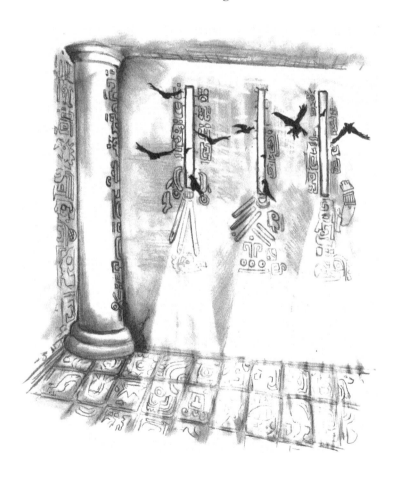

As the last of the birds flew away, Quint sat up. His left forearm tingled, a nasty gash dotted with blood.

Angélica squatted next to him, taking his arm in hand, grimacing down at his injury. "You need to see Teodoro."

"What happened?"

"Esteban and his clumsy feet."

Quint glanced around the chamber. "Where is he?"

"He fled with the crows." She smirked. "I've never seen anyone move so fast in my life."

She stood, holding out her hand to help him to his feet. The strength in her tug surprised him. Maybe she *could* drag him out of trouble.

"You okay? Any other injuries?"

His knee stung where it had connected with the floor, but his pants weren't ripped, so he kept quiet about it. "Just my arm."

He picked up his camera, brushed off a few feathers, and looked it over. It still worked. Good. He turned it off and shoved it into the leg pocket in his khakis.

"Teodoro's place is next to the mess tent, remember?" She glanced at his arm again, her forehead wrinkled. "It's the pole-and-thatch building. You think you can find it on your own?"

Quint waved off her concern. "I can just wrap a T-shirt around it."

"No, you can't. Look around you, Parker. This isn't the cleanest place. The closest hospital is over sixty miles away, and that's after you make it to pavement. Believe me, you don't want to get a bad infection out here in the jungle."

He could see this was a losing battle. She'd made up her mind. "All right, I'll go and be back in a bit."

"Don't come back. It'll be suppertime soon. Get some rest. You need to be ready to go again tomorrow."

Relieved as he was to escape the heat of the temple, Quint groused as he marched across the plaza toward Teodoro's quarters. Steel being here would probably keep Angélica on edge, meaning more tight-lipped than ever about anything related to Dr. Hughes. Maybe Juan would be more willing to share, but with Steel around, getting time alone with him might be a problem.

Teodoro had the only pole-and-thatch building in the camp, so it didn't take a Sherlock Holmes effort to find it. Quint hesitated at the weathered wooden door, closed fist in the air, not sure if the custom here was to knock or just enter. Before he could make up his mind, the door flew open and Teodoro stood there.

"Quint! Come in." Juan's voice boomed from the shadowy interior. "Teodoro was about to slip me one of his notorious voodoo potions."

Teodoro shook his head. "I do not know voodoo." He moved aside for Quint to duck through the doorway.

"The last time he made me drink a cup of that stuff," Juan said from where he sat on a cot in the corner, rubbing his jaw, "I howled like a monkey for hours."

Glancing around, Quint took in the dirt floor, rustic looking table and benches, and multitude of various shaped gourds hanging on the back wall. To his left was a wall-length shelf packed with dark brown, antique bottles of all shapes and sizes.

Quint turned back to Juan, noticing his face looked a bit pale. "What's wrong?"

"It's this darned tooth of mine. Ever since we found that curse, it's been giving me trouble."

There was that curse again. Quint thought about asking more about it, but he figured if Angélica caught wind of his snooping, she'd be even less likely to share information. Hell, she'd probably take today's lesson on the Mexican government one step further and cover the history of the damned country, starting with the Aztecs.

Teodoro came up beside Quint and grabbed his arm, turning it toward the light shining through the window.

"How'd that happen?" Juan pushed off the cot, joining Teodoro's examination of Quint's arm.

"Esteban ran into me when I wasn't looking."

Juan snorted. "That boy's ankles are made of rubber."

Teodoro let go of his arm and shuffled over to the shelf full of bottled concoctions.

Throwing caution to the wind, Quint asked Juan, "How do you know it's a curse?"

"Because I've been working among Maya ruins for a long time, and I've come across other curses." Juan returned to the cot. "Marianne found one at a site where she was acting as a visiting archaeologist, lending her expertise on reading Maya glyphs." He frowned at Quint. "It was that dig site she was leaving when her helicopter crashed."

Quint had read in one of the articles on Juan that his wife had died as a result of injuries from a helicopter crash in the jungle. If he remembered right, she'd lived through the crash, but had passed shortly afterwards in the hospital. "I'm sorry about your wife."

"Me, too." Juan sniffed and then cleared his throat. "Anyway, when it comes to the curse Angélica and I found, all I know is it reads like a curse. Whether or not anything more comes of it, only time will tell. However, since we found it, odd things have been happening around here."

"Like your motorcycle not working?"

"For one, yes. Having a tree fall and destroy our only means of reaching the outside world via phone and computer is another." Juan rubbed his jaw on his sore tooth side. "Do you believe in the supernatural, Quint?"

Was he serious? One look at Juan's expression left little doubt. Quint weighed telling Juan the truth. He'd experienced some crazy shit off and on over the last three decades, but he preferred to keep his theories to himself.

"Not usually," he lied, thinking of the protection charm that his Aunt Zoe had made, the one he carried with him wherever he traveled.

"I didn't use to when I was young." Juan eased onto his back, staring up at the thatched roof. "But too much has happened in my life now not to suspect there are things going on beyond our natural world."

"What about Angélica?" Quint wondered how she felt about her mother's demise in relation to the curse at that other dig site.

"My daughter is way too logical to buy into anything supernatural. She is a mirror of her mother on that thought. Marianne didn't for a moment believe she was in any danger after finding that curse. She always said I was too superstitious for my own good." He chuckled. "Angélica has recently echoed those very words when it comes to this Lord of Death curse. But I can't help it. I can't shake the feeling that we're in for more trouble."

Juan's words left Quint feeling antsy. What in the hell had he stumbled into down here? Had Dr. Hughes found the curse, too?

"Curse is bad," Teodoro agreed. The healer returned to Quint's side, lifted his arm, and without warning dumped what looked like iodine on the gash.

"Ouch!" Quint winced. "You could've warned me."

His complaint was met with a smirk from Teodoro. "No crying from you." He cocked his head toward Juan. "He cry two times today. That's too much. No more."

"I did not cry." Juan grinned. "He's exaggerating."

Teodoro looked at Quint and shook his head, refuting Juan's accusation. Then he splashed iodine on the gash again, soaking up the overflow with a rag.

Quint cringed until the sting eased. "Did this curse list specifics?" he asked through gritted teeth.

"No. It just talked about the Lord of Death and this village. I'd show you the glyphs, but Angélica is the only one around here who can read them."

That was okay. Quint doubted the bullheaded woman would appreciate her father sharing without her approval.

Teodoro slapped some green, petroleum jelly-like goop on Quint's wound, wrapped a wide strip of gauze around his forearm, and then sealed it all with duct tape.

It was crude, Quint thought, but it would definitely hold. He walked over to a piece of a tree trunk making do as a stool and took a seat. "Your daughter seems a bit stubborn."

"More than a *bit*. She takes after her mother."

"I asked about her mom today."

Juan looked over at him, both eyebrows raised.

"She refused to tell me anything about her."

"You're lucky she didn't bite your head off for asking."

Juan sat up as Teodoro approached him with a bowl made from the lower half of a gourd.

"I must have caught her in a good mood."

"Angélica doesn't like to talk about her personal life with strangers. The divorce only made her more closed-mouthed."

He wondered what she had to hide. Was it anything involving her ex-husband? "Did you get along with Dr. Steel when they were married?"

"For the most part. Jared can be quite charming when he wants to be."

Yeah, Quint remembered. He also remembered how much he lied and manipulated.

Teodoro motioned for Juan to open his mouth.

Juan frowned at the bowl in Teodoro's hand "What's that?"

Teodoro dipped his finger in the bowl and scooped out a pasty, beige substance. "It numbs tooth."

"Will it sting?"

"No. Open."

Juan reared back. "Let me put it on."

Teodoro wiped his finger on the edge of the bowl and dropped it on Juan's lap, mumbling something Quint couldn't decipher. He grabbed a full-size gourd from the back wall and left the hut, leaving him alone with Juan.

"He needs to work on his bedside manner," Juan said with a wink. He dipped his finger in the goop and rubbed it on his tooth and gum. The gagging face he made left no doubt as to the taste of the stuff.

Quint hid his amusement behind a closed fist.

When Juan finished, he wiped his finger on his pants. "Teodoro wants to perform a *Lolcatali* ceremony to calm everyone down and get things back to normal, but Angélica won't allow it."

"A 'local' what?"

"It's a ritual that's supposed to protect us from evil spirits."

A curse *and* evil spirits? This was beginning to feel like one of his Aunt Zoe's bedtime stories.

"Does Steel know about the curse?" Quint asked.

"Not from me."

Quint stared down at his duct tape. This curse business was bad news. With everyone feeling skittish, his chances of digging for the truth about Dr. Hughes' disappearance were slimmer than he'd figured. He decided to get down to business now that he had a few minutes alone with Juan. "Did you know Dr. Hughes?"

"Not as well as you did, apparently."

He met Juan's keen stare. "*Touché.*"

"I never met Dr. Hughes," Juan told him. "But I've known of him since Marianne and I took over the site. We learned a lot about his work from the copies of his notes that his wife sent to us back when we first started here."

Mrs. Hughes had been in contact with him back then? Did Jeff know about that?

"I have several binders of Dr. Hughes' work thanks to her generosity. Plus, she sent one of his journals that talked about the work he was doing down here."

Had she made a copy of the journal's pages first? Quint needed to see this journal. Tapping the tips of his fingers together, he wondered how he could get Juan to let him read Dr. Hughes' journal without arousing suspicion.

"You know, I've been doing some thinking since breakfast," Juan said.

Something in his tone made Quint's shoulders tighten. "Oh, yeah?" He tried to act like they were just two guys shooting the shit.

"How did you know Dr. Hughes?"

"I went to school with his son." That truth came easy.

"I see. And how is Mrs. Hughes doing these days?"

"She passed away last year."

Juan frowned, his surprise at this news appearing legitimate. "I'm sorry to hear that." His voice was sincere as he rubbed his jaw.

"Thanks. She was a kind-hearted woman." Dogged, too. She never gave up on finding her husband.

"She wrote to me several times over the past eight years," Juan continued, "asking repeatedly if I'd found any clues that would help explain her husband's disappearance."

Quint remained silent, his body coiled with tension. He had a feeling Juan was heading somewhere with this conversation, and he wasn't sure if it would end with him tied to the railroad tracks.

"But now she's gone." Juan crossed his arms over his chest. "And oddly enough, here you sit—someone who not only knew Dr. Hughes, but who also worked with him twenty years ago at this very site." His gaze bore into Quint. "Someone who worked here the last year Dr. Hughes was ever seen or heard from."

Quint held Juan's shrewd gaze. "That's correct."

"Don't you think that's an interesting coincidence, Quint?"

Chapter Five

Ek Chuah: The Maya god of merchants and warriors.

B usted.
Damn it.

Quint kept his face schooled, hiding behind a frozen smile while he scrambled to figure out how to keep his true agenda hidden from Juan's unblinking scrutiny.

It hadn't taken Juan long to pin the tail on Quint. Hell, a bottle of whiskey in a five-handed poker game lasted longer.

"Well," Quint said, licking his lips. "It might seem …"

The door banged open. Several of the bottles on Teodoro's shelf rattled and clinked against each other. Steel and Fernando squeezed through the doorway with Alonso in their arms.

Quint flew to his feet at the sight of Alonso's bloody pant leg. He raced over to help. Angélica's warning about the danger of injuries out here in the jungle replayed in his thoughts as he noticed the blood smeared on Fernando's hands and shirt from carrying Alonso. Before he had a chance to ask what had happened, Teodoro rushed inside and ordered Juan off the cot.

They laid Alonso down gently as soon as Juan stepped aside. The boy cried out, arching in pain.

Juan peered over their shoulders. "What happened to him?"

Teodoro cut away Alonso's pant leg. An ugly, jagged gash ran along the outside of the boy's calf. The coppery scent of blood, sweat, and dirt filled the small hut.

Steel made a retching sound, then covered his mouth and rushed over to the window, hanging his head outside.

Frowning in surprise, Quint stared at Steel's back as he visibly took several deep breaths. Apparently the big shot archaeologist had a problem with the sight of blood. Quint didn't remember that tidbit from when they'd worked for Dr. Hughes. Then again, he hadn't exactly exchanged scar stories with Steel back then.

"Pulley line broke," Fernando told Juan, wiping his hands and arms off on a rag Teodoro handed him. "A rock landed on his leg."

"Son of a …" Juan ran his hand through his hair. "Where's Angélica?"

"*No lo sé,*" Fernando said with a shrug. "But she sent Esteban to help us a little bit ago."

"That must have been right after I left her at the Temple of the Crow," Quint told Juan.

Grabbing the bottle of iodine, Teodoro motioned for Quint and Fernando to secure Alonso. "Hold him." He dumped iodine on Alonso's cut.

The boy cried out, thrashing for several seconds under their grip before slumping back onto the cot. Quint knew that sting well only his gash had been a lot shallower.

Teodoro delicately touched the area around Alonso's shin.

"Is it broken?" Juan asked.

"No." He pulled a handkerchief from his shirt pocket, wiping the sweat from his brow. "Maybe bad bruise."

Juan rubbed the sore tooth side of his jaw, his face scrunched with worry. "Who inspected the pulley lines this morning?"

Fernando finished wiping off most of the blood and tossed the rag in a basket by the wall. "Lorenzo."

"Is he still at the Sunset Temple?"

"Yes," Steel spoke, turning from the window, his face pale. "I saw him a few minutes before the bucket fell."

"Jared, come with me." Juan headed for the door. "Find Angélica," he said to Fernando. "Let her know what happened."

Quint watched Angélica's father stride away, wanting to help somehow. He darted outside ahead of Steel, jogging to catch up with Juan. "Is there anything I can do?"

"No." Juan continued walking. "This damned curse," he muttered. "Lorenzo's checked the lines many times. He knows what he's doing."

"Juan," Steel called out from behind them. "Hold up."

"I wonder how my daughter will rationalize this." Juan's brow was covered with beads of sweat, a drop rolled down from his temple. He clasped Quint's shoulder while they waited for Steel. "I appreciate your offer, but Angélica wouldn't like the idea of you being at the scene of the accident."

Quint blew out a frustrated breath. It wasn't like he planned to take pictures. "Okay. Let me know if I can help in any way."

Steel caught up with them, his gaze honing in on the duct-tape bandage on Quint's arm. "Another injury? You're quickly becoming more trouble than you're worth." He turned to Juan. "You realize that if Parker includes this accident in his article, you might as well say goodbye to hopes of future funding. A plague of safety issues will kill your chances of returning to this site anytime this decade, maybe next."

Quint ignored the dickhead's sneer. "I'll be in my tent if you need me, Juan."

"Thanks. Take care of that arm." Juan strode away with Steel.

With the afternoon sun baking his shoulders, Quint watched until they'd disappeared around the side of the mottled-gray, rectangular *Ik* Temple. He swung at a mosquito buzzing around his ear, trying to come in for a landing.

Damn, he hated this fucking jungle.

He smacked the blood sucker flat against his neck.

There had to be some way to convince Juan and Angélica to trust him. Some way that didn't require him to show his hand.

Scratching at his neck, he headed back to his tent. Once again he was back where he'd started—in need of a plan.

* * *

Angélica crept around the side of the *Ik* Temple, squatting low in the shadows. She paused, searching the plaza in front of her. Twilight had blanketed everything in shades of gray, framing the open area with a dark vignette that extended into the trees.

A rumble of voices drifted out through the mess tent entrance. Supper was still going full swing. Perfect. Now was her chance.

She tucked the newfound vase tighter into the crook of her arm. Dry weeds crackled under her hiking boots as she threaded her way through the tents and made it to hers without being seen. Once inside her tent, she zipped the canvas door closed and tied down the window flaps.

After pushing the jumble of paperwork and books to the side of her desk, she gently set the vase down, making sure it didn't tip over. Then she stepped back and stared at it in the semidarkness. Her ears rang in the silence.

Where was her father? He needed to see this. Maybe she should go get him. No, she should probably make sure her memory was correct and the vase had a connection to her mom's notes like she'd thought when she'd first found it.

Where was her lantern? She glanced around her tent, not

seeing its shape in the thick shadows.

A fresh coat of sweat covered her skin in the muggy gloom. With all air flow restricted, the heat seemed heavier. She grabbed a dirty T-shirt from the floor and wiped off the gritty sweat ringing her neck.

The sound of soft snores came from under her cot. She peeked underneath it. A familiar shape lay on its side next to Rover's sleeping form. She reached under and pulled out her lantern. He must have been playing with it again.

Turning it on, she set it next to the vase and leaned closer to inspect the designs on the vessel.

Outside, the frogs croaked louder as they wound up for their nightly performance. Crickets chirped in harmony. A breeze blew through, rustling the high treetops, blocking out the sounds of the crew eating supper.

She opened the bottom desk drawer and pulled out a stack of papers along with a couple of books, lowering them to the floor. The fake drawer bottom lifted out without a sound. She plucked out the old, frayed-edge notebook hidden there and set it down on her desktop.

Her chair creaked as she settled into it. Her mother's signature was scrawled across the bottom corner on the front cover of the notebook. With her finger, she carefully traced the curves in her mom's name, remembering the way her mom had held her pen, the intensity lining her face as she scribbled note after note for hours on end, the long braid of silvery auburn hair resting on her back. It seemed like just yesterday ...

No.

Angélica shook her head, clearing the memories. This was not the time.

She flipped open the notebook and sifted through it, searching for a certain symbol she was sure her mother had drawn in the right margin on one of the pages.

There!

She flattened the page and scanned midway down, slowing

when she found the related paragraph.

Several of the vessels contained images of Ek Chuah and his servants delivering goods to the king. However, two cylindrical vessels contained the image of a shell. One had the shell in Ek Chuah's hand. Another had a shell on a necklace worn by the king.

She frowned up at the vase, and then grabbed her magnifying glass. Under the magnifier, the subjects in the images encircling the vessel cleared.

Grabbing a pencil and a piece of paper, she wrote: *Cone-shaped shell, Ek Chuah, skeletal visage, and death god.*

She closed her mother's notebook, excitement bubbling in her stomach along with a growl of hunger.

Something nudged her leg. Smiling, she lifted Rover into her lap. "Hey, baby boy. Look what I found."

He snorted, undoubtedly praising her sleuthing skills.

"I never doubted her, you know." She scratched him behind the ears. *Even when everyone else ridiculed her.*

Rover snorted again, wiggling in her arms.

"I won't stop, either." She stroked his back. "Not until I prove her right."

Rover's stomach gurgled.

She chuckled. "Poor baby! You must be starving. I haven't fed you since lunch." That made two of them. Not eating supper was becoming a habit of late, something her father had chastised her about more than once after noticing how baggy her pants were getting.

The sound of footfalls approaching made her freeze. She held her breath, waiting for whoever was out there to pass on by, her arms tightening around Rover.

"Dr. García?" Quint's low voice came through the canvas walls.

Shit. She frowned at the vase.

Rover squealed, struggling to break free. She let him down, watching him race toward the zipper. Usually only food made him squeal like that, not good-looking troublemakers.

"What in the hell was that?" Quint said. "Angélica?"

She was stuck. He could undoubtedly see her lantern light leaking through the canvas.

"Hold on a moment," she called out. She carefully set the vase down on the floor next to her desk.

"Are you okay in there?"

"Yeah, sure." She tossed her mom's notebook into the bottom drawer and kicked it closed. "I just need to ..." she glanced around her living quarters. A pink bra dangled from the main support pole, several dirty T-shirts and pairs of underwear and socks littered the floor, and a bunch of books lay scattered next to her cot. "I just need to grab something." Like a big rug so she could shove everything under it.

"I brought you some food."

"You did?" That explained Rover's squeal. And why he was currently trying to bite the flap zipper. Her father had probably put Quint up to this visit while he was busy keeping Jared out of her hair over in the mess tent.

"This may sound like an odd question," Quint said, "but do you have a pig in there with you?"

She booted her pink bra and the rest of her dirty clothes and several books under her cot. After one last check to make sure none of her other unmentionables were scattered around for him to see, she nudged Rover out of the way and unzipped both flaps. "Hi."

He held out a plate of food. "Good evening."

"It's Rover," she said, taking the plate. "My *jabalí*."

"It is?" His forehead wrinkled. "Your what?"

"My pet javelina." She stepped aside, allowing him room to enter. "Please, come in."

He'd barely made it inside the tent when Rover head-longed into his ankles, greeting his shins with grunts and snorts and nuzzles.

"Holy pork chops!" He laughed, kneeling down. "I didn't realize javelinas were so cute as babies."

Angélica zipped the mesh flap shut, sealing them inside. Together. Alone. She stood over him, breathing him in. He smelled clean, fresh from the shower. She was tempted to do something stupid. Her gaze traveled down over his broad shoulders and strong forearms, her fingers flexing. Make that something downright asinine.

Oh, stop it, she scolded her silly libido and then settled into her chair. Besides, after spending the afternoon crawling around in temples, she was coated with dirt and probably stunk like monkey butt.

She switched her focus to the fresh baked tortillas he'd brought and the pile of fruit. Her mouth watered. "Thank you for bringing me supper." She pointed at Teodoro's trademark bandage. "How's your arm feeling?"

"Fine." He scratched Rover behind the ears.

She tore a piece off one of the tortillas and held it out toward Quint. "Give him this and you'll have a new best friend for life."

He dangled it in front of Rover's snout. The hungry javelina inhaled it in a single chomp.

Quint chuckled, patting Rover's back. "You want some more, little guy?"

Rover danced around in a circle in response, something her father had taught him when offered treats.

"Have you been teaching him English?" Quint asked, his eyes warm and sparkly in the lantern light.

"No, Dad has. 'Food' is Rover's native language."

"That makes two of us."

Angélica watched them play a few moments longer, then her stomach demanded a forkful of sustenance.

"So, what's Rover's story?" he asked.

She cut another bite, forcing herself to slow down and not inhale it like her javelina. "I found him a couple of weeks ago. He was caught in a trap in the forest about a quarter-mile from here." She handed Quint another piece of tortilla.

"Hurt your leg, huh, buddy?" He fed Rover and then

moved over to her cot, waiting for her nod of approval before lowering onto it.

Rover took a couple of steps toward her, sniffing the air, but then whirled in Quint's direction. He hobbled over to him and nuzzled his outstretched hand.

Angélica froze with her fork halfway to her mouth. "Amazing. He chose you over food. It must be true love."

"I think we may be related." Quint fanned his shirt, glancing at the closed window flaps and then her desk before returning to her. "I have a first cousin who looks remarkably like him, snout and all."

She laughed and then stuffed some dried mango into her mouth. For several moments, he played with Rover while she chewed. The lack of tension in the air was a nice change. Lately, her meals had come with a side of anxious whispers about that damned curse. Heartburn was served for dessert.

"Did Fernando find you earlier?" Quint asked.

She shook her head, wondering why her foreman had been looking for her.

"You haven't heard about Alonso, then?"

She swallowed. "What about him?"

"A pulley line snapped and a rock landed on his leg."

"What?" She pushed aside the last bits of supper, her hunger suddenly replaced with a clenching ache. "How is he? Is his leg broken?"

"Teodoro says it's just a deep bruise. His calf muscle took the brunt of the blow."

Damn it! She could imagine how fast this news had spread throughout the camp. She dropped her plate onto the floor for Rover, rising to her feet. Was everyone still in the mess tent? Maybe she should go address this newest incident, try to talk sense into the most vocal of her crew before they started scaring some of the newer hires away.

"Your dad and Jared checked out the pulley line." Rover left Quint's side and tore into her food. He watched the javelina for a second or two and then frowned at her. "Juan said it looked like it had frayed and snapped, but he mentioned that a small cut might have started the process."

A cut? Something done on purpose? To what end? To shut down the dig site? Ruin her father's career? Hers?

She leaned against her desk, the weight of possibilities heavy. She needed to talk to her father about this, somewhere away from the others. Maybe in one of the temples. "Thanks for bringing me supper, Quint, but—"

"Teodoro thinks it's the curse."

She groaned.

"Your ex-husband overheard Teodoro and your dad talking about it and insisted on learning all about your curse problem. He appeared to find it all quite interesting and even jotted down some notes, which didn't seem to settle well with your father."

She rattled off a long string of very unladylike swearwords.

Quint raised his eyebrows. "Did you work in the steel mill during your summers at college?"

"One of my professors liked to hire ex-cons to help with field work. A cheap but motivated labor force. They taught me a thing or two."

"Apparently. I think my ears are smoking."

"Sorry about that."

"Don't be. I like how you worked 'Dr. Pompous Bungweed' into it all. You think your ex would consider changing his name?"

That earned him a thin smile in spite of the shit storm flying around her. "How much did my father spill about the curse in front of Jared?"

"As little as he could."

Something on Quint's face told her there was an unspoken *but* in there. "But still enough to potentially hang him if Jared feels like using it against him?" she finished for him.

"Unfortunately."

Angélica dropped back into the chair. Excellent. Just fucking terrific. She closed her eyes and covered her face with her hands.

"What do you think about all of this curse business?" She cringed in anticipation of his response but needed to hear from someone on the outside. "Do we look like a bunch of superstitious, wild-eyed natives who've been worshiping the sun too much?"

"I prefer the moon—it's too damned hot down here to praise the sun."

"I'm serious, Parker."

"Okay. In all seriousness, when it comes to the curse and your crew, I think you're trying to herd marbles uphill."

She peeked out at him between her palms. "You've noticed, huh?"

"Hard to miss. I've also noticed several other things in the last twenty-four hours."

"Yeah?" She covered her eyes again, wondering if she should cover her ears, too, but then asked, "Like what?"

"Besides having a very nervous crew, you have an ex-husband poking around where he's not wanted, a healer who wants to have an exorcism to get rid of evil spirits, a father who is willing to bend over backward to keep his funding so he can continue working here with you, and a javelina who likes to cross dress."

A javelina what?

She lowered her hands. Rover sat on the floor between them. The strap of the pink bra that she'd kicked under the cot was wrapped around his neck.

"Rover, come here." She reached for him, her cheeks warming, but he dodged her hands and hid behind Quint's feet.

Quint reached down and untangled the bra from around Rover's neck. He stared down at it in his hands for one dreadfully long wince on her part. Then he dangled it between them, slamming her with a stare that was hotter than any temple she'd been in today. "I imagine this looks better on you than your javelina."

Her tongue felt thicker than normal, like she'd traded it for a dry sponge. "Well," she tried to think of something witty to toss back, or something that would pinch out this flame flickering between them before it spread any further. "I am a little less hairy than Rover."

Oh, jeez! Really? That was the best she could come up with? Maybe Quint would take pity on her and leave after she opened her desk drawer and shut her head in it a few times.

His brow wrinkled. "Only just a little?"

"Angélica!" The sound of Jared's voice made her jerk in surprise. She looked toward the mesh flap. Her ex-husband's face was pressed against it. "We need to discuss this curse situation."

No, they didn't. "I'm busy right now." If only she had a door to slam in his face.

Jared's gaze moved to Quint and then to the bra that still dangled from his finger. "What's going on in here?"

Chapter Six

Chachac: Traditional rain ceremony.

A long, long time ago in a kingdom far, far away, Angélica had married a man she had thought was Prince Charming. It turned out she'd been played a fool, hornswoggled by a handsome face whispering empty promises of securing her a teaching position with tenure at the same university where her father had taught for well over a decade.

So maybe the fault wasn't all Jared's.

Maybe her ambition had made her gullible when he'd painted the fairytale life they'd lead, working dig sites side by side like her parents had all of her life.

And maybe her attraction to the distinguished, well-renowned Dr. Steel had more to do with skipping a few rungs on her career ladder than actually enjoying his companionship.

And truth be known, she'd been so caught up in the fantasy of being as revered as her parents had been at the time—prior to her mom's downfall—that she'd overlooked his inability to meet her cravings both in and out of the sack. She'd even gone so far as to convince herself that there was more to marriage than love and good sex ... or even okay sex.

After all, she'd been around the block a few times by then. She knew how to take care of her own needs, which had become necessary in her marriage way too soon.

But that woman, the one who'd been driven at all costs to have everything her parents had shared, all of the professional accolades they'd received, had long ago awakened from that fairytale. Her carriage had turned back into a pumpkin and rotted; that sparkly glass slipper had given her blisters long before the ball was over.

As for Prince Charming, he'd granted her the divorce she'd wanted but at a cost to her career back in the States. She'd figured that relocating south of the border for much of the year, far from his reign, would save her from dealing with him, allowing her to live happily forever after in the jungle.

It turned out she'd been foolish yet again, as evident from the Prince's visit not only to her dig site, but now to her tent.

She glared at her ex-husband through the mesh flap. What in the world made him believe he could come down here and order her around like they were still bound by vows?

"Go away, Jared. I'm not in the mood to discuss anything with you right now," especially not that damned curse, "unless you are here to say '*Adios*' and need directions back to the village."

"Is that yours?" Jared ignored her jab, pointing towards Quint and the bra he was holding.

"Of course it's mine." There was no use denying it. "Who else would it belong to?" The only other female on the site was María, Teodoro's wife, and she was about two cup sizes larger than Angélica.

"Why is Parker fondling it?"

She looked over at Quint, who was now holding her bra up between them by the straps, as if sizing it to her chest.

His eyes gleamed with a devilish glint when they met hers. "I think I like this pink one best," he said, "but I'd have to see the others on you again to be sure. Maybe I can come back later after your company leaves."

She shot Quint a knock-it-off squint. "He's just joking around, Jared." She snatched the bra from his fingers and tossed it down by the vase she'd found earlier. "Quint was kind enough to bring me something to eat."

"You should be wary of Trojans gifting wooden horses."

She rolled her eyes. Jared had never had much imagination when it came to insults.

"I am not a Trojan," Quint said, sounding like Arnold Schwarzenegger.

Jared snorted. "Obvious from your erroneous accent."

Quint shrugged off Jared's criticism. "Although Angélica would give Helen a run for her money, don't you think, Steel?" He gave her a conspiratorial wink.

In spite of his obvious jesting, her stupid pulse fluttered. *Enough!*

Enough of Jared's meddling.

Enough of Quint's flirting.

Enough of her sitting here accomplishing nothing.

She collected her empty plate from the floor and stood, needing to get rid of both troublesome men and find her father. She had a much bigger problem to deal with than a pissing match over her dirty bra.

"Jared, I'll give you two minutes to speak your piece." She unzipped the mesh flap, glancing back before she stepped outside. "Parker, thanks again for supper. You know the way to your tent."

Jared backed up enough to let her out, placing a hand on her shoulder when she'd cleared.

Jeez, she hadn't seen him this possessive since he'd slipped that huge honking engagement ring on her finger. She pulled away from him. "What do you need?"

"Join me for a walk." He nodded toward the trees.

She'd sooner snuggle with venomous pit vipers.

"I'm a little busy right now." She glanced at Quint, who was squatting next to something on the floor by her desk. What was Rover getting into now? "Parker told me about the accident."

"It seems you've had a plague of these so-called accidents lately."

A series of snorts came from inside her tent followed by a happy squeal.

Jared frowned. "What was that?"

Quint joined them, holding Rover in the crook of his arm.

"Of all the disgusting …" Jared turned to Angélica, his nose wrinkled. "Surely you're not going to allow him to keep that revolting, smelly over-sized rodent in his tent."

"Rover is not a rodent," Angélica said, taking her little buddy from Quint's arms. "He's a peccary. And I just gave him a bath this morning so he smells like my citrus soap." She sniffed him. Or more like one of María's tortillas.

Parker scratched Rover between the ears. "Let me know if you need a javelina-sitter anytime soon."

"I'll keep you in mind."

"You do that." He cupped her chin and leaned in close, his gaze fixed on her mouth. "And I'll keep you in mind." Before she could find a direct line from her brain to her tongue and hit him with a smartass comeback, he brushed his lips over hers. "Sleep tight, Dr. García."

With her lips tingling, she watched him go. Of course his exit had all been a show for Jared's sake, but still … *Damn!*

"Do you think it's wise to be fraternizing like that with a man writing about this site for a national publication?"

No, and she knew better without her ex-husband rubbing her nose in it. "Shut up, Jared." She set Rover down inside her tent.

"What a brilliant way to secure future funding, Angélica. Men will line up with cash in hand to spend a couple of weeks in your tent getting the 'real' archaeological experience."

She crossed her arms over her chest, giving him her full-on scowl. What had she ever seen in the arrogant jerk? Oh, yeah, his lofty position in her father's university. Otherwise, beneath his classically handsome features, blue eyes, and dark blonde hair, he was about as appealing as a dung beetle.

"What do you want, Jared? Did you come here for some reason other than to insult me and my *jabalí*?"

"I want to talk to you about your father."

"What about him?"

"I'm concerned about his health."

She couldn't see where that was any concern of Jared's. "Dad can take care of himself." She turned back toward her tent, needing to grab a change of clothes for the shower before seeking out her dad.

Jared caught her by the upper arm and pulled her around to face him. "You've been too close to him these last few months to see the changes. He looks haggard, and that toothache is a sure sign of being overstressed."

She looked pointedly at where his hand gripped her arm until he let go. "What do you know of his stress? You just arrived here this morning."

"I know the university's decision on funding and grants can determine his future here on the Yucatán Peninsula. I'm sure that's not making sleep come easy for him."

"And what would you have me do to remedy this? We both know that I have no control over what they decide."

"No, but I do." His smile made her feel cold and clammy inside.

She lifted her chin. "And you're loving that, aren't you?"

"Come now, darling. Don't take that tone."

"I'm not your 'darling' anymore, Jared. I'm your ex-wife. Try to remember that EX part."

He ran his finger down the side of her neck. "That was not by my choice. You left me, remember?"

She brushed his hand away. "Don't touch me."

"Tsk, tsk, my love. Those frown lines will become permanent soon enough. Keep in mind that it would well benefit you and this dig site to work with me instead of against me."

Her patience for his games had long ago gone the way of

the great Maya kings. She held up her hand, counting off her fingers. "I'm not your employee. I'm not your co-worker. I'm not your *love*."

"I can't help the feelings I still have for you, Angélica."

Oh, please. "You never loved me." He'd been more interested in having her dressed to the nines and hanging on his arm like a trophy. "What are you really doing here on my dig site?"

"Deciding your father's chance at further funding from the university, something you would be wise to remember in the future when I tell you I need to speak with you."

There he was, the controlling Jared she'd known during their brief marriage, peeking out from behind that fake smile that barely made it to the corners of his mouth.

"Ah ha." She nodded slowly. "I had a feeling this would come down to a desperate game of blackmail at some point. I just didn't think you'd play your trump card so soon." After all of these years, he was still finding ways to play on her weakness—her love for her parents. "So, what's the price, Jared? What do I have to do to get your go-ahead for more funding for Dad? What's the going rate now for extortion by an ex-husband? A hand-job? Sex?"

His nostrils flared at her blatant crassness. "As tempting as you can be when you aren't covered in filth and sweat, darling, I'm not sure what you offer in bed is an equivalent exchange for my professional blessing."

Prick! "What then? A public ass-kissing in front of my crew?"

"For starters, get rid of Quint Parker."

* * *

Early the next morning, Angélica was still clenching her fists about her run-in with Jared outside her tent. After he had spelled out what he wanted, she'd walked away without a backwards glance in spite of his demanding she return and finish their conversation. She'd made a beeline for the shower, the one place she knew she'd find solace, and had scrubbed her hair with a vengeance. By the time she'd cooled off enough to pay her father a visit without letting him see any evidence of her agitation, it was well past his normal bedtime. So, she'd decided to show up on his doorstep first thing before they headed to breakfast.

And here she was, still wide-eyed and bushy-tailed about Jared. "Dad, I need to talk to you."

Juan unzipped the tent flap. He waved her inside to wait while he finished putting on his socks and boots.

"I have a solution to our problem with the curse," he said from where he sat on his cot.

"What?"

" A *Lolcatali* ceremony."

"Absolutely not!" She wouldn't give it a second thought. "Like I told Teodoro, there has to be some other way."

He frowned "I don't understand why you're so adamant about this. What harm could it cause?"

She couldn't believe he was considering it. "Don't you see? By allowing the ceremony, I'm acknowledging to my crew that this curse exists."

"Maybe, sort of, I guess, but if it calms them down—"

"It's not going to calm them down, only open the door for more accidents to be blamed on the curse." She could imagine how far some of the men would take it. "I don't need this to be blown out of proportion any more than it already has been." She thought of Jared's veiled threats. "Neither do you."

Her father waved her worry away. "If you're referring to Jared, don't sweat it. He already knows about the curse and doesn't give it any merit. I doubt how we handle this situation will play a role in his or the university's decision about funding my future projects."

After facing off with her ex-husband last night, she had a different take on that. "I don't give a fucking shit about that damned university!" Her frustration slipped out before she could catch it by the collar.

"*Gatita*! Such language. Your grandmother just rolled over in her grave."

She scrubbed both hands down her face, and then sighed, regaining control. "Sorry, Dad." She looked up at the tent ceiling. "*Lo siento, abuela.*"

His brow knitted. "Are you okay?"

She smiled—or at least tried to produce a facial movement that resembled one. She didn't want him stressing about her. Jared wasn't the only one who'd noticed her father's haggardness this dig season. Something was weighing on him, something he denied whenever she prodded.

"I was actually referring to your reputation in the archaeology community, not what my ex-husband thinks about the curse. What do you think your peers would say if they heard we were having exorcisms down here to cleanse the place of evil spirits? You'd be the joke of the year."

She'd already gone through her mother becoming a laughing stock with her "wild" theory. She didn't think she could stomach watching the same thing happen to her father's career, not when she had the means to prevent it.

He nodded, but she knew by the way he was chewing on his lower lip that he wasn't fully convinced.

"And what about Quint's article?" She continued. "Can you imagine the fun the press would have after his story comes out in *American Archaeology Today*? I can see the headline now, 'Archaeologists Ask the Dead for Help!'"

Juan chuckled, but still didn't agree with her.

She pressed on. "Then there's the Mexican government to consider. With all of the bad press, they'd kick me out of the country without even a *vaya con dios.*"

Running out of convincing reasons, she reached for his heartstrings. "And how are we supposed to prove Mom's theory and clear her reputation if we're banned from coming down here to work anymore?"

"All right, you win, *gatita.* The *Lolcatali* isn't such a great idea, but we have to do something."

Yes, they did. "Maybe if you'd talk to the crew …"

He shook his head and lay back on his cot. "No amount of talking is going to work. You know how they are when it comes to this supernatural stuff."

"Okay." She rocked back on her heels. "Think, think, think." Maybe Teodoro could help somehow.

Then it hit her. "A *Chachac* ceremony!"

"What?" Juan looked doubtful. "It's too early. They usually hold those later in the season."

"I know, but it never hurts to have a little rain."

He still didn't look convinced. "And how will this ease their fears about the curse?"

"By distracting them. A little bit of feasting and a lot of drinking will take their minds off the curse for a few days. Help it to begin fading from their memories."

Juan nodded slowly. "That might work. Can you convince Teodoro to perform this ceremony tomorrow? Is there enough time for him to prepare?"

"I'll talk to him after breakfast. I'm pretty sure we already have most of the food and supplies here. He can ride into the village and bring back whatever else we need this afternoon. There shouldn't be any problem fitting the rest on the back of the bike."

"Remind him to check for any mail for Quint."

She still wondered what could be so important Quint needed to have his mail forwarded down there.

"Okay. When Teodoro returns he can grab a couple of the men and head into the forest to hunt for a deer to use in the ritual. Tomorrow, with their help he can finish preparations. We'll plan to start it in the afternoon."

This would work out perfectly. After her crew heard the news, excitement would replace their fears. "I'll announce the ceremony at supper this evening," she told him, clapping her hands together. Done deal. Problem solved. Back to the business of digging up the past.

"I thought it took four days to make *balche*," Juan said.

"Teodoro always has some made up. He doesn't like to be caught without ceremonial wine on hand."

"Okay, *maybe* that will work." The twinkle in his eyes eased her worries for the moment. "But what about Jared?"

"I was thinking we could stuff an apple in his mouth, mount him on a spit, and roast him over the campfire."

Juan laughed. That made her relax even more. But as his laughter quieted, concern tightened his forehead again. "Has he cornered you yet?"

She kneeled down to tighten the strings on her hiking boots, worried he might see something in her face that would give away her secret. "Why would he want to talk to me? It's you that he's here to see."

"No. I'm just an excuse. He's here for you."

If that were the case, he'd have chosen sex last night in exchange for his blessing.

"The way he's constantly watching you, I think he's still in love with you."

A harsh laugh burst from her throat as she stood. "Please, Dad. Jared's only ever been in love with Jared."

He sat up, lowering his feet to the floor. "We'll see." He reached for his work boots. "But I bet if you asked, he'd go to the ends of the earth for you still."

"Maybe you're right," she smirked at her dad. "But would he promise to stay there?"

* * *

As far as Saturdays went, the day had gone like every other one in this steaming, bug-infested overgrown greenhouse. But tonight Quint was in for a treat according to Juan. After almost getting bit by a venomous coral snake this afternoon while paying a visit to the latrine, he could use a little pick-me-up.

"How long will Teodoro go on like this?" Quint asked as

he lowered himself into a dilapidated lawn chair that looked like it had been rescued from a junkyard compactor at the last minute. Teodoro had been chanting for several hours already according to Juan.

"Throughout the night," the older Dr. García answered, and then took a long hit from his cigar. "The *Chachac* ceremony is used to ask the saints and the *Chacob*—the Rain gods—to bring the rains."

Across the sunburned grass, Teodoro sat behind a small, narrow table made of saplings and cluttered with bowls and cups carved from green, orange, and yellow gourds. Over his head was an arch made of tree branches covered with leaves.

Juan had set up chairs for the two of them about thirty feet from the main attraction. Smoke from musky-scented incense filled the twilight, adding a surreal fog to the purple-tinged sky. The smell of baked corn cakes tickled Quint's taste buds as drafts of heat wafted their way from the underground pits dug earlier that morning.

Several of Angélica's crew sat scattered around on the grass. A few of them, including Fernando, had dragged pieces of firewood over and were using them as makeshift benches.

As Quint's gaze drifted from face to face, he nodded at those he'd worked with at the Owl Temple over the last couple of days.

Esteban lifted a hand in return, waving as he dropped into his chair with a full gourd cup, and then somehow managed to overbalance, falling ass-over-teakettle onto the ground. His cup landed on his shirt, upside down.

Quint looked away, choking back a chuckle. "What's in the gourds?"

"*Saca*," Angélica answered from behind him. She came around and graced him with a quick smile. "How's it going here?" She squeezed her father's shoulder.

Juan patted her hand. "You made a good decision."

"I hope so."

Quint watched as she settled in at her father's feet,

catching a whiff of citrus. She sat cross-legged, looking relaxed with her hair unbraided and tumbling down over her shoulders, her brow smooth in the flickering firelight. Something settled inside of him, something that made him feel content in spite of the mystery he'd yet to solve. "What's *saca?*"

"Maize gruel." Juan absently stroked his daughter's hair, as he probably had since she was a child. "*Gatita*, have you seen Jared?"

"He's back in his tent, fighting a migraine. He says it happens when he experiences a climate change, which was news to me." She looked up at Quint. "How's your arm?"

He held his arm out for her to inspect. She leaned closer, running her fingers alongside the faint scar that remained, tickling his skin. Goosebumps rippled clear up to his shoulder.

"It looks great."

"Teodoro says I'm mostly healed. That green jelly is some kind of miracle medicine." He sat back in his chair, his arm still tingling from her touch. Focusing on Teodoro, he reminded himself of the reasons he needed to steer clear of the siren sitting near his feet. "What's he singing?"

Juan crushed his cigar out on the chair arm. "Rosaries. It's all part of calling the *Chacob* and asking for rain."

"Do we need rain? I thought the dry weather was normal for this time of year." At least that's what the guidebook had said.

"It wouldn't hurt. They'll plant corn in their *milpas*—their fields—in another month or so. If the rains don't follow soon, the crops will fail."

A young man with a pencil-thin mustache, who Quint was pretty sure had helped dig the holes for the ovens this afternoon, began handing out gourd cups to several members of the group. Quint watched as each one took a drink and then passed it to another. Just then, the youth noticed Angélica had joined the group and brought her a gourd cup filled to the rim. The liquid splashed over the sides as he carried it.

Quint opened his mouth to ask, but Angélica beat him to it. "Jorge is passing *balche*." She took the cup from Jorge and thanked him. "It's a ceremonial wine Teodoro made from the bark of the *balche* tree. He mixes honey from his own hives with it and ferments it."

She took a sip and held it in her mouth a couple of seconds, closing her eyes. Then she swallowed and sighed in pleasure. Eyes open again, she held the cup out to Quint. "Try some. It's one of Teodoro's specialties."

Juan reared away from the cup as Quint grabbed it. "Be careful with that stuff."

Quint hesitated with the cup halfway to his lips. The look on Juan's face was almost comical.

Angélica laughed low and velvety. "Don't listen to him. The last time he drank too much *balche*, he shaved a strip of hair off the top of his head, duct-taped crow feathers to his chest, and tried to pierce his ear with a pocket knife."

"I was trying to reenact an ancient Maya rain dance, thank you very much. And those jade ear plugs just wouldn't fit in the hole Teodoro made with the bobby-pin."

Quint grinned, picturing the scene.

Angélica nodded at the cup. "Go on, try a sip. It will spark a fire in your belly."

Like he needed any more heat on top of the warm blasts drifting around him, making him sweat in his T-shirt and khakis. He took a sip expecting it to be bitter. But the lukewarm liquid coated the inside of his mouth with a sweet honey taste, leaving a warm trail as it slipped down his throat.

"Smooth." He took another sip before handing it to Juan. "Tasty."

Juan took a quick swig and then bumped Angélica's shoulder with the cup. "Believe me, after three cups of this stuff, you'll be singing and dancing for your own gods."

Quint licked his lips, savoring the remnants of the peculiar sweetness. Judging by the warmth still coating his throat, he didn't doubt Juan for a minute.

Angélica grabbed the cup and motioned to Jorge to bring them more. The easy-going relationship between her and her crew showed as she laughed at something Jorge mumbled when handing her another cup. She handed the drink to Quint, still smiling from the private joke.

With the firelight glowing on her cheeks, he couldn't stop staring.

"More?" she asked when he didn't take the cup.

Of what? Oh, right, the *balche*. Quint plucked the cup from her grasp and looked at Juan. He needed to get his mind back on the task at hand—the disappearance of Dr. Hughes—and off the images of a certain green-eyed temptress. Maybe if he got Juan a bit tipsy, he'd start telling tales about the site's past. "Another drink, Juan?" He offered his cup.

"No way! I'm still rubbing that goop on my tooth. With my luck, mixing the two will turn me into a frog again."

Quint had started to look over at Teodoro and did a double take. "Again?"

"Of course, the notorious frog episode," Angélica said, her voice soft with humor. "Best not to talk about that one after sunset."

"That's it." Juan stood and stretched. "I've taken enough abuse for this evening. I'm going back to my tent to read and rest my tooth."

Angélica clutched his pant leg. "Come on, Dad, not already. The ceremony is just getting its rhythm."

"Sorry, *gatita*. These old bones need a soft cot right now." He leaned over and kissed her on the forehead. "Be good." To Quint he warned, "Be careful. Don't let her trick you into drinking too much *balche* or you'll end up swimming in the *cenote* at midnight, and I can tell you from experience that the water will freeze off your tiddly bits."

"Gotcha." Quint liked his tiddly bits still attached and hoped to use them again someday.

"It's not that cold," Angélica said.

"It's cold enough." Rubbing his lower back, Juan limped off into the darkness.

Darkness? Quint looked around. When had twilight turned into night? Was the *balche* already messing with him?

"I worry about him sometimes." Angélica's voice was quiet, meant for his ears only.

"Because he works too hard?"

"No, because he's lonely."

Are you? The question sat on the tip of his tongue, but instead of asking it, he swallowed more drink.

The chair next to him creaked as Angélica lowered onto it. She leaned back, stretching her legs out in front of her. He could imagine how they'd feel wrapped around his ...

Crikey! What was wrong with him? He grunted inwardly and looked in Teodoro's direction again, watching as he poured a dark liquid into one of the gourds. That did not look like *saca*. "What's he doing now?"

"He's offering the gods chocolate." Angélica tipped back the last of her drink and then dropped the cup onto the ground. "Throughout the night, he'll continue to make such offerings, but no bloodletting. There's been enough of that going around here lately."

"Bloodletting?"

She nodded, staring dazedly into the firelight.

"How is that different from sacrificing?"

"The Maya people have always believed that gods were the source of all life. But only kings could converse with the gods. A Maya's soul is in his blood, so when a sacrifice was needed by the gods, blood was more important than bodies. On certain occasions, especially when a big sacrifice was needed, the king would give his blood to open the doorway to the gods."

"By 'give his blood', you mean he'd cut his finger or thumb?" He lifted the cup and took a drink. Swirling the honey-sweet warmth around with his tongue, he wondered what it would taste like on her lips?

"No, I mean he would pierce the foreskin of his penis with the spine of a stingray."

Quint choked on the wine, coughing. His nuts crawled up into his stomach and hid there.

She patted him on the back a couple of times. "You okay?"

"Yes," he wheezed, "but no matter how drunk I am later, please don't let me sign up for any bloodletting."

Her laughter sounded like water bubbling in the stream over behind the Owl Temple. He stared at her profile while she looked on at Teodoro. What would it be like to trace his fingers along her ... He reached for his cup again.

A couple of hours and several refills of *balche* later, he still had no new information on Dr. Hughes. To be honest, he'd stopped caring as soon as Angélica had begun to tell him her theories about what had happened at the site over a millennium ago. With the wine warming his stomach and his beautiful seatmate spinning tales of grandeur and demise, he was having trouble remembering why it was so urgent that he find out any details about Dr. Hughes' work tonight. There was always tomorrow.

"How about I grab you another drink?" Angélica started to rise.

"I'll get it." He put a hand on her arm to stop her and stood. The world spun for several seconds, taking him on a bobbing merry-go-round. "On second thought, I should probably call it a night."

Before he realized she'd risen, she was there beside him, taking his arm. Time was starting to move in fractured moments. "Can you walk to your tent?"

He tried a step, surprised his feet didn't fly out from under him and leave him sitting on his ass. "Sure," he said, and then stumbled into her.

"How about I walk you to your tent?"

After fighting the urge to put his hands all over her for most of the evening, he wasn't sure that was such a good idea.

"You should stay and enjoy the show."

She shook her head. "I have some notes to write about the turkey and deer bones we found today in the *Ik* Temple, so it's time for me to head back to my tent anyway."

He looked down at her. She split into two Angélicas. That was about three more than he could handle after all of that wine. He blinked her back into one. Why did Steel's ex-wife have to be so damned attractive?

"Okay," he said, concentrating to keep from stumbling as they started toward his tent. "But keep your hands to yourself, Dr. García. I may be a few sheets blowing in the wind, but I'm not easy."

* * *

Angélica smiled as she crunched through the plaza's dry weeds. Quint walked beside her, silent. Frogs croaked in the forest, filling in the quiet gaps.

She'd managed to keep him off the subject of Dr. Hughes and his history at the site all night. Now, if she could get him to his tent without any personal questions about her own past, she could mark off another day.

She peeked at him. Maybe he really was here to see the sights and sounds of a dig in process. She could be wrong to distrust him. She'd been wrong in the past. Look at the mess she'd gotten into with Jared.

A warm breeze trickled across her skin. The smell of the dried grass was mixed with smoke and incense from the ceremony. The flavor of Teodoro's wine still coated the back of her tongue. She crossed her fingers that tonight's ritual had taken care of her crew's fears about the curse, or at least dulled them with the help of the *balche*.

They reached Quint's tent too soon. Walking next to him in the moonlight had been comforting in a way she hadn't felt in a long time.

He paused outside the tent flap and looked down at her,

his eyes hidden in the shadows. "Thanks for telling me all of those stories, Angélica. I enjoyed them. Except for that bit about stingray spines and foreskin."

The memory of his reaction to that part of the tale made her chuckle. It was kind of him to thank her considering how she'd babbled on all night, well aware of the alluring guy periodically bumping knees with her the whole time. "You were a great listener."

"I like the sound of your voice." He stepped closer, trailing the back of his fingers down her cheek. "It's sultry."

His touch left a molten trail on her skin. She could smell the wine on his breath. A wave of wanting crashed through her, followed by an ache for so much more than flirty teases and tender touches. She waited, wondering if he were going to kiss her again, and half afraid she might kiss him back this time if he did … and not stop at just a kiss.

"Very sexy." He cupped her chin, tipping it up. His thumb brushed across her lower lip. Her mouth opened to his touch. "Coming from very tempting lips."

Which happened to be very dry all of a sudden. She dabbed them with her tongue.

Quint groaned, leaning toward her. "Steel's ex-wife," he whispered right above her mouth.

She wasn't sure if he was reminding her or himself of her past mistake. Either way, it cooled her blood as effectively as liquid nitrogen pumped through her veins. Once bitten, twice shy and all of that shit. She took a step back, slipping out from under his spell.

To reaffirm what she'd suspected since Quint's visit to her tent a couple of nights ago *and* to reinforce the chains of control now tethering her libido, she asked, "Did you kiss me the other day to piss off Jared?"

He stared at her in the moonlight. Shadows shifted on his cheeks as his expression sobered. Several seconds went by with only the frogs croaking.

He turned his head, blowing out a breath. "Yeah, I did."

Sometimes she hated being right. His answer stung more than it should have, and she didn't want to think about why.

Her face felt tight, like an unwieldy rubber mask that took effort to hold in place. She tried to laugh. It came out brittle. "I thought so."

"Angélica, I …" He hesitated, jamming his hands in his front pockets, focusing down on his boots. When he looked back up his smile had returned, only it looked formal, platonic. "I'll see you tomorrow at breakfast."

"Sure." She took another step back. She needed some distance from him before she did something really stupid, like showed him how much she wanted another kiss in spite of the whole Jared bullshit.

Pride took the wheel, thankfully, and she managed a friendly wave. "*Buenas noches*, Parker."

She heard his tent zip as she strode away.

What the hell was wrong with her? She kicked at a tall patch of weeds, spreading seeds over her pant legs. She was too old to have a crush on a man she barely knew.

Once inside the safety of her own tent, she turned on the lantern and surveyed the mess surrounding her. It was much like her life outside the four canvas walls.

"Fuck me," she grumbled, yanking off her top, wadding it up, and whipping it across the tent. It made a less-than-satisfactory thud against the canvas wall.

Rover snorted at her from his snoozing spot on her cot.

"You know what, Rover? There are too many breeding males sniffing around and marking territory at this dig site." She dropped down next to him, patting his head. "Maybe it's time for me to do some castrating."

Chapter Seven

Artibeus Jamaicensis: A Jamaican or Mexican fruit bat often found in more exposed areas of caves.

"Quint Parker can kiss my ass," Angélica told the glyph-covered walls surrounding her in the Temple of the Water Witch the next morning.

Steel's ex-wife.

Arghhh!

Those two words had replayed in her head over and over throughout the night. They'd burrowed under her skin, making her beat up her pillow deep into the early morning hours until she finally gave up, got dressed, and focused on what she did best—divorce.

Wait! Make that work. Work was what she did best. She mopped sweat from her forehead and blinked away all thoughts of Quint ... again.

She picked up another piece of semi-transparent rice paper and held it in place so that it covered two particular glyphs. Another layer of perspiration popped up on her brow as she rubbed a piece of charcoal over the paper, beginning to see the relief markings of a headdress from the first glyph.

The room felt much warmer than it should have for this early in the morning. A few hours had passed since she'd left her cot and tried to find a distraction that would help her feel like less of a pariah for her choices in past bedroom partners.

Steel's ex-wife.

"What? I'm tainted now? Defiled? A soiled dove because I was stupid enough to fall for Jared's charm and exaggerations when I was still wet behind the ears?"

She lowered the charcoal and blotted her face with her sweat-dampened T-shirt. "It's not like I picked up any sexually transmitted diseases from him."

With Jared, most physical contact in the bedroom had been clinical at best. She used to joke to herself that his version of safe sex included a hazmat suit, thick rubber gloves, and a post-coital decontamination shower. She scoffed, blowing charcoal dust off the rice paper. Looking back, it was no wonder their sex life had been problematic. The jerk had practically insisted on being vaccinated after every orgasm.

She leaned forward, scraping charcoal over the paper again. Who cared what Parker thought? She didn't need his validation. His approval wouldn't make or break her.

Besides, Jared wanted her to get rid of him in four days. Her ex-husband hadn't minced words naming his price when she'd checked on him last night before she had headed to the Chachac ceremony. If Quint wasn't gone by Thursday, she could say goodbye to her father's university funding.

She hadn't wasted time arguing about the price, just nodded and walked away. That didn't mean she was going to let him have his way. If she sent Quint packing, it was going to be because …

Her breath caught at a carving in the corner of the glyph that showed more clearly in relief as she rubbed over it. She pulled the paper close enough to touch her nose. "What have we here?"

Turning down the intensity of the lantern so it wasn't much brighter than a jar of fireflies, she grabbed her flashlight and shined it on the actual glyph. The direct beam washed out the carving so she angled it, giving the carving's shadow more depth.

"Holy javelina!" Goosebumps broke out on her arms. Taking up her drawing pad, she sketched out the figures.

She reached for the lantern, tossing aside the flashlight. Its light beam spun around the chamber before coming to rest on the passageway into the room. Removing a paintbrush from her tool belt, she swept over the carving, clearing aside granules of dust hidden in the minute crevices. She needed the pitted surface as clean as possible to see the detail on the king's jade necklace.

Leaning closer, she squinted at the glyph. Small skulls had been carved into every other bead. In the center, almost hidden by the torch held over the king's chest, was—

"Angélica."

She let out a squawk of surprise at the sound of her name coming from behind her.

Fernando joined her in the room, speaking in Spanish as he usually did when they were alone. "Your father thought I'd find you in here."

With her heart still doing the Macarena, she chastised him. "You scared the hell out of me."

She'd been so engrossed in what she'd found that she hadn't heard his footfalls. Considering what she was trying to accomplish for her mother, she needed to be more aware of what was going on around her at all times.

Fernando picked up her flashlight, shining it around the walls covered with glyphs. "How much time do you think it took to carve this?"

"A lot." She stood and wiped the dirt off the back of her khakis. "What's going on? Does Dad need me?"

"No." Fernando killed the flashlight. "He had to go to Cancun."

"What? Why?"

"His tooth. He woke up with it abscessed."

"How is he getting to Cancun? The motorcycle isn't running yet. Don't tell me he's walking out of here."

Fernando shook his head. "When Rafael rode his bike into the village this morning for Sunday service, he called Pedro. Lucky for your father, Pedro was between tour jobs. All he needed to hear was that Juan was in pain. He flew in and picked him up. I'm surprised you didn't hear the helicopter."

Angélica wasn't. The walls of the Temple of the Water Witch were thick, and she was several layers deep. She wasn't surprised that Pedro had raced to the rescue. Juan was more of a parent to him than his own had ever been.

She frowned around the room at nothing in particular. "I knew that toothache wasn't caused by any curse."

"Teodoro wanted to pull it. He even sterilized his pliers and pocketknife, but Juan threw some gourds and a plate at him when Teodoro tried to get near him."

That made her frown disappear. "Did Pedro say he would fly him back after Dad gets the tooth fixed?"

"Yes, but not until tomorrow afternoon."

That meant she had to take care of Quint and Jared in the meantime, which wasn't going to leave her much time for further work in this chamber, damn it.

"I need your help with Quint and Jared."

Fernando nodded. "Pedro says he's flying back here again on Wednesday. He's staying for a week or two to help."

"Good, I can use him." She took a drink of water.

"There's something else."

The tone in Fernando's voice made her gulp. "What?"

"Carlos also rode into the village this morning, taking Alonso with him."

"How? Isn't Alonso's leg too sore for that?"

"Carlos peddled while Alonso sat on the seat."

Where there was a will, Angélica thought.

"It was a one-way trip," Fernando continued. "Both boys won't be coming back this year."

She swore under her breath. "Let me guess: the curse."

"Their mother refuses to allow them back here until the evil spirits are sent away. And since you won't let Teodoro perform a *Lokatali* ceremony ..."

She slapped away his words in mid-air. "Their mother has always been too superstitious for her own good. I guess I'm out two men for the season. Cross your fingers that's all this year."

She gathered her drawing pad and the tracings she'd made, shoving them into her backpack. "Let's go eat breakfast. We'll figure out what we are going to do with our photojournalist and visiting archaeologist."

"Breakfast has been over for hours. It's almost lunchtime."

"What?" She held her watch up to the lantern. The hands had barely moved since the last time she'd checked. That couldn't be right. The battery must be dying.

Well, crud. She'd sneaked out of her tent while the birds were still sleeping, figuring on getting a few hours of work before breakfast. Those few hours had turned into seven or eight in between her dozing off, telling off Parker, and tracing glyphs.

"All right, then you take Parker for the afternoon and have him help you clear out that chamber in the Owl Temple."

Fernando turned to leave.

"Remember," she said to his back, "keep him off the subject of Dr. Hughes. I want Parker so busy he doesn't have time to think up questions."

"Okay." Fernando waited at the mouth of the passage for her to follow. "What are you going to do with Jared?"

She grinned, thinking of the perfect place to take the arrogant prick. "Feed him to the bats."

They left the Temple of the Water Witch, Fernando making a side trip to the latrine while she headed for the mess tent.

Besides María, who was cleaning up after lunch, Jared was the only one in the tent. Angélica grabbed a few tortillas and the small plate of salad and chicken María had set aside for her before heading over to where her ex-husband sat, drinking coffee while wearing a fancy pair of leather work gloves. He'd always been a stickler about protecting his hands, keeping them callous-free and regularly manicured. He said it was a necessity in the professional world, but she suspected it had more to do about his fastidiousness when it came to being clean.

She would have preferred to have eaten in the kitchen, catching up with María, but she couldn't afford to slight Jared today. She sniffed her T-shirt, wrinkling her nose. After sweating all morning in the temple, she had a natural force field to keep the blowhard at bay.

Leveling her shoulders for battle, she sat down opposite him. "Hi, Jared. Have you seen Parker?" She needed to set them both straight on how the next two days were going to go without her dad around.

Jared squinted at her over his coffee cup. "I have no interest in that man's whereabouts." He lowered his drink. "Except when he visits your tent."

She ignored his catty remark. "I didn't ask if you cared where he is." She picked up her fork and dug in. Daylight was wasting. She needed to eat, go change into some fresh clothes, and then head back out into the field.

"Your pal," Jared's lip wrinkled when he said that word, "rushed out of here about twenty minutes ago with a letter one of your crewmembers brought to him."

Rafael must have checked for mail while he was back in the village for Sunday services. "Did you see where the letter was from?" It wasn't really her business, but her curiosity got the best of her.

"One of the Dakotas, I think."

South Dakota? His home state? She took another bite. What was in the letter? Well wishes from home? Or something from Mrs. Hughes' son? Something pertaining to the disappearance of his father?

"You'd better keep a close eye on Parker."

She frowned across at Jared, not liking that their minds were traveling along the same path. "You're paranoid."

"He's not trustworthy and you know it."

Of course she did. She hadn't managed to secure her own dig site from the Mexican government by being a gullible chump. "Neither are you."

He shrugged off her rebuff. "You should be careful around him, especially with your father gone."

"You heard about Dad, I see." She took another bite.

"I found it difficult to ignore a helicopter landing within sixty feet of my tent."

"You were wrong," she said after she swallowed. "He has an abscessed tooth. It's not stress."

"I'm wrong about many things, darling. I let you divorce me, didn't I?"

She clunked her coffee cup on the table. "Not today, Jared. We're stuck working together. I don't want to spend it living in the past."

He smirked. "That's ironic, considering you choose to spend each day studying the habits and customs of people long dead."

"True, but the key word there is *dead*. They don't keep coming back to annoy me."

"According to your crew, you're wrong about that. Funny things, those curses. They sure have a way of wreaking havoc."

She pushed the last of her lunch aside. "It's not a curse."

"I don't imagine it is. Curses are illogical hypotheses formed in the minds of those who can't distinguish reality from mythology." He stood, looming over her. "I wonder how the university feels about curses."

"The university can go fuck itself." She refused to be intimidated, swirling the last of the coffee in her cup.

"I'm sure those words will go over well when the board is debating the necessity of your father working with you here in the future."

She stretched her neck from side-to-side. "You can knock off the blackmail shit, Jared."

"I'm making sure that you don't let anything sway you from the task at hand."

After gulping the last of her drink, she stood and collected her plate. "And what guarantee do I have that you'll uphold your end of the bargain?"

"My word."

His smarmy smile made her want to upchuck down the front of his name-brand camp shirt. Shaking her head, she walked toward the counter María was busy wiping down. "*Gracías.*" She handed her dishes to the older woman.

"Where were you this morning, darling?" Jared followed her lead, handing over his cup.

"My whereabouts should not be of any interest to you since I no longer work for the university."

"Considering our investment in some of the work at this site, both you and your father's actions are of supreme interest to me."

"I already told you how I feel about the university." She headed for the exit, cursing her father's abscessed tooth for sticking her with her ex-meathead for the day.

He followed her out into the sunshine, his jaws locked onto her ankle like an angry honey badger. "Where were you that you didn't come running when the helicopter landed?"

She stopped suddenly, making him almost crash into her. "In the Sunset temple excavating and diagramming Sub Chamber Q."

"All morning?" he persisted, his gaze narrowed, suspicious. "You didn't make it to breakfast either."

"What can I say? I love my job. I get lost in my work." From Jared's taut face, she could tell he wasn't buying her bullshit. Too bad, that's all she was selling today. End of story. "Meet me back here in half an hour. We're shorthanded, so you're going to need your tool belt today."

"But I—"

"And keep those gloves handy. I'd hate to see you ruin one of your manicured fingernails on my watch."

* * *

From the time Steel had first arrived at the dig site, Quint's neck had bristled whenever the dickhead had come near. But his dislike for Steel had more to do with their disagreements decades ago while working for Dr. Hughes than anything present day. He'd known since the first time he'd met Steel not to turn his back on the snake. He hoped the article Jeff had mailed to him would now provide the proof for his suspicions.

He glanced at the mesh tent flap. Should he zip the concealing flap, too? Or would that look too suspect if Angélica walked past? Or Steel? He'd sure been eyeing the envelope in the mess tent, especially after Quint flipped it address side down.

Dropping onto his cot, he opened the envelope and unfolded the enclosed paper. The title read: *Dean Rogers Appoints Dr. Steel as Dean of Anthropology.* He continued, reading under his breath.

After several months of rumors regarding a possible blossoming relationship between Dr. Catherine Rogers and Dr. Jared Steel, it seems the gossip mongers have mistaken love and affection for a political courtship.

"Schmoozing," Quint muttered, to be more accurate.

He read further, learning how Steel wriggled his way up from being a run-of-the-mill professor to the god of the department.

Lowering the article, he rubbed his knuckles over the stubble along his jaw, trying to fit puzzle pieces together. Steel's ambition to run the show undoubtedly had to do with his monster ego, but Quint had a feeling there was something more going on.

With Steel in charge of the department, he'd have some control over Juan and what funding he'd receive. As was obvious from meeting both Dr. Garcías, Steel only needed to have power over one to control the other.

So why was he down here? Why not send someone else to check up on Juan and report back? Quint would bet a kidney that it had something to do with Angélica. Something Steel planned to use to gain leverage over her via her father.

But to what end? Could it be as simple as him still being in love with her? Wanting her back? Steel did tend to watch her when she was near with an intensity that made Quint's skin crawl. Was he dangerous? One of those ex-husbands who'd sooner kill his wife than allow her to escape?

Or was there something in it for Steel that would boost his career? Some power that came with corralling Angélica? Something to do with an artifact they'd come across at this site that had more importance than they realized?

Quint swiped away the sweat rolling down from his temple. Maybe he should talk to Angélica, bounce some of his suspicions off her.

Or not.

There was no way he could talk to her about any information Jeff had shared without hurting his credibility in the process. She'd want to know his source and why he was so interested in Steel's past. Things would only tumble downhill from …

He looked up at the sound of footfalls coming near.

"Parker?" Angélica called. "You in there?"

Shit! He stuffed the article under his pillow, and then he noticed the torn envelope lying on the desktop. He shot to his feet, but he was too slow to reach it.

Angélica peered through the mosquito flap. "I need to talk to you. You have a moment?"

Frozen in the middle of his tent, Quint forced a grin. "Sure. Come in."

As she unzipped the flap, he glanced over at the envelope.

He'd have to let it sit there in broad daylight. Dropping onto his cot, he rested his arm on the pillow covering the article. An envelope could contain anything, but the article about Steel would be tough to explain.

She stood just inside his tent, clasping her hands together in front of her. With her hair tucked back in a braid, her cheekbones looked more defined, exotic. Her T-shirt brought out the green in her eyes, turning them into dark emeralds.

Under his scrutiny, she lifted her chin. A trail of dirt ran down her neck. What had she been up to all morning? She'd missed breakfast and the whole Juan and Teodoro circus act.

"I'm assuming you know that my father's gone." Her tone was all business. The soft huskiness from last night after the Chachac ceremony nowhere to be found.

He nodded.

"Due to his absence, you'll continue working with Fernando at the Owl Temple today."

"What about Steel?"

Her eyes narrowed for a fraction of a second. If he hadn't been locked onto her gaze, he'd have missed it.

"I need Dr. Steel's expertise this afternoon. He'll be working with me."

Fingers of unease trailed down Quint's spine. He didn't like her working alone with Steel. What kind of expertise, anyway? He opened his mouth to ask her, and then bit back the words.

Not his business.

Not his problem.

Angélica was a big girl. She knew what she was doing. But that didn't stop Quint from feeling antsier about Steel's motives for coming down here. Based on Mrs. Hughes' collection of articles about the esteemed Dr. Steel, she hadn't trusted him either. But while her reasoning was still a mystery, Quint suspected that his distrust had a bit to do with Steel's past, but a shitload more to do with the woman standing in front of him.

"Okay," he said, unable to see a way for him to change her mind about spending time alone with her ex-husband without showing his hand. "Works for me."

"Good." She turned to leave but then stopped, looking back at him. "I hear you received a letter."

Quint resisted the urge to cover his pillow with his other hand. "You must have paid a visit to your ex-husband before stopping by."

Steel probably couldn't wait to tattle and give Angélica another reason to keep her eye on Quint.

"I trust everything is okay back home?" she fished.

He cocked his head to the side, wondering how much this was eating at her. Apparently enough to make her ask. "You want to know who it's from?"

"No!" She flushed a shade darker. "I mean, of course not. It's your business who sends you letters."

Yes, it was, but Quint didn't want this to become a barrier between them. He needed her to trust him, share details of the past, open doors that would allow him to dig for more on Dr. Hughes. "I don't blame you for wondering."

"You don't?" She wrung her hands together, then pulled them apart and frowned down at them as if catching them in the act of giving away her secrets. With a sigh, she jammed them in her pockets. "You're right. I want to know who sent the letter, even though I have no right to ask."

She was playing nice. He'd given her plenty of reason not to trust him from the start. Here was an opportunity to change that around, continue with being honest with her, like he'd been last night when she'd prodded about his reason for kissing her.

"The letter is from Jeff Hughes."

Her forehead creased. "Mr. Hughes' son." It wasn't a question, more like an accusation.

"Yes. Jeff wondered how things are going down here." That was true. "He's been cleaning out his mother's place and found some old memorabilia and wanted to tell me about it."

That was true, too, just a little vague.

"How long have you known Jeff?"

"Since second grade when he hit me in the face with a dodge ball and made my nose bleed. He felt so bad about it that he gave me the ball so I could hit him back and give him a matching bloody nose."

"Did you?"

"Nah, I told him to give me his Wolfman hat and we'd call it even. We've been friends ever since."

"You're lucky to have such a good friend."

"What about you?"

"What about me?"

"Do you have any old friends you keep in touch with still?" If he could distract her from the letter, maybe she wouldn't get him in a position where he'd have to choose between telling too much or hiding behind a lie.

She shook her head. "I grew up on dig sites like this one. That didn't leave opportunity for making friends."

"What about school?"

"My parents home schooled me throughout the day and in the evenings." His expression must have relayed his sad feelings for a lonely little girl stuck down here in this jungle, because she held up her hands. "No, it wasn't as bad as it sounds. I was lucky to get to play in tombs and swim in shallow *cenotes* all day long. How many kids are encouraged to get their hands dirty every day instead of sit still and listen in a classroom?"

She had a point. School was not his favorite pastime, especially not on warm, sunny days.

"It wasn't until college that I realized how lucky I'd been to be raised the way I was—a little wild, but free."

"And then you met Steel."

A cloud shrouded the light that had been in her eyes. "Right. Let's not forget about that colossal blunder."

Damn it, that's not what he'd meant. She was shutting down just like she had last night when he'd mentioned her ex-husband while trying to remind himself why he shouldn't kiss her in the moonlight and taste Teodoro's sweet wine on her tongue.

"Listen," he started, standing, "about what I said last night. I—"

"Stop. Please." She glanced toward the tent flap. "I'd rather not go there."

Whether he intended it or not, he'd found a way to get her out of his tent. He took a step toward her on purpose, testing. "Maybe we should talk about what happened."

"No!" She forced out a chuckle that sounded breathless, kind of sexy. "I had a little too much *balche*." She fumbled with the mess flap's zipper. "My lips were drunk." She finally got a handle on the zipper. "And stupid."

He moved closer, driving her out into the sunshine. "Yeah, but they're nice lips, and you looked really good in the moonlight."

Truth be told, she'd looked damned hot, but he'd had enough sense left to fight his attraction. Getting involved with Steel's ex-wife could mess up what he'd promised Jeff he'd do down here.

"Yeah, well, thanks, I guess." She put a few feet of distance between them. "But let's forget that ever happened."

Quint didn't think that was possible, but he nodded anyway. He fought back a grin at the obvious discomfort the big, bad boss lady was fighting on his account. It was nice to see that she was human after all.

He took mercy on her now that she was safely away from Jeff's letter. "Where should I meet Fernando?"

The flush faded from her cheeks. "You can head over to the Owl Temple whenever you're ready. Fernando and some of the men are already working on clearing a chamber over there."

"Where will you be?" His business or not, he wanted to know.

If his nosiness bothered her, she didn't show it. "At the

big *cenote*." She pointed toward a trail leading into the jungle. "There's an underground cave a few yards from it where several sacrifices occurred."

"You mean the bloodletting type?"

"I mean the tie your wrists behind your back, whisper messages in your ears to deliver to the gods, and push you into the underground river type."

Quint grimaced. "Does it make you nervous to go into that cave?"

She shrugged. "Not much about this place makes me nervous anymore. The cave is dangerous though," she warned him. "It's slippery in places from all of the bat guano and moisture. If you're not careful, you could fall into the river and get sucked into one of the underground limestone caverns. That's why I've made it off-limits to everyone."

Got it, boss lady. "And Steel is going in there with you? He must not be squeamish about working in caves."

"To my knowledge, there are only two things that get Jared excited, and one of them is blood."

"I noticed that." He remembered the incident with Alonso. "What's the other?"

Her smile came quick, her eyes sparkling with devilry. "Bats."

* * *

Angélica woke before dawn on Monday morning to the sound of a scream. She bolted upright in her cot, nearly tumbling out onto the floor.

A dark quiet cloaked her. She strained in the silence, listening. Not even the trees made a creak or shiver. Had she really heard a scream or had it been a nightmare? She fumbled for the lantern, but found her flashlight instead.

Another scream rang out before she could turn it on.

She dropped the light, her heart going off like a tommy gun. When she felt for the light again, it was nowhere to be found. "Dammit!"

Who was screaming? She hopped out of bed and landed partially on Rover. He squealed as if he'd been mortally wounded. She yelled along with him in the darkness, stumbling across the clothes-covered floor, tripping over a boot. Her right knee slammed into the desk. "Son of a b—"

"Angélica!" Teodoro called from right outside her tent.

"I'll be right there," she said through gritted teeth while hopping around on one leg, holding her throbbing knee. In the darkness, she grabbed what felt like a shirt and threw it on, then shuffled through the pile of clothes next to the desk and found a pair of shorts.

Where were her shoes? Where had she taken them off? She grabbed the boot she'd tripped over, slipped it on, and after feeling around the floor for a few seconds, found one of her shower flip flops. It was for the same foot as the one wearing the boot. *Shit-criminy!* It'd have to do.

She shoved the left shower shoe on her right foot and limped out into the moonlight. Teodoro waited long enough for her to zip up her tent before rushing off into the feeble moonlight toward his place.

"Teodoro, would you slow down?" she said in a loud stage whisper. When she rounded the corner, she saw there was no reason for keeping her voice low. Half of her crew was standing outside his door, twittering excitedly like a bunch of newly hatched chicks.

She stopped and took a deep breath, not sure she was ready to deal with the fears and irrationalities that were sure to come with whatever had caused the screaming. Several of the men noticed her and rushed toward her. She lowered her head and pushed through them, ignoring the questions about the curse and concerns about how she was going to get rid of the evil spirits haunting the site.

Fernando stood waiting in the doorway. She looked up at him, searching his face. The frown lines rippling up his brow made her wince in anticipation. "What is it?"

He stood aside. "You need to see for yourself."

"Oh, God! What now?" She hobbled past him, approaching the group of men huddled around the sick bed.

They parted as she neared. Teodoro stood directly next to the bed, holding a lantern over its occupant. The sweat on his forehead glistened.

She followed his gaze. Her hand flew to her mouth, barely catching her gasp.

On the bed, sprawled face down with his pants around his ankles, was Jorge. Or rather, Jorge's bare ass, covered with huge, inflamed, horrible-looking blisters.

Whimpering, Jorge reached back and began scratching his right cheek.

Teodoro caught his hand. "It will only make it worse," he told the boy in Mayan.

Jorge cried for his mother.

Teodoro looked over at Angélica, his face craggy with wrinkles, his hair all askew.

"What do you think happened?" she asked.

"Looks like the curse got the latrine, too."

Chapter Eight

Chechem Tree: The "black poison-wood" tree. Resin from this tree causes itching, blistering, and swelling.

There was nothing like a couple of hair-raising screams in the night to make a guy fall out of his cot and land flat on his face.

Thanks to Quint's nose plant, it'd taken him a few minutes to get dressed. To make matters worse, the zipper on his tent flap had stuck and ended up breaking off in his hand.

Now that he'd managed to get himself both vertical and outside, he couldn't seem to find anyone in the shadow-filled predawn light. But he could hear their low murmurs. Maybe they were at Teodoro's hut.

Gingerly pressing on the cartilage below the bridge of his still-throbbing nose, he rounded the corner of the mess tent and ran smack-dab into Angélica. His elbow jammed into her shoulder, which in turn rammed the heel of his hand into his nose.

"Yowch!" He reared his head back, his eyes watering.

She let out a yip of surprise and stepped backward, tripping over a tent stake, her arms flailing.

Quint caught her wrist, pulling her back toward him before she fell into the tent wall. "Gotcha." He steadied her, holding her by the shoulders while he blinked away his pain.

She looked frazzled in the pale light. Wisps of hair floated around her face, pillowcase wrinkles lined her cheek. The tag of her tank-top stuck out at chest level, bobbing slightly as she breathed. The shirt's seams were showing.

"Sorry about that," Quint said. "I should've been watching where I was going."

She leaned into him slightly, like she needed a kickstand to stay upright. "I'm the one who should've been more careful."

Taking a closer look at her, he noticed the dark shadows under her eyes. Sweat dotted her upper lip. She looked more than tired; she was almost haggard. "That wasn't you screaming was it?"

The scream had been high-pitched but not quite at the female level.

"No, not me." She stared blankly off to her left, and then shuddered at whatever was passing through her thoughts.

"What's going on? Where is everyone?"

Steel came around the corner right then, following in Quint's wake. He stopped at the sight of them, his face pinching into a scowl. "Well, isn't this cozy."

Angélica snarled at him. "Don't start, Jared. I'm in no mood for your high-and-mighty shit."

He looked at Quint's hands, which were still clutching her shoulders. "Are you taking her prisoner, Parker?"

Quint ignored him, focusing on the tousled, obviously troubled woman in front of him. "Are you okay?"

"Ask me that again when the sun is setting."

"Unhand her, Parker."

Unhand her? Were they lords and ladies? Apparently, he'd missed the trumpeted announcement. Hell, and here he'd gone and left his rapier in his other pants.

Quint slid his hands down to Angélica's elbows before releasing her, enjoying the feel of her soft skin under his fingers.

Steel muttered something not very gentlemanly.

"What happened?" Quint asked her.

"Nothing that concerns you," Jared answered.

"I don't remember yanking your chain, Steel." Quint kept his focus on the woman in front of him.

"Uh, nothing really." She crooked her head side-to-side, stretching her neck. "Just a minor glitch in this morning's routine."

Damn her for trying to close him out again. "Either I hear the truth from you or from your crew, Dr. García. Who's it gonna be?"

She nailed him with a squint. "I don't want this to show up in print."

"It won't."

"You understand I'm very concerned about my crew's reputation as qualified field workers."

"Completely." He held her squint. "You have my word."

"Don't trust him," Steel advised.

"Jorge has experienced an incident that caused several large blisters to form on his skin."

Quint grimaced, wondering what the boy had gotten into. "How did—"

"Dr. García," Fernando interrupted, joining their little party. "*Nada.* Not on the seat, the walls, or the door handle."

She threw up her hands, cursing in a rapid-fire mixture of English and Spanish.

"Teodoro says it smells like resin from a *chechem* tree," she said after catching her breath.

"He can actually smell that?" Steel asked.

She nodded. "He sent Enrico out to gather some juice from a *chacah* tree."

Quint looked from Angélica to Fernando and back, lost in the middle of the conversation. "What does that do?"

Angélica glanced his way. "Cures the rashes caused by the *chechem* resin."

"What should I do about them?" Fernando thumbed in the direction of the cluster of men hovering outside of Teodoro's door.

"Send them to the mess tent. I'll be there shortly to deal with the ripple effects from this." As Fernando walked away, Angélica sniffed the air. "I smell coffee."

Quint sniffed, too, noticing only the scent of his tent canvas coming from his clothes, which reminded him of something. "I broke my tent zipper. It was jammed or something, and when I tried to force it, the zipper broke off in my hand." He pulled the piece of metal out of his pocket and showed it to her.

"You'll have to switch to the other supply tent."

"Which one is that?"

"The one next to mine."

"Parker should remain with the other workers," Steel commanded, as if it were his decision. "Give him the one I'm using, and I'll move into the one next to yours."

She hit Steel with a testicle crushing glare. "Damn it, Jared! This is my dig site. Try to remember that while you wait for me in the mess tent with the rest of my crew." She returned to Quint. "You can move after breakfast." Squaring her shoulders, she limped off toward her tent.

Quint noticed her boot and flip-flop ensemble and grinned.

"Pretty convenient, your zipper breaking like that."

"You should see me work my magic with buttons." Quint continued to watch Angélica until she slipped between tents and disappeared.

"You're up to something, and I'm going to catch you in the wrong place at the right time," Steel threatened.

Jesus, this pissing contest was getting old. "Oh, yeah? Catch this." He tossed the zipper at him.

Steel snared it with a bandaged left hand, sucking in his breath in pain. He dropped the zipper into his other palm, wincing as he flexed his injured hand.

Quint eyed the bandage. The wrap job didn't look like a Teodoro Special. "Ruin your manicure in the bat cave?"

"Stay away from my wife, Parker."

There was an underlying menace in his voice that made Quint pause. His gut warned him there was more to Steel's animosity than petty jealousy. "I have a news flash for you—she's not your wife anymore."

Steel's nostrils flared. "She's my wife until I say otherwise."

The son of a bitch really needed his face rearranged. "Tell you what. How about you just stand here living in your fucked-up fantasy world while I go grab a cup of coffee and enjoy reality without you in it."

"Remember," Steel snared Quint's sleeve. "I'm watching your every move."

"Fine." Quint yanked free. "Watch me move into the tent next to hers."

* * *

Inside the safety of her tent, Angélica dropped onto her cot and covered her face with her hands.

What in the hell was going on? First Esteban's arm, then Alonso's leg, now Jorge's ass. Over the years, they'd had incidents at the dig site but just the average sprained ankles and sore backs. Nothing like this. Maybe she was working them too hard. Maybe she needed to give them a longer *siesta* after lunch. Maybe …

"I see some things haven't changed," Jared said.

She lowered her hands, frowning at her ex-husband who was peeking inside her tent through the mesh flap.

"Mind if I join you?" He let himself inside the zippered flap.

Tents really needed to come equipped with doors with deadbolts.

He eyed her messy tent with an expression of distaste.

Like she needed this shit right now. "I told you to wait for me in the mess tent."

"Your standards have lowered greatly."

She considered telling him that he was mistaken, throwing back that she had divorced *him* after all, but she didn't feel like getting into an argument after this morning's mess. "Why are you standing inside of my tent, Jared?"

"I need to talk to you."

"So talk." She plucked a pair of clean underwear from a stack of clothes next to her cot, and then stood and unhooked her bra from the tent pole where she'd draped it to dry yesterday.

"You used to wear satin and lace."

Was she actually awake? Was this madness real? Here she had yet another crewmember injured, inciting more whispers about that stupid ass curse, and now her ex-husband wanted to reminisce about past lingerie choices.

"What can I do for you, Jared?" She crossed her arms.

"There's another reason why I came down here, other than the university's needs."

No shit. "Can we talk about this another time? I'm a little busy right now."

"As you've probably noticed," he plowed right over her. "I'm still in love with you."

She blinked. No. This couldn't be happening.

He stepped over a pile of boots and socks, closing the distance between them. "I'd like you back as my wife. Living without you all of these years has made me realize how valuable you are to me. We could do so much together for the archaeology world."

She blinked again. Maybe there was a curse after all.

"Angélica, darling." With uncharacteristic awkwardness, Jared reached for her, capturing her shoulders. He pulled her closer. "I've missed the scent of your skin."

Really? He missed the smelly parts and all? No way.

He lowered his head, zeroing in for a kiss.

She sidestepped. "Jared, it's way too early in the morning for blisters and kisses."

"Come on, my love," he said, snaring her hand. He lifted it to his mouth and kissed her knuckles. "We were so good together in bed."

He remembered their sex life a lot differently than she.

"Jared, stop." She tugged free of his grip. "This isn't going to work." The Yucatán Peninsula would freeze over before she even considered swapping spit with him, let alone signing up for another tour of his version of wedded bliss. However, she needed to use a dump truck load of tact while making her feelings crystal clear. Her father's future was at stake here.

"I know you still enjoy my touch." He tucked a tendril of hair behind her ear. "Why fight the feelings you have?"

He was right. She should stop fighting and choke the arrogant son of a bitch to death. "We tried the marriage thing, remember? It caused more harm than good. Maybe it's best if we keep this," she pointed back and forth between them, "the way it is."

"Ah. I see." His smile had way too much confidence behind it. "You need some time to consider my offer."

Sure. The rest of eternity might be enough. "I don't think so."

"You don't *think*? So, there is an element of uncertainty still." He took a step back. "How about I give you a little time to work through this morning's unfortunate event and let my proposal sink in. Then we'll revisit this later."

"Okay." Fine. Groovy. Whatever it took to remove him from her tent before she clobbered him with her boot. "How about this time next year?"

"Oh, how I have missed that dry wit of yours." Jared stepped over her mess of clothes on his way toward the tent flap. "It reminds me of all the good times we used to have."

Huh. She wondered if he'd put in a change of address at the post office now that he was living in Fantasyland. "Jared, there's no use digging up bones. Let's keep to the present."

"You dig up bones every day. Just think about my proposal."

She'd sooner weigh the pros and cons of lighting her hair on fire. "I'll do that. Now leave so I can get dressed."

He left, zipping both tent flaps closed behind him.

As his footfalls faded, Rover waddled out from under the cot and snorted up at her.

"My thoughts exactly." She scratched behind his ears. "So, what am I going to do about the other guy?"

* * *

Later that afternoon, she was still working on that answer while sitting across from Quint in the small burial chamber two layers inside the Temple of the Crow.

She'd made the choice of keeping Quint with her today rather than Jared. Listening to Jared talk about their past for hours would've driven her headfirst into a *cenote*, hands tied and all—especially after the crazy rumors flying around at lunch. She'd barely had a chance to eat while trying to convince her crew that Jorge's blisters were not caused by some supernatural devil that blew in on the wind along with that damned curse.

Expecting Quint to spend their time together plying her for information for his article, she was surprised at how quiet he was today while they worked. She should have been doing the Snoopy dance at his lack of chatter. Instead, she kept glancing his way, watching the frown lines sweep over his face like cloud shadows over the desert valley floor at her dad's ranch.

What was going on in his head? Was he regretting coming down here after learning more from Fernando about what had happened to Jorge? Was he unhappy with having to move to the tent next to hers? Did his pensiveness have anything to do with that letter he'd received from Jeff Hughes?

Her vision blurred, her eyelids growing heavy. The heat of

the temple was building, draining her. They shouldn't stay in here much longer, but the soft glow of the lantern and the sound of Quint's breathing lulled, making her want to curl up and catch up on all the sleep she'd missed lately.

She leaned her head against the warm wall, her eyelids drooping, thoughts scattering ... her father rubbing his sore tooth, Teodoro sending her worried glances, Quint digging in a chamber, Jared holding out a diamond ring, Esteban screaming, her mother crying in her tent, Jorge whimpering, Quint cupping her face ...

"Dr. García." His voice seemed to come from far off, echoing, yet she could feel his breath caressing her skin. *Tell me, Angélica.*

She reached for him, coming up empty. Where was he?

"Angélica," he whispered in her ear. *Tell me what you want.*

She wanted him, damn it. Right here in this hot, pitch-black chamber where nobody would see her lose control, hear her cry out when he touched her. She could smell his skin, hear his clothes rustling. Her imagination took over, slamming her with sensations and stimulating fantasies, filling her with aches and longings.

Her hand flailed until she touched something solid, warm. "Quint." She grasped his shirt, tugging him down.

"Angélica," this time his voice was clear and strong, right in front of her.

Her eyelids flew open. Quint leaned over her, his hazel eyes close, his mouth even closer thanks to her grip on his shirt. Sweat glistened on his skin in the lamplight.

"What?" she gasped more than spoke, letting go of his shirt. She slid upright against the wall, putting space between them.

"You talk in your sleep." His smile lit up his face. The corners of his eyes crinkled. "Did you know that?"

Her dream about having her way with him here on the chamber floor pinballed through her brain. Oh, dear Lord, no. Her whole face burned like she'd stuck it in a blast furnace.

"What did I say?"

His gaze centered on her mouth for one long head rush, then he sat back on his heels and looked at the glyph-covered wall behind her. "Nothing much. It was mostly mumbling and a few moans."

Moans? Like lust-filled, desperate for sex moans? Shit. Really? She wanted to hide inside her turtle shell.

"What happened with Steel and the bat cave?"

She latched onto his change of subject like it was a rope dangling from the cliff next to her. "I've never seen Jared's face so pale, especially when he slipped on some guano-covered rocks and hurt his hand when he fell."

"That explains the bandage."

Silence stretched like taffy, starting to sag in the middle. "How is the article coming along?" she blurted out.

"Great. You've given me a lot to get started."

It would have to be enough to finish, because he had to be gone in three days per Jared's blackmail demands. Although, she hadn't yet figured out how she was going to manage that. "Good, good. I'm glad to hear it."

Wonderful, first she tried attacking him in her sleep and now she was bumbling like a crush-filled teenager. Where was that bottle of rum she kept hidden in her tent when she needed it?

He twirled the paintbrush he'd been using throughout the morning to clean the bone shards she kept finding. "Why don't you let me dig for a bit?"

"I have a better idea." She pushed to her feet. "Let's get out of here before we melt to death." Or she fell asleep and did something even worse.

"Your wish is my command, my master." He bowed, handing her the paintbrush.

She avoided his eyes while they cleaned up, still fretting over what she might have said in her sleep. They trekked in silence as they made their way out of the temple.

"Dr. García!" Esteban met them just inside the exit.

Her stomach dropped at his wide eyes and hitching breath. "Jesus, what now?"

"It's your father."

"What about him?" She stumbled backwards a step, right into Quint, who grasped her shoulders, steadying her.

"He needs you right now."

"Where is he?"

"Outside." He wiped a stream of sweat from his temple with the shoulder of his T-shirt.

He'd made it back from Cancun, thank God. So why was Esteban standing in front of her out of breath and sweating all over the place?

"What's wrong? Did something happen to him?" She leaned into Quint, afraid of what she was about to hear.

"*Sí.* He dropped the key to the safe box into the *cenote.*"

She choked back a bout of hysterical laughter and pushed past Esteban. That was it. She was going to duct tape her father in his tent for the rest of the dig season.

* * *

Spread out on the king's chest is a necklace containing eight jade beads, four of which look to have skull visages carved into the face of the bead.

Angélica stopped writing and yawned, blinking away sleep. She looked at her travel clock, and then leaned closer to it. Either the light from her lantern was dimming, or she'd reached the point where sleep deprivation was affecting her vision. She plucked it up and frowned at the clock hands. Was it really three already?

She stood and stretched, needing a little more energy to finish her analysis before catching an hour or two of sleep. Maybe she'd actually sleep during the afternoon *siesta* break instead of working.

Rover snorted in his sleep, his legs jerking as he raced

through his dreams. He was probably running from María after tearing up her garden again, the unruly little *jabalí*. Splint or not, he managed to keep sneaking out of her tent and getting into trouble.

Her focus returned to her notes. It was time to wrap things up. She sat back down and picked up the tracing she had made Sunday morning in the Temple of the Water Witch when all hell had been breaking loose with her father, his tooth, and Pedro. Holding the tracing in front of the lantern, she bent over the paper and wrote:

In the center of the eight beads is a shell. While this glyph is pitted with age, details of the carving seem to show a cone-like shell with three flaring layers resembling a small Christmas tree. There are ten points rounding the bottom of the shell. According to my research (using "The Wayfarer's Guide to South American Shells"), this shell looks like a member of the Astraeinae family of the Gastropoda Orthogastropoda class. After looking at photos of several specimens of this family, I believe it is either an Astraea Tecta or an Astraea Latispina. I would need to see the actual shell to give an official ruling on …

"Angélica!"

She jumped at the sound of her father's voice right outside her tent. "What?" she whispered loudly, wishing everyone would stop sneaking up on her.

"Can I come in?"

"Of course."

Juan unzipped the mesh flap and stepped inside. He had on the hole-ridden, white T-shirt and worn gray cotton shorts he wore to bed each night.

"What are you doing?" He moved over to where she sat at the desk and picked up the lantern. "What's this?" he crooked his neck and looked down at her scrawls.

"Notes on what I found in the chamber Sunday morning."

"Anything that will help?"

"Possibly, but I don't think we have a leg to stand on unless we actually find one of the shells. Paintings and carvings are too indistinct and easy to mislabel."

He grunted in agreement, and then held the lantern right in her face. "Do you realize how late it is?"

She squinted, wincing in the light. "What's your point?"

"What are you still doing awake?"

"I can't sleep."

"Is it Jared?"

More like Quint, but her father didn't need to know about that particular pickle. "Jared's part of it. What are *you* doing out of bed? Is your tooth doing okay?"

He scraped his hand over his beard stubble. "My tooth is fine, but we've got a problem."

"What now?" She collected her notes and the tracing and stuffed them all in the drawer with the fake bottom. "Did you sacrifice the spare key, too?"

"Very funny, *gatita*, but this is serious."

She was afraid of that. She slammed the desk drawer closed. "Which one of my crew is it now?"

"It's not your crew this time."

Her breath lurched. "Quint?"

He shook his head. "Jared."

Chapter Nine

Subín Tree (commonly known as Bullhorn Acacia): A tree covered with thorns and biting red ants.

¡Dios mio!" Angélica gripped the doorjamb on Teodoro's threshold, trying to hide her recoil at the sight in front of her. "What happened to you?"

Jared looked up at her from the cot where he lay shirtless while Teodoro applied ointment to tiny red welts covering his chest, neck, and face. "Ants."

She shuddered, her legs starting to itch. She'd had a run in with biting ants as a kid when she'd poked a stick into a red ant hill on her dad's ranch. Turned out the stick wasn't long enough. While she was busy messing with their home, a war party had crawled up inside her jeans and attacked her legs. She'd kicked off her pants and run around in circles screaming until her mom had sprayed her off with the hose, and even then some of those little fiery buggers had held on tight, requiring a more persuasive shooing.

Her father nudged her inside the hut so he could shut the door behind them.

"How did this happen?" she asked nobody in particular.

Juan dropped his arm around her shoulders and led her toward Teodoro's cot, forcing her closer than she wanted to be. The memory of what her father still laughingly referred to as *The Mexican Ant Dance* still haunted her. Those bites had hurt.

"*Gatita*, I think you might want to sit for a moment."

"Really?" At his sober nod, she slumped onto the edge of the cot. She braced herself for what was to come, scratching at an itch on her arm. A glance in Jared's direction left her grimacing. The tendons and muscles in his neck were visibly taut in the lantern light. Sweat ran down his face, mixing with the glistening ointment covering his cheeks and jaw.

"We have a problem." Juan squeezed the bridge of his nose, a gesture she'd seen often during the brief time her mom had been in intensive care. He wasn't nearly as pale and worn-out looking this time though. Not yet anyway.

Teodoro grunted at Juan, pointing at the lantern.

Juan grabbed the lantern and moved closer, lighting up the angry bites even more. He frowned at her. "I found a *subín* branch in Jared's cot."

In his cot? How did it get up in his cot? And why?

"And ants scattered throughout his sheets. There were too many to count."

She turned to Jared. "Did you notice anything odd before you crawled into bed?"

"No."

Grimacing, she scratched her lower back. "So, you think someone sneaked into his tent while he was sleeping and slipped the branch into his cot?"

Juan shrugged.

"Why would someone do that?"

"Personal vendetta?"

Angélica opened her mouth to dismiss his idea but then closed it. Just about every person at the site could be labeled guilty on that count, including herself. Jared was about as well-liked by her crew as the ants he'd been sharing his bed with tonight. "Any other ideas?" Any that wouldn't alert the *federales* to start snooping around her dig site?

"The curse," Teodoro spoke in Mayan.

Angélica nailed him with a glower. She should have seen that one coming. "Any other *logical* ideas?"

"What about Rover?" her father asked. "Maybe he dragged the limb into Jared's tent. We've both witnessed him climbing up on your cot even with his bum leg."

She considered that. "I don't think so. He may like to pilfer from María's garden, but he's a picky eater when it comes to insects." There was another possibility, one that gave her goosebumps.

She needed to talk to her father. Alone.

Rising, she scratched at a tickling on her scalp. "I'm going to go scout around Jared's tent and look for signs of anything peculiar."

"I don't think that's wise, *gatita*."

"It's my dig site." Her crew. Her responsibility. Hiding in her tent wasn't going to make this lunacy stop. "None of this leaks out to anyone else, understand?" She locked gazes with each man, emphasizing her words with a warning glare.

Her father pressed his lips tight, holding his two cents inside. He didn't need to speak. His disapproval lined his forehead. "What do you want us to do with Jared? Wrap him like a mummy and hide him in one of the tombs?"

What a great idea! If only it were that easy to get rid of her ex-husband.

"Jared." She avoided looking directly at him, focusing on the cot next to his head while scratching at a tingle on her hip. "Stay in your tent all day today. If you have to use the latrine, wear a hat and sunglasses. I don't want you to be seen by anyone until the swelling on those bites goes down a bit." At his nod, she turned to her father. "I need to talk to you outside as soon as you're done helping Teodoro."

Grabbing a spare flashlight off the shelf, she escaped into the waning moonlight, itching all of the way.

Damn! She wanted to throw the flashlight as far as she could, but settled for kicking at a rock on the ground instead. "Damn, damn, damn," she growled under her breath for good measure, flicking on the flashlight.

The leaves on the trees rattled softly as a small breeze blew past, mixing with the croaking of the frogs down by the *cenote*. She peered across the plaza at the thick shadows around the base of the Dawn Temple.

It would be so simple for someone to sneak around this place, especially in the dark.

Something crashed through the bushes behind her.

She whirled, shining the light into the thick canopy of trees and clusters of underbrush. Several low branches at the edge of the jungle bobbed slowly up and down. It was too dark further under the canopy to see beyond the jungle's outer skin. Tiptoeing toward the bushes, she aimed the beam of light at several thorny branches.

A hand clamped down on her shoulder.

With an inward gasp she leapt sideways, wrenching free, but then dropped the flashlight. It hit the ground with a small *clink* and the beam of light disappeared.

Darkness swallowed her whole, quaking heart and all.

She could hear someone breathing.

It wasn't her.

Her knees turned loose and wobbly. "Who's there?"

"Santa Claus," her father said. "Who do you think?"

"Dammit, Dad!" She kneeled down, feeling around for the flashlight. "You scared the crap out of me."

"Didn't you just tell me to meet you out here?"

"Yes, but you didn't need to sneak up on me like that." Her fingers bumped the flashlight casing.

"I didn't sneak. I'm an old man." He flicked on his flashlight, shining it around on the ground near her hand. "My sneaking days are long over. There it is, near that bush."

"You're not that old." She reached for the light.

A rustle in the bushes near her outstretched hand made

her jerk back. A rat zipped past her hand, darting out of sight under the bush next to her. She cursed at it for making her adrenaline spike again.

"What's with you?" Juan snickered. "Got ants in your pants?"

Oh, man, that was lame. She scooped up the light and pushed to her feet. "I don't know, I guess I'm feeling a bit antsy tonight."

Juan laughed aloud.

She reached up and covered his mouth with her hand, shushing him. "We're terrible."

He pulled her hand away from his mouth, using it to draw her into a hug. "Maybe so, *gatita*, but only at four in the morning." He rested his chin on the top of her head. "The rest of the time we're just incorrigible."

With her forehead pressed against his chest, she soaked up the strength he was offering. His love warmed away the chill that had followed her out of Teodoro's hut into the darkness. He always knew when she needed a hug and when to give her space. Long, long ago, her mom had told Angélica one of the reasons she'd married Juan was because his hugs were filled with magic elixirs, able to light up her heart in even the blackest of temples.

But not even Juan's arms could save her mom from the shadows that had swallowed her up at the end, damn it.

Sniffing away the memories of her mom, she focused on the task at hand and stepped out of her dad's hold. "Come on." She led him toward the mess tent.

Inside the tent, she turned on one of the lanterns from the kitchen counter. "Are you thinking what I'm thinking?"

Juan sat at the closest table, watching her pour a cup of cold coffee, waving off her motion to fill one for him. "This is no accident."

She set the light and the coffee on the table, dropping down across from him. "Someone's messing with us."

"One of our own or someone else?"

"You tell me." She sipped the cold drink, grimacing at the bitterness. She should have added some sugar. "You know what's scary?"

"Jared coming to Thanksgiving dinner this year."

She flicked his arm. "I'm serious."

"So am I."

She ran the tip of her index finger around the rim of the coffee cup. "I have no idea how to begin to protect us."

His gaze measured her for several blinks. "You think it's that serious?"

"Remember the *chechem* resin incident that I told you about the other morning?" At his nod, she continued. "I was having trouble buying that it was caused by Jorge wearing the same underwear for four days in a row." That had been the front-running rumor, other than that damned curse, of course.

"Maybe some prankster from the village heard about our curse and decided to have some fun with us. Was there anyone you didn't hire this season who wanted to be part of the crew?"

"I hired everyone on the sign-up sheet after our decision to take on extra crew this year."

"Right. Extra crew. Well, fiddlesticks." He rubbed his eyes. When he blinked them open again, he hit her with a stern look. "You're not going out to look around until it's light out." It wasn't a question. He'd used his *fatherly* voice, the same one he'd been using since she'd started brushing her hair on her own.

Fine. With dawn just another cup of coffee away, she wouldn't have long to wait.

She stirred sugar into her coffee, thinking about a certain hazel-eyed man. "I'd like you to work with Quint today. But I do *not* want him finding out about this." She tapped her finger on the table for emphasis. He already knew too much for his own good … or theirs.

Juan's brow crinkled. "You still don't trust him, huh?"

"Not entirely."

Quint had a ways to go to earn that. Not that he had much time left to work on it if she bowed to Jared's ultimatum. Somehow, she needed to give Quint the boot without ruffling his feathers. She should probably let him know soon that he had to go, giving him time to finish acquiring all of the information necessary. If she played things right, she would have both his article and Jared's recommendation helping to ensure her father's future for another year or two, maybe more.

"I'm still not thrilled about you scouting about on your own, even in the daylight. Why don't you take Teodoro with you?"

"It's probably going to be a waste of time." She doubted she'd come across whoever put the branch in Jared's cot just sitting outside the camp boundary waiting to be caught. "Besides, it's Tuesday, Teodoro's regular day to get supplies at the village. I don't want to cause any suspicion by switching his schedule."

Juan leaned closer and took her chin in his hand. "If you aren't back by lunch, I'm going to recruit some men and come looking for you, your stubbornness about keeping this all one big secret be damned."

"I know this jungle like the back of my hand, Dad. I'll be fine." When he kept frowning at her, she added, "I'll take a machete with me."

"What happened to my docile, innocent little girl?" He let go of her chin. "You used to wear the cutest, frilly dresses."

"For the record, I only wore a frilly dress once." And she'd promptly stained and ripped it while chasing the jackrabbit Juan had told her was the Easter bunny. She gulped the rest of her coffee and then stood. "I'll check on Jared when I get back."

"Where are you going?"

"Back to my tent to change." She pointed at her shirt. "I'm still wearing yesterday's clothes."

"You should try to get some sleep."

"I'll sleep when the dig season is over."

He snorted his disapproval. "Oh, one more thing. Guess what Jared asked for earlier when I helped him to Teodoro's hut?"

"A new cot?"

He shook his head. "My permission to marry you."

* * *

The Dawn Temple was like all of the other structures at the site—miserably hot and muggy, dusty and musty, and claustrophobic as a coffin. Quint would rather skinny dip with jellyfish than spend another afternoon helping Juan take measurements of every wall, doorway, ceiling, and whatever else he could find. Hell, working outside with the swarms of bugs would have been less aging on his heart than tooling around in this death trap.

He looked over at Juan, who was measuring the width of the short, narrow doorway they had entered to get into this sub chamber, as Juan called it. The silence felt cottony in there, interrupted only by the sound of their breathing and Juan penciling numbers on his notepad.

After a morning of Juan evading most of his questions, Quint strongly suspected that Angélica had ordered her father to keep quiet about Dr. Hughes and stick to high level details only about the site.

She was doing a bang-up job of keeping Quint at arm's length and he didn't like dangling out there one bit. Damn her need to control every little thing that happened on *her* dig site. He wondered how she'd react if he barged into her tent later tonight and gave her a thorough tongue lashing for playing these games with him.

And when he'd finished with her mouth, he'd peel off her clothes and study her skin inch by inch, using one of those little paintbrushes from her tool pouch. A fresh coat of sweat slicked his skin as his mind took him places he shouldn't go with the boss lady, starting with her …

"Earth to Quint, Earth to Quint," Juan's voice interrupted his sweaty thoughts about the older man's daughter. "Can you write a few numbers down for me?"

"Sure," Quint said, swiping the sweat and all thoughts of Angélica's curves from his mind. He took the notebook and started listing numbers as Juan read them.

In between the measurements, he stared up at the web-like cracks spreading across the limestone ceiling. When Juan finally finished, he reached up and touched one of the larger cracks. "This chamber looks like the roof is about to cave in."

"Don't do that!"

Quint yanked his arm back. "Why?"

Juan tucked his pencil back behind his ear, a smile rounding his cheeks. "No reason. I just wanted to see you jump."

"Wise ass." Quint leaned against the opposite wall of the narrow chamber. He tried to come up with a subtle way of asking where Angélica had been this morning. Ever since they'd left the mess tent after breakfast, he'd been waiting for their conversation to turn in her direction, but Juan had other plans and kept spewing facts about Maya history.

Juan measured the height of the walls on each side of the chamber's entrance. He glanced at Quint before picking up his notepad again. "Have you noticed how stale the air is in here?"

Quint had noticed that and many more nerve-wracking tidbits. The room they were in was no more than ten feet long by five feet wide—small enough to make a tall guy a little fidgety. He had to stay hunched over or risk scraping his head on the uneven ceiling.

"We're actually in a section of the structure that is too deep in the ground and far from any openings to get much fresh air. The only air movement comes from you and me stirring it up." Juan pulled a hand-held instrument from his tool kit. "I use this to keep track of the oxygen levels when we get this far into the temples just to be safe."

Quint looked at the chipped fragments of frescos lining the walls. "It must've been hell to excavate this room."

"According to Dr. Hughes' journal, he had to work in here alone. None of his crew was willing to venture this far into the temple."

He wanted that journal, dang it. "Because of the lack of airflow?"

"No, because of the instability of the surrounding passageways. Fernando and I shored up these walls about four years ago. Before that, I didn't allow any workers to come in here. The cracks you see in the ceiling are evidence of the temple's weakening structure."

Quint eyed those cracks again, his mouth drying. Several seemed wider than they had a moment ago. Were those new? How much more weight could the ceiling take before giving in to gravity? Would it crack before the sky fell? Or would it come crashing down, crushing …

Closing his eyes, he talked himself down off the ledge. Juan wouldn't have led him in here if it weren't relatively safe. He reached down, picked up his hard hat, and dropped it on his head. Then again, no need to take chances.

"It must have been a hell of a job," Juan mumbled, holding his pencil in his mouth as he measured the width of ceiling at one end of the room and then the other.

"What's with all of the measuring?"

Juan took the pencil from his mouth. "Every year, I measure the same chambers, watching for any change that would indicate a structural shift." He jotted something on the paper, scratched his head, and then added another couple of numbers.

Quint thought about Dr. Hughes, working alone in here with only a flashlight or lantern while his wife and son went about their daily lives back in Rapid City.

What in the hell had happened to Dr. Hughes? Quint had gone over the notes Jeff had given him again last night wondering how someone could disappear without a trace.

He'd almost crossed over to Angélica's tent more than once, thinking up one excuse after another to prod her for answers, but his need to see her had more to do with *her* than talking about the past. So he'd stayed put, listening to the sounds of her moving around not twenty feet away.

At some point, he needed to talk to her alone. To explain why he'd come clean about the kiss he'd stolen that day in front of Jared. To make it clear he would be honest with her from here on out. No more lies. No more secrets.

But his promise to Jeff made him pause. If he opened himself up to Angélica and she asked too many questions, he might find himself on the road to the village without any answers for Jeff. He didn't want to risk that now, not after all of the sweat and bugs he'd put up with down here. He wasn't going to show up on his friend's doorstep empty-handed.

Where was Dr. Hughes' body?

Hell, Jeff had found out his mother's suspicions about his father's murder only when she was taking her last breaths. Before that revealing moment, Jeff had made peace with never knowing what had happened to his father. But then Mrs. Hughes had whispered words of murder in the jungle, telling Jeff about her investigation into his father's death, making him promise to find out the truth after she was gone.

When Quint found out Jeff was thinking of flying down to the dig site where his father had last been seen, leaving his newborn son behind, Quint had volunteered to take Jeff's place. It was easy enough for him to solicit a job working on a Maya dig site. Plus he owed the Hughes family for their kindness. But mostly he couldn't risk something happening to Jeff with a baby who needed a father there to raise him. History was not going to repeat itself on Quint's watch. Losing one Hughes to this place was bad enough.

Quint looked at Juan, whose features were scrunched as he scribbled numbers and notes. There had to be some way to coerce information from the older man, an honorable way of getting that journal. He screwed up the courage and blurted,

"What's the chance of my borrowing Dr. Hughes' journal for a night or two?"

Juan peered at him over the rims of his reading glasses for what felt like a Maya calendar year. Quint did his best not to squirm. "Would this be for your professional or personal reading pleasure?"

"Personal."

Juan closed his notepad and shoved it in his back pocket. "At least you're honest."

Most of the time. "I don't like to lie." Especially not to people he respected.

He nodded slowly, as if weighing Quint's words. "I have two conditions for you to meet before allowing you to borrow the journal." He took off his glasses, cleaning them with the hem of his camp shirt. "First, you must swear you will not take any excerpts from the journal to use in your article about this site."

"You have my word."

Juan folded his glasses, tucked them into a small black case, and shoved them into his shirt pocket. "Second, I'd like an explanation."

"About what?"

"Why are you so interested in an old journal?"

"What makes you think I'm *that* interested?"

"Because the last time I mentioned it to you, your eyes widened and you tapped the tips of your fingers together just as you are now."

Quint looked down at his fingers. Damn it. He'd have to be more careful around Juan. That wide grin hid a sharp mind. "I'd like to see if Dr. Hughes mentioned anything about his family."

"That's it?"

"Maybe I'm also curious if he came across any oddities at this site."

"Like a curse."

"Sure." Or something more logical that would explain his

absence for the last twenty years.

"All right. I guess that's good enough … for now."

"I noticed Dr. Steel wasn't at breakfast." Quint switched the subject before Juan changed his mind about letting him read the journal.

Juan pushed back his hard hat, scratching his forehead. "He's fighting off some kind of bug. Angélica decided the smart thing to do is to keep him quarantined."

"Quarantined?"

"Yep, for a day or two anyway. It's best if you keep clear of him, too."

If he never saw Steel again, it would be a lifetime too soon. "That won't be a problem for me."

"I noticed there's not much love between you two boys."

Quint hadn't been called a "boy" in quite a few years. For a moment, he felt a bit gangly in the arms and legs again. "What gave it away? The hair standing up on the back of my neck every time he comes near?"

Juan chuckled. "More like the way Jared starts marking his scent on everything when he sees you coming."

"We seem to have some twenty year old tension that we haven't quite resolved yet. Sorry about that."

"Oh, it's not a problem with me so long as you both act relatively civil with each other. But it does make me wonder if this tension between you two has anything to do with Jared's request this morning."

"What's the request?"

"For my permission to marry Angélica … again."

That hit Quint like a mule kick to the solar plexus. What in the hell was Steel up to now? "What was your answer?"

"The same thing I said when he asked the first time. She isn't mine to give away." He picked up the lantern, holding it up to a large fissure in the wall. "She's her own woman."

"Yeah, I noticed that."

"I thought you might have."

Quint stared at the back of Juan's head, trying to figure

out if there'd been an undertone in that statement or if he'd imagined it. "You think that's the main reason Steel came down here? To reunite with Angélica?"

"That's what he says." Juan ran a finger along the ridge of the fissure and frowned. "But I don't quite believe that."

"Why do you think he's here?"

Juan rubbed the grit from the crack between his thumb and forefinger. "I'm still figuring that out."

"Do you think he's dangerous?"

Juan glanced over. "Jared? No. He gets squirmy around caterpillars and dust bunnies." He turned back to the fissure, pulling out his tape measure. "I think he's down here to see if he can worm in on something Angélica and I have been working on for a few years."

"What's that?"

"Nothing much." Juan jotted down another number in his notebook. "Just a theory about some old stuff."

He'd been taking lessons from his daughter on how to be vague, or maybe she'd learned from the master. "If it's nothing much, why would Steel want to be part of it?"

"They're cutting funds left and right at the university, and he hasn't been on a dig site for a couple of years now. He's probably feeling parasitic, and my daughter is the perfect host. She's going places he'd like to be."

An interesting theory and definitely possible, knowing what Quint did about Steel's ambition. But Juan was up to something, sharing ideas and thoughts he normally held out of reach when Quint worked with him. Like his mention of Dr. Hughes' journal, and now this. "Why are you telling me this?"

Juan shrugged. "Maybe it's because I like you."

Quint raised an eyebrow, waiting for a more likely reason.

"Or maybe it's because I have received a rather high commendation on your character recently."

"From whom?" Had Jeff written to Juan, too?

"Let's just say that Jared's not the only one who shares a history with you."

Chapter Ten

Blancos: White men.

Later that afternoon, Quint felt like chucking Dr. Hughes' journal into the *cenote* along with all the other cryptic articles and notes Mrs. Hughes had left behind.

"Christ," he muttered, scratching the stubble on his cheeks and chin. He'd given up on shaving two days ago. Maybe it was time to give up on this damned mystery. He glared at where Dr. Hughes' journal lay on the end of his cot.

This dead-end shit was getting old. So was hitting his head on the brick wall Angélica kept reinforcing.

A glance at his watch told him *siesta* hour was almost over. Juan would be waiting for him back in that suffocating catacomb he called a temple.

"This sucks." He leaned down to stack the papers he had spread out around his cot into a pile, wiping off a drop of sweat that had dripped from the end of his nose onto them. Why couldn't Hughes have studied the Eskimo culture?

So many puzzle pieces, but none of them fit together. Mrs. Hughes had supplied plenty of articles and pictures, but she had no notes explaining why she kept them. Dr. Hughes, on the other hand, had left plenty of detailed notes about his work, but nothing that indicated a reason why Mrs. Hughes would want to focus so much energy on Steel.

Sitting back on his heels, Quint surveyed his tent along with his situation. He'd been here for a week, and all he'd managed to accomplish was to break one tent and make everyone suspicious of him. At this rate, he'd win the Worst Detective of the Year award, hands down.

Back on his feet, he picked up the journal again and flipped through the pages, scanning, still coming up empty. He might as well give the damned book back to Juan. The funky drawing on the inside of the back flap was the only thing of interest.

Flipping to the back, he stared down at the two masks sketched in pencil. Quint had no idea if they had any meaning or if they were random drawings. They looked similar to what Esteban had produced that first day in the Temple of the Crow when he'd been copying the wall.

Angélica would know if the masks represented anything, but Juan had made it very clear when handing over the journal that he didn't want his daughter to know he was sharing the book.

Quint could bug Juan about the drawings, but that might make him more suspicious of Quint than he already was. Besides, Juan had told him several times since they began working together that he couldn't read glyphs like Angélica, which meant that Juan would have to ask her to help. Quint was back to square one with a drawing of two masks and no way of finding out the meaning behind it.

Clue or not, he knew better than to rely on his memory when it came to Maya symbolism and glyphs. He ripped out a piece of paper from his notepad and began tracing the masks.

While he did his best to copy the sketches, he came up with a plan. He'd keep an eye out for similar masks in the temples where he'd be working, carrying his copy of them at all times. If only he had access to the books on the Maya that he'd seen in Angélica's tent.

That reminded him of something he'd read in the handwritten notes she'd had on her desk that night he'd first met Rover. He wrote *cone-shaped shell* and *skeletal something* below the drawing. What else was there?

He opened the flap of the holder containing the other pieces from Mrs. Hughes. Sifting through her collection starring Jared, Quint flipped past the recognition awards, the announcements regarding his public and private grants, and several reviews of his book.

Where had he stuck it?

There it was.

He pulled out a crinkled piece of paper containing the list he'd made of her notes, dropping the holder onto the cot, and grabbed the copy he'd made of the masks. He scanned the list: *Cone-shaped shell, Ek Chuah, skeletal visage, and death god.*

Ek Chuah?

What the hell was that? His focus shifted back to the masks. Maybe one of them was a death god. They kind of looked like skeletal visages though.

Giving up, he lowered both. This was going to take time to figure out, a commodity that was in short supply at the moment thanks to the schedule Angélica had him working.

Tonight at supper, maybe he'd ask her if he could borrow one of her books to read. He could tell her he wanted to learn more about the Maya as background information for his article. With any luck, she'd believe him.

That was if she made it to supper. He hadn't seen her since last night, and with Steel dishing out marriage proposals, Quint wanted a moment alone with her to address that kiss. Or rather the discussion about the kiss.

The sound of footfalls approaching made him look over at the tent flap zipper. He waited for it to move.

Instead someone fell into the side of his tent. As he stared at the canvas, the person slid down the outside of it, landing on the ground with a *thump* and a grunt.

Quint glanced over at the file holder lying on his cot with several articles about Steel spilling out.

"*Ayyy, me duele la pierna*," a familiar voice said from the other side of the canvas.

Esteban.

Quint unzipped the flap and looked out to see his clumsy buddy sitting on the ground rubbing his thigh. Next to the boy's leg was a wooden tent stake sticking about four inches out of the ground. It was still broad daylight, right? How could Esteban have not seen the stake? "You okay?"

Esteban nodded, still rubbing his leg.

Stepping outside, Quint helped him to his feet and then brushed the dirt off his back.

"*Señor* Parker," Esteban started.

"It's Quint, remember?"

"*Sí, Señor* Parker."

Quint gave up and wiped his hands off on his pants. "*Que paso*, Esteban?"

Esteban licked his lips, frowning in concentration. "Doctor García say to bring you to mess tent." Esteban motioned for him to follow and started limping away.

The mess tent? He thought Juan had said they were working in the Dawn Temple again this afternoon. "Tell him I'll be there in five minutes," he told Esteban's back, slipping inside his tent to hide his stuff.

"*Sí, Señor* Parker," Esteban called back, "but no *es* Doctor Juan. *Es* Doctor Angélica who wants you."

* * *

"Quint, I'm sorry, but you have to leave tomorrow," Angélica practiced in the empty mess tent.

No, that was too blunt.

She wrung her hands and paced in front of the counter. Okay, how about, "I'm sorry, Mr. Parker, but due to unforeseen circumstances, you must leave first thing tomorrow morning."

Nah, too formal.

She chewed on her knuckle. "Listen, Quint, as much as Dad and I have enjoyed your company …"

She blew out a sigh. Jeez, she really sucked at kicking men out of her life. Maybe some coffee would spark a better exit line. She poured a cup, adding a hit of sugar to the lukewarm liquid.

Damn Jared for forcing her into this situation.

And damn her for wanting Quint to stay.

After gulping down the coffee, she set the cup down with finality. "Quint, I have some bad news for you …"

No, she shouldn't lead with so much negativity.

Groaning, she grabbed the jar of dried mangos María had left out for the men to snack on, dumped several slices out on the counter, and shoved two in her mouth at once, chewing away her troubles. If only she could click her heels together and escape from this place.

"What's the bad news?" a voice spoke from behind her.

She whirled around. Quint stood, arms crossed over his chest, leaning against one of the wooden support poles at the tent's entrance. She swallowed the fruit. "Good afternoon, Mr. Parker."

His head tilted, his gaze narrowing with suspicion. "What bad news do you need to talk to me about, *Dr. García?*"

Shit, this breakup run of hers had a worrying limp fresh out of the gate. She leaned against the counter, deciding the straightforward approach was the way to go. "You have to leave tomorrow."

"No." He didn't even pause to consider her words.

Of all the arrogant … she took a step toward him. "What do you mean 'no'?"

"If this is concerning my publishing something about your curse, you're wasting our time. I won't."

There was no damned curse, and it certainly wasn't hers. "It's not, and you're leaving in the morning. Period."

"Why?"

Because she said so and it was her dig site, her rules, damn it. Keeping in mind the article he was writing on her father's behalf, she reined in her tongue. "Things are getting too unsafe here for foreigners."

His jaw hardened. "Bullshit."

She lowered her head, determined to finish what she'd started, and plowed forward. "In addition, my father and I don't have time to babysit you anymore."

That came out a little harsher than she'd wanted, but she owned up to it, meeting his glare head on.

"No."

"You seem to be confused. I'm not asking."

He pushed away from the pole, closing the distance between them. "Juan didn't mention a word this morning about my leaving. Don't you think that's odd?"

"He doesn't know about this." She hadn't yet figured out how she'd explain to her dad why Quint had to leave without giving away that it was blackmail born.

"And why wouldn't you tell him?" He stopped at the end of the counter. "He's the one who worked the deal with me. Shouldn't he be included in this decision?"

"I'm the one in charge of the crew, the site, and who comes and goes during a season. When it comes down to it, Dad works for me. If I say you go, then you go, whether he agrees or not."

"No."

She threw up her hands. "Where in the hell do you get off thinking you can just tell me no?"

"Does this have to do with Steel's marriage proposal?"

Heat shot up her neck, roasting her cheeks. Son of a ... *DAD!* She had *not* wanted Quint to find out about that. "That's none of your business, Parker."

"I'm making it my business." He matched her gritted response. "Are you going to marry him again?"

"I can hardly see why that would be any concern of yours,

unless you plan on including *that* in your article."

He cursed at the ceiling. "Would you forget about that damned article for one second?"

"I can't!"

Between that article and the crazy shit happening lately, including Jared's talk of resuscitating what she considered to be a long-dead horse, her stress level had shot into the red zone.

She strode over and poked him in the chest. "Ever since you walked onto this dig site, everything I say and do could show up in print. Do you have any idea how hard it is to speak casually to my crew in front of you, knowing that if I let my guard down for one second and something goes amiss, I could end up the laughing stock of the archaeological community?"

His face softened as he looked down at her. "I would never do that to you."

"What guarantee do I have?"

"My word."

"You already lied to me once."

He shook his head. "I didn't outright lie."

"You might as well have."

"And I already apologized for misleading you."

"So I'm supposed to blindly trust you now?"

"Well, maybe not blindly, but—"

She scoffed.

"*But* I'm telling you the absolute truth now."

She started to turn away from him, hating how torn he made her feel, but he caught her arm.

"Angélica, listen to me. I swear that I will not publish my article until I get your approval on its contents."

God, she wanted to believe him, but he'd fooled her once. She wasn't willing to take a chance at being made the fool twice. "Okay," she pulled free, but held her ground. "If you're being honest, tell me why you really came down here."

"To write this article."

"Is that the only reason?"

"Not entirely."

"Ah-hah!"

"I also wanted to revisit the last place Dr. Hughes was seen."

"Why?"

"Because he was my best friend's father."

"Why else?" She wasn't buying it was only for sentimental reasons.

He rubbed the back of his neck. "Because he helped me out of a rut twenty years ago."

"So this is some self-discovery, getting in touch with your inner feelings, mumbo-jumbo journey?" There had to be something more driving him to come down to a jungle he obviously hated.

"Me and my inner feelings are touchy-feely enough, thank you for your concern."

"You're still not being totally honest with me."

"You're a hard woman to please."

She slammed her hand down on the counter. "Damn it, Quint, tell me why you are—"

"Because I have trouble believing he's really dead."

Finally, they were getting somewhere. "And now that you've been here and seen all there is to see, what do you think?"

"I don't know."

He didn't know? "Well, he's not here, I can tell you that."

Quint raised both eyebrows. "What makes you so certain?"

"I've been in and out of each of these temples for eight years now. Don't you think I would've seen something of him if he were here?"

"Maybe. Probably." He sighed, scraping his palm down his face. "Hell, I don't know."

"Listen, Quint. I'm sorry that Dr. Hughes disappeared like he did, but life here in the jungle had to go on, and it has. My father and I haven't forgotten who started the work here, and with every paper I publish on the findings, I always try to mention Dr. Hughes and his work." She wished she could do more for Quint, but she knew what she had to do to protect her father's future. "When you get back to the States, tell Mrs. Hughes that—"

"She's dead."

Brakes screeched in her head. "What?"

"Mrs. Hughes died a couple of months ago."

"Oh." She grimaced. "I'm sorry."

He waved her off.

"Is that what spurred your interest in Dr. Hughes?"

"Sort of. The funeral brought back memories."

She nodded. "That's understandable." But the fact of the matter hadn't changed: Quint needed to leave, pronto. "I'm sorry we couldn't do more to help you, but I have to ask you to—"

"I'm not leaving, Angélica." A muscle twitched in his cheek.

"You have to."

"Why? I don't have any pressing engagements."

"Damn you, Quint!" She grabbed a mango slice and threw it at him.

He caught it against his chest. "No, damn you, Angélica. I was honest with you about Dr. Hughes. Now it's your turn. Tell me why I have to leave in such a big rush."

An eye for an eye. Fine. "Because if you don't, Jared's going to convince the university to pull Dad's funding." There, it was out. If only that could free her from her ex-husband's stranglehold.

He clenched the mango slice in his fist. "I knew it had something to do with that asshole."

"Yes, well, now you know. So, please, leave tomorrow."

"That's not going to happen."

"Why not? You have enough information to write your goddamned article, and don't try to tell me otherwise." She'd made certain of that.

"Angélica." Quint caught her arm. "Are you going to marry Steel again?"

"I told you before, that's none of your business."

"Have you put any thought into why he's forcing you to get rid of me?"

"Yes." Several hours' worth and usually in the middle of the night.

"And?"

She shrugged. "Something happened twenty years ago between you two, and he hasn't gotten over it." She glanced down at where he held onto her, feeling the callouses on his fingers, the heat of his palm. Maybe there was a girl from the village they'd fought over, or a female grad student here helping Dr. Hughes. "Did you steal his girlfriend?" she jested, sort of. Curiosity weighed in, too.

"No. Not yet anyway." The rousing look he shot her made her pulse do jumping jacks. "I think there's more to it than the past."

"Like what?"

"I'm still trying to figure that out."

As much as she wanted him to stay, he needed to figure it out somewhere else. "Whatever Jared's reasons are, you need to leave."

He let go of her arm as if she disgusted him, his expression tight with scorn. "I can't believe you're going to let your ex-husband push you around."

Her go-to-hell glare didn't seem to ruffle him.

"Where were you this morning?" When she didn't answer, he pushed further. "Were you with Steel?"

Her chin rose along with her defenses. "None of your business."

His eyes flashed white-hot. "Quit shutting me out."

"Quit prying."

"You're so damned stubborn."

"You're one to talk." How many times did they need to lock horns until he understood she wasn't backing down?

He growled in his throat, all bristly, predator like. "Just answer the question, woman."

"I was busy."

"Doing what?"

Her heartbeat drummed in her ears, her breath coming short and fast. This battle of wills had gone far enough. "Mr. Parker, as an employee of the Mexican government, I am asking you one last time to remove yourself from these premises tomorrow morning."

"You don't really want me to go, do you?" His eyes issued a challenge.

She ignored him. "If you fail to heed my request—"

"Were you with Jared this morning?"

Unfortunately she had been, and she still itched every time she thought about those damned ants. She continued, "I will be forced to involve the *federales*."

"He sure has you wrapped around his finger."

"God damn your hide!" She grabbed Quint by the shirt collar and yanked him down to her level. "I was not *with* Jared this morning! At least not in the connubial sense."

He leaned closer, his nose almost touching hers. "Then where were you?"

The scent of his skin wafted out from under his collar, his cologne or deodorant spicy, very male, kindling a flare of lust. She let go of his shirt and stepped back, needing distance to keep her head in the game instead of under the bleachers with him. "I was in the jungle looking for signs of whoever has been sabotaging our camp."

"What?" His brow wrinkled.

"Happy now? Write that in your article."

He hit her with an exasperated glare. "Can it about that stupid article."

"It's your fault."

He didn't take her bait. "You think someone is behind these incidents? They're not just accidents?"

She nodded. "We found out for certain early this morning.

Like I've preached from the start, it's not a curse. What's worse, the games are getting dangerous."

He gaped at her. "And you went out looking *alone?*"

Sheesh! He must be taking lessons from her father. "This is another reason you should leave tomorrow. I can't guarantee your safety if you stay any longer."

"Don't worry about me. I can take care of myself."

"Fine. Whatever." She was tired of trying to take care of everyone anyway. "Just remember, I tried to save your ass."

"Who's going to save your ass?"

She didn't answer.

The intensity of his stare multiplied so fast it stole her thoughts. "Are you considering marrying Steel again?"

She struggled for words, trying to come up with something coherent. "That's a rather personal question."

"I've been feeling 'rather personal' lately when it comes to you."

What did that mean? "Of course I'm not going to marry Jared again."

"Good." He stepped toward her, his intentions written all over his face. It didn't take a decade of studying glyphs to read him.

She backed into the counter, her heart tapping an S-O-S against her ribs. "Quint, don't. Stop."

He placed his hands on the counter on both sides of her, cutting off all escape routes. "I won't. Not this time."

She gulped. "There was a period between *don't* and *stop.*"

"I didn't notice it." He stared at her mouth.

She scrambled for something to detour him. "I'm Jared's ex-wife." That had brought him to a halt the night of the *Chachac* ceremony.

"Who gives a shit about that?"

She thought he did. "It'd make things easier if you left."

"Too bad. I'm staying." He crooked his head, lining up his lips with hers.

She could feel the heat radiating from his skin through his

shirt. "Why?"

"I can't stop thinking about you." He traced her lower lip with the pad of his thumb.

The tingling started at his touch and fire-balled south. "You can't?"

The back of his fingers trailed down her neck. "I'm not going anywhere until I do something about it."

She couldn't stand this much more. It'd been too long since she'd felt anything even close to it … Hell, since she'd felt anything at all.

She captured his hand. "Stop it," she whispered, her throat constricted along with her lungs.

This time he listened. His eyes searched hers, hesitation lurking in their green depths.

To hell with it all. She was tired of being hungry for more whenever he was around.

"Stop teasing me unless you plan to kiss me." She lifted his hand to her mouth, running her teeth down the length of his index finger.

He sucked in a breath, his eyes darkening as she lightly bit the web of skin between his finger and thumb. "Oh, sweet Jesus, I do." Using his hand that she still clutched, he drew her against him and nudged her chin up with his knuckles. "Lick your lips, boss lady."

She did as told.

A groan rolled up from deep in his chest. "I don't know what's sexier, your wet lips or you listening to me without fighting back for once."

She flirted with him from under her lashes. "Shut up and kiss me, Parker."

"Yes, ma'am." His lips brushed over hers—soft, feather-like, testing. He drew back to look into her eyes, searching.

That wasn't enough by far. Sinking her fingers in his hair, she dragged him back down, showing him what she really wanted.

This time there was no dithering in his response. While his

mouth took over, coaxing moans and gasps from her, he ran his hands down her sides, gripping her hips through her khakis. She suctioned herself tighter against him, craving more of the rugged terrain of his body.

"*Dios mio*," she breathed when he gave her time to catch her breath. "You really know how to kiss."

"I know how to do other things, too." His lips trailed along her cheek.

"Like what?" She closed her eyes, her body turning into liquid fire from the inside out. She moved against him, really, really interested in finding out firsthand.

"Quint?" Her father's voice penetrated the lust that was making her head rummy. "Are you in here?"

Angélica gasped, leaping out of Quint's arms.

But it was too late. Her father stood frozen just inside the mess tent entrance. The wide-eyed look on his face made her want to hide under a table. Then he grinned, his face lighting up, and she knew she was up shit creek.

"Well, hello, you two." Juan sauntered toward them, handing a cardboard envelope with *Express* written on it over her shoulder to Quint.

Quint cleared his throat. "Thanks, Dr. García."

"Oh, it's Dr. García now, is it?" Juan crossed his arms over his chest. "So formal all of a sudden, huh, Quint? What were you two doing in here anyway?" He blinked with exaggerated innocence at both of them.

Angélica trilled out a handful of Spanish curses. She'd never hear the end of it now.

"Just what are your intentions, young man?" Juan's grin grew even wider, his enjoyment soaring right along with her humiliation.

"Dad, knock it off." She blazed past him, her skin practically in flames. She needed some fresh air.

"But I'm just starting my Spanish Inquisition," he called after her.

Quint's low rumbling of laughter followed her out into the

hot sunshine. The grass crackled under her boots as she strode toward her tent.

She smacked the palm of her hand against her forehead. "Way to maintain control of your emotions around the guy, dummy." What in the hell was she going to tell Jared when Quint was still here come Friday morning? She kneaded her hands together. More important, what in the hell was she going to do about Quint and what had happened back there?

Maybe she should sleep with him and get it over with.

She smacked her forehead again, aiming for the voice inside of it that wasn't helping one iota.

"*Gatita!*"

She paused without looking back, waiting for her father to catch up.

He grabbed her arm when he reached her side. "Where're you heading?"

There was a worried tone in his voice that made her look at him. Tension lined his eyes. "Back to my tent, why?"

He wrapped his arm around her shoulders, turning her toward his tent. "I need to talk to you alone."

She blew out an exasperated sigh. "If this is about what happened between Quint and me back there …"

"I wish it were only that."

Come on! What now? She halted in her tracks. "I'm getting really tired of this crap, Dad."

He kissed the top of her head. "I know, *gatita*, but we have a problem."

Chapter Eleven

Stela: An ancient inscribed stone monument.

Quint waited until he had reached the safety of his sauna, aka tent, to tear open the express envelope from Jeff. He was tempted to open the window flaps so he could breathe while melting to death, but decided to see what he had in his hands first.

Inside the envelope he found four sheets of paper. The top piece was a note from Jeff. The next one was a letter from Dr. Jared Steel requesting his own high school records. Judging by the Eastern Valley Catholic High School logo on the upper right corners of the last two sheets, they were the requested records.

Fanning himself with the cardboard envelope, Quint dropped onto his cot and read Jeff's letter.

I'm still going through those boxes of Mom's that I found in the attic above Dad's office. So far, all of it seems fairly trivial, mostly more random articles from the university newspaper about Dr. Steel. These school records arrived in the mail yesterday morning. The envelope had our mailing address wrong, so it's a wonder it made it here. The original post date is close to the time

Mom passed away. There was no letter of explanation or anything, which makes me wonder if she'd hired that private detective to get this, too. I don't understand why she would have wanted these. Then again, I don't understand why my mother was obsessed with Dr. Steel at all. Anyway, I thought maybe you could make some sense of it. If I come across anything else of interest, I'll send it your way. I hope you're having more luck than I am.

Don't let the Yucatán bed bugs bite—or the snakes and spiders. Ha!

Quint let Jeff's letter drift to the floor and focused on the school records. The top third of the first page listed his hair and eye color, as well as his height and weight for the ninth and tenth grade. The eleventh and twelfth grade slots were empty. The rest of the records noted several instances when Steel had been given detention and why. Quint smirked as he read, remembering his own checkered school life.

At the bottom of the second page, there was a handwritten note:

Jared's parents died last week in a boating accident. The state has decided to place the boy with a local foster family. He will be allowed to finish the final quarter here, but will be moved into a public high school next year.

Quint felt a pang of sympathy for the kid, being orphaned at such a young age. He tried to picture a younger version of Steel, with blue eyes, dark blonde hair, and a lot less hostility, but he came up blank. That was the only side of Steel he'd ever known.

Gathering the documents, he stuffed them back into the envelope. He started to stash them under the mattress, but then changed his mind. Rolling the cardboard into a tube, he jammed it into the middle of his backpack instead.

He cinched his pack tight and stared at the canvas wall. Sweat trickled down his neck. "Okay, so now what, Sherlock?"

He was still missing some crucial pieces of the puzzle when it came to Mrs. Hughes' fascination with Steel. He had all kinds of articles and documents on the jerk, but nothing connecting them. No notes on why she went through the trouble to gather all of it.

If only he could figure out a way to bring it up to Angélica without her getting bent out of shape. Being Steel's ex-wife, she probably knew things about his past that would link the clues Mrs. Hughes had left behind. But after what had just happened between them in the mess tent, if Quint pressed her for information on Steel, would she think he had been warming her up in order to get her to spill personal details?

He scoffed. Of course, and she'd probably also suspect he was going to use whatever she shared in his article.

Fuck. He tossed his backpack on the floor. The damned hard-headed, distrustful, bossy woman! She could light his fuse like nobody else.

His mind flashed back to the moments when she'd raked her teeth over his skin, pulled his mouth down to hers, moaned against him. She knew how to fire him up, too. It was too bad Juan had interrupted them.

Closing his eyes, he replayed that kiss, getting sweaty all over again. Her mouth had tasted sweet from the mangos she'd been eating, while her skin had smelled like coconut sunblock. The two fruits had made an intoxicating combination, especially when she was pressing against him, all soft curves and wet …

The sound of someone unzipping his tent flap yanked him back to the present. He turned, watching the zipper slide slowly along the bottom of the flap.

Somebody was trying to be very quiet about sneaking into his tent. Was it the same person who was terrorizing the rest of the crew? The dig site's saboteur?

Quint looked around for something to use as a weapon. He looked at a cardboard shipping tube. No, too soft. Maybe that coil of rope hanging by the window. No, his lassoing skills were rusty. There, he zeroed in on a handful of tent stakes tied with a strip of hemp … and what, he'd stab the intruder in the heart? This was turning into an episode of Scooby Doo versus Count Dracula.

He swiped the long handled flashlight from his desk, flipping it around, waving it like a police baton. That was more like it. He crept into position, raising the flashlight.

It was time to put an end to this game of cat and mouse.

* * *

"So, how many of them are leaving?" Angélica asked as she slumped onto her father's cot.

"Only two—Horatio and Octavio," Juan answered. "Where's that book on seashells, the Wayfarers one? Is it somewhere in your messy tent?"

"No, it's on your desk, right there under those books on structural architecture." How could he think about seashells while members of her crew were fleeing the dig site like mice from a burning *milpa*? "Have you tried talking some sense into either of them?"

Juan pulled out the book on shells. "It's no use. They're convinced it's the curse."

"Way to go, Jared." She wrinkled her lip. "I told him to keep a low profile. I knew something like this would happen if anyone saw him."

"It was a case of bad timing. He thought he'd waited long enough to avoid running into anyone after breakfast."

"I think it was a case of arrogant stupidity." She rubbed her temples, trying to push aside her frustration and figure out a solution.

Juan fished his glasses from his shirt pocket. "Teodoro noticed this morning that some of his *balche* was missing. He suspects the two boys dipped into that last night and that's why they were lagging behind the others and ran into Jared." He used his shirt tail to clean his glasses, a crooked smile forming on his mouth. "We've all had our share of those mind-numbing *balche* hangovers."

"Maybe we could offer some kind of incentive for them to stay."

"Like what?" He slipped on his glasses and flipped open the book. "More money?"

She laced her fingers together, running through numbers in her head. "I can't give them more pay without giving everyone more, and my budget is already maxed out. Due to the extra crew we took on, I had to cut into our supply allotment in order to give these guys a semi-decent wage."

"Lord knows the university won't help." He was too busy scanning one of the book's pages to notice Angélica's grimace.

And if she didn't provide Jared with a good explanation for Quint staying past Thursday, they'd have an even bigger problem with money from the university.

"There's the *Lolcatali* ceremony," Juan suggested as he turned pages.

"You already know how I feel about that."

He glanced at her over the top of his glasses. "That stubborn streak of yours comes from your mother's side of the family."

She stuck her tongue out at him. "I could offer a bonus to all who stay the duration of the dig season, deliverable in their final paycheck."

Juan lowered the book. "You just said you didn't have that kind of money left in the budget."

"I could pull from my personal savings."

"I don't like the sound of that."

"Take it out of one of my retirement accounts maybe."

"The penalties for early withdrawal are brutal."

"I'll do whatever it takes." She touched his sleeve. "We're so close. The proof is within our grasp."

"You're obsessing again."

She hated it when he was right. "We all have our vices."

His focus returned to the pages of the book. "There has to

be another way."

"When you think of it, let me know. Until then the best I can come up with is the bonus option." She rolled off the cot, sticking her nose in the book along with his. "What are you looking for?"

He turned a few more pages and then pointed at a black and white picture. She recognized the shell at once, telling him, "That's a member of the *Astraeinae* family."

"I've seen this." He tapped the picture.

"I know you have. I showed you a likeness of it the other night on that glyph in the Temple of the Water Witch."

"No, I mean I've seen it elsewhere."

As his words sank in, her excitement welled. She squeezed his arm. "Where?"

"In the Dawn Temple, when Quint and I were working in there this morning."

"Show me."

"I will later tonight after everyone is in their tents."

"Was it on another glyph?"

"No. It was on a *stela*."

She let go of his arm. This could be the key that led them to the proof they needed. "Did it have a date on it?"

"It might have at one time. A corner of it was broken off

and nowhere around."

"Why didn't we notice this *stela* before now?"

"I was showing Quint some stability modifications I had done years ago in one of the chambers. It's in a structurally sound part of the building, so I haven't been concerned about monitoring it since then." He closed the book and dropped it onto his desk. "I practically tripped over the thing. Talk about good luck."

She looked up at him, pausing. "Did Quint see it?"

Juan grinned. "He was too busy worrying about the cracks in the ceiling. I'm beginning to think that boy is a good luck charm."

Oh, he was a real charm all right. He certainly had some kind of magnetism that sucked her right in, dang it. "Just be careful around him."

"I don't understand why you don't trust Quint yet." He crossed his arms over his chest. "Pedro does."

She did a double-take. "Pedro knows Quint?"

"They worked together here with Dr. Hughes."

"You're kidding me." Talk about a small world. "I didn't realize Pedro had been here back then." Why hadn't he ever mentioned that? Maybe she'd forgotten that detail.

"He was just a kid then, like Quint. When I flew to Cancun to get my tooth fixed, Pedro told me that your boyfriend used to help him with his English in exchange for cigarettes."

"He's not my boyfriend."

Juan's grin made an appearance. "I could swear I saw you two kissing earlier."

"That was an accident."

"Oh, I see. You two *accidentally* bumped lips and you got caught up on his mouth?"

"Real funny. Ha ha."

"Did you *accidentally* use glue instead of lip balm today?"

No, she'd accidentally lowered her guard and let her body rule over her head. "Drop it, Dad. I was just showing him something."

"Well, judging from his reaction, I think he is going to want to see it again."

She chuckled at that one. "Smartass."

Dropping onto the cot again, she pondered this new information about their visiting photojournalist in light of the current situation. "Did Pedro mention any animosity brewing between Quint and Jared back then?" Something that would explain the current hostility between them, and Jared's demand that she kick Quint off the site immediately.

"No. But I didn't ask either. He did say that Quint had been pretty close to Dr. Hughes, almost like a son."

Like a son, huh? What had Quint told her? That he had trouble believing Dr. Hughes was dead? A tightness in her chest told her that there was more to Quint's story than a bout of melancholy for a friend's father.

She needed to be very careful around Quint. Just because she wanted to do naked things with him didn't mean she was gullible enough to let him off the hook. "Who was that *Express* letter from?"

Juan shrugged. "It had some South Dakota address on it. Teodoro picked it up at the hotel while he was at the village today. Why?"

"No reason," she lied. "I was just curious."

"You're just getting *this* into trouble." He tweaked her nose. "You should be more concerned with your ex-husband than our photojournalist."

She gave him a wary look, wondering if he'd overheard her earlier when she'd told Quint about Jared's blackmail deal. "Why?"

"I think Jared is on to us."

"What makes you say that?"

"For starters, he's certainly not paying much attention to what I'm doing for the university down here. Every time I try to talk to him about my work, he changes the subject to something about you."

"Maybe Jared's not into Maya architecture."

"Maybe not, but there have been a couple of days when his only interest is what you've been doing." Juan sat down next to her. "At first, I figured it was because he was still in love with you."

"Trust me, Dad, the only person Jared pines for is Jared."

"But the more I think about all of the university cutbacks, the more I believe he wants to be part of something that's bigger—something that secures his place there. He knows as well as we do that there are more PhDs in this field than paying jobs."

"Yes, but Jared is one of the best at charming and schmoozing. You and I both have firsthand experience with that."

"True." Her father rested his elbows on his knees. "But even silk flowers fade with time. Jared knows that, too."

"Going forward," she said, "you keep an eye on Jared, and I'll watch Quint."

Juan snickered. "Are you going to be watching Quint with your eyes or your lips?"

She backhanded his thigh. "Forget you ever saw that, because nothing else is going to happen between us." That didn't sound very convincing even to her ears.

"That's too bad. I like the boy."

So did she. That was the problem.

"If Horatio and Octavio go," she counted on her fingers, "that leaves us with sixteen men, right?"

"Not including Fernando," he added.

"We can finish out the season with that many, but we can't afford to lose any more. I'll talk to the men at supper tonight about a bonus if they finish the dig season with us. We'll see if they're willing to fight their fears for a little extra cash in their pockets."

Juan sighed. "I still don't like the idea of you dipping into your savings. Let's see how many stay to the end. We'll figure out where to get the money when the time comes." By the stern look on his face, she knew better than to battle him on this right now, but there was no way she'd allow him to dip into his pension to help.

He stood and held his hand out to her. "I'll take Quint with me this afternoon." He pulled her to her feet. "Fernando needs your help over at the Owl Temple."

She caught his arm when he turned to lead the way outside. "Dad, promise me that you won't ask Quint about what happened back in the mess tent."

"*Gatita*, would I do that?"

"Definitely. At the first opportunity." She glared at him. "Promise me."

"All right. I promise." He waved her off, shaking his head as he unzipped the mesh flap. "You sure know how to take the fun out of an old man's day."

They stepped out into the bright afternoon sunshine. Waves of heat rose from the plaza floor. Angélica felt a bead of sweat slip and slide down her spine into the waistband of her pants. It was going to be hotter than hell in the temples this afternoon. She should probably grab a fresh bottle of water on her way to the Owl Temple.

"Sassafrass!" Juan grumbled. "It even smells hot out here." He mopped his brow with his handkerchief. "What did you find while scouting around this morning?"

"Not a single darned thing." She frowned at the thick patch of trees and bushes to her left, wondering if they were being watched even now.

"What's next?"

"I don't know." As far as she could see, they were in a pinch until somebody actually witnessed something. She had debated about warning the crew but was afraid that would drive more of the guys away. "I was thinking about starting night watches, but let's see if Pedro has any bright ideas when he gets here tomorrow morning."

"That reminds me of another thing that Pedro told me about Dr. Hughes. He said Hughes' wife contacted him a couple of weeks before her death."

Angélica's eyes narrowed as she looked up at him. "I didn't realize you knew she was dead."

"Quint told me."

She noticed that her father seemed more preoccupied with the jungle suddenly. What else had Quint told him? "So what did she want from Pedro?"

"To schedule a trip to this very dig site via his helicopter."

She took a step back in surprise. "What? When did she plan on coming?"

"Prior to our arrival to set up for the season."

Why would Mrs. Hughes want to visit the site alone? Did she realize that visitors were not allowed at the dig site without the government's permission—or Angélica's? Something wasn't right about this.

"Pedro never heard back from her after that initial call," Juan continued, "so he figured it had been a whim on her part and forgot about it until I mentioned Quint's name."

Angélica worried her lower lip. "Why would she want to come down here after all of these years?" Was it the need for some kind of psychological closure? Curiosity?

"According to Pedro," Juan lowered his voice, leaning close to her ear, "she wanted to collect what was left of her husband's body."

Chapter Twelve

Chakan: Xtabay in the form of a snake.

The jungle sizzled the whole damned day.

Quint's ass was fried by the time he'd scaled the steps of the Owl Temple. Once inside the entrance and out of the sun's relentless bullying, he leaned against the wall, panting. His eyes adjusted to the shadows in the limestone-enclosed sauna while sweat dripped from his chin.

"What are you doing here?" Angélica asked from where she and Fernando were kneeling over a tattered map of some sort spread out on the floor. "Is my dad coming?"

Fernando gave Quint a nod in greeting and then focused back on the map. Angélica's gaze stayed locked on him, waiting for his answer.

"Your dad wanted to go back to his tent to analyze the measurements we collected in the Dawn Temple, so he sent me here."

"Oh, okay. Good. I thought maybe …" She pinched her lips together. "Never mind."

"He told me to tell you that you need me."

"Why would I need you?"

He slanted her a grin. "You want me to show you?"

Her eyes widened and then narrowed just as quickly. "Lucky me. I have two comedians here to entertain the crew this year. You boys are a regular USO Comedy Tour."

"You ain't seen nothin' yet, Sarge. Stick around, I'm just getting warmed up."

"I can see that by your shirt." She picked up the bottle of water lying next to her. "Here. Use this to cool your smart-ass back down." She tossed it his way.

Quint caught it, unscrewing the cap. "There's something else mouth-watering that I wish you'd give as freely." When she nailed him with a warning look, he held up the bottle. "Ice cubes, boss lady. A tub of them for me to soak in after we're done tonight. What did you think I meant?" he teased.

Her cheeks darkened.

"What's the plan?" Fernando asked, snagging her attention.

She bent back over the paper, studying it. "I'll go check it out and see what I can find." She pointed to the lower left corner of the sheet. "I think I remember seeing it over here somewhere."

Quint inched closer, taking a sip of warm water, trying to see what they were studying. Turned out it wasn't a map, rather some kind of blueprint, but of what he had no idea.

He returned to holding up the temple wall, feeling beaten and whipped. He really wished he could go back to his tent, curl up in a fetal position, and sweat to death without anyone bothering him, but this was an opportunity he couldn't pass up. With any luck, he'd have Angélica to himself for a while and maybe find a way to squeeze some information out of her.

Or just squeeze her. He had a few places in mind where he'd like to start.

"I'll take Lorenzo with me," Angélica said, rising along with Fernando, who rolled the blueprint and shoved it into a black cardboard tube that had seen better days—like the one in Quint's tent. She glanced in Quint's direction. "You come, too." She led the way outside.

Wonderful, back into the roaster. In another half hour, he'd be well-done.

"Where are we going?" he asked, trailing behind her down the narrow, crumbling steps to the ground.

"The GOK pile."

"The gawk what?"

"GOK pile, as in G-O-K. It's an acronym for God Only Knows." She rounded the corner of the temple. "Years ago, before Dr. Hughes' time, some amateur archaeologists stumbled across this place." She sidestepped several large chunks of limestone strewn randomly in their path. "Be careful. We've had several men stumble on these stones and end up with nasty cuts and bruised bones."

Quint dodged and weaved, remembering Dr. Hughes mentioning some "damned golddiggers" twenty years ago.

"These amateur idiots were hell bent for gold and jewels, and in their greed they destroyed some important architecture." She cleared the last of the rock rubble, waiting for him to catch up. "Fortunately, they focused mostly on the Owl Temple and didn't damage all of the surrounding temples as well."

Shielding her eyes, she squinted toward the jungle's edge. Quint followed her line of sight. Lorenzo and two others were working in a shallow pit inside of the tree line.

"*Lorenzo, necesito tu ayuda, por favor,*" she called, asking for his help.

The boy waved. "*Un momento, Dr. García.*" He leaned down and picked up a small shovel.

When Quint turned back, Angélica was gone, striding away in her usual rush. "So what did these amateur archaeologists do?" he asked as he caught up with her. His memory failed him on any details from Dr. Hughes' complaints.

"They gutted parts of the temple and threw the broken glyphs along with other fallen chunks of limestone into one big pile behind it." She pointed out three piles of gray rocks in front of them. "Over the years, we've worked on dividing up the pile, putting together pieces that we think should go together and trying to figure out what glyph went where."

He followed her to the pile on the left, where she picked up a football-sized rock. "Take this piece, for example. Judging by the list of dates here, it looks like it could belong to a partially demolished wall in Sub Chamber B." She held it out for him to see. "We have plans to work on that wall next year." She set the rock on the ground, brushing off her hands. "That is, if Dad gets the funding."

Quint didn't like the troubled look lining her face. Steel was a real son of a bitch for adding blackmail to her list of problems. There had to be something Quint could do to help her out of the bind that his sticking around would cause.

"So." She lifted a second rock, flipping it over, examining it for a moment. "When are you going to tell me why you're really here?"

Whoa. She didn't pull that punch. "We've been over this, Angélica. I'm here to write an article."

"That's partly true, I'm sure." She lowered the stone to the ground. "But you're hiding something from me."

His poker face nearly cracked under her gunslinger glare. Jesus, she was something to behold. After their hot-blooded bout in the mess tent after lunch, this steely side of hers only made him itch to climb back in the ring for Round Two.

"I want the truth, Parker. All of—" She stopped, her attention shifting behind him. "Shit, here comes Lorenzo. Don't move. I'm not done with you yet."

The feeling was mutual, only Quint suspected she wasn't thinking about getting naked while they finished.

He waited as she met Lorenzo halfway and pulled out a notepad from her back pocket. "I'm looking for the top part of this," he heard her say, and then she showed Lorenzo something on the pad. The boy nodded, made his way carefully to the other side of the pile, and began going through it stone by stone.

Angélica returned to his side. "Where were we?"

"You were about to show me what I'm looking for here." Maybe whatever she had in that little notebook would help him with those drawings he'd found in the back of Dr. Hughes' journal. Quint pointed at the notebook she still held. "Let's see it."

Her expression guarded, she flipped open the notepad. "We have the bottom half of a glyph that put together should look something like this." She showed him a rough sketch of two faces and a funky looking frog-like animal. "We need to find the top, and I think I remember seeing it in this pile last year."

"Where do you want me to start?"

She picked up a rock the size of a ten-pound bag of flour and shoved it at him. "Right here."

A half an hour later he peeled off his shirt and wrung it out. After a gulp of water, he surveyed their progress. They were a third of the way through the pile with nothing to show for their efforts yet. As he screwed the lid on the bottle, he heard Lorenzo cry out. He looked over to find Lorenzo cupping his hand.

"What happened?" Angélica was beside him in a flash. Quint joined them.

Lorenzo held up his hand. Quint winced when he got a good look at the boy's fingers. Two of the four were bleeding under the nails, and a third had only the lower part of the nail left.

"*Ay, dios mio.*" Angélica pulled a Swiss army knife from her pocket, sliced the hem of her shirt, and ripped off a small strip of it. She gently took Lorenzo's hand and wrapped his fingers with the cloth, then lifted his hand above his heart. "Keep that up high and go see Teodoro," she told him in Spanish. At least that's what Quint thought she'd said. His Spanish was still rusty.

His face etched with pain, Lorenzo nodded and headed

off toward Teodoro's hut.

Angélica watched him go. "Listen, Quint, if you want to pack it in for the day and go back to your tent—" She stopped mid-sentence when she turned to look at him, her eyes darkening as they drifted downward.

In the commotion with Lorenzo, he'd forgotten to put his shirt back on. "And miss out on doing more back-breaking work in this wonderful heat and humidity? I don't think so." There was no way he'd pass up this opportunity to spend time alone with her.

"You seem to have lost your shirt somewhere."

"I have it right here." He held up the sweat-soaked cotton.

"Ah, mystery solved. Good job, Magnum P.I. You should probably put it back on before you get burned."

"You're worried about me. I'm touched."

"You are …" She appeared to be having trouble focusing north of his chin. "I am … uh …"

Trouble getting words out, too.

"You okay, Dr. García?"

"Yeah, sure." She blinked several times, glancing away. "I think the heat is starting to get to me."

"Maybe you should take off your shirt, too."

Her gaze jerked back to his. "You are one cheeky man, Parker. Put your shirt on before you get eaten up by bugs."

"Yes, boss lady." He slid the wet shirt over his head with a grimace. Christ, he hated this fucking jungle.

"You could go get a dry one from your tent."

"Nah. I don't want to wake up Rover."

"What do you mean?"

"He's sleeping in my tent."

"He is?"

"I caught him sneaking in this afternoon." Rover had been his uninvited guest earlier. "He's pretty good with zippers."

Her mouth gaped. "You're kidding me."

"Nope. I think that explains the chew marks on the broken zipper from my last tent."

"And how he keeps escaping and ending up in María's garden."

"I fed him the snack pretzels they gave me on the plane ride down here. He inhaled them and then rolled under my cot and crashed."

"I'm sorry about that. I'll grab him after we're finished."

"Don't worry about it. I like your javelina." He liked her even more. Maybe she could come eat pretzels with him later and roll around on top of his cot.

No.

Slow down there, pilgrim.

He needed to tread carefully here. Before things could progress to more than kissing, he needed to tell her some of his secrets or risk her skinning him alive. But if he opted for full disclosure, she'd probably really kick him off the site—Jared's prompting or not. Maybe if he helped her out with Jared's blackmail, she'd be more open to the whole search for Dr. Hughes.

The silence between them grew heavy, awkward almost.

Quint searched for something lighthearted to say. "Shall we continue here with our game of Clue? My guess is the frog-faced glyph with the sword of Ra in the Owl Temple."

"Ra is Egyptian and you know it," she said with a huskiness in her voice. She picked up another stone and handed it to him. "So, what has my father told you?"

"What do you mean?" he purposely played dumb, frowning down at the carvings in the limestone.

"About Dr. Hughes?"

"Nothing much."

"Baloney."

He put the stone down, grabbed another one, and handed it to her. "Who do you think is behind the trouble you've been having?"

She took one look at it and shook her head, dropping the stone onto the grass. "I can't think of anyone who'd have a grudge against any of us."

"No ex-boyfriends or wanna-be stalkers of yours?"

She grinned, lifting another stone without replying.

"Nobody who'd be insanely jealous if some random photojournalist was to sweep you off your feet?"

"See, I knew you were here for some reason other than that article." There was a jesting lilt in her tone.

"Guilty as charged." Quint took the stone from her, enjoying the way her eyes twinkled when she teased. He flipped over a lichen-covered rock. "Hey," he angled his head, taking a closer look. "I think we have a winner."

"Let me see." She stepped closer, her breast bumping against his arm repeatedly as she ran her hand across the stone's surface, tracing carved lines.

"Angélica."

"Yes?"

"If you don't stop rubbing against me like that, I'm going to drop this stone and do something that will probably make you slap me."

She stilled but didn't step away. "Are you saying you're up for a bit of slap and tickle this afternoon, Parker?"

Temptress! "You're making this hard."

One of her eyebrows cocked upward. "Isn't that how it works?"

"Now who's being cheeky?"

"You're right." She put some space between them. "I'm also being very unprofessional."

"I think we pretty much blew any last remnants of a professional relationship out of the water back in the mess tent."

"True, but we should put a stop to what's happening here before it becomes a problem." She snorted. "Well, a bigger problem."

"Yeah, but here's the glitch in your plan—I can't." He put the rock down between them. "And neither can you."

"We should at least try."

"Why?" He knew why he shouldn't let it go any further,

but that wasn't enough of a deterrent apparently.

"Because I don't trust you yet, Quint."

"So start." What would it be like to have her trusting him? To have her look at him without suspicion?

"I have this dig to run."

"I'm not stopping you."

"We can't be seen carousing in front of my crew."

He grinned. "My ideas for you don't include carousing."

"My ex-husband is here."

That made him pause. "Is that a problem for you?"

She rubbed her hand down the right side of her face, leaving a smudge of dirt on her cheek. "Kind of."

"Why?"

"Because if I don't make you leave, he's going to stop my father's funding for next year."

An idea hit him out of the hot humid blue—a solution for her problem. "Angélica, would you be willing to make a deal with me if I take this problem with Jared off your hands?"

Her brow wrinkled. "Define the deal."

"If I can get Steel to drop the blackmail, you help me with something that I don't have the time or resources to figure out on my own."

"What makes you think you can get Jared off my back?"

"I have an idea." He held out his hand. "Deal?"

She hesitated before shaking on it. "Okay, it's a deal."

He resisted the urge to hang on to her hand longer than appropriate. "Good."

"So, what is it you need to figure out?"

He reached into his back pocket and pulled out the folded drawing he'd traced from the back of Dr. Hughes' journal. "Look at this."

Flashing him a wary glance, she unfolded it. After staring at it for a couple of seconds, she let out a laugh. "This is it? This is all I have to do and you'll save the day?"

He nodded, not sure what to make of her frivolity.

She handed the paper back to him. "They're head

variants—glyphs with animal or human faces. These were often used more commonly than the actual signs."

Head variants? Why did Dr. Hughes sketch them in his journal? "So what are these two in particular?"

She pointed to the one on the left and then the other on the right. "The Sun god and Venus as they rise from the horizon at dawn."

Quint frowned down at the paper. "That's it?"

"Yes. Why? What were you expecting?"

He wadded up the drawing and stuffed it in his front pocket. "A bit more than that."

"Where did you get them?"

"I saw them in the Temp ..." He stopped, the lie catching on his tongue. He wanted Angélica's trust. The only way to earn it would be with honesty. "They're sketched in Dr. Hughes' journal."

Blotches of red stained her cheeks. "God damn it!" She shoved past Quint, stomping toward the tents.

"Hey," he called after her. "What about this stone I found?"

"Take it to Fernando." She didn't break stride.

"Where are you going?"

"To torture my father." She walked backwards, pointing at him. "You better hold up your end of the deal, Quint Parker, or I'm calling the *federales* and telling them to drag your ass back to the border!"

* * *

Someone screamed.

What was that?

Angélica sat up from where she'd fallen asleep at her desk, her eyes wide, every cell listening.

Shadows quivered in the soft lamplight, the tent canvas rustling in a breeze.

Her pencil lay motionless in her fingers, a line drifting off the paper from the last word she'd written before falling asleep.

Had it been a dream?

No, she'd heard something.

At least she thought she had.

What time was it? What day was it? Wednesday? Yeah, it had to be Wednesday. Where was Rover? Was he squealing in his sleep again?

She reached for her open water bottle.

A shout echoed through the camp, making her jerk in surprise. She bumped the bottle. It teetered like a bowling pin, and then fell off her desk. Water chugged out onto her tent floor, running toward the stack of research books she was using as a makeshift night stand.

"Dammit!" She grabbed the bottle and set it upright.

"Angélica, wake up!" Quint's voice outside her tent made her jump anew, bumping the bottle, sending it tumbling again. This time she watered her notes instead of her books.

"Stupid bottle." She scooped up the bottle and threw it across her tent.

"Angélica?"

"I'm coming!" She plucked a clean T-shirt from a pile María had left on her cot and threw it on her notes to sop up the mess. Then she unzipped the flap.

Quint hit her with a flashlight.

She winced in the brightness. "Let me guess, we have another problem." She shoved him aside, stepping out into the early morning darkness. "At least I have my shoes on this time."

"True." His flashlight traveled south. "But you're missing your shorts, Dr. García."

She looked down. Sure enough. She'd gotten halfway undressed last night before getting distracted by something she'd remembered needing to jot down.

A squawk escaped from her mouth. Covering the front of her underwear with her hand, she made a mad dash into her tent.

Quint's laughter followed her.

"It's not funny," she hissed, her whole body burning in mortification as she yanked on a pair of shorts.

"Were those tiny pink hearts?"

She joined him outside once again, avoiding his eyes.

"I'd ask you to be my Valentine," he joked, "but all of my chocolate has melted in this damned heat and we're fresh out of cupids last time I checked."

Her stomach did a silly little flip-flop at his flirting. "Shut up, Parker."

Another shout rang out.

Angélica recognized Teodoro's voice. "Come on." She caught Quint's arm. "Let's go see what's going on."

"I'm right behind you."

They hustled toward the crew's tents. The murmur of voices grew louder with every step. Outside of Diego's tent, she saw a group of men huddled together, wild-eyed in the shadows. She stopped in front of the tent. "What is it?"

"*Chakan*," Esteban said in Mayan. "It bit Diego," he added, his voice reaching a high shrill.

"What did he say?" Quint asked, drawing up beside her.

She frowned up at him. "A *chakan*. That's what the Maya call *Xtabay*—an evil spirit—when it takes the form of a serpent."

"Snakes. Just great." Quint sounded anxious. "Why does it have to turn into a snake? Why not a jungle rat? Or something cute, like a baby monkey?"

This year's dig might as well be flushed down the toilet now. No amount of money was going to calm their fears when it came to a *chakan*, not even the cash bonus she'd offered them last night at supper if they'd stick around until the end of the dig season. Those who had been hooting and trilling at the idea of more money were now looking here and there with the white of their eyes showing.

She heard a groan come from inside the tent, then

Teodoro stepped out, his face pale. She rushed to him. "How is he?"

"Okay, but he'll have a sore leg for several days."

"Did you kill the snake?"

"Yes."

"What kind was it?"

"Coral." He crossed himself. "It used its venom."

"An accident?" she whispered for his ears only.

He shook his head.

The need to scream in frustration clawed its way up her throat. She gulped it back down. "Where's Dad?"

"Inside."

She looked over at her crew, wondering who would be trying to hurt them. And why? She had no idea how to stop this from getting any worse, not without knowing who or what they were up against.

"Don't let them see the snake," she told Teodoro.

The murmurs grew louder all of a sudden, mixed with gasps and cries of fear. Esteban pointed at the tent and ran several feet away.

"Too late," Teodoro said and stepped back inside.

"What now?" she growled, pushing aside several men. One of them stepped back quickly, coming down on her toes. He apologized and moved aside, giving her a clear view of the instigator.

Rover!

She cursed about both her throbbing toes and her *jabalí*.

The little shit squealed happily up at her from where he stood in the middle of the circle, the snake dangling from his mouth.

Chapter Thirteen

Lolcatali: A ritual that protects a village from evil spirits.

What a huge catastro-fuck!

Angélica collapsed onto her cot, hiding out in her tent after a breakfast loaded with frustration and indigestion.

Once the hubbub about the snake had died down, three more crewmembers decided to leave the dig site, not willing to risk running into *Xtabay*, not even for extra cash. No amount of hot air from her could convince them it was a stupid snake and not some evil spirit brought about by a nonexistent goddamned curse.

Now she was left with a meager crew of thirteen plus Quint. She grabbed her pillow and covered her face.

She was going to need one hell of a big sacrifice to the Maya gods to fix this mess. Something akin to the bloodletting days of old.

Hey! Where was Jared? She'd happily pierce his penis with a stingray spine.

The whooshing of helicopter blades coming closer made her lower the pillow. It was Wednesday. That meant the helicopter now hovering overhead carried her knight in shining armor: *Pedro!*

She unzipped her tent flap and found Jared standing there watching the helicopter descend. The Maya gods must have taken her bloodletting idea seriously. She'd need to sharpen her stingray spine.

Nah, on second thought, leave it blunted.

"What do you need, Jared?" she hollered over the whooshing of the blades.

He frowned down at her. "Pedro's here."

No shit, Sherlock. "I noticed." She zipped her tent.

"Is he taking your father somewhere?"

"No. He's coming to help."

"For the day?"

"For the next two weeks."

The helicopter landed, powering down. She heard her father shout out Pedro's name.

"You're looking a bit frazzled these days, darling," Jared told her.

"Thanks for noticing."

"How is the boy who got bit by the snake doing?"

"Teodoro says he'll be sore for a few days, but otherwise fine." She nodded toward where Pedro had landed. "If you'll excuse me, I'm going to head over and see Pedro."

"Wait." He caught her shoulder. "You need to keep a tighter leash on Parker."

This territorial hokey-pokey was really getting old. "Quint is not your concern, Jared."

"He is as long as he's still here. Have you considered that he may have his own agenda for being down here? Something to do with Dr. Hughes? Something that may require him to interfere with your advancements here? Even sabotage your work?"

"Of course I've considered that." Well, maybe not that part about Quint hindering her goals for a reason having to do with Hughes, but Jared didn't need to know that.

"Have you informed him he's leaving?"

"I don't want to talk about this right now."

"Because I'd hate to have to tell your father that this is his last year down here."

She shoved his hand off her shoulder. "You know, you haven't changed a bit over the years. One minute you're telling me how much you care about me, the next you're trying to tear me down."

"I'm only looking out for your welfare. I know how much this dig site means to you. Remember, I've known Parker a lot longer than you."

"You knew him twenty years ago."

"A tiger doesn't change his stripes."

She glared up at him. "No, he sure doesn't, does he?"

"Angélica, don't let our past differences interfere with your admirable, logical, level-headed good sense."

"Fuck you."

She left him standing in front of her tent. Quint had better come through on his part of the deal they had made yesterday, because otherwise she'd just sealed her father's fate.

* * *

Mornings in this hellhole were legendarily awful, with biting flies and sweltering humidity. All Quint needed was a three-legged dog, an empty wallet, and a broken heart and he'd have an award-winning country song on his hands.

He finger-combed his hair as he walked back to his tent, his jaw stinging from shaving with plain old soap. Here he was fresh from the tin-bucket shower, and he was already sweating. That was just a Porta-Potty full of wonderful.

Earlier, after wrestling the snake from Rover's jaws and getting coated in snake blood and javelina slobber in the process, he'd skipped breakfast in lieu of a scrub down. He'd been scraping off the last of his beard stubble when he'd heard the helicopter coming in.

As soon as he dropped off his shampoo and razor, he was

going to head over and find out who had arrived for the party … or if the helicopter was here to rush someone away. He hoped Diego's leg hadn't taken a turn for the worse.

He turned the corner of his tent and saw Steel standing across the way outside of Angélica's zip flap.

The jerk challenged him with a scowl.

Speaking of snakes, Quint thought with a lip curl. He paused long enough to toss his stuff inside his tent and then headed over to deal with more venomous vermin.

"You misplace your stick?" he asked Steel.

"What?"

"You know, the one that's been jammed up your ass since you showed up here?"

The skin around Steel's mouth tightened. "What's it like for you, Parker, trying to fit in with the more intellectual crowd and always falling abysmally short?"

And the gloves were off again. "You and I need to talk."

"I have nothing to say to you—except when are you leaving?"

Quint planted his feet, ready to lock horns. "I'm not."

"I believe that's Angélica's decision, but if I were you, I'd start packing."

"She told me yesterday I could stay as long as I needed."

Steel sniffed. "That's her mistake then."

"Something told me you'd take that attitude. Why are you so determined to get me out of here?"

"You're not trustworthy."

"Trustworthy or not, I have a legitimate reason for being here, unlike you."

"You're a liar. When Angélica finds out how deep your lies go, she'll tear you apart limb by limb."

Quint rubbed his smooth chin, studying his adversary, deciding tactics. "Where did the love go, Steel? Does this animosity you're still clinging to after twenty long years have anything to do with my turning you in for being too rough with that young Maya kid?"

Steel's jaw jutted. "He needed to be disciplined."

Maybe, but not beaten senseless. "Or are you still bellyaching because Dr. Hughes trusted me with secrets he refused to share with you?"

"You did nothing to deserve his esteem. You were a selfish brat brought down here to be taught how to work hard and respect authority."

Quint didn't deny that. He'd been fresh out of school, full of rebellion, and high from an overinflated ego. Had it not been for Dr. Hughes, he probably wouldn't be where he was today. "Dr. Hughes recognized my potential, and in case you've forgotten, his respect wasn't given freely. I earned it that summer through sweat—lots of sweat."

A vein pulsed in Steel's temple. "Why are you here, Parker?"

"You know exactly why I'm here." *To find a ghost.* "To write an article."

"I hope you don't have some romantic notion that you'll find Dr. Hughes holed up in one of these temples, waiting for you to rescue him, because he's long dead."

Interesting that Steel would mention that. "What makes you so sure of his demise?"

"Five years ago, a plane was found in the Guatemalan jungle, two hundred and fifty miles southwest of here, half swallowed by the bush."

"I'm sure there are downed planes strewn throughout the Central and South American jungles. What does that have to do with Dr. Hughes?"

"Hughes is dead." Steel took a step closer as if to reinforce his point. "He was on that plane when it crashed and burned twenty years ago."

Quint tried to hide his surprise behind a stony mask. "What proof is there that Dr. Hughes was on that plane?"

"The tail broke off during the crash. They found his luggage near the wreckage, along with other personal belongings."

"How come Mrs. Hughes wasn't aware of this?"

"She was, but she chose not to believe it, clinging to some foolish hope of finding her husband alive in some remote village with his memory wiped."

He didn't want to believe Steel. Hell, part of Quint was holding onto hope, too. Hope that Dr. Hughes was still around, impossible as that seemed.

Until he could investigate this nugget of information further, he decided to change the subject. "Drop the blackmail threat, Steel. I'm not leaving tomorrow."

Steel inhaled through his teeth. "Angélica told you about our little arrangement, did she? How unfortunate for her father."

"Drop the blackmail or deal with the consequences."

"This is really a bit over your head, Parker."

"Okay, let me speak in your vernacular," Quint said. "If you don't drop the blackmail threat, I'm going to call up the editor of *American Archaeology Today*, who happens to be a good friend of mine, and explain to her that you are using blackmail as a means to get me kicked off this dig site."

Steel's face hardened so fast Quint was amazed it didn't split in two.

He continued, "We'll see how your superiors like having their university criticized in print for using petty treachery and interfering with not only the public's awareness of the past, but also the scientific community's advancement in knowledge about the Maya people." Quint crossed his arms over his chest. "Trust me, you aren't going to be well-liked when this article comes out. Hell, who knows, you might even lose your job, along with respect from your peers."

If looks could burn a man to death, Quint would be nothing more than a poof of smoke.

He rocked back on his heels. "So what's it going to be, Steel? Are you going to back off, or do I have to hike to the village this morning and make a phone call?"

* * *

By the time Angélica caught up with her father and Pedro in the mess tent, Juan had already spilled most of the beans.

"The blisters were where?" Pedro grimaced.

"You heard me," Juan said. "And then Jared ended up with biting ants in his cot."

"No!"

"He was covered with red welts for over a day. Angélica made him wear a hat and sunglasses whenever he left his tent. He looked like some kind of polka-dotted clown. And then—"

"Dad!" Angélica interrupted. "Don't you think that's enough muckraking for one day?"

"It's not really muckraking since we're not exactly prominent people, *gatita*. Besides, it's just Pedro."

"What's 'muckraking' mean?" Pedro asked.

"It's still humiliating."

"You're overreacting." He turned back to Pedro. "Diego was bit by a coral snake this morning."

Pedro winced with his whole upper body. "*Ay yi yi.*"

"He'll be okay, thanks to Teodoro's quick thinking, but that leg is going to smart for a while."

"So all of this is because of her curse?" Pedro nodded in Angélica's direction before taking a sip of his coffee.

"My curse?" Her dad must have filled him in on everything else when he had flown to Cancun to get his tooth fixed. "Really, Dad?"

Juan had the decency to look a little sheepish.

"Sounds like hanging around here isn't going to be good for my health." Pedro lowered his cup to the table. "Especially if someone will be muck-cracking me."

"Pedro, not 'muckcracking,' it's *muckraking*," Angélica explained. "And you're staying for two weeks no matter what." She needed him more than he could imagine.

"Of course I am, *mi angelita.*" He patted her hand in his

usual brotherly way.

"Angélica thought maybe we could start having a couple of men pull night watches," Juan stirred more sugar into his coffee. "What do you think?"

"*Es bueno,*" Pedro agreed.

"We can't spare any men completely from the day shift," she said. "But maybe if we split the nights into four-hour shifts, it won't cause that much of a ripple effect in the workload."

Pedro finished his coffee, bringing his cup down hard like a judge's gavel. "I'll cover the first shift tonight. Have Rafael pull the second."

"You sure? You just flew in."

"I'm well-rested and fresh compared to the rest of you."

"True." Juan leaned toward Pedro, a fat grin popping up on his face. "You'll never guess who I caught Angélica with in this very tent yesterday morning, and they weren't in here drinking coffee."

Her mouth fell open.

"*Por favor*, don't tell me it was Dr. Steel?"

"Nope. It was—"

"Dad!"

Pedro might be practically family, but some things did not need to be shared.

"Would you look what's falling out of the sky these days," Quint's voice behind her made her jump. "Pedro Montañero in the flesh. I'll be damned."

Angélica hoped like the dickens that Quint hadn't heard what her father had been saying a moment before. She lifted her coffee cup to her lips, trying to hide behind it.

"Quint Parker!" Pedro stood as Quint rounded the table. "A big, old birdy told me you were here." He pumped Quint's hand. "Have you been staying out of trouble all these years?"

Angélica peered over her cup at Quint. Freshly shaven, damp hair combed back with a few wavy tendrils already breaking free, smelling of soap, he looked good enough to eat in one tempting bite.

"Hell, no." Quint grinned. "Where's the fun in that?"

Pedro patted the bench seat next to him. "Join us, *amigo.*" After Quint grabbed some coffee and settled in across from her, Pedro elbowed him lightly. "Quint, what does 'muck-er-aching' mean? Angélica keeps saying something about it to Juan."

"She does, huh?" Quint shot Angélica a raised brow. "It's kind of like mudslinging."

Pedro's whole face rounded in a whopping smile. "Ah, *sí.* I've seen those shows—two women in bikinis covered with mud while they fight. *Ay yi yi.*"

"*Ay yi yi* is right," Quint said with a wink at Angélica.

Angélica wrinkled her nose back at him, then squeezed Pedro's hand across the table. "Pedro, you have a wonderful way with English, but that's not the kind of mudslinging I'm talking about."

"What I said was not exactly muckraking," Juan said to Quint. "I was filling Pedro in on what's been going on around here."

"Ah, gotcha." Quint looked at Pedro. "It's sort of like whistle-blowing."

Angélica stole a line from Lauren Bacall in *To Have and Have Not*, one of her mom's favorite movies. "You know how to whistle don't you, Pedro," she said, her voice smoky. "You just put your lips together and … blow."

Quint's gaze was glued to her mouth. He puckered and let out a quiet wolf whistle, finishing the scene Bogart style.

Pedro tried to copy Quint's whistle, but it sounded weak, so he gave up and trilled instead, which made Juan laugh.

"Try again," her father encouraged.

While Pedro and her dad fooled around with whistling, Quint tapped her wrist, getting her attention.

He leaned across the table and spoke low. "I ran into someone outside your tent."

Jared! Her grip tightened on her cup. "What a coincidence.

He was just asking about you this morning."

"That should be the last time. My side of the deal is done."

She blinked in surprise. "That was quick."

"I don't mess around." He sent her a cockeyed smile. "Except with women who know how to whistle."

Flirt! Okay, now that the whole blackmail mess was behind them, she needed to get back to business, to keep her mind on her work—not Quint. "I believe I owe you a big thanks."

Quint shot her a smoldering look. "Or something else."

Her new resolve buckled just like that. She gulped some coffee, careful not to swallow her tongue.

"What does whistling have to do with the curse?" Pedro asked, bringing them back around to where they'd started.

Juan snapped his fingers. "I know! Think of it as being dragged through the mud."

"Why would she think you were dragging me through the mud?" Pedro asked Juan.

She needed some fresh air. Too many of her senses were suddenly tuned into the All-Quint-All-Night radio show going on in her head. Standing, she told Pedro, "I meant he was exposing what's been going on around here."

Pedro shrugged. "Teodoro fills me in every Tuesday when he calls from the village."

"You knew about all this?"

"Not all. I missed Teodoro's call yesterday. But I knew about the curse."

She growled in her throat. Was there no such thing as a secret around this place? That was it. She needed a few hours alone in the Dawn Temple to find her happy, orderly, get-her-shit-together place.

Pointing her cup at Quint, she changed back into boss mode. "You're with Fernando again today. Dad, you take Jared and Pedro."

"Will do," Juan picked up his coffee. "As soon as I finish this. Where are you running off to?"

"I have a report to write," she lied.

"Right." He stirred his drink. "Be careful, *gatita*. Sub Chambers Q and V are extremely unstable."

* * *

This trip to jungle hell was turning into reunion central. First Steel and now Pedro. Quint snorted. If only Dr. Hughes would make an appearance, he could turn in his name badge and leave the party.

Or not.

He had a few things to sort out with Angélica first.

"Quint!" Pedro called, catching up with Quint just outside his tent and handing him a large manila envelope. "I have something for you."

Quint held up the envelope. "From you?"

Pedro shook his head. "From Jeff Hughes."

"I didn't realize you know Jeff."

"He called three days ago, said he found *mi nombre* and number in some of his *madre's* things and wondered why."

Quint wondered why, too. Maybe the answer was in the envelope in his hand.

"I told him you and I used to work together for his *papa* and I would be seeing you soon. He asked if he could ship this to me to bring to you."

Quint squeezed the envelope. It felt like some kind of thin book. He itched to open it, but not in front of Pedro. "Thank you for making sure I got it."

"*No problema.*" Pedro hitched his bag over his shoulder. "Now which of these tents was Alonso's? Juan said I can sleep there."

Quint pointed across the way. "That green one." He picked at the corner of the package, working it loose.

"*Gracías.* Wish me luck. I'm working with Jared this morning. He is … what do you say? A fun blower."

"You mean a fun-sucker."

Pedro chuckled. "Some things never change, *sí?* Save me a seat at lunch."

He watched Pedro walk away, debating whether he should ask him to keep quiet about Jeff's delivery. No, that might make him curious.

As soon as Pedro was out of sight, Quint tore open the top of the envelope. What could be so important that Jeff had to ship it via Pedro? Why had Mrs. Hughes been in possession of Pedro's name and number?

"Quint!" Juan was headed his way.

He lowered the envelope, trying to discreetly tuck it behind him.

"Fernando wants me to take you over to where he's working." Juan came to a stop in front of him. "He moved inside the temple to one of the chambers."

Of course he had. It was undoubtedly hotter, tighter, and a helluva lot more dangerous inside. Quint couldn't wait to dig in.

"It's like a maze in there," Juan added. "Can be dangerous if you don't know where you're going."

Juan was doing a bad job of selling today's task, but Quint had no choice. Angélica needed the help, and he needed to get to the bottom of these Dr. Hughes' clues. He rubbed his thumb over the torn piece of envelope. Jeff's package would have to wait until later, along with the new questions Pedro's news had drudged up.

"Let me grab something from my tent."

At Juan's nod, Quint stepped inside, glancing behind him to make sure Juan didn't follow. Unable to resist, he peeked inside the envelope and saw a letter clipped to the front of a notepad. He opened the envelope wider and read: *I finally found Mom's notes! They were in...*

"You coming, boy?" Juan's voice interrupted.

"Be right there." He stuffed the envelope under his cot, his pulse rat-a-tat-tatting about what answers he was going to find in that envelope.

* * *

Angélica ducked under a broken support beam and carefully stepped into the dark chamber in the heart of the Dawn Temple. Shining the beam of her flashlight around the walls, she stared at the fissure cracks splintering across them like spider webs without really seeing them.

Instead, she was busy racking her brain, trying to come up with who would be trying to shut down her dig site this year and why.

Was it some drug cartel members who wanted the site to grow cocaine or store guns? No, they'd just come in with guns blazing.

Could it be another archaeologist who'd found out what she and her father were up to? Someone who had located clues at another site that led to this one? She'd heard of some unorthodox competitive personalities in the field, especially with so few new career-boosting finds happening these days.

Could Quint be behind it like Jared had hinted? Could he be charming her on one hand while trying to destroy her career with the other? But why? Dr. Hughes had done some monumental work at this site, but nothing extraordinarily newsworthy. At least nothing that she or her parents had found in their years here.

A warm body bumped into her, bringing her back to the present and her search.

"Where are we?" Pedro whispered in the dark chamber.

"Sub Chamber Q."

"Didn't your dad say we should NOT come in here?"

"No, he just warned that it's dangerous." The air smelled stale, felt heavy; this chamber's dust hadn't been stirred for over a year.

"Oh." He directed his beam of light downward. "What are all of these stones doing on the floor?"

She took hold of his light and shined the beam at the ceiling. "They used to be up there."

He cursed, using a few combinations of the Spanish language that she hadn't heard before. "Maybe I should wait in the hall."

"Go ahead." She hadn't wanted to drag him in here anyway. He was supposed to be helping her father.

He didn't move. "Is finding this piece of rock really worth risking your life?"

"Yes." It was what she'd lived for the last few years.

He sighed. "Fine. I'll stay, but I'm not happy about it."

"I don't know why you're here in the first place." She stepped further into the chamber. "I told Dad to keep you with him."

"He said he'd feel better if I came with you." Pedro reached up and ran his finger along a crack in the ceiling. "Now I know why."

"Pedro, you don't have to stay in here. You can wait out front."

"Yes, I do," he said with finality. "What makes you think you can find this rock in here? There are more rocks on the floor than in the walls and ceiling."

"Well, it wasn't in Sub Chamber V, so it has to be in here. We checked the rest of the temple last night."

"What if it's not in here?"

She stepped further into the room. "I don't want to think about that. It's in here." She rolled a stone over and checked it with her flashlight. "It has to be."

"If you say so, but I think you should have the *Lolcatali* ceremony," he said switching subjects mid-sentence.

Where had that thought come from? She glanced over at him. He was still checking out the ceiling.

"No, Pedro."

"You're not thinking of your men and their needs."

She checked two more stones. "I offered more money."

"That's not enough. Fear is stronger than greed."

Angélica turned to him, hands on her hips. "And you think the ceremony will keep them here?"

"*Sí.*"

"It's just a ceremony, not magic."

He shined the flashlight on her, making her shield her eyes. "To you it's just a ceremony. To them, it's like a … what do you call that thing in *Star Wars* … a force-field. It protects them from future *Xtabay* attacks."

She didn't want to think about the mess she was in with her crew right now. "Come on." She tugged his arm, pulling him over to a small pile of rocks with a large flat one on top. "Help me move this."

Pedro nudged her aside and lifted the rock. "Teodoro said he could be ready to have the ceremony within a day."

"When did you talk to him about this?" She had a feeling her father had something to do with it.

"I didn't. Your father did."

Bingo.

"*Angel*, this rock isn't getting any lighter."

She scrambled to grab a stone the size of a grapefruit that had been hidden under the bigger one, and told Pedro to put down the rock.

"There are a few key things my father isn't considering when it comes to the ceremony."

"What?"

"For one thing, if I allow it and the Mexican government finds out, they will question my ability to handle my crew."

"Nobody but us needs to know about it."

"Jared will know, and I can't see him keeping his big mouth shut." She examined a couple more stones. "It could tarnish my credibility among my peers."

"You would be praised by the Maya people for thinking of your men's needs," Pedro shot back.

"Quint might publish something about it."

"He won't if you ask him not to."

She peeked over at him. He was shining the flashlight through his closed fingers, looking at his bones and blood vessels. "What makes you so certain?"

"Because he likes you."

She felt her cheeks warm for a whole other reason than the heat trapped in the temple. "How do you know?"

"And you like him."

"No, I don't." She'd be damned if she was going to admit it, even to Pedro.

"Liar, liar. Your underwear are on fire."

"It's supposed to be my pants."

"Those, too. I saw the way you looked at him at breakfast. There were birds in your eyes."

Birds? Angélica frowned at him. "You mean stars?"

"*Sí.* Quint is a real hottie."

She laughed. "Where did you hear that expression?"

"Some businessman brought his family down and chartered a private flight to Tikal. He had two teenage daughters." He held the flashlight under his chin, grinning like a madman. "Admit it. You like him."

She chuckled, shoving him away. He was hopeless, and she loved having him here with her, even if he was more distraction than help.

"Who I do and do not like is my business, Pedro." Lifting several rocks from another pile, she checked each one before lowering them back to the dirt floor.

"Your father and I approve of him."

She rolled her eyes, turning over a triangular-shaped rock. They'd approve of anyone who didn't have the last name of *Steel*.

"And it's about time you got laid," Pedro added.

She gasped. "Pedro!"

"What? You're too uptight."

"Shut it," she ordered, and socked him lightly on the arm to emphasize her feelings on the matter.

"*Ay chihuahua.*" He rubbed his arm. "The truth hurts."

"It will hurt even more if you bring up the subject in front of Parker." She shined the light on the triangular rock, and her breath caught in her throat.

"I couldn't think of a nicer guy to—"

"Pedro, look!" She dropped to her knees. "I found it!"

He came over, squatting next to her. "That's it? That's what you were searching for all of this time?"

"Yes!" Finally, she was going to be able to put the pieces of the puzzle together.

He grabbed her arm, his stare insistent. "You have to let Teodoro do the *Lolcatali* ceremony."

Ah, what the hell. She needed her crew more than ever now. She blew a raspberry in defeat. "Fine. He can perform the damned ceremony. Happy?"

"No. But I will be when we get out of this death trap."

He was beginning to sound like Quint.

She ran her palm over what she hoped was going to be the key to finding the shell. "But if this ceremony causes any problems for me," she told him, "I'm going to tell Dad that you broke his favorite Lone Ranger and Tonto statue, not that gecko you blamed it on."

He kissed her cheek. "This is going to work, trust me."

"It better." Because nothing else seemed to be.

"*Por favor*, can we leave this creepy place now? It's giving me a case of pringles on my arms."

She wasn't even going to touch that one. Clutching the broken piece of *stela* to her chest, she stood. "Come on, let's go find a shell."

Chapter Fourteen

Itza: The ruling family of Chichen Itza, "Water Witch."

Quint escaped to his tent, zipping the mesh flap closed behind him. After spending all afternoon helping the crew clear rubble from behind the Owl Temple, he wanted to fall onto his cot and sleep for half a day.

Grabbing his shower towel, he used it to dry the sweat from his face and hair. The lantern on his desk cast a soft light, pushing back the early evening's shadows. His stomach rumbled as he lifted the cot and pulled out the envelope Jeff had sent via Pedro.

He sat down on his cot while opening the envelope and drew out a notebook. Its green cardboard cover was worn white along the edges. He laid it on the cot next to him. Reaching into the envelope again, he pulled out a single sheet of paper with Jeff's handwriting.

"I finally found Mom's notes! They were in Dad's chair. She'd made this hidden compartment under the seat cushion. It was a pure accident that I found it, and I have a bump on my head to prove it. Good luck figuring out what she wrote. I look forward to hearing from you."

Quint returned the letter to the envelope and picked up the notebook. The answers to why she'd been watching Steel for years had better be inside. If not … well, he wasn't usually a quitter, but after Steel's news about the plane wreck, he wondered if there was anything of Dr. Hughes left down here besides memories.

The scrawls on the pages made him grab the lantern and bring it closer. He'd forgotten how hard it was to read Mrs. Hughes' chicken scratch. He flipped through, scanning, stopping when he saw mention of a plane wreck.

October 17th: I got a phone call this morning from a representative of the Mexican government. They found the wreckage of a plane in the jungle, somewhere near the Guatemalan border, and said they were sorry to inform me that my husband was on it. His luggage was found near the wreckage and is being sent to me. There was evidence of him inside the plane—his satchel and college ring. Close by on the jungle floor was a boot with his name written in it, something Henry did ever since his stint in the Navy. Some of his foot was still in it they said, mostly just bones. They figure an animal dragged away what was left of his body, because they couldn't find it. They are sending me the ring and satchel. I told them to keep the boot. It's been fifteen years since I last saw my husband. Why does the pain still feel so fresh?

October 18th: They say he was on that plane, but the more I think about it, the more I don't believe them. He never wore his lucky ring. He carried it in a small leather pouch that I'd sewn into the liner of his luggage. Something isn't right here, but I can't quite put my finger on it.

Steel was right, Mrs. Hughes had known about the accident. Even after fifteen years of no contact from her husband, she'd still been in denial.

Quint rubbed the back of his neck, grimacing at the grit. He frowned down at the pieces of dirt on his palm. Had his whole trip down here been a waste of time? If so, maybe he should write the damned article and catch the first bus back to the airport.

He turned back to the notes. With the weight of the tragic ending to the Hughes' marriage heavy on his heart, he read on:

October 20th: I keep remembering pieces of conversations I had with Henry that last season, and the troubles he was having with that grad student who continually challenged his authority. I've been trying to remember his name but can't place it.

"Jared Steel," Quint told her. She'd obviously figured that out though. Was this the beginning of her obsession with Steel?

"Would you stop wiggling, you little shit," Angélica said from somewhere outside.

He froze, listening. Was she coming closer?

There was a muffled snort and then footfalls in the dry grass. Her laughter rang out low and soft, rousing his curiosity.

His gaze landed on an old boot Rover had left next to his cot—the perfect excuse to talk to her. He stuffed the notebook under his mattress and practically tore the mesh flap open in his haste to see her.

"Angélica."

She looked over from where she stood bathed in the last rays of the day's sunlight. Rover squirmed and twisted in her arms, doing his best to break free. "Hi, Quint," she said with a hint of a smile on her lips.

Rover laid eyes on him and squealed, struggling harder.

"Okay, okay." She let the little guy down. Rover bounded over to him as Quint drew near.

With the sun setting at her back, she had an ethereal radiance behind her. The loose tendrils of hair that had escaped her ponytail were lit like little live wires. Floating pieces of dust glowed like tiny fireflies around her face. To his tired eyes, she looked like a slice of heaven.

Then again, maybe he was delirious with heat exhaustion

and hunger and was starting to hallucinate. That didn't stop him from wanting to drag her back to his tent and do naked things to her.

"You weren't at lunch today." He kept it easy between them, not wanting to scare her off with a "Me Tarzan, you Jane" chest beating display.

"You weren't at supper," she shot back.

Rover nuzzled his ankle, making an odd snorting-grunting sound.

She glanced down, wrinkling her nose. "He's sliming your sock."

"After all of the sweat it soaked up today, it needs to be burned." He held her chewed hiking boot out in front of him. "He left his toy in my tent."

She took the boot. "At least it wasn't my pink bra this time."

"I might not have given that back."

Her cheeks darkened, but she held his stare. "Then I'd expect something in trade."

"Oh, yeah?" He shoved his hands in his pockets to keep from touching her. "Like what?"

"Well, certainly not your sock."

That surprised a laugh from him. When he quieted, the silence stretched between them. The sun slid below the horizon, leaving them alone in the twilight.

She shooed away a mosquito. "How did it go today?"

Hiking barefoot through hell would have been preferable. "Good. I think we actually made progress."

"That's great. You're working with Fernando again tomorrow, right?"

"If that's where you need me."

A chorus of frogs broke into a croaking frenzy in the jungle behind him.

"Yeah," she nodded, "that's where I need you." She pointed at her tent. "I should get some work done. I guess I'll see you at breakfast tomorrow."

"You will."

She turned toward her tent and then looked back at him. "Quint, as you've probably gathered, I'm not really comfortable talking about my feelings, but I want to let you know how much I appreciate your help. I don't know what we … what *I* would do without you these days."

The sincerity in her eyes was his undoing. Angélica needed his help. At that moment he happily would have steered his ship full speed ahead into the rocks, whistling as it crashed into pieces and sank into Davy Jones' locker. The importance of whether or not he figured out the details of Dr. Hughes' death barely mattered. For this particular damsel in distress, he'd put up with bugs, snakes, sweat, and whatever else this godforsaken place threw at him.

"Angélica?"

"Yes?"

"You have a smudge of dirt," he lied, reaching out and rubbing his thumb down over her cheek.

She brushed the back of her hand over the area. "Did I get it?"

He tilted her jaw up and to the side pretending to inspect her cheek. "Yes, but you missed the other spot."

"Where?"

"Right here." He lowered his head, brushing his lips over hers. She tasted salty with a hint of María's orange special sauce. At her moan of submission he returned for more, letting the spark between them catch fire and flare.

A hard tug at his ankle pulled him back from the deep. He broke the kiss, looking down at where Rover was yanking on his sock.

"He's a demanding little shit," she said, her voice husky.

"We need to find a Rover-sitter."

She chuckled. "Did you get it?"

"Get what?"

"The spot on my lips." Her eyes flirted.

No, not even close. "For now."

As much as he wanted to follow her into her tent and peel her clothes off, he stepped back. There were too many secrets. If this thing between them were going to be a one night stand, secrets wouldn't matter. But there was no way one night with her was going to be enough. He wanted more. A lot more.

He jammed his grab-happy hands back into his pockets. "I may need to check for dirt smudges another time though."

"Oh, yeah?"

"Definitely."

"We'll see." She reached down and grabbed Rover. He let out a squeaky grunt as she lifted him. "Goodnight, Parker." Giving Quint a parting wave, she disappeared into her tent.

His body still rigid and pining for the auburn-haired siren, he returned to his tent. She was so close yet still just out of reach.

Secrets …

He stared at the corner of the cot where he'd hidden the notebook. Maybe it was time to come clean about why he was really here.

* * *

The jungle was still asleep.

Angélica wasn't. She'd been awake since way too early in the morning, unable to stop thinking about all of the what-ifs filling her head. Instead of staring at the ceiling while her anxiety stacked up, she'd gotten up.

At first she'd figured on heading to the Dawn Temple to take another look at that *stela*, see if she could find the altar stones that would usually be next to it. But then she'd heard Quint groan in the darkness and decided to stay put, studying the charcoal relief copy she'd made of both the *stela* and the broken piece. There was something comforting with him only a tent away, something she hadn't felt since she'd had both of her parents on the dig site with her.

An hour had passed before she knew it. Her vision blurred

as she stared down at where her pen touched the paper. Blinking away sleep, she stood and massaged her lower back. Now was not the time to take a nap. She had more to decipher and another full day to dig, dig, dig.

After doing a couple of stretches, she dropped back into her chair, pulling the relief copy of the *stela* front and center. With the broken piece back in place, she'd figured out that the date of the king's death was close to the time when the merchant would've been traveling with the shell, which fit within the limits defined by her mom's theory.

But the scribe who'd carved the glyphs had used an unfamiliar head variant to represent the name of the temple where the king was buried. She frowned down at the charcoal lines that made up the strange symbol. She needed to figure out what that head variant meant in order to know where to begin looking.

Rubbing her eyes, she tried to go over what she knew. Someone had moved the *stela* from its original location, because there had been no altar stones in front of it when her father had found it. Unfortunately, she didn't have the time this season to search every temple for altar stones without an accompanying *stela*. She was already way behind schedule and low on manpower.

As cliché as it seemed, she needed to work smarter now, not harder. Although that was often more of a pipedream than a reality given all of the things that could go wrong—and lately had.

She yawned and then pounded the heel of her palm against her forehead. Come on brain. What next?

Variables … variants.

That was it! Head variants.

She grabbed her mom's favorite old epigraphy reference book from near the bottom of her nightstand stack. As she fanned through the several hundred pages, she wondered where to start.

In the thick quiet of the predawn jungle, she heard Quint's

cot creak. She looked up, listening, thinking about when he'd kissed her earlier. If Rover hadn't interfered, would she have pulled him into her tent and finished what he started?

Shaking off the semi-naked images that followed along with that idea, she directed her attention back to the damned book. Maybe the Table of Contents would lead her in the right direction. She scanned down the chapter headings for something relevant.

The words blurred. She stroked her cheek, following the path of his touch. What would his fingers feel like elsewhere?

She buried her face in her hands. This was hopeless. Her brain was stalling out, spinning wheels on subjects better left unexplored.

Closing the books, she killed the lantern and stretched out on her cot. Over by her desk on his makeshift bed of old rags, Rover snorted in his sleep, probably tearing up a dreamland garden.

"Damn it, Quint," she whispered. "What's it going to take to get you out of my head?"

There in the safe darkness of her tent, she let go. There were no visions of sugar-plums dancing as she drifted off, only fantasies involving the man next door and what she'd like to do to him.

Preferably while he was tied to a bed.

Naked.

Mostly.

* * *

This jungle was going to be the death of him.

After a long night of tossing and turning on his cot, bouncing from one bad dream to another, and then an even longer day trying to keep up with Fernando, Quint could barely lift the *balche* to his lips.

"I'm too old for this shit," he told Juan, who sat next to him on a rickety lawn chair in the growing shadow of the

Temple of the Water Witch. A haze of incense hovered above their heads, perfuming the early evening air. "Twenty years ago, I could handle working in this heat, but not anymore."

"Quit your crying, Junior Mint." Juan blew out a mouthful of cigar smoke. "You're not going to let my little girl show you up, are you?"

"Hell, yes. Your daughter is a machine. I'm beginning to think her energy source is nuclear-based."

"She's a carbon copy of her mother. I never could keep up with Marianne."

He wanted to press Juan for more details about the curse Marianne had found, and if Angélica believed it had anything to do with her mom's death, but he settled on a more neutral subject. "So, why are we having this Local-whatever ceremony here next to this particular temple?"

"We found the curse glyph here, and the evil wind blew right after Angélica read it aloud. All of the men here know that, so Teodoro thinks that this would be the best spot to perform the protection ritual."

"Protection from what?"

"Evil spirits like *Xtabay*."

"And more evil winds," Pedro added as he dropped into the chair on the other side of Quint. He pointed the cup of *balche* in his hand at Steel, who sat across the fire. "We need a ritual to protect us from that one."

"I thought there was." Juan raised his cigar. "It's called 'divorce,' but apparently it doesn't always work."

Pedro sipped while Juan puffed.

Quint's attention shifted to Teodoro, who was chanting something while standing at an altar under an arch made up of bent and tied sticks. The altar looked similar to the one used at the *Chachac* ceremony last week. Candles and gourds littered the altar surface and the ground surrounding it.

Pedro tapped Quint on the arm. "You going somewhere after the show, hot stuff?"

While Pedro had on his usual jeans and T-shirt, Quint had

cleaned up and donned his least stained khaki pants and a short-sleeve, black button-up shirt. With all of the talk he'd kept hearing about this ceremony, Quint had figured he'd better shower, shave, and wear something nicer than his usual duds. Now he looked like a tourist among the natives.

"I have a date," he joked.

Juan winked. "I'm sure Angélica will appreciate it."

Heat crawled up Quint's neck. "That's not what I meant."

"Really?" Juan raised one eyebrow. "You two-timing my daughter with one of the boys?"

Quint's tongue was bumbling around in his mouth still, so he changed direction. "Where is your daughter?"

"Don't know. Haven't seen her all afternoon."

"She's probably back in that damned death trap," Pedro muttered. He pushed to his feet. "Time for a refill. Anyone else need one?" When he got no takers, he headed off.

Quint pulled his shirt away from his chest, fanning the material against his skin. The setting sun tie-dyed the sky in a mix of blues, purples, and pinks. He should have brought his camera, but he'd promised Juan that he wouldn't write about this ceremony in his article, so he'd left everything back in the tent.

"How's Jeff doing?" Pedro asked as he settled back into his lawn chair, sloshing some *balche* onto his pants. He muttered a string of curses in Spanish when he realized what he'd done.

Quint shot a glance at Juan before answering, checking if he was paying attention. The good doctor was staring into the flames, appearing to be lost in fiery thoughts. "As good as can be expected, I guess."

"Jeff said he's been going through his mother's stuff for the last few weeks, finding some interesting things."

Quint wondered how much Jeff had said, but with Juan here, now was not the time to get too inquisitive. Besides, he needed an answer from Pedro to a question that had been churning in his mind all day. "Did you know about Dr.

Hughes being in a plane crash?"

"I have a friend who was part of the investigative team. He works for the government, inspecting plane crashes. I called Mrs. Hughes after I'd heard. She told me she didn't believe her husband was in that plane." He swilled his *balche*. "I didn't argue with her."

"Do you believe he was in that crash?"

"*Sì*, but I didn't want to cause her any more pain."

Sitting back, Quint pondered Pedro's words. If it were true, if Dr. Hughes had been on that plane, then the great mystery was solved. Game over.

Across the flames, Steel sat alone, a book open on his lap while he stared off into the dark jungle. Maybe Mrs. Hughes was a bit off her rocker. As much as he'd like to justify his distaste for all things Steel, the jerk might be guilty of nothing more than being a Grade-A asshole.

He might as well do the only thing he could at this point—keep reading Mrs. Hughes' notes.

In between helping Fernando all day, he'd managed to get through a few more pages before falling asleep during the afternoon *siesta*. Mostly her scrawls were random thoughts about articles on Steel and snippets of conversations with her husband. Nothing worth staying awake over apparently.

Teodoro's chanting grew louder, capturing his attention. Quint watched him take a drink from a piece of gourd fashioned into a bowl. "He's drinking *balche*, too, right?"

"Yes," Juan answered. "Now that he's walked around the temple ten times, he has to drink twelve bowls of it. Then he'll pray to the *alux*."

"*Alux?*"

"Forest spirits," Pedro said. "Tricky little dwarfs who have protective powers."

"Good evening, boys," Angélica interrupted, standing next to her father.

Quint's pulse sped up at just the sound of her voice, which was pretty goddamned pathetic. He was turning into her puppy dog.

She eyed him for a moment, taking in his shirt and pants. "You look very nice tonight, Parker. Which one of these two jokesters told you there was a dress code?"

Pedro laughed. "*¡Demonios!* I wish I'd thought of that."

She squatted next to her father's chair, patting his knee. "How was your day?"

"*Bueno.*" Juan reached over and ruffled her hair, which looked damp, freshly washed. "Where have you been, *gatita*? You've missed some of the good stuff."

Her whole face lit up from her smile. "I figured it out."

"Really?"

She nodded. "Where's Jared?" she whispered.

"Sitting over on the steps."

Her smile faded at the sight of Steel. Then she focused back on her dad, her eyes glittering in the firelight.

"Well?" Juan prompted.

She glanced pointedly toward the temple looming over them. "*Itza.*" She spoke loud enough for only the four of them to hear. "I didn't recognize it because it was a style used a couple of hundred years before the one I'd learned."

"You mean it's been in the Temple of the Water Witch all along?"

"Shhhh." She shot a look at Jared while nodding.

Pedro leaned in closer. "I bet it's in *the chamber.*"

Quint gazed from one to the next, feeling like the odd man out. "What are you talking about?"

She measured him up and down for a moment. "Ask me the next time we're alone." He appeared to have passed inspection.

Something warm flickered to life in his chest. Maybe it was the *balche*, or maybe it was being accepted into Angélica's inner circle. He didn't want to move a muscle, afraid he'd break the spell now that she was actually going to trust him with something. And something very important, judging by the way the three of them were acting.

She watched Teodoro for a moment. "Has he petitioned the spirits already?"

"Over an hour ago." Juan took a draw from his cigar.

"Dang. That's my favorite part." She shifted, sitting cross-legged at her father's feet. "Where are Esteban and Rafael?"

Pedro lowered his empty cup to the ground and leaned back, his chair squeaking as he settled into it. "They're getting the chicken."

"Right, the chicken." Angélica grimaced as she took the two cups of *balche* Francisco had brought her. After thanking him, she offered one of them to her father.

"No way."

"Come on, don't be a wimp about it." She softened her words with a grin and offered the cup to Quint. He held up his own to show her he already had one.

Pedro snickered. "Remember that time Juan got so drunk on *balche* that he strapped himself to the altar with duct tape and chanted for twenty minutes?" He took the cup she held out to him and continued. "And when you cut him loose, he tore off his clothes and jumped into the *cenote* with nothing on but his underwear?"

"Mom made me dive in and save him. She would have done it, but she was laughing so hard she didn't think she could swim."

Juan grunted. "I explained to all of you ya-hoos that I was momentarily transformed into a *Chilam Balam*."

"What's a *Chilam Balam*?" Quint asked.

"A Jaguar priest of the ancient Maya," she said. "*Chilam Balam* would predict the future."

"What was your prediction?" Quint asked Juan.

Juan stroked his index finger over his chin, frowning in thought. Then he shrugged. "I don't remember."

Angélica nudged his leg with her shoulder. "Didn't it have something to do with the Lakers winning the championship?"

Juan snapped his fingers. "That's right. And they did, too!" When the laughter settled, Juan snorted. "You two need to get new stories and leave this poor old man alone."

Pedro hiccupped. "Poor old man, my ass! I'll never forget that time you talked me into rubbing *achiote* seed paste on my arms."

"I really thought it'd get rid of the chigger bites."

"It took two weeks to get my skin back to brown."

Quint leaned back in his chair, breathing in the fog of incense surrounding them. He sipped his cup of *balche*, letting the sweet wine swill on his tongue. He could get used to this …

Two hours later his lips were numb, and he couldn't feel his toes.

Juan snoozed in his chair, his chin resting on his chest. Meanwhile, Pedro was trying to count the lines on his palms but kept losing his place and having to start over.

Angélica still sat on the ground with her legs stretched out in front of her. She stared into the fire, her thoughts obviously elsewhere.

Steel and several of the others had disappeared, probably retired to their tents.

When Quint lowered his drink to the ground, standing up to stretch, she snapped out of her daze.

"What time is it?" she asked him.

"Just after eleven."

"I would have thought Esteban and Rafael would've been back with the chicken by now." She pushed to her feet, staggering slightly. "My foot's asleep," she explained when she turned down his hand to help steady her.

"They did come back, don't you remember?"

"Nuh-uh."

"Oh, that's right. You went to the bathroom."

"Good, I missed it. I hate that part."

He watched Teodoro carry a wooden cross and a gourd cup toward the Temple of the Crow. "What's he doing?"

"This is another step in the ritual. He's going to place the cross, some rum, and a piece of black obsidian on the ground to protect us. He'll do that three more times, as if in the corners of a square. Then he'll make more offerings to the *alux*, burn more incense, and chant at the altar for a while longer. Eventually, intoxicated by all the *balche* he's been drinking, he'll have a vision of the future and share it with the men. We're hoping his words will reassure them that the wind spirits have been called to protect them."

"And then they'll stay?"

"Keep your fingers crossed." She searched the area. "So where are Esteban and Rafael now?"

"Juan mentioned they were cleaning up at the *cenote*."

"How long ago did they leave?"

He thought for a moment and then looked down at her. "Maybe half an hour ago."

She watched Teodoro move to the next corner. "I'm going to go to the *cenote* and make sure the boys find their way back okay."

"Not alone, you aren't." Not with someone possibly waiting in the forest to do who-knew-what to her.

She studied Quint for several seconds, her lips pursed. "Okay, you can come with me. But be careful where you step. The snakes are hard to see at night." She headed toward the forest.

Quint grabbed his flashlight, jogging to catch up with her. "What kind of snakes are we talking about here? The venomous ones?"

Dodging a low-hanging limb, she stepped onto a well-worn path, her light leading the way. "The ones that eat the rats hiding in the bushes next to the trail."

Great. Snakes and rats. Didn't they have any cute, furry bunnies down here? Hell, he'd take an ugly possum over another venomous predator.

The glow from the fire disappeared as they moved deeper into the forest. Darkness cloaked them, broken only by their flashlight beams and shafts of moonlight. Angélica maneuvered through the shadow-filled brush as easily as if she were threading through tables in the mess tent.

Now that he had her to himself, maybe it was time to tell her about Mrs. Hughes and why he was really here. After all, with the new information about the plane crash on the table before him, it didn't look like he needed to spend any more time figuring out what had happened to Dr. Hughes.

She led him around a large tree standing in the middle of the path. "We're almost there." She looked over her shoulder at him. "You doing okay?"

"Angélica," he started and then tripped over a tree root. He stumbled into her, his weight shoving her off the trail. She corrected course, holding onto him, but then toed a stone jutting out into the trail. Still tangled up, they both hit the ground, rolling as the path dipped down a steep hill.

Her grip on him slipped as they tumbled. Quint lost track of her while trying to stop himself by grabbing onto tufts of grass and bushes. He heard her grunt somewhere below him, and then she grasped his leg as he slid past her. But he had too much momentum. Instead of stopping, he spun around and skidded headfirst for several more feet, dragging her along until they finally came to a dusty stop.

"Shit." He spit out a mouthful of dust. He rolled over onto his back and wiped his mouth on his shirtsleeve, cleaning the grit off his tongue.

The half-moon shone through the opening in the tree canopy overhead. The jungle was silent for several breaths, and then the nightly serenades started up again.

Angélica leaned over him, the moon lighting half of her face as she stared down at him. "Are you okay, Quint?" She ran her hands over him. "Is anything broken?"

He tested his limbs, moving them slowly. "No, I think I'm fine. What about you? I heard you grunt."

"Lucky for me, a tree stopped me from falling into the *cenote*." She pointed over his head.

He twisted his neck to look. A black hole yawned in the earth a few steps away.

"Shit, that was close." He stared back up into her face. "If you hadn't grabbed my leg …"

"I'd have been jumping in after you."

"How far down is it to the water?"

"Twenty feet or so."

He replayed the whole circus act over in his head. Laughter bubbled in his chest and then floated to the surface. "Hot damn, boss lady. You sure know how to show a guy a good time."

She kissed him, hard and demanding, knocking every coherent thought out of his head. Her lips tasted sweet from the *balche*, and when she touched her tongue to his, he forgot to breathe for several seconds.

She sank down onto him, all soft curves and heat. Her lower body pressed against his, her legs straddling him. He groaned, his hands traveling south over her curves, rounding her hips. He shifted her against him, starting a friction that shot fire through his veins.

She pulled back slightly. "Oh, Quint," she whispered. "I really like that."

Rolling her onto her back, he trailed his fingers up along the side of her breast, tracing the contour. "You're gonna like this even better."

He slid his hand under her T-shirt, skimming his fingers along the soft skin of her stomach. She arched into his touch, her breaths short and fast as he made his way north.

There was a rustle in the bushes across the *cenote*. Something splashed into the water below.

He hesitated, squinting in the moonlight toward the direction of the sound.

"What was that?" She sat up, twisting around. "Did you see anything?"

"No."

She rose to her knees and peered over the edge of the *cenote*. "I think there's something down there in the water."

He grabbed onto the waistband of her pants to keep her

from falling in. "What is it?"

"I'm not sure." She strained further. "It kind of looks like …" Her body stiffened. She gasped.

"What is it?"

"Oh, no!" She yanked free of him, leaning further.

Quint joined her at the edge. "What?" He saw nothing beyond the moonlight reflecting off the water below.

"It's Esteban." She shoved to her feet, glancing wildly at the bushes surrounding them. "I've got to do something."

Quint realized her intention a moment too late. He reached for her leg. "Angélica, don't …" but he missed.

She leapt over the edge of the *cenote* and vanished into the darkness.

Chapter Fifteen

Tok: An obsidian blade used in bloodletting.

Angélica burst up through the *cenote*, searching for Esteban across the surface of the dark, cool water. There he was off to her right, floating on his back. Reflections of moonlight glittered like diamonds on the small waves she made as she paddled over to him.

"Esteban?" She grabbed his arm, towing him closer. "Esteban, can you hear me?"

He didn't answer.

She touched his neck, searching for a pulse while treading water.

"Angélica," Quint hollered from above, his deep voice echoing off the limestone walls.

Don't be dead. Please don't be dead. She closed her eyes in concentration, focusing.

"Angélica, are you okay?"

She moved her fingers slightly, trying not to shake as she waited for a sign of life.

Rustling sounds came from overhead. Pebbles plunked into the water at the edge of the *cenote*. "Angélica, answer me or I'm coming in."

She felt it! Weak and slow but definitely a pulse.

"Wait!" she called to Quint. "I'm all right." She pulled Esteban closer, amazed that he was out cold yet floating face-up. What was keeping him from flipping over?

"What about Esteban?"

"He's unconscious." She ran her palm over his head and paused when she felt an egg-sized bump at the base of his skull. "He's got a bump on his head."

"Any other injuries that you can tell?"

"I'm checking." She skimmed her hands over his shoulders and ribs, then down the side of his baggy shorts toward his legs, sweeping over what felt like a piece of plastic.

What was that? She dug into his front short pocket and pulled out a sealed plastic sandwich bag. A silver watchband gleamed in the semi-darkness. She reached under him and checked his other pocket, drawing out another bag with a Rosary stuffed into it. "You've got to be fucking kidding me."

So that was what kept him face-up. The sandwich bags had saved his life. She was flabbergasted. There must have been just enough air in each of them to keep him from rolling. What were the chances?

She stuffed them back into his pockets. The way things looked down here at water level, she needed all the help she could get at the moment. As she pulled her hand back, her fingers touched a piece of rope. She followed its length. Her breath caught when she realized that it was binding his wrists together.

"What in the hell is this?" She fished her Swiss army knife from her pocket and cut the rope. As she snapped the knife closed, it slipped from her wet hands and plopped into the water. She tried to catch it as it sank but missed in the dark water.

"Damn it." She cursed her clumsiness and threw the cut rope off to the side of the *cenote*. This was no curse and definitely no accident.

"What's going on down there?"

"You don't want to know." She lifted his left eyelid, unable to see the pupil in the weak moonlight. "I need your flashlight," she hollered up at Quint. "I dropped mine when we fell down the hill."

"Is it waterproof?"

"All of the flashlights at the dig are waterproof. They float, too."

"Heads up. It's to your right." A small splash sounded as it hit the water. "You need to take off your hiking boots, Angélica. They're too heavy to tread water for long."

She swam over and grabbed the light, then paddled back. "I can't. They're laced up all the way and double-knotted. Besides, I don't have time." She lifted Esteban's eyelid again, shining the light into his pupil. "Oh, shit." She opened the other lid.

"What?"

"His pupils aren't dilating, his pulse is weak, and his breathing is shallow." She shined the beam around the limestone walls. "I have to get him out of here fast."

Where was the goddamned rope ladder?

"Quint, I need you to look around the edge of the *cenote*. There should be a rope ladder somewhere up there."

She tried to ignore the balloon of anxiety expanding in her chest. Panic was not the solution at this point.

"We usually leave it hanging down into the water in case somebody slips and falls in," she called up, still holding onto Esteban. "But I don't see it anywhere."

Quint had been right about her boots. They felt like ten-pound barbells dangling from her ankles. She released Esteban, using her arms to keep afloat. She needed to save the strength in her legs for the climb up the ladder with him in tow.

More pebbles cascaded over the edge from above and plopped into the water.

"Come on, Quint," she whispered, a chill seeping up her

legs.

"I can't find it," he called down.

She hit him in the face with the flashlight beam.

He squinted in the brightness. "Not without that light anyway."

"Damn it." She directed the beam back on Esteban. His lips were starting to look blue. She had to get him out of the water, or he'd go into shock ... if he hadn't already.

"There are some vines in the trees," Quint said. "I could lower one down and pull you out."

"It won't work. Not with him unconscious. There's no way I can hold his weight." She blew out a breath, knowing what she needed to do. Her chest tightened at the thought of doing it. "Listen, Quint, I have a plan."

"I can tell by the tone in your voice that I'm not going to like it."

"There's an underwater passageway between this sinkhole and the cave that I dragged Jared into last week."

"How do you know?"

"Because this *cenote* is part of an underground river system. A couple of years back, we hired a hydrogeologist to visit the site along with some divers. They mapped the tributaries leading in and out of the *cenote*." She paused to catch her breath.

"Nope. I definitely don't like this plan. Come up with another."

"According to the divers," she continued, "the tunnel is about four feet in diameter most of the way." She didn't want to think about the section at the end that supposedly narrowed before emptying into the river.

"No, Angélica. Do *not* try it."

"It's only about fifteen feet long if I remember right. With your light, I think I can swim both of us through—"

"That's an insane plan, woman!"

"—the passage and into the river. You can meet me in the cave, and we'll carry him back to the site." She waited for another comment from him, but none came. "One more thing, make sure you take the left fork, not the right."

"Here's a better, more sensible plan. You wait right there for me to go get help."

She checked on Esteban. His breathing was too shallow. "We don't have time for being sensible. I need to get him out of this water. If he stops breathing, he'll start to sink, and then we're in big trouble."

"Christ," he growled.

"Besides, you were right about my boots. My legs are getting tired. I don't think I can tread water for another ten minutes while I wait for you. If I go through the tunnel, we could be out of the water in half that time."

"He can't hold his breath when he's out cold. You're going to drown him taking him under there."

He had a good point, but by the looks of things, another ten minutes in this water and Esteban would go into shock, and who knew what would happen then. Her odds were better taking the underwater passage. "I know CPR. I can bring him back on the other side if he swallows water. Just meet me in the cave."

"I can't! I don't even know where the damned thing is."

Oh, hell! She hadn't thought about that. "Okay, go back and get Teodoro, Pedro, and Dad. They know where the cave is. While you do that, I'll take Esteban through the passageway. Tell Teodoro to bring his bag and some blankets. He may have to work on Esteban in the cave if he's too far gone."

"There has to be another way."

"I wish to God there was."

"I don't want you to do this."

"I don't want to either, but I don't have much choice."

She looked around the *cenote* walls, trying to get her bearings, remembering the details of the underwater map. The passageway to the cave was on the north side, the entry point twenty-four feet from the lip of the *cenote*. When the water table was low, and the sun was overhead, she could see it under the surface. Lucky for her, it had been a dry year so far. She shined the light under the water at the wall in front of her, searching left and right.

There it was about five feet down—a dark circle.

"Quint, do you think you can get back to the site without a flashlight?"

"Yes."

"Good, because I'm tired of talking about this." She shined the light at him. "Now go! And keep an eye out for Rafael on your way. He might have witnessed what happened to Esteban." She prayed she wouldn't run into Rafael below the waterline. Dead.

"Okay, I'm going." Quint shielded his eyes from her light. "But you get your ass in and out of that passage as fast as you can. You understand me, woman? No fucking around in there."

"Trust me, I won't dilly dally."

"Good, because you and I have some unfinished business." He disappeared from view, leaving her alone with the moon glowing overhead and the water lapping around her.

"Quint was right," she whispered, drawing Esteban toward her. "This is insane."

She treaded water for several seconds, trying to build up her courage.

Esteban wheezed next to her and then coughed.

"Esteban." She shined the light across his profile. "Open your eyes if you can hear me." She spoke in his native tongue in hopes of getting through to him.

His lids opened a little, then even wider as he looked around. He began to struggle, but he was too weak to do more than squirm in her arms.

"Esteban, be still."

He obeyed, groaning in pain, staring dully up at her.

"Esteban, listen closely to my words. We're in the *cenote*. I need to get you out of here, but you're hurt and the only way out is for me to take you under the water and through a short passageway. We will come out in the river inside the cave." Fifteen feet was sort of short anyway. "Do you understand what I'm saying?"

His eyes started to roll back in his head.

She squeezed one of his arms hard. "No, Esteban! You have to stay awake for me."

His eyes opened, blinking. He looked dazed but awake.

"You have to hold your breath for thirty seconds. Do you think you can do that?"

He frowned. "Yes," he said, barely audible.

"Okay. I'm going to count to three. Then I want you to take a deep breath and hold it until you reach the river. We'll get you up on the bank and help will be there soon."

She hoped.

She wrapped her arm around his ribcage. "Ready?" Ignoring her pounding heart, she took several quick breaths. "One, two," she drew in as much air as her lungs could hold, "three!"

She dove under the water, dragging Esteban down with her. She kicked hard, struggling, trying not to lose her grip on the flashlight as she towed him with her. As she swam into the tunnel, she had to let Esteban slide toward her feet. She kept a firm, one-handed grip on his arm, careful not to kick him with her boots as she swam. The current helped to pull them along the passage as it flowed out of the *cenote* into the river.

She pointed the flashlight in front of her. The beam cut through the clear water. Keeping her mind on the task at hand, she tried not to focus on the walls of the passageway getting tighter and tighter.

Up ahead, she saw a dark hole where the tunnel met the river. The divers hadn't exaggerated. It was a narrow hole. They'd have to squeeze through one at a time to make it.

She was able to move quicker now, using the walls of the passageway to propel them along. She stretched her hand forward and reached for the edge of the dark opening.

Something caught her foot, yanking her backwards.

She bumped into Esteban, sending him into the tunnel wall. A shine of light in his face showed his cheeks puffed out with air, his eyes darting around the tight space.

Angélica tugged on her foot but couldn't pull free. She looked down, the glow of the flashlight dimmer down by her legs. Her bootlace was snared on something she couldn't see in the swirling water.

Shit! Her heart pummeled her ribs, determined to break out and swim to the surface.

She had to get Esteban out of the tunnel, or they were both going to drown in here. Waving her hand in front of his face to get his attention, she pointed toward him and then the hole.

He frowned, pointing back at her.

Angélica shook her head and started pulling him up past her and then pushing him toward the opening. He grabbed the edge of the tunnel and with a final shove from her, squeezed through.

As his feet disappeared from view, fear took hold of her, chilling her to the bone along with the cold water churning and bubbling around her.

Her lungs were starting to burn.

Her legs ached from swimming so long in her damned boots. Her muscles were slowing, starved for oxygen. She probably had twenty more seconds to free herself or she was up shit creek. Or under it.

She shined the beam on her boot, bending down to take a closer look. Her vision blurred, panic trying to take over. She shook her head, forcing herself to focus on her boot lace. The loop of her shoestring was lodged in a narrow crevice between a piece of rock jutting out and the cave wall. She tried to tug the string out the way it had gone in, but it wouldn't budge.

Just her fucking luck! She'd bought these damned industrial strength laces last fall. If only she hadn't dropped her knife in the *cenote*.

Several bubbles of air escaped through her nose.

Her eyes felt like they were bulging out of their sockets.

She tried to loosen the double knot, but it wouldn't give. *Son of a bitch!*

She let out several more bubbles, starting to feel a bit lightheaded.

Her ears began to ring.

Grasping the heel of her boot, she tugged down on it, trying to wrench her foot free. But the laces were too tight up top.

She pulled and pushed, slicing her finger on one of the eyehooks.

Panic won, gripping her. Any last bits of control bubbled out and up as she struggled for freedom.

Her lungs were on fire.

Her leg muscles were shaking uncontrollably, along with her arms.

This was not how she'd hoped to leave this world. Not twenty thousand fucking leagues under the *cenote*, damn it!

Burrowing her finger under the laces where they crisscrossed up on the ankle of the boot, she heaved on one of the strings until it felt like it was digging into her fingers. She stretched it as far as she could, and then forced it over the eyelet hook holding it in place, cutting her fingers again. Through her panic, she forced herself to focus and slipped the loose lace over another hook and then another. As soon as she had enough slack near the knot, she freed the other lace, too. When she had the laces unwound from all three sets of hooks, she yanked her foot free of the boot.

Fired up with adrenaline, she swam like demons were at her feet.

She scraped her way through the opening, slamming her knee into the side.

The last of her air bubbled out, the pain in her lungs stabbing, burning a hole clear through them.

Kicking and clawing her way toward the surface, she inhaled. Her body sought oxygen, but she swallowed water instead and kept swimming up, up, and … She breached the surface, erupting into the dark cave.

She coughed out water, gasping on oxygen. Her lungs filled with delicious, musty cave air. Oh, sweet Mother Mary, she was alive.

Holy fuck.

That had been close.

Esteban!

Still coughing out water, she shined the flashlight around her. "Esteban," she called.

She allowed the flow of the river to carry her along a little way, thinking that he might have passed out again and be floating downstream.

What if she never found him? What if she'd sent him through that hole to his death? She slapped down her fears.

"Esteban, where are you?" she hollered, searching the shoreline.

A low groan came from further up the bank.

There he was sprawled out on the rocks.

She sloshed out of the water and bent over him. "Esteban, we made it."

"*La cabeza*," he groaned, reaching up to rub his head.

As his arm passed in front of the flashlight beam, she saw something red on his wrist. Had he cut himself going through the tunnel?

She caught his hand and flipped it over, focusing the light on his palm and then slowly moving it down. Watery blood dripped out of a deep cut in his wrist. Oh, Jesus. How long had he been bleeding?

Then she remembered the rope that had been binding his wrists. Her pulse jumpstarted anew. She grabbed his other wrist and checked it with the light. It also had a horizontal slice across his skin oozing blood.

Esteban went limp in her hands.

She lowered his arm and sat down next to him, pulling him into the warmth of her lap. They were several yards down from the opening that led to the underground cave, but she decided against moving him any further. He was too weak. He'd never make it without more help.

She was running out of time. If Quint hadn't made it back to the site yet—no! She couldn't let her mind go there.

She shifted under Esteban's weight and her tender knee collided with something hard in the back of his pants. Reaching down, she unsnapped his back pocket and pulled out a thin, triangular-shaped stone about the length of her pinkie. Its point had been sharpened.

She wrapped it in her fist. This was some holy fucked up shit!

She peered into the shadows surrounding her, her teeth beginning to clatter. The sound of rushing water drowned out almost everything except her jackhammering heart.

No matter how many ways she tried to bend the truth, she couldn't deny the evidence before her.

Esteban hadn't fallen into the *cenote*; he'd been sacrificed.

She had the *tok* to prove it.

* * *

"Good morning, boss lady."

Angélica lifted her forehead from the table and stared across the mess tent. Quint leaned against the counter, his arms crossed. Except for the dirt stains on the khaki pants that he still wore from the night before, he looked like he'd been touring the site rather than rolling around on the jungle floor with her.

She was so whipped she hadn't even heard him come in. She tried to smile, straining to lift the edges of her mouth. "How is he?"

"Weak but stable. He's still unconscious. Teodoro says he doesn't think Esteban will be capable of answering any questions for a day or two."

"Did he say anything about Pedro flying him to the hospital in Cancun?"

"No. Juan said Teodoro is insisting the boy will be okay after some rest and a visit to the little clinic at the village."

Her father stepped inside the entrance, patting Quint's shoulder on his way to the coffee carafe. "You found her; good job, Watson." Juan frowned when he turned and really looked at her, coffee in hand. "*Gatita*, you should go to bed. You look—"

"Like hell, I know," Angélica finished for him. She felt like petrified dinosaur dung. Her lungs still ached, her knee throbbed, and her head pounded. "I just need more coffee, and I'll be fine." She lifted her cup to her mouth, grimacing at the taste of bitter coffee. She hadn't had the energy to seek out cream and sugar this morning.

"I'm not sure coffee has that kind of power," Quint said, sitting across from her.

Juan headed for the kitchen. "You need to take a day off," he told her in his fatherly voice before disappearing from view.

"You doing okay?" Quint asked. At her nod, he asked, "What happened to your boot?"

"It fell off."

His eyes narrowed. "It just fell off, huh? Laced all of the way up and double-knotted."

She shrugged and then winced at the pain that came with it.

He pointed at the bandage on her finger. "What about that?"

"I sliced it on a sharp rock when I was crawling out of the river," she lied. The embarrassing moment of her panicky attempt to free her bootlace was her secret. No one needed to know how close she'd come to losing it down there in that tunnel.

"How's Rafael?" She changed the subject.

"Shaken up, sore, and suffering from one hell of a headache. He didn't get the full treatment Esteban received, but the goose egg on his head feels as hard as an elbow. Looks as big as one, too."

"It's too bad he doesn't remember anything. They must have been jumped close to the same time. It makes me wonder how many thugs we're dealing with here." And why would they sacrifice Esteban? Were they cult members? Or was that a show of their strength? In her opinion, they were a bunch of goddamned cowards, afraid to step out of the jungle and face her.

"Who was watching the camp last night?" Quint asked.

"Lino's shift started at ten, but he says he didn't see anything suspicious."

Juan came out from the kitchen with a leftover *gorda* tortilla stuffed with tomato and beans and sat down next to Quint. "From now on, let's put two men on patrol for each shift. Jared volunteered to step up tonight."

She stared down at the black liquid in her cup. "How many more are leaving?"

"Five, including Esteban," Quint said. "Teodoro is taking him to the village clinic tomorrow as soon as he feels Esteban can travel. The others are heading out at dawn."

She shook her head in defeat, too tired to do more right now. The *Lolcatali* ceremony had been a waste of time.

"That leaves us with eight men, not including Fernando. Doubling up is going to put a crimp in what we can accomplish while the sun is shining."

Juan reached over and gently squeezed her hand. "There's more, *gatita*. Teodoro said there are rope burns on Esteban's wrists."

"I know. I freed his wrists while we were in the *cenote*. Someone must have tied them behind his back after they sliced them." She reached into her pocket and pulled out the triangular stone she'd been hanging onto since she'd made it out of the river. "I found this small *tok* blade in his pocket while I was waiting in the cave for you guys."

Juan paled. "*¡Dios mío!*"

She palmed it again. "Esteban was sacrificed."

"Why?"

"Maybe it's some weird cult," Quint replied, picking up on her earlier wavelength.

"We need a gun," Angélica told her father. "Sticks and harsh language aren't going to stop whoever is messing with us."

"We're not commandos, *gatita*. We're scientists. I haven't fired a gun in over a decade, and that one was full of pellets."

"I'm tired of sitting here on my hands while my men are picked off one by one."

"We could search the surrounding jungle," Quint suggested. "Play some offense instead of defense."

"It's no use," she said. "There's a lot of jungle out there. We'd have better luck finding Bigfoot. Plus we risk somebody getting lost or bit."

"Maybe we should call in the *federales*," her father said.

"No!" Angélica shot to her feet. That was not an option. "We do that, and they'll shut down the dig for the rest of the season."

Juan frowned. "You don't know that for sure."

"I've seen it done at other sites, Dad. They'll want to do a thorough investigation. And if they don't find who's behind this right away, they might not let us start up again next season." She crossed her arms over her chest. "We can't risk that. Not when we're this close."

He pinched the bridge of his nose, shaking his head, but didn't argue further. She'd convinced him, for now.

"You'd rather risk more lives?" Quint butted in.

He didn't understand the full penalty of shutting down this dig site, the years of work that would be put on hold indefinitely, including their search for the proof. Without that shell, she'd never be able to save her mother's reputation.

"I'd rather find out who is behind this and take care of it myself than involve the Mexican government and all of its red tape."

She didn't want to discuss this anymore. Her head hurt, her body ached. She wanted to go to her tent, close her eyes, and forget about it all for several hours.

"And what about what your men want?" Quint wouldn't let it go.

This was her dig site, her crew, her huge fucking disaster. Who was he to question her choices? His job was to write a damned article and that was it.

"My men need money to feed their families. *Wants* often

take a backseat to *needs* down here."

"Angélica, listen," Juan started in his peacekeeping tone. "You're tired and not thinking clearly at the moment. Maybe we should all—"

"And if they don't want to stay?" Quint pushed, going head to head with her.

"The exit door is open for everyone." She leaned over the table, bearing down on him. "Including you."

Chapter Sixteen

Hypothesis vs. Theory: Hypothesis implies insufficient proof to provide more than a tentative explanation. Theory implies a greater range of proof and a greater likelihood of truth.

Lunchtime rolled around all hot and sweaty.

Quint loaded his plate with a fat *panucho* and carried it over to where Juan was sitting alone at a table, reading a thick book full of pictures of Maya symbols.

"I've made a decision," he told Juan, taking the seat across from him.

Juan peered at Quint over the rim of his glasses. "What's that?"

"For my next article, I'm writing about the Polar Bear plunge. Want to throw on some swim shorts and join me in the icy water?"

"You'll freeze your kibbles and bits off."

"Nah, they already melted away this morning."

Juan grinned. "Tell you what. If you stick around and help us wrap up the season here, I'll jump in with you."

"A couple more weeks in this heat?"

"I'll even go commando."

"Deal." He perused the mess tent as he chewed on a piece of María's tangy chicken, noting the empty lunch tables. The place felt like Bourbon Street on Ash Wednesday. Where was Angélica? Was she still pissed at him? "So, has your daughter always been this stubborn?"

"No. She's getting worse with age."

"Where is she anyway? Sleeping?" He tried to keep his interest casual sounding.

"Last I checked her tent was empty." Juan pulled a handkerchief from his pocket, took off his glasses, and began to clean them. "But knowing Angélica, she's probably in the Temple of the Water Witch."

Didn't that woman ever sleep? Quint took another bite of his *panucho*, trying to remember Juan's words during the ceremony last night about that temple. What had he said? That something had been in there all along?

Quint glanced up to find Juan watching him with one raised eyebrow. "Why do you ask?" Juan asked.

"I need to talk to her about what happened this morning." He'd overstepped his boundaries and wanted to clear the air.

"You do realize she was exhausted after the whole Esteban accident? That's the only reason she said what she did to you."

"She was right. It's not my place to interfere."

"You've been working alongside of us. That gives you as much right as anyone else on this site to question her reasoning, whether she likes it or not."

"That's easy for you to say. You're her father." Quint swatted away a fly trying to land on his plate. "I'm just a journalist here to write a story."

As far as they were concerned anyway.

"Well, you started out that way." Juan slid his glasses back on, stuffing the handkerchief in his pocket. "She needs your help. We both do. In case you haven't noticed, we're short a few men. We need you to meet Angélica's objectives set for this year."

"What happens if she doesn't meet her objectives?"

"She'll be written up by her superiors, possibly even be pulled from future work at this site."

Quint paused, his next bite halfway to his mouth. "Just because she didn't meet her objectives for one year? That seems irrational."

"It comes down to the fact that she's not local. She may live south of the border for much of the year, but she's not a Mexican citizen. There are a lot of local archaeologists who would love to take over this site. As long as she keeps meeting her goals, the National Institute of Anthropology and History will continue to allow her to work at this dig site and possibly others as requested. But if she fails, she could end up as an assistant on some less prestigious dig and not be able to set foot on this site again until they open it to the public."

Her stubbornness was beginning to make sense.

"So you see, we need your help for however long you are willing to give it. Pedro has agreed to stay here for a week more than he originally planned, and if I can get Jared to take on part of the workload, Angélica could still reach her objectives this season."

Juan could get more than he bargained for from Steel. Quint had trouble believing the snooty professor would be willing to contribute without a steep price.

"But more important than any of those reasons," Juan leaned forward, "I need you to stay for my daughter's sake."

Quint frowned, not certain what that meant.

"I may be old, but I'm not blind. My daughter hasn't shown so much interest in a man since the early days with Jared."

"I ... uhh ..." He shoved a bite of tortilla in his mouth to fill the useless gaping hole.

"Or frustrate her as much as you do."

He gulped down the bite. "Pissing off women is my specialty."

Juan grinned. "I see that. I also see that you can give her something the rest of us here can't."

As much as this conversation with the father of the woman he'd been lusting over lately was making him want to slide under the table, curiosity got the best of him. "What's that?"

"A ch—"

"¡*Díos mío!*" Pedro cut in, dropping onto the bench next to Quint. "I feel like someone hit me on the head with a bag full of coconuts." He rested his head in his hands.

Juan pushed his coffee cup toward him. "Drink up. It's María's magic elixir."

"What time is it?" Pedro grabbed the cup and swallowed it all down. He slammed the cup down on the table and winced at the noise it made.

"Lunch time."

"Damned *balche*." He glanced around the mess tent. "Where is everyone? This place is like a town of ghosts."

"Well, sleeping beauty, while you were busy sawing logs last night, Angélica was doing her best to save Esteban, who'd been sacrificed in the *cenote*."

Pedro hadn't been there when Quint raced back for help getting Esteban out of the cave. Juan told him later that Pedro had stumbled back to his tent soon after Quint and Angélica had gone to find the boys.

"No!" Pedro sat up straight, his eyes wide. "Is he alive?"

"Yes. Teodoro and a couple of the crew took him to the clinic in the village this morning. They should be back anytime now."

"Good. Where's Angélica?"

"In the chamber."

"Am I working with her this afternoon?"

"No." Juan closed his Maya symbol book and stood. "Quint is."

"I am?" That was news to Quint. He'd been in the Owl Temple with Fernando all morning.

Juan nodded. "Pedro will take your place with Fernando. I'd rather not have anybody working alone anymore, so plan on staying with her throughout the day."

"Okay." But he had a feeling Juan's daughter wasn't going to be happy about this change-up.

"Plus, Angélica needs to talk to you."

"About what?"

"Ask her." Juan flashed him a wink. "Pedro, Angélica wants to know if you carry a gun on that rig of yours?"

"A flare gun."

"Well, as much as I like roasted marshmallows, that's definitely not what we need with the jungle tinderbox dry right now. Never mind." He bade them goodbye and left.

"Where's Jared?" Pedro asked when they were alone.

Quint shrugged. He hadn't seen Steel since he'd helped carry Esteban out of the cave last night.

There was something about that whole rescue scene that made Quint uneasy. Neither bats nor blood had deterred Steel from helping. Sure, adrenaline could have been a factor. Maybe Steel had a superhero fantasy. Or it could be that Steel was desperate to impress his ex-wife and was giving it his all to win her back. Desperation would certainly explain the way his gaze locked onto Angélica whenever she was around, following her around like a love-starved puppy.

Then again, if Mrs. Hughes was on to something with Steel, maybe Quint's uneasiness was due to an underlying threat.

He finished the last bite of his *panucho* and then asked Pedro, "How well did you know Mrs. Hughes?"

Pedro shrugged. "We talked on the phone several times, but I never met her. *¿Por qué?*"

"I keep thinking about Dr. Hughes going down in that plane. I can't believe that after all of this time, that's all there is to the mystery of his whereabouts."

Pedro rubbed his temples. "Dr. Hughes was a good man. Pretty funny, too, when he wasn't working too hard." He stretched his neck from one side to the other. "You know one thing that I do not understand?"

"What's that?"

He focused on Quint, his gaze hawk-like. "You know how detail oriented Dr. Hughes was, right? Why didn't he call his wife and tell her he was taking a different flight home?"

* * *

Angélica was hiding from the world in the Temple of the Water Witch. The sub chamber was steamy, dark, and musty, but she was alone. No crew. No Jared. No Quint. Only ghosts and their stories carved into the walls.

She was being a big, fat chicken shit and she knew it. But between finding Esteban sacrificed and coming way too close to spending eternity in a watery tomb, burying her head in the past seemed like the thing to do. At least until she could breathe without feeling tightness in her chest and get a handle on what was happening at her dig site.

She leaned over the paper copy of the glyph she had just charcoaled, blowing off the excess dust. Her vision blurred as her thoughts strayed.

If only she hadn't morphed into Medusa in front of Quint this morning. Her father knew the stress she was under. He'd forgive her and understand the reasoning behind her harsh words about accepting the risks to her crew.

Quint, on the other hand, probably saw her for the snake-haired bitch she was. If he were as smart as he seemed, he'd be on his way to the nearest airport to catch a flight back to the States by now. This dig was sinking faster than the Titanic.

The sound of footfalls clapping on the dirt floor behind her made her neck prickle. She twisted around. Quint's shoulders filled the narrow entryway into the sub chamber as he angled into the small room.

Apparently, he wasn't that smart after all.

Or maybe he was the bearer of more bad news.

"What's wrong?" she asked, going up on her knees. "Did something else happen?"

"No." He couldn't stand fully with the low ceiling, so he squatted.

"Then why are you here?" As soon as the words escaped her lips, she winced. "Sorry. I didn't mean that to sound so bitchy."

He waved off her apology. "Your dad sent me here." He held out a piece of paper. "He even made me a map so I wouldn't get lost."

She took the paper without looking at it. "Why?"

"He doesn't want anyone working alone anymore, so he assigned me to you."

"Oh." Having a shadow wasn't going to work for her, and her father knew exactly why. Maybe he was referring to daytime work.

"He also said you need to talk to me."

Damn her all-too-knowing father. She did need to talk to Quint but not here, not yet. She still wasn't sure what to make of her growing attraction to him, and she needed to get a handle on her feelings before she fumbled through another intimate conversation with him. "I'm not sure what he's referring to," she said, buying time.

Turning back to the task at hand, she tried to remember what she'd been doing before Quint had filled the sub chamber with his presence and scrambled her brainwaves. Oh, right—the shell.

"Since you're here, you may as well grab that rice paper over there and help me copy glyphs."

Scraping sounds were followed by paper rustling. Then he was kneeling beside her, paper in one hand and flashlight in the other.

"What do you want me to do?" He shined the light on her notepad lying open on the floor next to her.

Fighting the urge to close it, she motioned to a diagram on the floor in front of him. "That's a chart of this wall, split into proportions that equal eight by ten inches when blown up to actual size."

He picked up the diagram and studied it under the light.

Leaning closer to him, she pointed at the numbers in the corner of each section. "These match the numbers on the relief copies. Upon completion, we'll be able to pin these copies on a wall in the lab and continue analyzing the meaning of all these glyphs in the comfort of air conditioning."

She was so close she caught a subtle whiff of his cologne or soap. It had a cedar scent with some sandalwood notes. A glance up made her realize she was close enough to count his eyelashes. They were thick and long. Not fair. Also not fair that he didn't seem at all flutter-pated about being so close to her while she was on the verge of a stroke from a sudden tidal wave of high blood pressure.

She moved away, putting some good ol' musty air between them, and began busily organizing the copies in front of her.

This chamber was too small for the both of them, damn it, and her father knew that. Playing matchmaker, was he? Two could play at the cupid game. There was a certain widow just down the road back home in Arizona who had taken a shine to her dad lately. Maybe Angélica could invite her over along with her collection of molted snakeskins.

"What are these marks on this diagram?" Quint asked.

"Those are the glyphs I've copied. I'm only about halfway done, as you can see." She grabbed a piece of charcoal from her tool pouch and placed it on the floor in front of him. "If you could make relief copies of as many of the remaining sections as you have time for today, and then label each with the appropriate number and place it on the stack to your right, it would be a big help. There's an extra lantern over there in the corner if you need it."

"Couldn't you take a bunch of pictures with a digital camera and use them instead?"

"We have pictures already, but they don't show details hidden in relief like charcoal does."

"Okay. I'm on it." He placed a sheet against the limestone and began rubbing the charcoal over it.

She wrote the number of the current copy on the paper in front of her, glad to have work to do. If Lady Luck was on her side, they could avoid any personal subjects and work in silence.

"I've been thinking about what you said this morning."

She blew out a big sigh. What had she done to piss off Lady Luck these days? Was this about that broken mirror in the showers? If so, that was Jared's fault for pissing her off with his blackmail bullshit.

"Listen, Quint." If he was going to take this road, she might as well head him off at the pass. "I was out of place earlier." She looked over to find him watching her, his piece of charcoal hovering in midair. "You raised some valid points about the welfare of my crew. I'm sorry for blowing up at you." Apology offered, now for the begging part. "And while you are more than welcome to leave, I need you here with us. Will you please consider staying on for a bit longer? I can pay you—"

"Stop right there." He lowered the paper and charcoal. "First of all, I won't take a dime from you for anything I do here. Second, you say you need me, right?"

She nodded.

"What do you mean by that?"

She knew exactly what he was fishing for, but there was no way in hell she'd bite on that hook. "I need your help. With so many from my crew gone, I don't know if I'll be able to meet my objectives." She tapped her pencil on her notepad, sending a prayer to the Maya gods that he'd let it go at that.

After staring at her so long she began to wonder if she had something on her face, he placed the paper against the wall again and brushed the charcoal against it. "That's not good enough for me, Angélica."

Come on! "What would be?"

"You kissed me last night." He kept his focus on the

paper.

Her blush made the chamber feel even warmer. "I did."

"Why?"

"It seemed like the thing to do at the time."

He rubbed charcoal in silence for a lengthy, unnerving moment. She picked up her notebook, crossing her fingers that they could now return to chronicling Maya life.

"Your father told me you haven't been interested in a man since you divorced Steel."

Her mouth fell open, her jaw weighed down by both embarrassment and exasperation. She fanned herself with her notebook. "My father needs to stop talking about me behind my back."

Quint glanced over, his eyes raking down her in a way that made her fan her notebook even faster.

"When all this is over, boss lady, you and I are going to go away somewhere for a while—alone." He handed his finished rub to her. "Then I'm going to show you why you really need me."

A bead of sweat rolled down the front of her shirt, soaking into her bra. "Is that part of the deal to keep you here until the dig season ends?"

"Nope." He grabbed another piece of paper and held it up to the next glyph. "It's a promise to you from me." He rubbed the charcoal over the sheet. "I'll stay on and help as long as you *need* me, if you'll come clean about something."

She braced herself. "What?"

"What are you looking for in this temple that's worth risking everything meaningful in your life?"

She hesitated, lowering the notepad to her lap. "What guarantee do I have that you won't publish what I say?"

"My word. That's all I can give."

She watched him work for several beats. "If you breathe one word of what I'm about to tell you to another soul, Quint Parker, I'll …" she paused, not sure how to finish.

"Angélica." He looked at her, no smile or grin or even a

twinkle in his eyes. "Trust me."

"That's easier said than done."

"I promise your secret is safe with me. Now spill it."

She stared down at the pencil in her dirty fingers, figuring out where to start. "My mother had a theory—not just a hypothesis. She published it a couple of years before her death. In it, she spelled out the reason for the mysterious disappearance of the Maya from large urban centers in this part of the Yucatán toward the end of the Classic period."

Angélica drew a heart in the dirt with her pencil eraser, remembering how excited and nervous her mother had been on the eve of her article coming out in one of the top archaeological magazines of the time. They'd all gone out to dinner to celebrate, toasting to a whole new future for her mother's career.

"But that theory made her the laughing stock of her peers in the archaeological community. They didn't believe her, but she didn't let that slow her down. 'Think of how many great scientists have been mocked early in their career,' she explained to me when I wanted to do something to shut them up. I even tried to convince her to sue for libel at one point." Angélica scratched out the heart in the dirt. "Instead, Mom continued searching to add to the proof she already had— namely, shells."

"Wait," Quint interrupted. "According to Fernando, you guys find shells in a lot of the tombs around here."

"That's true." She started drawing a cone-shaped shell next to the scratched out heart. "But the shells Mom was looking for specifically are called *Astraea Tecta*. They come from a very localized area in South America." She added the points on the bottom of the shell, then sat back to scrutinize her finished piece. "Mom's theory was that a South American tribesman got lost at sea and somehow ended up on Maya shores. Unfortunately for the Maya people, along with shells for trading, he also brought a nasty disease that none had been exposed to before."

"Mom found glyphs at Tulum, which is just southeast of here, that tell of the arrival on the coast of a strange merchant and the shells he carried with him. She searched Chichen Itza for signs of the shell but came up empty. She did, however, find a *stela* for a king who had died at a very young age. His death was around the same time as the demise of several other communities. Around this king's neck was a necklace with a shell that looked like an *Astraea Tecta*."

"Then wouldn't the shell be there somewhere?"

She shook her head, crossing out the drawing of it. "Some of the graves there had been looted in the early forties. We suspect the shell was one of the items stolen." She threw her pencil at her destroyed dirt masterpieces. "After that, Mom began to focus her energy on this site, but she died before getting very far on her research here. Since then, Dad and I have continued the search for the shell."

Leaning back, she rested on her hands. "Several weeks ago, I found a glyph in this temple that told of death arriving with a merchant—what you know as the 'curse' glyph. Since then, I've found several other artifacts with images of a king with a shell on his necklace. This shell fits Mom's description."

"Is this one of your objectives?"

"Not officially for the Mexican government, no."

"Is this the chamber you disappear to until late at night? Where you sneak off to early in the morning?"

"You've been listening to my comings and goings."

"There's not much to do around here after the sun goes down, and the TV in my tent doesn't seem to pick up any channels other than crawling ants and snow."

"How'd you score a TV?" she joked back.

He winked. "I do special favors for the boss."

"They're not special enough to score a TV." She waited for him to finish laughing and then returned to her story. "A couple of nights ago, Dad found a *stela* with a carving of the same king as before and the necklace with the shell. The carving was made *after* the king's death. But the *stela* was in the wrong temple, most likely moved by those amateur archaeologists I told you about. The corner was broken off, so I wasn't sure of its original location. But then Pedro and I found the corner a couple of nights ago, and then last night I was able to decipher that it belonged in the Temple of the Water Witch."

"Now we have plenty of signs pointing to this temple, but no actual shell as of yet." Sitting forward, she pulled her knees into her chest, wrapping her arms around them. "Somewhere within these limestone walls is the proof I need not only to clear my mom's name but also to put her life's work in history books for the world to read."

Lines formed on Quint's brow. "That's a noble cause, but is it worth risking your life?"

She scoffed. "I've spent the last three years looking for this damned shell. I'm not about to let whoever is trying to sabotage the dig stop me when I'm this close."

He nodded but said nothing.

"So, Parker, I've now held up my end of the deal." She rested her chin on her knees, wondering if she'd made the biggest mistake of her life by telling him her secret. "Are you going to stick around a little longer to watch the fireworks finale at the end?"

A smile crept up his face. "I'm not going anywhere without you, Angélica, especially if fireworks are involved."

Chapter Seventeen

Kinich Ahau & Kan ek' (the Sun god and the morning star, Venus): Sometimes shown together as they rise from the horizon at dawn.

Gatita, wake up."

Angélica opened her eyes.

The world had fallen over onto its side.

Wait. False alarm. She lifted her head, grimacing in the morning light. She pushed her hair out of her face and brushed off a paperclip that had stuck to her cheek. "What is it, Dad? Is something wrong?"

"Yes." He leaned down and kissed her forehead. "You've missed breakfast again."

"That's it?" She rubbed her eyes with the heels of her palms. "Nobody has been stung, bitten, cut, or sacrificed to the Maya gods?"

"Not yet but the day is young."

"Real funny. What day is it anyway?"

"Saturday. *Gatita,* you can't keep falling asleep at your desk like this. You're no spring chicken anymore. You'll get a crick in your neck and your back."

She wiped the sleep from her eyes. "Why are you really here, besides to harass me?"

He pulled a plate of scrambled eggs, bacon, and papaya out from behind his back. "To provide nourishment."

"Ah, *mi amor*," she said, taking the plate.

"Are you calling *me* your love or the food?"

"Both, but especially the bacon."

"Speaking of pig." He pulled out two thick tortillas. "I brought something for Stinky Poo, too. Where is he?"

"How many times do I have to tell you that Rover is not a pig, nor does he stink … not yet anyway." She stabbed her fork into her eggs and shrugged. "I'm not sure where he is this morning. He's been spending a lot of time in Quint's tent lately."

"Joint custody it is. That's nice."

"Knock it off. Quint feeds him more than I do. Rover's stomach rules his actions."

"What? It's nice you've found a new *friend*." He pushed aside a stack of books on her cot and sat down. "You know, I'm not getting any younger and neither are you."

"Where's this going?" She crunched on the bacon.

"It would be nice to hear the pitter patter of little feet around this place."

She should have known. "I'll buy you some baby ducks. They can waddle behind you wherever you go."

"I'm serious. Quint is a nice young man, and—"

She held up her hand. "Stop right there."

"What do you have against him?"

"Dad, I don't even know him."

"He's been here for almost two weeks. How much more time do you need to work your magic?"

"Jared and I were together almost a year before we got married."

"And look how that worked out for you. It's plain to see that giving you too much time to get to know a man isn't the solution. You need to speed things up."

"Well, then, why don't *you* court Quint for a couple of weeks and let me know when the time is right for me to jump in and get hitched."

"That's absurd."

"What's absurd is us having this discussion."

"You still don't trust him."

"Not completely, no." She popped a piece of papaya in her mouth.

"He's staying on to help us out."

"True, but how do I know that he isn't staying for the sake of that damned article, which," she paused in emphasis, "I haven't seen hide nor hair of since he arrived. And have you considered that maybe he's staying for some other reason that has to do with Dr. Hughes?" It would be shortsighted to totally ignore Jared's warning.

"Dr. Hughes is dead. Why would Quint want to stay because of him?"

"Hell, I don't know. At this point, I'm keeping both Quint and Jared under a microscope."

"You're wasting energy watching Quint. Jared, on the other hand, is a whole other case."

"Jared is nothing more than a paper tiger."

"Maybe so, but I'd rather he not be here when we find the shell." Juan plucked a couple of clean socks off her pillow and folded them together, reminding her of her mother. Next he would be telling her to clean her tent, just like old times. "He wants something down here."

"How do you know?"

He shrugged. "Call it father's intuition."

"I'll call it 'father's in an institution' if you keep up this kind of talk about Quint and me."

"Cute, *gatita*, but mark my words. Jared is up to no good. I can see it on his face when he watches you."

She wiped her hands on a dirty T-shirt drooped over the back of her chair. "Well, I can't find the shell, so it doesn't matter how he looks at me."

"What? I thought the answer was in that chamber."

"If it is, then I'm blind."

"Have you read through all of the glyphs?" Juan asked.

"Most. They tell factual things such as the date when the king died, his lineage, which takes up lots of space on the wall, and details of his wealth. But nothing about the shell."

"How can that be? The *stela* showed him with the shell on his necklace."

"I know. Maybe there are two different kings with similar names." She rubbed her forehead. "Maybe the carver of the *stela* was using artistic license to exaggerate what the shell really looked like."

"That shell is in that temple, *gatita*, but you're tired and frustrated and a little overstressed, so it's easier to give up right now than dig in and figure out the truth."

She studied the lines fanning from his eyes. "I don't know where to look next."

"I'll tell you what. Finish that last piece of papaya, take a shower, put on some fresh clothes, and go back in there tomorrow with Quint and just let your mind wander."

"I'll go back, but I'm not taking Quint."

"Angélica," he started in that stern, fatherly voice. The one that made her feel twelve all over again.

"No, Dad. We can't spare the manpower. We're behind schedule as it is. Believe me, I'll be better off working alone than with Quint sitting there watching me."

He sighed in resignation. "Fine. I'll take Jared with me in the Dawn Temple and send Quint and Pedro with Fernando to work on clearing out the rubble from Sub Chamber M in the Owl Temple. When Francisco gets back from the village later this morning, he can direct the others as they finish going through the middle GOK pile."

Juan stood, coming over and squeezing her shoulder. "We'll take care of the Mexican government's To-Do checklist for this year. You find that shell."

* * *

For lunchtime entertainment in the mess tent, Steel and Juan were performing a high-noon, verbal shootout. Quint watched the bullets flying back and forth along with Pedro and Fernando, none of them saying a word.

"While I concur that you have more experience in the field of structural architecture," Steel said to Juan, "I believe that your methods are antiquated."

Taking the last bite of his tangy, pork-filled taco, Quint's gaze bounced back and forth between the two archaeologists. Juan's face was lined with tension while his body appeared relaxed. Steel's face showed no emotion as he methodically cut his taco into smaller and smaller symmetrical pieces.

Who cuts a freaking taco? Nut jobs, that was who.

Juan took a sip of his coffee, his eyes narrowing as if he were either weighing his next words or the effects of dumping his drink on Steel's head. Quint couldn't tell which, but hoped like hell for the latter.

"Trust me," Juan spoke evenly. "The beams will hold."

"I didn't say they wouldn't. I said there are better, more modern methods to use that are less costly. Something you need to consider when petitioning for future grant money."

Pedro grunted something that sounded like "asshole" in Spanish, then he rose from the table with his empty plate and headed toward the counter.

Juan set his cup on the table with a small *thud*, splashing some coffee over the rim. "Point taken, Jared. Thank you for the advice."

Fernando shook his head, standing with his plate in hand. He looked down at Quint. "See you after your *siesta*."

"Actually, Fernando," Juan said, "I need Quint this afternoon. I believe Jared would be of more use to you."

Fernando's lips thinned.

Juan pointed at Fernando with his cup. "He could help you with the reconstruction of the fresco-covered wall."

A muscle at the back of Fernando's jaw twitched.

"Ah, yes, that fresco." Steel laid his fork on his half-finished plate and frowned up at Fernando. "I noticed the last time I was in there that your grids were not lined up properly."

Fernando gave Steel a flat stare, and then he turned to Juan and said something in Mayan. Juan fought back a grin but said nothing. Without another word, Fernando walked away, dropping his plate on the counter with a clang.

Juan looked at Steel. "Fernando can't wait to hear your thoughts on how to finish the wall."

Chuckling under his breath, Quint checked the tent entrance for the umpteenth time since he'd arrived for lunch. Where was Angélica? She'd skipped breakfast this morning; probably too busy working on deciphering the copies of those glyphs to remember food equals energy. He'd noticed Juan leaving the mess tent with a plate full of food and figured it was for her, which had killed his excuse for going to see her earlier. Now he wondered if anyone was taking her lunch.

Francisco appeared in the entrance, his gaze locking onto Quint.

"*Señor* Parker." Francisco joined them, holding out a package covered with Express labels.

Quint took the package. "*Gracias.*" He scanned the return address before stuffing the package partly under his thigh. It was from Jeff.

"Who's that from?" Steel nosed in.

None of your damned business. "A friend."

"You've received a lot of those Express envelopes since you arrived."

"What's your point?"

"You must have a lot of these so-called friends, or one in particular who misses you dearly." Steel pointed his fork at Juan. "Doesn't it make you wonder why your photojournalist keeps receiving all of these mysterious Express packages? What could be so important that it couldn't wait for him to get back home?"

Quint kept silent. He wasn't going head to head with Steel in front of Juan today. For one, Angélica's father was too sharp and might catch something Quint let slip in the heat of battle. For another, it was too damned hot to fight.

Juan shrugged, swishing the coffee in his cup. "Not really. Quint's business is his own." He glanced up at Quint with a devilish glint in his eyes, and then returned to Steel. "You of all people should understand that, Jared. If memory serves me right, you once had a talk with me about interfering with your marriage."

A spasm of irritation flashed across Steel's features. "I'd forgotten about that. It's interesting how time dims the importance of such minor annoyances."

"Interesting, indeed." Juan stood. "Quint, if you're up to it, I'd like to skip a *siesta* and get busy at the Dawn Temple as soon as possible."

Quint would rather find out what was in the package. Mrs. Hughes' notes were getting him nowhere fast. But that would have to wait. "I'm right behind you." He grabbed his plate and the package, rising.

"Parker." Steel had waited until Juan was out of earshot to speak.

Quint paused.

"I wonder how Angélica is going to react later tonight when I tell her that you received another package."

The fucker just had to have something to hold over everyone's heads. That was how he'd controlled the crew back when Dr. Hughes had ruled the roost, and probably how he'd manipulated Angélica and her father for years. It was no wonder she'd left him; she was way too headstrong for Steel to keep under his thumb for long.

"Good luck with that." Dealing with Steel was like stepping in dog poop. No matter how hard he tried to scrape the piece of shit off the bottom of his shoe, Quint couldn't quite get rid of the dickhead—nor his nastiness. Not even after twenty long years.

Steel smirked, stabbing a bite of taco. "I wanted to let you know ahead of time so you could start packing."

Christ! Were they still fighting over this bone?

"There's something you need to get straight." Quint leaned over the table, waiting for Steel to meet him eye-to-eye. "When it comes to this dig site *and* your ex-wife, I'm not going anywhere."

* * *

"Do you mind if I take a few photos in here?" Quint asked Juan as he followed him through a maze of corridors and shoulder-scraping passageways in the Dawn Temple.

After two weeks, he should be acclimated to the heat by now, but oh no, his blood was being stubborn about thinning. He swiped away a stream of sweat dripping from his chin.

"Not at all," Juan said, "But you might want to wait until we reach the sub chamber. There's some rubble up ahead from the ceiling falling apart that's dangerous if you aren't paying attention to where you're walking."

Quint groaned. "Great. I love walking through tunnels where the roof is partly on the floor. Makes a guy feel all warm and fuzzy inside."

Juan chuckled and continued forward. Several minutes later, he stooped under a very crooked beam. "Ah, here we are," Juan whispered in the gloom.

Quint tiptoed in after him, frowning when he saw the thirty-degree slant of the rock slab making up most of the chamber's ceiling. "Are you sure it's safe to bring visitors into this room?"

"Well, I wouldn't bet my retirement account on it, but sure, it's mostly safe." Juan turned on his lantern and tossed the flashlight he'd been using to Quint. "The ceiling doesn't move unless you hit the wall with something hard." He picked up a bat-sized piece of timber. "Something like this."

Juan swung the piece of wood at the wall.

"No!" Quint reached for the mad man.

Stopping the makeshift bat just short of the wall, Juan looked back at Quint, his eyes crinkled with laughter. "Gotcha." He dropped the wood and pulled a tape measure out of his front pants pocket.

Quint stumbled backward into the wall, holding his stampeding heart. "Pedro is right. You're insane."

"And you're gullible. But not as gullible as Pedro. He won't even come in this temple with me anymore."

He couldn't blame Pedro. Quint was surprised he hadn't pissed himself when Juan had swung.

"This room is relatively stable considering the looks of it," Juan mumbled around the pencil in his mouth. "It hasn't shifted since I got to this dig site."

Taking in the funhouse-like look of the room, Quint didn't feel comforted even a little by Juan's words.

"Go ahead and take some pictures." Juan pulled his glasses from his pocket. "If you can capture the tilt of the walls and ceiling, this place will look great in the magazine."

Quint moved silently around the room, snapping shots of the walls and ceiling, cracks and fallen rocks, and Juan as he took his measurements. The slide of the tape measure, the whispering of numbers, and the digital snapshot click were the only sounds as the two of them worked.

Shining the flashlight on a lower section of the wall furthest from the door, Quint moved closer and tried to make out the figures he could see on the pitted and worn fresco. He aimed his camera and snapped a picture, then paused as something below one of the figures caught his eye. He directed the beam on the picture, recognizing it with an inward gasp.

"Hey, would you look at this," he said, touching it.

He heard footfalls behind him. "What?"

"This." Quint pointed at the image. "It's a head variant for the Sun god."

Juan patted him on the shoulder. "Yes, *Kinich Ahau*, the

Sun god—very good. Where did you learn that?"

"Angélica told me when I showed her the drawing from the back of Dr. Hughes' journal. This head variant is on the back page."

"Oh, that's right. I'd forgotten about that." Juan sounded surprised.

Quint looked at the other images surrounding it, not recognizing any of them. "Interesting that it's here," he said more to himself than Juan as he walked away.

"Not really."

Quint turned, watching as Juan measured the width of the entryway. "It's not?"

"No. You can find some type of representation of the Sun god in several chambers in this temple. Same with *Kan ek'*, Venus as a morning star."

"Are they ever together?"

Juan nodded and shoved his pencil behind his ear. "Of course. Together they often signify *dawn*, as in sunrise. That's why I named this place the Dawn Temple."

Quint stared blankly at the head variant. Was Dr. Hughes referring to this temple with that drawing? Or was there something more to it? Was he giving a clue of some sort, or did he just like to doodle head variants?

He opened his mouth to ask Juan if he knew why Dr. Hughes would have drawn those head variants in his journal but stopped before uttering a word. He needed to think about this for a while. He wasn't sure if actually questioning Juan or Angélica about it was wise.

"If you're finished with your pictures, we can head down to the next chamber." Juan said, bringing Quint back to the present.

"Yeah, sure." He moved toward the entrance. He'd keep his eyes open for the rest of the afternoon. Maybe he could figure out what the drawing meant, if anything, on his own.

Juan waited for him in the hall, then led him deeper into hell, aka the Dawn Temple. Quint locked his focus on Juan's back to keep from grinding his molars down to nubs with every visible crack and crevice.

"While we're on the subject of Angélica," Juan said over his shoulder, "I have a question for you."

When had they been on the subject of Angélica? Oh, right, she'd explained the head variants. "Sure. Shoot."

"How old are you?"

What did that have to do with Juan's daughter? He ducked under another low beam, grimacing at the splintered crack running the length of the beam. "I'll be thirty-nine in a few months. Why?"

"Are there any little Quint Parker juniors running around back home or in past ports of lading?"

That question surprised Quint into standing upright, which resulted in smacking his head into the ceiling. "Ouch." He rubbed his head.

"I told you to wear that hard hat." Juan knocked on his own. "It only took me about two dozen hits to the old noggin' for me to learn my lesson. You okay?"

Quint nodded. "To answer your question, no, I have no offspring out there."

Juan led him into another sub chamber, shining the light over the patch of rubble on the floor, then up to the fractured-looking ceiling. "How do you feel about children?"

Rubbing his throbbing bump, Quint frowned at Juan. What in the hell did children have to do with any of this? Maybe he was making small talk or trying to distract him from the fact that they were bumping around in this death trap.

"That depends on the kid," he answered. "I love hanging out with my sister's twins. Whenever I'm back home, I spend as much time with them as possible."

Juan turned the beam on Quint's face, making him wince and shield his eyes. "You misunderstood my question. How do you feel about *having* children?"

Chapter Eighteen

Mentir: To tell an untruth; lie.

Quint had lied … sort of.

He'd told Juan that he hadn't thought about having kids because he'd been too busy building his career. Truth was he'd considered having kids ever since his sister had given birth to her twins almost a decade ago, but with as much traveling as he did each year, even finding a long-term girlfriend was tough.

But he wasn't comfortable telling the father of the woman he'd like to whisk away to some hidden bungalow and spend days and nights exploring every part of her body—and her mind—that he would like to have a kid or two someday. That might give Juan ideas about long-term commitment, and Quint knew from experience that women did not like being in a relationship with someone who was gone more than he was home.

After Quint's answer, Juan hadn't questioned him further about anything else domestic. Instead he'd wanted to hear about what being a photojournalist was like, the places Quint had traveled, the adventures he'd lived. The afternoon had passed quickly with plenty of laughs to distract Quint from the fact that he was sweating to death in a creepy tomb.

Now, after a shower to wash off the grit from the temple and a chicken-laden *panucho* filling his belly, Quint was having trouble keeping up with Juan's supper conversation in the mess tent. More than anything, he wanted to escape back to his cot, read whatever it was Jeff had sent in that envelope, and drift off to dreamland. These long-ass days of work and sweat were for younger men. But he hated to leave Juan to finish up supper alone.

"I can't find the damned thing." Angélica's voice jerked Quint out of his post-*panucho* daze.

Where'd she come from? He had listened outside of her tent before coming to eat and hadn't heard a peep.

"Good evening, *gatita*. Why don't you join us," Juan patted the seat next to him, "and have something to eat."

"I ate earlier." She slid onto the bench next to her dad. "I can't figure it out. All clues lead to the Temple of the Water Witch, but it's not there."

"Are you sure you've deciphered every glyph on that wall correctly? You know how the slightest variation can skew the meaning."

"I've gone through the copies several times using Mom's notes. I'm telling you, we've hit a dead end."

"Maybe we need a fresh perspective." He turned to Quint. "What do you think?"

Quint pointed at his chest. "Me?" At Juan's nod, he threw out the first thing that came to mind. "Backtrack."

"That will put us further behind—" Angélica started.

Juan held up his hand to hush her. "Backtrack how?"

"Well," Quint continued, "maybe there's something more to be found in the Dawn Temple." After going through chamber after chamber with Juan, he had a better idea of the size of that ruin. "Something close to where you found the *stela* that might offer another clue."

He needed to take his own advice about backtracking

when it came to Dr. Hughes and the plane crash. But then, maybe whatever Jeff had sent would answer his …

He suddenly realized something that had escaped him until this moment. Why hadn't Jeff ever said anything about the plane crash? Had Mrs. Hughes not told him about it when she had gotten the phone call? If she hadn't told her son his father might have perished in a plane crash, why not? Why withhold something like that from Jeff even after he was an adult?

"… looked everywhere," Angélica was saying when Quint tuned back in. "Besides, like I said, we don't have the manpower to waste on this. We're already running everyone ragged with the night watches." Angélica grabbed her father's cup and took a sip. "Jared told me he caught Benito sleeping on the job earlier and had a hard time waking the boy up."

"What about that vase-like piece in your desk?" Quint asked, still backtracking. "The one with the broken neck. It has a king and a necklace on it. Where did you get that?"

Her eyes narrowed. She stared at him for a long, silent moment as she lowered the cup to the table. "How do you know about that vessel?"

"It was on your desk that night I brought you supper. You know, the first time I met Rover."

She cocked her head to the side, still drilling him. "What else did you see on my desk that night?"

Damn! Instead of helping, he'd managed to get mired in some quicksand. "Let's see, there was a magnifying glass, a dirty sock, a stained T-shirt, and a broken pencil."

Juan snickered. "He passed that test."

She lightly whacked her father on the shoulder and then turned back to Quint with a warning frown. "You'd better not be playing games with me again, Parker."

Jesus, this lack of trust shit was getting old. Coming clean about his search for Dr. Hughes was probably going to make it worse. Part of him hoped that Dr. Hughes had died in that plane crash. Then he could do what she thought he was here to do—write a damned article and that was it.

In the meantime, he needed to deal with her suspicion. "Why would I sneak into your tent, Angélica? What would I gain from that?"

She searched his face, finding what he had no idea. "I don't know. I'm sorry. I guess I'm not thinking clearly."

"If you're done interrogating our guest, *gatita*," Juan winked at Quint, "I'd like to get back to the task at hand. Where's that shell?"

"I wish I knew."

"Was there any other mention of *Ek Chuah* on the wall other than on the glyph with the curse?" he asked.

She shot Juan a frown. "Don't make me say it."

"Yeah, yeah, there's no curse. Just answer the question."

"There were several. According to the carvings, the king was buried in what they refer to as 'his royal chamber.'"

"His body must be there, somewhere."

"Then I'm blind."

"You're smart like your mother. You'll figure it out." Juan stood, dropping a kiss on her temple, and then nodded at Quint. "If you two will excuse me, this old man needs his beauty rest."

Quint watched Juan leave. When he turned back, he slammed into Angélica's squint.

"Why are you really here, Parker?"

It was the moment of truth.

Well, it could have been if telling her about Dr. Hughes wouldn't result in her serving him his head on a copper Maya platter. As it was, with her in a distrusting mood already, he preferred to keep his head intact this evening.

"To write an article about your dig site, Dr. García." That was half of the truth.

"Then why do you keep getting Express envelopes from Dr. Hughes' son?"

Steel. That son of a bitch.

"Angélica!" Steel raced into the tent. His face pale, his eyes wide.

Speak of the goddamned devil.

"Come quick!" Steel said. "There's another man down."

She turned to Quint, her face lined with angst.

He took her hand, squeezing it.

She didn't pull away. "Who is it?"

Steel raked his fingers through his blond hair, opening and closing his mouth like he was struggling to get it out. "Sweetheart, I'm so sorry. It's Pedro."

* * *

When Quint and Angélica arrived on the scene at the Owl Temple, Juan was already there shouting orders. Steel must have caught him on his way to the mess tent.

Angélica raced over to where Teodoro bent over Pedro, who lay on his back in between the pieces of limestone.

Quint joined Juan. "What happened?"

"I couldn't tell for certain before Teodoro pushed me away, but it looks like when Pedro fell he landed on the screwdriver he was carrying."

Grimacing, Quint craned his neck to try to get a better look. "Where did the screwdriver go in?"

"His outer thigh. It missed the femoral artery, thank God. Teodoro is pretty certain it's not as bad as it looks."

Steel and Benito rounded the corner of the temple carrying a stretcher between them. Teodoro waved them over, and then he turned and motioned toward Juan. Quint followed, completing the circle.

The first thing he noticed was the blood staining Pedro's pant leg and smeared across Teodoro's shirt.

Under Teodoro's instruction, they all worked together to move Pedro onto the stretcher. Quint winced at the sight of the screwdriver sticking into Pedro's leg. Blood didn't bother him, but he sure didn't want to be in the room when Teodoro pulled that free. Just the thought of it made his balls hurt.

Angélica looked up at him. "Fernando is going to take one end of the stretcher. Can you carry the other? Benito is too shaken up right now, and Jared doesn't do well with blood."

"Of course." He and Fernando lifted on the count of three with a grunt of effort. "Pedro needs to cut back on María's super-sized *panuchos*," he told Fernando, who nodded with a small grin.

As they dodged and weaved through the limestone, Angélica walked beside them, worrying over Pedro. When they cleared the rubble Quint told her, "Why don't you go on to Teodoro's and help him get ready for us." The healer had run on ahead to prep for their arrival. "We'll be there shortly."

By the time they reached Teodoro's place, Quint had soaked through his T-shirt. They angled their charge inside with care. Juan and Angélica helped them transfer Pedro onto the patient cot; his eyes remained closed.

"Why is he out?" Quint asked Teodoro. "Did you give him a tranquilizer?"

Juan answered for the healer. "Pedro was out when we arrived. All we can figure is he knocked himself out when he fell."

Grabbing the scissors from Teodoro's supply shelf, Angélica began cutting away Pedro's pant leg around the screwdriver. Meanwhile, Teodoro was mixing up some concoction in a gourd. María came through the door with some water and clean rags.

Quint looked at Fernando then Juan. "I'm stepping outside for now, giving them some space."

At Juan's nod, he left. Fernando followed.

"Should we wait here?" he asked the foreman.

Fernando shook his head. "Go back to your tent and rest. You're on first watch tonight."

A few minutes later, Quint zipped his tent flap closed and turned on the lantern on his desk.

Rover rubbed against his boot, his whole body wiggling as Quint scratched the little guy behind the ears. "How are you doing, buddy? You're getting better with zippers, I see."

After spending a few minutes playing sock tug-o-war with Rover, Quint headed over to the showers and washed up again, putting on a dry shirt.

It was full dark by the time he returned. Kneeling next to his cot, he shined his flashlight under it. Rover was there, his belly rising and falling as he slept on top of the Express envelope. Quint extracted Jeff's package without waking the javelina.

He tore it open as he crossed to his desk.

"Fernando," Juan called outside.

Quint paused, listening to the footfalls coming closer. By the sound of it, Juan was heading toward Angélica's tent.

"Will you please go to Teodoro's and tell Angélica that she needs to come to her tent immediately?"

"Sí."

"If she resists, mention that I found her javelina in María's garden, and I need her help with him."

Quint glanced over at his cot. Rover was still asleep under it. What was Juan up to?

He heard Fernando pass in front of his tent on his way to Teodoro's. The sound of Juan unzipping Angélica's tent flap was clear in the quiet night. Quint would find out Juan's plan soon enough.

Dropping into his chair, he returned his attention to the package. Inside was a thin book with a thick cover. He pulled it out and read *Olympic Mountain High Memories*.

A yearbook? He flipped open the cover and found a note from Jeff.

I found this in a shoebox marked "Proof." It's Jared's senior yearbook. I thought this might have something to do with those school records I sent you last week. Mom circled a picture of him on page fifty-one, but there's no explanation why. Maybe there's something in her notebook about this.

Quint turned to page fifty-one and found a black and

white picture of the Spanish Club members circled in green marker. As Jeff had written, there were no notes about it on the page. He fanned the pages prior and after, looking for any other comments or circled pictures but came up blank.

Flipping back to the Spanish Club picture, he pulled the lantern closer. There were twenty-some kids in the picture, the back row standing and the front row sitting. A younger version of Steel sat third from the left in the front. He studied the names listed from left to right, matching them with each face. Wait a second. He counted and compared again, then leaned back rubbing his jaw.

Huh. He could have sworn that was Jared.

He found Steel's name and the face to match, second from the right in the back row. The kid also looked like Steel. Twins?

"Is that what this school thing is about?" he whispered.

He looked up the name of the boy in the front again: *Roy Bumm*.

What a name.

He looked back at Steel's picture.

"So what happened to your twin? And why is his last name different?"

Maybe those school records had something about a brother in them that he didn't catch last time. Mindful of his sleeping visitor, he reached under the frame of the cot and extracted his file holder.

Back at his desk he drew out the school records. As he scanned he looked for anything hinting at a brother but found nothing. The records made it sound like he was an only child. Maybe he was. Maybe Roy was a cousin.

While reading the physical description on the school records again, he glanced several times at the black and white photo. Eye color didn't matter. He couldn't tell Steel's blue eyes from green in the photos. The height looked about right.

"Shit." He tossed the papers onto his desk. This was getting him nowhere.

Why couldn't Mrs. Hughes keep a journal of her thoughts? These pictures and articles without much explanation behind them were making Quint want to bang his head against a temple wall.

What about the senior pictures? They would be in color.

He grabbed the yearbook and whipped through the pages to the senior photos. Starting midway through the letter B, he scanned the names under the photos: Borton, Bostly, Bozeman, Buhler, Burke, Caberrini.

He ran through them again. "Where is he?"

Several pages later, he found: Sobrinski, Solinger, Spakeman, Stadnyk, Stegger, Stephanos, Sutherland.

But no Steel.

He scratched his head. "Where in the hell are they?"

Two pages further, he found a list of names of seniors whose pictures were not shown, including Bumm and Steel.

Damn it! He slammed the book shut and shoved it away from him.

Why had Mrs. Hughes considered this proof? It did nothing but raise more questions. Like who was Roy Bumm? Was there some significance to neither boy having their senior pictures in the yearbook? And what did any of this have to do with Dr. Hughes' disappearance?

He rubbed his eyes. Frustration wasn't going to get him anywhere. It would be a lot easier to give up and walk away from all of this.

But there was that promise he'd made to Jeff.

Fuck.

"You mean you lied to me?" Angélica's raised voice right outside his tent made him jerk in surprise.

He turned in his seat, staring at the tent flap. Should he leave and give Juan and Angélica some privacy?

Curiosity kept him right where he sat.

* * *

"No, *gatita*," Juan told Angélica. "I used a small fabrication in order to get you out of Teodoro's way."

"Damn it, Dad." She needed to get back to Pedro.

"Don't swear at me, child. You need some rest. Pedro will be fine. Teodoro is watching him like a new mother. As soon as he wakes, you'll know. In the meantime, as your father, I'm ordering you to go lie down in your tent."

"I'm no longer eight years old, you know."

"Well, then your nap should be a lot longer than those I made you take back then."

She sighed, knowing he meant well. "Listen, Dad. I—"

"No, you listen." His voice hardened. "Someone out there is trying to stop us for some reason. You need to be sharp at all times or you could be the next one lying on Teodoro's bed covered with blood. As it is, you look like one of those walking dead people."

"It's called a zombie, Dad. You're hard on a girl's confidence."

"And you're snapping at your friends like a cornered turtle."

"A turtle?"

"Take a little advice from your old man. He knows what's best for you. Go to bed and get some rest."

There was too much to do to rest. "But—"

"Go!" He pointed at her tent and then ruined his strict order with a smile. "Please, *gatita*. I can't lose you, too."

"Fine." She unzipped her tent. "You're so mulish sometimes."

"It's called being a loving parent," Juan said after she stepped inside.

"Oh, so that's what you call bossing me around these days."

"Ungrateful child," he growled.

She grabbed the zipper. "Stubborn mule." She softened her words with a kiss on his cheek and then zipped the flap closed.

After he left, she frowned at her cluttered tent, worrying her thumbnail about Pedro. For several minutes, she walked around picking up her dirty clothes and putting them back down, her mind back in Teodoro's hut.

"Angélica." Quint spoke from the other side of the canvas. "Can I talk to you for a moment?"

She hesitated. Her tent looked like a tornado had gone through it, followed by a tidal wave of dirty clothes.

She heard a grunt and then a snort from the other side of the tent flap. *Rover!* He must have sneaked out again.

Hell, she needed to talk to Quint anyway. "Sure." She unzipped the flap, standing back so he could enter.

He joined her inside, smelling as fresh as a daisy. Wait, did daisies even have a scent? She couldn't remember at the moment. Anyway, he smelled clean and she stank like a troll's armpit.

Rover snorted and wiggled in Quint's arms until he lowered him to the floor.

"Hey, squirt." She scratched Rover's back as he nuzzled her leg. "You've been bugging Quint again, huh?" She looked up at Quint. "Sorry he keeps going to your tent."

"Don't worry about it." He glanced around, his gaze landing on the plate of food on her desk. "You said you ate. It doesn't look like you even touched your food."

"I wasn't hungry." Nor had she been for the last couple of days, not with the prickly ball of anxiety rolling around in her gut. She'd been forcing food down her throat in an attempt to keep up her energy, especially since she wasn't sleeping much … or well.

He frowned at her, leaning back against her desk. "How's Pedro?"

"Still unconscious when I left him. Teodoro has him all patched up."

"Did you figure out what happened? Was it an accident?"

"I don't know." She dropped onto her cot, her knees suddenly weak now that her adrenaline had come and gone.

"We won't know anything for certain until he wakes up, but there's something fishy about this whole thing."

"What do you mean?"

"If Pedro slipped and fell, the only logical way that he could've been knocked unconscious was if he'd hit his head. But Teodoro couldn't find any bumps on his skull, so why was he out when we found him? His heartbeat was regular; his breathing was steady. The only other thing I could come up with was that he fainted from the pain when he fell on the screwdriver."

"Have you ever witnessed Pedro in pain before? Does he tend to pass out?"

"I've seen him hurt himself here and there over the years, but I've never seen him pass out before." She glanced at the tent flap and then back at Quint, lowering her voice. "Fernando told me that Benito thought he saw a dart next to Pedro when he and Jared first came upon him. But after Jared and he returned from getting help, the dart was gone."

His brow wrinkled. "You mean like a tranquilizer dart?"

"Yes, and that would explain Pedro's unconscious state, but nobody has been able to find it."

"What about Steel? Did he see it, too?"

"No. Jared didn't see a dart, but he clarified that with all of the blood, he barely looked at Pedro before having to turn away or throw up."

"But Benito swears it was there?"

She nodded.

"Could Jared be lying?"

"Why would he do that?"

"Who knows with Steel."

"I don't think so. I think whoever is fucking with us did something to hurt Pedro."

"You think they stabbed him in the thigh with the screwdriver?"

"I don't know. Probably not. But they may have put something in his water bottle when he wasn't looking."

"So what do we do now?"

Hiding behind her hands, she knew the right thing to do no matter what it meant to her future. She peeked out between her fingers. "I'm thinking about sending everyone home with full pay."

Quint's jaw gaped. "What?"

She lowered her hands. "Hell, four of them are already skipping out first thing in the morning. They'd leave now, but they're too scared to walk through the jungle at night."

"If you do that, it means you won't finish what you need to by the end of the dig season."

"I've put everyone's lives in jeopardy for long enough. I can't risk any more for the sake of my future."

"Would you be leaving, too?"

"Of course not."

"What about Juan and Teodoro?"

"It's up to them, but Dad will probably stay. I don't know about Teodoro and María. They usually split their time between here and the village, coming to the site weekly during the rainy season to check up on it. They act as the caretakers. They may want to take a break until this all blows over." She sighed in resignation. "Fernando may stay as well. That's up to him."

Quint crossed his arms. "I'm not leaving."

She was too worn out to do more than glare at him. "You'll go if I say you go."

"Not without you."

"Parker, don't you understand what we're up against here? I'm not talking about small time pranks like lighting firecrackers outside your tent at night. Whoever is behind these attacks is aiming to seriously injure if not kill."

"That's why I'm not going anywhere without you."

She growled at the ceiling. "Why do you have to fight me on everything?"

He went down on one knee in front of her, capturing her hands. "Angélica, think about it. What if something happens to your dad in one of the temples? You can't carry him out on your own."

He had a good point, damn it. "I'll manage."

"Bullshit."

"I've always managed on my own before."

"Christ, you're so damned obstinate!"

"Said the kettle!"

He stared at her long and hard. "Whether you like it or not, woman, I'm staying. You need my help."

Why couldn't he see that what she needed was for him to leave so he wasn't the next one carried into Teodoro's hut with blood pumping out of him? She didn't want Quint to go, but she didn't want him getting hurt or worse because of her determination to find that damned shell. This was her obsession, her madness. Not his.

She tugged her hands free of his grip. "I don't need anyone," she lied.

He grabbed her by the front of her shirt, pulling her toward him. She let him, wanting him to kiss her and make her forget about everything that had gone wrong this season, at least for a while. She watched him, waiting with her pulse pounding for what came next.

Mere centimeters from her mouth, he stopped, hovering. "Liar," he whispered, his breath hot on her skin.

Then he was gone, zipping the tent flap closed behind him and leaving her alone with Rover and her worries.

Chapter Nineteen

La Verdad: The truth.

What a messed up dig season this had turned out to be.

In spite of all that had gone wrong, Angélica was breathing easier the next morning when she found out that Pedro was okay. Her father had confirmed Pedro was up and hungry as a bear when he'd met her coming out of her tent. She'd grabbed a plate of food from the mess tent and headed for Teodoro's place in search of answers.

When she entered the hut, she found Pedro sitting up on the bed, arguing with her father. They both looked over when she shut the door behind her.

"How do you feel?" she asked Pedro, joining them, wondering what was going on between him and her dad.

"Hungry and mad!" He pointed at Teodoro. "He keeps poking me with sharp things and *su padre* refuses to let me go back to work this morning."

She looked at her dad. "Don't you two know better than to poke the bear?" She pulled out the plate of food from behind her back. "Especially when he's just come out of hibernation?"

"*¡Dios mio!* You really are an angel," Pedro said with a huge grin. He gave her a loud smooch on the cheek and took the plate from her.

Juan moved over next to her, putting his arm around her shoulder. "Whew! You saved us from getting mauled."

Angélica turned to Teodoro, who was busy grinding something on a *metate* at the table. "I thought you said he was injured," she spoke in Mayan.

"His leg is, not his stomach," Teodoro replied in the same tongue.

Pedro tore off another huge bite, his cheeks puffed out with food.

"Look at that appetite, Teodoro." Juan chuckled. "I guess we won't have to take him out back and put him down after all."

Pedro finished the last bite, dropped the plate on the chair next to the bed and sighed, smiling contentedly at her as he lay back on the bed with his hands behind his head. "Life is good."

"Except for the hole in your leg."

He waved her off. "That's better than a hole in my head."

Angélica could use some of his optimism this morning. As much as she'd like to relax along with him, she needed those answers now to help her make a final decision about keeping the rest of the crew or sending them home.

"Four more men left this morning," she told the three of them as she sat down on the end of the bed, careful not to bump Pedro's leg. "I need to know what happened yesterday, Pedro."

Pedro's eyebrows drew together. "I was making my way through the rocks, trying to be careful because I'd twisted my ankle there last dig season."

Angélica nodded. "I remember."

"Then it felt like something stung me on the back of my neck." He was silent a moment, appearing lost in thought. Then he shrugged. "The next thing I know, I'm waking up screaming."

Angélica shot Teodoro a frown. "He was screaming?"

"Not screaming," Teodoro clarified. "Crying, like your father when he needs fixing."

"I have never cried."

Teodoro harrumphed.

Juan's face darkened. "Okay, maybe once. But you didn't have to stab me with that extra-long needle *there*. You could've put it in my arm."

Teodoro was smiling when he returned to his grinding. "Pedro can work after lunch," he said in Spanish over his shoulder. "He needs more sleep first."

"What?" Pedro sat up. "I'm fine now. A moment ago, I was walking around here with barely a limp."

"After lunch," Teodoro iterated, putting his shoulders into his work.

Grabbing her hand, Pedro implored her with his dark eyes. "You need me, *Angel*. I'm fine. Let me help this morning."

Why was everyone around here telling her what she needed these days? "I need you strong and healthy," she told him, pushing him back onto the pillow. "I also need another answer from you."

After wrinkling his nose at Teodoro's back, Pedro looked up at her. "Shoot, *bebé*."

"Benito said he saw a dart in the rocks next to you, but when we got there, it was gone. Do you think that sting you felt could have been from a tranquilizer dart?"

"Maybe. That would explain why I blacked out and didn't wake up even when I fell on my screwdriver."

"My thoughts exactly." She exchanged a worried glance with her father.

"Why shoot me with a tranquilizer? Who would do that?" Pedro rubbed the back of his neck at the base of his hairline. "Why not just shoot me with a bullet?"

"I don't know. Someone is getting more serious about

getting rid of those of us still here." She rose from the bed and crossed the room, keeping her face averted as several "what ifs" flew through her thoughts.

When she turned back, Juan was checking the area on the back of Pedro's head. But it didn't matter if they found a dart hole or not. She believed Benito. It made sense with the way Pedro had blacked out.

"Why do you have to have so much hair?" Juan grumbled. "Maybe we should shave him bald again."

"Get away from my head." Pedro slapped at Juan's hands. "I still haven't paid you back for that last time."

"You're the one who wanted a Mohawk."

"I was drunk on *balche* when I told you to cut my hair."

"That made two of us. The next time we reenact the *Barber of Seville*, we should probably at least start out sober."

Their banter lightened the bleakness in Angélica's heart, but it didn't make the task in front of her any easier.

"You know what this means, Dad."

Juan looked at her, his expression growing somber. "Maybe we should let this set for another day. Make doubly sure first."

"Sure of what?" Pedro's brow lined as he searched each of their faces in turn. "What are you talking about?"

Fuck. She'd worked so hard for so long to get her own dig site, to prove herself. Fury burned in her chest at the cowardice of whoever was behind the sabotage.

"No, I have to let them go today." She blinked back tears of frustration.

"Oh, *gatita*." Juan crossed the room and pulled her into a hug. "It'll be okay. We'll make it through this together."

"Let who go?" Pedro asked.

She closed her eyes, burrowing into her father's arms.

"Everyone," Juan answered for her. "She's going to shut us down."

* * *

Quint stopped in to check on Teodoro's patient after breakfast. While Teodoro's back was turned, he slipped Pedro some tortillas in case he needed a snack.

"*Gracias, mi amigo.*" Pedro stuffed the tortillas under his pillow. "How do you like working with Juan in the Dawn Temple?" His face split into a big fat grin as soon as the question left his lips.

Quint shuddered and told Pedro about Juan's batting practice. "If I ever have to step foot back in that over-sized coffin it will be one damned day too soon."

An hour later Quint stood inside the Dawn Temple once again, sweating his ass off, cursing at the cracks in the ceiling.

Oh, the irony.

From up on a stepladder, Juan held out his hand for some nails from the box Quint was holding for him. "I need a few more."

He dropped the nails in Juan's hand.

"Okay, now hold that right there while I sister this onto the header," Juan muttered through the nails sticking out of his mouth. He hammered a nail through the board Quint was holding up overhead.

Flinching with each pound, Quint ducked his head, keeping the board pressed against the cracked header beam. The echoes reverberated off the chamber's crumbling walls and ceiling, making him sweat even more.

"Okay, that should do it." Juan climbed down. "Now just the two jack studs on each side to support that reinforced header and the entryway should hold for a few more years."

Eyeing Juan's work, he doubted even rebar and concrete would keep this place from crumbling *for a few more years.*

"Angélica wants to send everyone home," Juan said. "Including Fernando and you."

That had come out of left field. "Does that mean her theory about the tranquilizer dart is true?"

"She told you about that, huh?" When Quint nodded, Juan smiled. "Interesting."

"We talked about it last night in her tent."

"Even more intriguing."

"What? That she told me her theory?"

"Yes, *and* that you made it in and out of her tent alive. That place is one dirty sock away from becoming a superfund site."

Quint chuckled. "Does her eviction order include you? Or are you staying?"

"Staying, of course. We still have work to do. What about you?"

"I'm not leaving. Not unless she goes, too."

"Excellent." Juan patted his shoulder. "I was counting on you being too bullheaded to obey her order."

"Although," Quint said, stepping out into the passageway and lifting one of the studs with a grunt, "I'm sure she'll put up a fight." He glanced over at Juan as he carried the timber over and hefted it into place. "What about Pedro?"

"He's staying and so is Fernando, whether she likes it or not." Juan climbed up the stepladder and pounded several nails into the steel bracket that fastened the jack stud to the header.

"What about Steel?" Quint asked when Juan finished.

Juan flexed his hammering hand. "He's staying, too."

"Shit." Quint collected the other stud from the hall. "That man is like a tapeworm."

"Or a tick. He sure sucked the lifeblood out of my daughter."

Quint smiled as he carried in the timber. That was one of the things he liked most about Juan—his mutual dislike for Steel. He set the jack stud in place. "At least their marriage didn't last long."

"Yeah, but it changed her. She used to be more carefree. Not such a workaholic."

Really? He would have liked to have seen her then.

"And this whole distrust issue of hers now drives me nuts." Juan pounded nails into the bracket holding the other jack stud in place.

"You mean she hasn't always been that way?"

"Nope." Juan climbed down off the stepladder. "She used to have a lot more faith in people."

Shit. This didn't make telling her about his search for Dr. Hughes any easier.

"Nowadays, she trusts only those closest to her, the ones she really cares about."

So what happened if she cared about someone and then found out he'd been hiding part of the truth from her? Would Angélica ever trust him again?

While Juan inspected his work, pushing on the jack studs, studying the walls and ceiling, Quint pondered why earning Angélica's trust mattered so much to him.

He wasn't sure he liked the answer.

"You've got it bad, don't you, boy?"

Quint grimaced. "Is it that obvious?"

"Well, you do get pretty bristly and territorial around her." Juan pulled a pair of leather gloves from his back pocket. "Play your cards right, and you might win."

He'd be smarter to fold and walk away.

It was time to change the subject. "So, what's next in here? We move to another chamber?"

Juan clapped Quint on the shoulder. "Unfortunately for our backs, Mr. Photojournalist, we get to spend the rest of the day moving these rocks out of here."

Studying the huge pile of limestone pieces taking up two-thirds of the room, Quint tried to figure out Juan's goal. "How are you going to keep the ceiling from caving in further?"

"Using those timbers outside on the ground. We'll shore it up as we go."

"And you're sure that's safe?" Quint scrutinized the cracks riddling the ceiling.

"*Safe* is a term I like to use loosely."

"Great." He really hated this temple. "I'm a dead man."

"Think of it as a new weight-lifting routine to build your

upper body strength."

"I'd rather stick with lifting a *panucho* to my mouth."

"Pedro would agree with you wholeheartedly."

"How long ago did this cave in?"

Juan shrugged. "I don't know. It was like this when we started working at this site. We haven't gotten around to cleaning it up until this year."

That was typical of Quint's luck. He should have come a year earlier.

"Normally, there would be about four more men working on this with us." Juan kicked a small baseball-sized stone toward the pile. "As it is, we're it."

Quint's back ached just looking at the pile. "Where do we start?"

"Grab that wheelbarrow I left around the corner. We'll take a load of rocks out and bring in the timbers."

Quint went out in the passageway, making sure the path outside was relatively smooth. When he wheeled back into the room, he found Juan standing off to the side of the pile of rocks, a perplexed look on his face.

"That's curious," Juan said.

Quint parked the wheelbarrow next to him. "What's curious?"

Juan pointed his flashlight beam at where the pile butted up against the wall, about twelve feet back. "Near the very bottom there—do you see that?"

Quint leaned forward, noticing something lighter in color than the rest of the rocks around it. "What is it?

"I think it's a hat."

* * *

Finding what looked like a hat in the Dawn Temple was the top story at the lunch table. Who knew a hat could rouse so much excitement, Quint thought, as he described what it looked like to Pedro, which was mostly a dust-covered, smashed, barely recognizable hat. Juan figured it belonged to a member of Angélica's crew from years before, maybe even from when her mother and he had run the site.

"What makes you so sure it's a hat?" Steel asked, seeming to pay attention for the first time since he'd joined them fifteen minutes ago.

"We're not," Juan answered after swallowing his last bite. "But it's definitely not a piece of the ceiling."

Steel lowered his fork to his plate. "What sub chamber are you clearing?"

"L."

"You never mentioned clearing that area of the temple in the plans you submitted to the university."

Juan swallowed. "The university shortchanged me this year, so we had to modify our plans when money ran low for supplies."

"You should have updated the board with your plan modifications." Steel's lips were pressed thin as he stabbed his food. "That's standard procedure."

"You're right. I'd forgotten the university's rules."

"How far did you get on the pile?" Fernando asked.

"What do you think, Quint? About three feet in?"

"If that."

Juan sipped from his coffee cup. "The darned wheelbarrow tire kept going flat. We had to stop and pump it up four times this morning."

"I told you not to buy that cheap wheelbarrow," Pedro told him. "This jungle will chew up a good wheelbarrow in a week."

"You should have tried harder to convince me back when we were picking up supplies for this year's dig."

"So, it's my fault now, old man?"

Juan grinned. "Isn't it always?"

"*Sí.*" Pedro swallowed the last of his lunch, wiping his mouth with a napkin. "I'm working with Fernando this afternoon, right?"

Juan shook his head.

"Teodoro gave me a clearance to work, remember? The screwdriver didn't go very deep. It's mostly a flesh wound."

"I know and I do remember what Teodoro said *and* you will be working this afternoon, but not with Fernando."

Pedro's eyes widened. "No!" He pushed his empty plate away. "I'm not going in that temple with you, you're *loco*."

Juan twitched purposefully several times. "I'm only crazy in the morning, boy. Come afternoon, I'm just slightly insane."

Turning to Quint, Pedro said, "I count my ducks lucky every time I walk out of that temple alive after working with him in there."

Juan snorted with laughter, which in turn made Quint start chuckling and even garnered a grin from Fernando. Steel, on the other hand, seemed bent on playing the straight man.

The sight of Angélica in the entryway quieted Quint. He noticed a rosy glow on her cheeks when she joined them, a plate of food in hand. For the first time in over a week, she was quick to smile, which seemed odd since today should be one of the worst days of her career.

"What's so funny?" Her gaze traveled from one man to the next as she lowered onto the bench next to her father.

Wiping tears from his eyes with his napkin, Juan explained, "Pedro is being Pedro. Same as always."

Pedro pointed at Juan, frowning at Angélica. "I'm not working with him, *Angel*. I'd sooner spend the day scrubbing down the latrines. Or working with Fernando."

A grunt came from the foreman at Pedro's backhanded compliment.

"Fernando is working with Dad this afternoon," she said, tearing into her *panucho*. "So is Jared for that matter. We're shutting down the work in the Owl Temple for the season to focus more energy on clearing and stabilizing the Dawn Temple." She took another big bite, making quick work of her lunch.

"What about you?" Pedro asked her.

She held up her finger until she swallowed. "I'm going to close up the other temples for the season."

His face suddenly sober, Juan tapped her on the wrist. "Did you tell them?"

"Yep. They're packing as we speak. Not too happy about it either." She grimaced at her plate before taking another bite.

Fernando stood with his plate in hand. "Full pay?"

She nodded.

"Plus the bonus?" Juan asked.

She nodded again, and then wiped her mouth with the back of her hand. "They earned it for their commitment, even if they weren't able to stay through the end."

"That's expensive," Steel said, pointing out the obvious.

"Yeah, well they were willing to put their lives at risk."

"When are Teodoro and María leaving?" Pedro asked.

"Tomorrow morning. María wants to make us some extra food before she leaves."

"One of these days I am going to steal that wonderful woman away from Teodoro, mark my words," Pedro joked.

Angélica swallowed another big bite of *panucho*. "I don't think you're man enough for her."

Looking at Quint, Pedro asked, "Why do I put up with this harassment?"

"Because you love us and we're the only family you have," she answered for Quint, laughing at the face Pedro made at her. "How's the leg?"

"Sore, but healing. That goop Teodoro uses is magic."

"He'll be happy to hear that. He's going to put together a first aid kit so I can take care of your leg after he's gone."

"So much for our nightly watches," Steel said, dropping his fork on his plate.

Juan sighed. "It doesn't seem right, ending it this way."

Wiping her hands on a napkin, she grabbed her empty plate and stood. "It could have been worse, Dad," she said, dropping a kiss on his temple. "Much worse." She pointed her plate at Quint. "If you're about finished, I need your help with something."

Quint pointed at his chest. Holy chicken *mole*! Did she actually say she needed him? Was Rover flying around outside? "Me? Right now?"

"Yes, you. Since you refuse to leave with the rest of the crew like I ordered, I'm going to put your ass to work."

God, he loved it when she got feisty with him.

He pushed to his feet. "Let's roll!"

* * *

Angélica wasn't kidding around; she really did need Quint.

However, rather than helping to close up the other temples, she needed him in the Temple of the Water Witch. Quint was the only logical choice of helpers since Pedro was injured. Her father and Fernando had to keep Jared busy and distracted. Besides, Quint acted as the perfect repellent for Jared. Her ex-husband had told her again yesterday how much he disliked working in the same room as Quint in the midst of lobbying once again for her to kick Parker off the dig site.

As she led him into the Temple of the Water Witch, she explained all of this to him. But she waited until they had reached their destination—the chamber with the curse glyph that had started the whole mess—to show him what she'd found.

"Guess what?" She grabbed his arm and towed him over to the wall adjacent to the glyph-covered wall. "This morning, a mouse showed me where the king's tomb is hidden."

He raised one eyebrow. "Were Minnie and Donald Duck with him?"

"No, smartass."

He leaned over and peered into one of her eyes and then the other. "How much sleep did you get last night?"

"Enough."

His eyes narrowed to a squint. "Were you out gathering magic mushrooms in the jungle this morning?"

"Parker, I'm not hallucinating. I threw the mouse a piece of one of María's tortillas that I was planning to take back to Rover. The mouse grabbed it and slipped through that thumb-sized crack over there." She pointed her flashlight at the crack. "The king is on the other side."

Quint squatted in front of the wall. "Right here?"

"Yes."

"You don't think he has a little burrow in the crack?"

"No." She dropped onto her knees next to him. "For one thing, it's too narrow for a mouse his size."

"True. I imagine those big yellow shoes of his would cause problems in that tiny crack."

She punched him lightly in the shoulder.

"Ow, you brute," he complained, chuckling. "You're going to need to kiss that better later. And while you're kissing places on my body, I have another spot that needs your—"

"Anyway," she interrupted, ignoring his flirting. "My theory is that there is a cavity on the other side of the stone block." The thought of the artifacts that might be hidden there made her heart zing. Maybe she'd even find the shell, which could possibly save her career after this year's dig site fiasco.

"No wonder you were so happy at lunch."

"I was that obvious, huh?"

"Well, I was paying close attention." He ran his hand over a different carving of the king in which he was getting his tongue pricked with a stingray spine. "So how do we break through without ruining the carvings on this wall?" He surveyed the wall from floor to ceiling. "Or bringing the whole thing down on us?"

"That's the tricky part. Normally, I'd have Dad in here with me, and he'd have all of these ideas on what is the safest bet structurally. But he has to babysit Jared, so you and I are on our own."

He looked at her, his gaze smoldering, giving her all sorts of naked ideas.

"Knock it off, Parker. We have a lot of work to do."

"That's too bad All work and no play makes me hot and sweaty, and not in a fun way." He grabbed the small hammer and chisel from her tool pouch. "Okay, boss lady, show me where to start."

"I think if you loosen the joints on this block," she pointed at the one with the crack, "you'll hit the edge of these two glyphs. I've already photographed and made charcoal rubs of this section in detail, so I'm willing to take the gamble that whatever is behind this wall is worth the possibility of marring it."

… An hour later, Quint had the two-foot square block wiggling.

Angélica put down her notepad and scooted over next to him. "How are you doing?" She held out the jug of water she'd brought along after lunch. The back of his shirt was soaked, but he hadn't spoken a word of complaint. "Want me to take over?"

"What? And have a woman do a man's job?" he joked. "Maybe in a little while." He swigged a drink of water.

She inspected his work, appreciating his care with the surrounding glyphs.

"You know what I don't get?" He handed the water back to her. "If you compare the joints on this wall to those on one of the walls in the Dawn Temple, the workmanship is as different as night and day." He pointed at one of the joints. "See how smooth and tight this is? Someone worked very hard to practically mold these together. Hell, if this stress crack hadn't developed, I bet this wall would've lasted for another millennium without a problem, especially since it's protected inside the outer temple walls. So, what's the difference? The builder? Or is the Dawn Temple centuries older than this one?"

She tucked her pencil behind her ear, happy to share her ideas about what had happened here long ago. "According to the glyphs in this room, the king who had this chamber built seemed to be paranoid about his wealth and possessions. My guess is that this wall was purposely designed and built to keep strangers like you and me out."

"I hope that guy got paid well for his hard work." He swiped the sweat from his forehead. "You really think the shell is behind here?"

"I sure hope so. I'm out of places to look if it's not, and probably out of a job. You interested in hiring someone to carry your tripod?"

His smile made her forget about how much it hurt to say goodbye to her crew this morning. "In my line of work, tripod carriers are a dime a dozen." He wiped his hands off on his pants and picked up the hammer and chisel again. "What I need is a beautiful woman experienced in exotic dancing and intimate massage. Interviews will be held later in my tent if you're interested in applying."

... Two hours later, Angélica stopped hammering for a moment and reached for the water jug. She pushed against the loosened stone with her boot. The block shifted in its bed.

"If only this wall was outside," she told Quint. "The exposure to the elements would have made this job much easier." She gulped down the water and then splashed some on her face.

"Whatever possessed you to marry Steel?" Quint asked, his voice soft, like he'd woken from a dream.

His question stopped her short. She could see him out of the corner of her eye, lying on his side about three feet away, his head propped up on his elbow as he watched her.

She lowered the water, slowly twisting the cap on as several answers played through her mind. In the end, she settled on the truth: "I was pregnant."

"Whoa."

She stared blankly at the block they were working on, slipping into the past.

"We'd been engaged for several months before tying the knot, so it wasn't like it was a shotgun wedding or anything. I never told my parents about the baby."

"Why not?"

"When I first told Jared, he insisted on secrecy and pushed me to marry him as soon as possible. At the time, I thought he was being romantic." She rolled her eyes at her own stupidity. "Looking back, I see how naïve I was. He was worried about his reputation and what his colleagues would say about him having a pregnant fiancée."

"Have I mentioned my dislike for your ex-husband?"

She doubted Quint's feelings for Jared came close to hers after the bullshit he'd put her through.

"I lost the baby in the third month, about two weeks after our wedding. At the time I was devastated, but now I realize how fortunate it was for all parties involved." She let out a hollow chuckle. "Jared isn't exactly the best father material."

"He's certainly no Andy Griffith."

The memory of how brokenhearted and alone she'd felt at the time still made her feel melancholy. "I don't think he would have let me walk away from him so easily if we'd had a child."

"He didn't own you."

"No, but I did let him run my life for a while." She realized suddenly what she'd just disclosed and to whom. "Anyway," she waved off the concern on Quint's face, "it's ancient history—my specialty."

"Did you ever tell your parents about the baby? Even after you left Steel?"

She shook her head. "Only Jared and I knew about it."

And now Quint. She hit him with a warning glare. "I'd rather nobody else found out either, if you get my point."

"Not a word, I promise." He placed his hand over his heart.

"Thank you." She wiped away the drop of sweat making a beeline for her eye and then lifted the chisel again.

"Why'd you tell me that?" His voice stopped her.

She wasn't completely sure. "I guess I wanted you to know the truth about why I married Jared."

He flinched slightly and looked away, rubbing the back of his neck.

"I know how much you detest him," she continued, "and I wanted you to understand the main motivation that drove me to the altar. Had it not been for the baby, I probably would've come to my senses before taking that vow." She focused back on the wall, feeling all kinds of foolish for sharing something so personal.

"Why else did you tell me?"

"There is no other reason."

"Your father told me that you only trust those you care about."

A red-hot blush made her sweat all anew. "My father causes me a lot of grief." She was going to duct tape his mouth shut if he didn't stop giving details about her. She shoved the chisel toward him. "Enough talking. It's your turn."

He grabbed the chisel and took her place. "Let's clear the air on another truth before I start."

"Okay, shoot." She tried to brace herself for whatever was to come, schooling her face.

"I understand why you married Steel. I understand even more why you divorced him. But in case you think I have an issue with your past love life, you need to get it through that overly brainy head of yours that I don't." He ran his finger down her cheek. "My only concern since I met you is who comes next."

She had little doubt, but the suspected consequences kept getting in the way. For now she needed to keep her focus on finding the shell.

"You want to know who's next?" She batted her eyelashes at him, needing to diffuse the sexual tension that filled the chamber before she did something really, really stupid. "Well, I do have a few candidates in mind."

He laughed and focused back on the wall, raising the chisel. "Let's hurry up and find that damned shell."

Chapter Twenty

Descubrimiento: Discovery.

They'd come so close, Angélica thought later that evening. She sat at her desk inside of her tent, her head in her hands. How in the hell was she going to figure out a way to get that damned loose stone out over the lip that was blocking it without bringing the whole wall down? She'd have to take her dad in there tomorrow without raising Jared's curiosity. Or maybe she could wake him later and they could go in the middle of the …

"Angélica," Quint's voice came from the other side of the tent flap. "I need to talk to you."

A glance at the dirty clothes, books, artifacts, and notes strewn around her tent made her wrinkle her nose. She decided to meet him outside, stepping out into the sticky night air.

The lantern light filtering out through the mesh flap cast a soft glow across Quint. His shirt was unbuttoned halfway down, giving her a glimpse of his chest.

"I had an idea while I was showering," he told her.

She dragged her gaze north. With his wavy hair slicked

back and a couple days' worth of stubble on his chin, he looked good enough to eat. She probably shouldn't have skipped supper again.

Pretending she wasn't thinking about joining him in the shower some time, she played along. "An idea about what?"

"How we can move that block out of there without having the wall collapse on us," he said in a quiet voice and glanced around suspiciously. "Can we go inside your tent to discuss this?"

Oh, hell no. Besides her tent being a pit, she stank like three-day-old underwear and didn't doubt she'd do something to embarrass herself within minutes. "How about we go in yours instead?"

He led the way.

When they were zipped inside, she made sure to keep a safe distance between them. "Okay, tell me how we can get it unstuck." She kept her voice low to be safe.

"We use a bar with a rope tied around it."

"I don't follow."

He hung his towel from a hook on one of the tent poles. "We'll need to chisel out about two to three feet of the floor in front of the block in order to remove that lip and make the floor level with the surface under the block. Then we'll shove the bar through that hole we made today and pull the block out using the rope."

She cocked her head to the side, weighing his idea. "I think we have some pieces of rebar left over from a project years ago. It's behind the Temple of the Crow. Maybe there's a piece small enough to use for this."

He leaned against the pole with his towel hung on it. "Rebar would work perfectly. It's strong, and the texture of it would help the rope stay in place when we shove the bar through."

"All right then." She unzipped the tent flap, needing to leave his tent before she licked something more than her dry lips. "We have a plan. Meet me tomorrow at six outside the mess tent. We'll get an early start on this."

He followed her outside. "Where's the fire?"

"No fire." She cleared her throat, trying to get that telling husky sound out of her voice. "I feel dirty and gritty is all. Seeing you fresh from the shower makes me want to go take one myself."

"You need any help?"

He must have been reading her mind.

Her body hummed at the thought of him joining her. But sex with Quint would lead to nothing but trouble, not to mention that her father, pseudo big brother, and ex-husband were all within hearing distance of the shower.

She hid her hankerings behind a lightweight smile. "Nice try, Parker. I'll see you tomorrow."

She felt his gaze on her as she returned to her tent. When she stepped back outside with her towel and some clean clothes in hand, he was gone, his tent zipped up tight.

Showering in the dark usually didn't bother her, but with all of the attacks on her crew lately, she didn't linger.

Her thoughts returned to Quint as she stepped into her underwear. He'd worked hard today without complaint, not even as the day wore on and the heat climbed inside the temple to a melting point. She pulled on the tank top she slept in, the cotton soft on her skin now cooled from the cold water she'd used to rinse off.

Not a single grumble as he worked, she mused as she towel dried her hair. And tonight he was still trying to help her, even willing to return tomorrow and sweat his ass off again. Why? What would make him go back into what she'd heard him previously refer to as a hell hole and death trap?

She wrapped the towel around her waist and slid into her shower flip-flops, combing her hair with her fingers. As she walked in the dark back to her tent, she ruminated about his quickness to laugh, her eagerness to share her hopes and ideas about this place with him.

When she drew near his tent, she slowed, listening for any

sounds coming from inside.

His cot creaked.

Papers rustled.

Her feet came to a stop in front of his door flap.

Don't be an idiot, the logical voice in her head said. *He's a crewmember. Off limits. End of story.*

But what if he was something more? She opened her mouth to say his name, but then pinched her lips together.

You take this step and there's no going back, the voice warned. *It can't be undone.*

She looked over at her tent, knowing what waited for her inside of those canvas walls. It was the same thing that waited for her every night while she lay awake, alone in that cot, fretting about her dad's health, her mom's reputation, her future, and those unfulfilled dreams for something more.

Your father is just across the way, right next to your ex-husband. Besides, what if he rejects you? How will you work with him tomorrow and the next day? You need his help more than his body.

She glanced around in the darkness, not seeing any movements, not hearing anything beyond the jungle's regular nightly soundtrack.

Go back to your tent and bury your head in your work like usual. He's not worth taking this risk.

Before the voice she'd listened to for so many long, lonely nights convinced her otherwise, she grabbed the zipper of his tent and opened it.

He looked up from where he lay on the cot reading from a notebook, his eyes wide in surprise. "What's up?"

She unzipped the mesh bug flap and stepped inside.

Sitting up, he dropped the notebook on the floor on top of some yellowed newspaper clippings and a handwritten letter. "What's wrong?"

She put her index finger to her lips, shushing him, and then zipped both flaps closed.

When she turned to face him, he was standing, his face lined with a mixture of concern and confusion. "What's going on?" he whispered. "Did you hear something out there? Do you want me to go take a look?"

His feet were bare. So were his legs. He stood there in his black briefs, ready to go to battle for her if she yelled *Charge!* That was some heady shit.

She shushed him again with her finger against her lips.

Her gaze traveled to his shirtless chest, her eyes trailing along the ridges and plains partially hidden by a sprinkling of hair that arrowed south.

Raising her eyes to his, she dropped her towel on the floor. Before she could lose her nerve, she followed it with her tank top.

In the quiet of the night, she heard him suck his breath in through his teeth. His focus lowered, locking onto her bared skin for so long that she wondered if she'd made yet another mistake with a man. There'd be no living with that damned voice in her head now.

His Adam's apple bobbed. "Angélica, there's something I need to tell you before I get sidetracked."

She shook her head, pretending to zip her lips closed. Then she held open her arms and waited.

"Sweet Jesus," he said. His chest lifted and fell visibly. His face contorted, fists clenching, a battle apparently waging within.

Her nerve started to wane, uncertainty filling her.

"I tried," he muttered to himself with a shake of his head. "Mark my words." Then he was across the tent, yanking her against him, his lips coming down hard on hers.

His hunger matched hers kiss for kiss. She linked her arms around his neck, leaning into him, letting him hold her up. His hands were everywhere at once, skimming down along her chest to her waist, up to her neck, and then returning to slide over her hips. Squeezing, cupping, pulling her even closer.

Her heart pounded loud enough to wake the dead king in his tomb. It had been so long since she'd let a man close, reveled in his strength, his hardness.

She wanted him now, immediately, afraid if they took too long they'd be interrupted, or one of them would come to their senses. Hooking her thumbs in the waistline of his briefs, she tugged them down, pushing them to the floor.

The force of his kiss increased, nearly bending her backwards. His hand slid up her spine, holding the back of her neck as his tongue toyed with hers, teasing.

She trailed her nails along his hip bones, then forward, down. She explored with her fingers, and then gripped, squeezed, stroked. He groaned, clasping her wrist, stilling her hand.

Dragging his mouth away from hers, he searched her face, looking for something. She'd show him something all right. Stepping out of her panties, she held the piece of cotton and lace up for him to see.

That sparked him back to life. He threw her panties behind them. His eyes darkened until they looked almost black in the lantern light. He grunted, fierce and brutish. His mouth crushed hers, the beast taking over.

Succumbing, she writhed under his palms as his tongue tormented hers. This was what she had missed. The feeling of passion filling her up, drowning all other thoughts in her head, allowing her to escape.

Quint's mouth left hers, prowling down her neck. He backed her into the center tent pole, and then lifted her hands, wrapping them around the pole.

She grabbed onto it, understanding the game, licking her lips in anticipation as he dropped to his knees in front of her. Her heart raced as he stared up at her, his intentions crystal clear.

His mouth hovered over her flesh, his breath tickling, making her writhe.

The feel of his tongue on her skin almost sent her over the edge. Her head lolled back, eyes closing. Her need for him was so strong it throbbed.

His hands feathered up her legs. His beard stubble

scratched her thighs, stomach, ribs.

Angélica's breath came in short, hard gasps. She turned to liquid, ready for him since she'd stepped inside his tent.

His teeth grazed her hip.

A zing of lust left her aching. Her eyes flickered open, her brain struggling to grasp that this was really happening.

His tongue … Oh, his tongue!

She buried her fingers in his hair, holding him against her as he made her spiral faster and faster. His mouth grew bolder, his touch more intimate. Lifting one of her legs, he wrapped it around him, his palms searing her bare skin.

Quint … She swallowed a moan filled with his name. The ability to think beyond what he was doing to her was long gone.

And then she went over the edge, clutching his shoulders, her body pulsing with release.

He continued touching until she finished and then pulled her down onto her knees, too.

When she opened her mouth to gush over him, he put his finger over her lips, shushing her. His smile warmed her inside and out.

Two could play at this teasing game. She pushed him back onto the floor. He watched as she straddled his waist, his eyelids heavy with lust.

Leaning over him, she lowered her mouth to his, almost touching, but held back. Her breasts brushed over his skin. A spasm of need mixed with pain flitted across his features.

He clasped her hips, pushing her toward him, but she dodged. "Damn it, woman," he growled.

She covered his mouth with her hand, shaking her head.

His fierce stare promised retribution.

She laughed without making a sound, teasing him with her body until his muscles were tight and sweat slicked his skin. Then she slid up his torso, nibbling her way up his neck, sucking on his earlobe.

His hands clutched her waist, his body bowing. When she

pulled back, his eyes were wild with hunger.

Giving him a sultry smile, she slid down, taking all of him at once.

"Angélica." Her name came out as a gasp. He held her still for a moment before tugging her down to him. "Wow," he whispered against her lips and then kissed her senseless while moving inside of her, building a bone melting friction.

His mouth trailed down her neck, his tongue circling, making her arch into him. The feel of his teeth on her was the final straw, her body giving way, bliss melting her limbs.

As she stilled, his moves grew more frenzied, his muscles straining. "I can't hold on much longer."

"So don't."

He frowned. "We're flying protection free here."

It dawned on her why he was holding back. "I've got us covered." She pushed him flat onto the floor and rocked against him several times, taking his hands in hers and moving them over her chest, playing, fondling.

That was all it took. He pulled free of her grip and locked onto her hips, his whole body bowing in pleasure.

When it was over, he collapsed flat on the floor again, a hitch in his breath.

"Damn, woman." He rested his left arm behind his head, using it for a pillow, and smiled up at her.

"There." She leaned over him, eye to eye. "You've been 'wowed' again, Quint Parker."

"That was like a 'wow' times one hundred." He toyed with a wavy tendril of auburn hair that hung down from her temple. "You are way better than my imagination."

"I want to do that again."

"I'm at your command, boss lady."

"That's more like it." She shifted against him, but he didn't move. "I thought you said you're at my command."

He chuckled. "Well, not right this moment." He ran the back of his fingers down her breast. "Here I'd figured on trying to be satisfied with only getting to fondle your pink bra."

"Been thinking about that bra, have you?"

"More like obsessing about it."

She was glad their obsession was mutual. "Good. Maybe I'll let you—"

The sound of his tent flap being slowly unzipped shut her up. She shot Quint a frown. He was already wearing one of his own.

Without a sound, she pushed to her feet, grabbed his towel from the pole, and tossed it to him. She picked up one of his folded T-shirts from the stack of boxes next to his cot and slipped it on over her head. The hem came to her mid-thighs.

If this were her father stopping by to smoke a cigar and chat, she was dead meat. She looked over at Quint, who was now standing securing the towel around his waist. Hell, she was dead meat no matter who it was.

Her gaze darted around looking for her panties. Quint's notepad was at her feet. Where were they? She glanced at the slow moving zipper. Please don't let it be her dad.

The sound of a snort came through the thin walls. Then a little snout poked through the bottom of the tent flap.

"Rover!" she said quietly, holding her heart. She dropped to her knees as he wiggled his whole body through the hole he'd made in the bottom of the flap.

Quint ran his hand down his face, relief lighting his expression as he watched the javelina limp-waddle to her.

She scratched Rover behind the ears, grinning as he circled, making a mess of Quint's papers, sitting down on a newspaper photo of Jared's and her engagement picture.

"You scared the …"

Hold the phone!

Her eyes zeroed in on the picture under Rover's butt. She nudged him aside, the blood draining from her face as she registered that Quint had a newspaper copy of Jared's and her engagement photo. She grabbed it, staring down at it as all kinds of questions stampeded through her brain. When she turned to Quint, all she could get out was, "What?"

He made a wincing grimace back. "There's an explanation for that."

"What," she started again, managing to add "the fuck?" at the end this time.

"I tried to tell you this earlier, but you wouldn't let me speak."

"Tell me what?"

He crossed his arms over his chest. "It's complicated."

Her vision tunneled. She looked down at the other papers Rover had scattered about. Most were articles about Jared, his promotions, society shit, all of the crap she'd hated during their marriage. She picked up the notebook, flipping through it, trying to put the puzzle pieces together. The yearbook from Jared's high school lay underneath it all. It didn't take her PhD to realize those letters from Jeff Hughes had been about his father and that Quint's real reason for being on her dig site probably had nothing to do with a goddamned article.

She slammed the notebook down. Her leg muscles shook when she got to her feet. "You lied to me!" she whispered harshly, keeping her voice down.

The last thing she needed right now was somebody to come running to see what was going down in Quint's tent. If Jared showed up, it would be a regular Jerry Springer episode—sex, lies, and complications.

"Not exactly."

"By omission."

"I'm here to write an article."

"Why else are you here, Quint Parker?" Before he could answer, she strode over to him shaking the copy of her engagement photo in his face. "How many goddamned times have I asked you that since you showed up? And every single time you lied to me."

"I couldn't tell you, especially when I first got here."

"Why not?"

"You would have sent me packing."

"You're damned right I would have." She covered her eyes. "Jesus, I wish to hell I had gone with my gut instinct and kicked your ass out of here from the start." Damn her father for inviting Quint in the first place. "And now I've really messed shit up by having sex with you." The logical voice in her head was doing the *I-told-you-so* dance at the moment. She shook her fist in the air, looking at the ceiling. "How could I be so stupid?"

"Having sex with me was stupid?"

"Hell, yes."

"Why's that?"

"You have me over a barrel now. Was that what you wanted from the start? Was all of this flirting with me, telling me how I needed you, a way to worm your way in deeper so you could blackmail me?"

"Whoa! You're taking this in a completely wrong direction. What we have going on between us has nothing to do with my looking for clues to Dr. Hughes' disappearance. *We*," he pointed back and forth, "happened because I have a weakness for women in distress."

Her jaw fell open.

"Wait," he held up his hand. "That didn't come out—"

"I'm a woman in distress? This was you being a good Samaritan? Oh, look, poor Angélica hasn't had sex in years. She needs me to screw her brains out?"

"What? No! Christ, can't you hear how nuts that sounds? You need to put crazy in the closet and bring Angélica back out so I can explain everything to her."

He was right. She was out of control and she knew it. The pressure valve holding back her stress over the last few weeks had blown right off at the sight of that engagement picture, and ugly stuff was spraying out all over. She could feel it coating her, suffocating feelings Quint had brought to life in her. Turning away from him, she bit her knuckle, trying to stem the flow.

He touched her shoulder. "Please, listen. It's not anything like what you're cooking up in that big brain of yours."

This was not good. She needed time to clear her head, cap the well of distrust and insecurities, figure out how to clean up the mess she'd made.

Pulling free of him, she walked over to his tent flap, unzipping it.

"Angélica, don't go. Let me explain."

She turned back to him feeling numb, empty. "What's to explain? You came down here to find Dr. Hughes, baiting my father with an article in a national publication as a means to get me to let you stay on my site. Does that pretty much sum up the truth?"

He growled out a sigh. "Yes, but there's more to it."

"Oh, that's right. I forgot the ending: You decided to seduce me to get information about Jared, whom you have some kind of hard-on for apparently based on that shit over there about his past. As a bonus, I instigated sex with you, which ensures you can continue to stay at my dig site as long as you want to get what you need."

His face grew stony. "Now you're confusing me with your ex-husband." He closed the gap between them. "Look closely, sweetheart, my eyes are hazel, not blue. The name's Parker not Steel, and I don't sleep with women for personal gain."

"They're green," she snapped back.

His forehead wrinkled. "What?"

"Jared wears blue contacts, but his eyes are really green." She nudged her chin at the papers by his cot. "Didn't your digging through the past tell you that? Some private dick you are."

His eyes narrowed. "How long has he worn blue contacts?"

Who cared? This was an absurd turn in their fight. "He never told me. Why don't you go ask him? I'm sure you two have a lot to talk about between all I've shared and what you have there on the floor."

"Don't walk away like this, Angélica. Stay and let me explain my version of it all."

At the moment she felt like spitting fire at him. That wasn't exactly conducive to listening. She needed to go somewhere and get herself back under control.

For now she slipped into her boss-mode, emotionally detaching. "Change of plans. You're working with Dad tomorrow." She needed to think of Quint as a crew member, that was all. "I appreciate your hard work today and the extra time you've put in over the last couple of weeks. I'd be happy to pay you for your time and help with our endeavors here, including the bonus I offered the rest of the crew."

He glared at her. "I don't want your fucking money."

"My fucking money?" Her smile was icy, like her heart at the moment. "I wasn't offering to pay you for the orgasms. You owed me those for manipulating information from me. We're even now. Consider all debts paid."

Without another word, she tore off his shirt, wadded it up, and whipped it at his face. Scooping up her tank top on the way out, she walked out into the dark jungle naked as a jaybird and didn't give a shit who saw her. With her dignity left in shreds, she had nothing left to lose.

* * *

"Wake up, sleepyhead. I need to show you something."

Quint lifted his head from his desk and slowly opened his eyelids. Juan stood over him smiling.

"Good morning," Juan said in a way too chipper voice.

Quint grunted and dropped his head back onto Steel's open yearbook. "What time is it?" he mumbled, his lips brushing a page of the book as he spoke.

"Dr. Hughes time."

"What do you mean?" Had Angélica paid her father a visit after she'd stormed off last night? He checked to see if Juan had a bat or two-by-four or something to beat the crap out of him.

Juan backed toward the tent flap. His eyes practically sparkled with excitement. "I've found something I believe will interest you."

Quint stood up. Was this some weird kind of post-traumatic fight dream? "What are you talking about?"

"Follow me." Juan stepped out through the flap.

Quint grabbed his shoes from the floor and headed after him but then remembered the yearbook and paused.

"Hurry up," Juan whispered loudly from outside. "Before someone sees us."

Hell, he'd probably be only a couple of minutes. Quint headed out after him. Juan was already crossing the plaza.

"Wait up, damn it." Quint slipped on his tennis shoes without untying them. He jogged up next to Juan. "What's so interesting that you couldn't have waited to show it to me in another hour when the sun is actually up?"

"You'll see." Juan led him toward the Dawn Temple.

Quint's feet slowed. There was nothing like starting his day in a claustrophobic death trap, especially after staying up half the night trying to figure out how to fix this Chernobyl-level disaster with Angélica. After he'd gotten sick of stewing on the trouble he'd made with her, he'd tried to come up with a reason why Steel's school records listed his eyes as blue instead of green. Was it as simple as he had worn colored contacts even then? In the end, he'd bombed on both fronts and passed out at his desk.

The rich pink hues in the sky and patches of early morning haze added a surreal air to the temple as they approached. Taking a deep breath as he climbed the first few steps, Quint caught a whiff of damp musty air coming from the dark passageway in front of him, cranking up his anxiety.

At the entrance, Juan handed him a flashlight.

Quint raised an eyebrow. "Should I have brought my camera?"

"Not this time."

He followed Juan back to the chamber they'd been clearing, the one with the hat.

"Do you see it?" Juan asked.

Quint followed the beam of light from Juan's flashlight. "See what?"

"There, about two feet above that cube-shaped rock."

The only things Quint saw were some glyphs carved into the wall. "What exactly am I looking at?"

"Hold on." Juan pulled Dr. Hughes' journal out from under his shirt, opening it to the back page. "This."

Quint frowned down at the drawing of the head variants. What was the big deal? Juan had mentioned that these could be found all over this temple. "I must need some coffee, because I don't understand why you think this is so important."

Juan pulled his glasses out of his pocket and slid them on. He stood next to Quint, holding the book out in front of them. "Last night, I was reading through Dr. Hughes' journal and noticed that he mentioned something about the number of loose stones with glyphs on them that he had found in this temple. That got me thinking about this drawing of his in the back of the journal. You see these swirls here and here," he said, pointing them out.

Quint nodded.

"These aren't typical with the majority of the head variants I've seen around here. As a matter of fact, I've only seen them once to date."

"Where?"

Juan pointed the beam of light back at the glyphs on the wall. "There."

Squinting, Quint took a step closer. "How can you see that much detail from here?"

"I couldn't. Before I came to get you, I climbed over the rocks to take a closer look." He shut the journal. "I noticed them yesterday when we were all working in here, but it didn't strike me as anything unusual until I took another look at this journal."

"What do you think this means?"

Juan shrugged, taking off his glasses. "Maybe I'm taking a big leap here, but I think there's something in this room."

"You mean an artifact? Or something having to do with your wife's shell theory?"

"No." He stuffed his glasses in his pocket, his face solemn. "Something that was important to Dr. Hughes."

Chapter Twenty-One

Nohoch tata: An esteemed elder.

The sweat trickling down Quint's spine had nothing to do with the already thick humidity in the Dawn Temple this morning.

Dr. Juan García was no fool. Quint should have known better than to think he was pulling the wool over Juan's eyes.

"You know why I'm here, don't you?" Quint asked.

"You're trying to find out what happened to Dr. Hughes."

Finally he was free! Relief made him feel ten pounds lighter. He'd been hiding behind that sort-of lie for way too long. Now to dig himself out of the hole with Juan ... and eventually Angélica, if that were even possible. "I can explain."

"No need."

He studied Juan. "There isn't?"

"We all have our secrets, and most of us have perfectly good reasons for keeping them."

"But I hid the truth from you and your daughter."

"I hid the truth, too," Juan said. "Remember how Angélica didn't know you existed until you showed up here ready to write an article that you and I had agreed on over a month before? I had plenty of time to talk to her about it, but I opted for keeping it from her."

"I hadn't thought about it." He'd been too busy feeling the noose around his own neck since arriving and finding out that Angélica was not only here but also running the site.

"And don't you think I realized that you believed I was the 'Dr. García' in charge down here when we were planning your visit? I could have made it clear that my daughter was the head archeologist, but I didn't. I kept the truth from both Angélica *and* you." Juan laughed quietly. "Hell, I think Teodoro is the only one who knew everything that was going on."

"What about Pedro?"

"I told him all about it when he flew me to Cancun to get my tooth fixed. He warned me that I was going to catch hell from her, but it was a risk I was willing to take. I'm sure you've noticed that she can be very inflexible sometimes."

He'd actually found her very *flexible* in certain situations. Amazingly so. Quint glanced down at his feet, trying to shut down all thoughts of Juan's daughter in her birthday suit. "Yep. Inflexible."

If Juan picked up on the direction of Quint's thoughts, he didn't show it. "But if all ends well between you two, it'll have been worth it."

After last night's blow up in his tent, Quint wasn't sure if she'd be talking to him again, let alone considering any future that included him. Angélica must not have mentioned anything about their fight to her father.

"But you'd better have a heart-to-heart talk with her before long. If she finds out from someone else, she'll—"

"Have me castrated." Too late, his nuts had already been left on the chopping block.

Juan chuckled. "That's one way of putting it."

"I have a feeling I've waited too long already."

"If she likes you," Juan patted him on the shoulder, reassuring, "she'll get over it."

"You sure about that?"

"Well, maybe not right away, but she has a good head on her. I've always found that if I give her a little time and space, she forgives. She doesn't always forget, but time is the great healer, my mama used to always say." He pulled his handkerchief from his pocket and wiped his brow. "Now how about we haul some of these rocks out of here and see if the block with that glyph is as loose as it looks. I'll go get the wheelbarrow."

Juan paused to pick up a flashlight lying next to the doorway and tossed it to Quint, and then headed out into the dark passageway.

A dusty, sweat-filled hour later, they'd made it a few feet closer to the head variants.

While Juan went out to dump another load of ceiling pieces, Quint rolled off more stones from the pile. Dust filled the chamber thanks to their sifting and moving rocks that had been collecting dust for Lord knew how long. He'd stripped off his T-shirt shortly after they had started, wrapping it around his head as a dust mask.

He stood, stretching his aching back. His stomach rumbled wondering where in the hell breakfast was. It had been spoiled by María's food for the last couple of weeks.

Checking his watch, he frowned. What was taking Juan so long? He must have taken a piss break. Or maybe someone had come looking for him, someone with wavy auburn hair and a pickax to bury in Quint's back. The same someone he kept trying not to think about and failing miserably—and feeling miserable because of her, too.

Rocks. He had to focus on the rocks.

Bending down, he hefted another large piece toward what Juan was calling the loading area. As the dust settled, what sounded like a muffled shout came from the dark passage outside of the chamber entry.

Quint stood, aiming the beam of light into the shadowed hall. "Juan?"

Silence.

He picked his way down off the pile and leaned out into the passageway. "Juan?" he called a bit louder.

Dust particles were the only things moving.

A stone rattled further down into the darkness.

Shit, he hated these creepy old temples.

"Juan?" When there was no answer, he headed toward fresh air, figuring he'd start there and then go on to the mess tent for the food María had planned on leaving behind. At the least he needed coffee before his head started pounding from a lack of caffeine.

He followed the tire tracks up the narrow tunnel toward the temple entrance and around a couple of corners. Up ahead, he caught a glimpse of something white on the floor next to the overturned wheelbarrow.

Something white … wasn't Juan wearing white?

His blood chilled. What had happened? Heat stroke? Heart attack? What?

"Juan?" He raced toward him dropping down beside him. "Dr. García?" One of the older man's legs looked funny, then he realized it was bent the wrong way. The coppery smell of blood was in the air, a pool growing under Juan's broken leg.

Oh, no. More blood ran down Juan's neck.

No, no, no, no, no. Not Juan.

He shined his flashlight on Juan's oddly bent leg. What the fuck was he going to do? He couldn't move Juan, not without … Teodoro! The healer was leaving this morning.

Quint started to get up, figuring if he hurried—wait! First he needed to make sure of something.

Lifting Juan's limp wrist, he searched for a pulse.

* * *

Angélica sat alone in the empty mess tent, memories of what had been only weeks ago moved like ghosts through her thoughts. The rumbling of voices, banging of pots and pans, occasional shouts and bouts of laughter.

She could still smell María's *panuchos,* but probably because Teodoro's thoughtful wife had barely slept last night. Instead she'd been in here preparing food for those they were leaving behind. Angélica knew this for a fact because after she'd stormed back into her tent and put on some clothes, she'd come to the mess tent to grab some cold coffee and sit in the dark alone and think.

Only it hadn't been dark, and she hadn't been completely alone. To keep her mind off the soap opera that was now her life, she'd joined María in the kitchen, sitting on the counter as she had off and on over the years when she needed someone to "mother" her. María had fed her warm tortillas while catching Angélica up on her family's lives, some local village gossip, and the elders' weather predictions for this year. By the time María had gone off to pack, Angélica had eaten too many tortillas and drunk enough coffee to stay up for a week. She'd done everything she could to keep her mind off what had happened back in Quint's tent.

She had nearly teared up when she'd waved María and Teodoro off. It wasn't so much saying "goodbye," since she'd see them again in a week or so. It was everything else that had gone wrong piled on top of feeling worn thin.

Her anger from last night had ebbed back to sea, leaving her stupid heart flopping around on the sand.

Damn Quint for lying to her.

Double damn him for making her feel things for him, things that ran deeper than attraction and lust.

Now as she stood alone in the dark tent listening to ghosts, she realized how foolish she'd been from the start about Quint. Hindsight being 20-20 and all of that bullshit.

"Angélica!" Quint yelled, racing past the mess tent entrance like the hounds of hell were nipping at his heels, heading in the direction of her tent.

Speak of the devil. Only this devil wasn't wearing a shirt? What had him so full of energy this morning? It couldn't be coffee because she'd drunk it all and hadn't made any more yet. She stepped outside to see what had him all excited.

"Parker!" She followed his path toward their tents. "Where are you?"

He burst from her tent flap and rushed over to her, his face pale, eyes wide. "You have to come with me right now." Grabbing her wrist, he pulled her toward the plaza.

She yanked free of his grip. "What in the hell is your problem? And where's your shirt?"

He turned back. "You can kill me later for what happened last night and everything else."

"I'd prefer to torture you instead."

"Fine, torture away, but later. Right now you need to come with me and hurry." He latched onto her forearm and practically dragged her behind him.

As she struggled to get free, she noticed a streak of blood on his arm. Blood? Why was there bl—

She dug in her heels and pulled him to a stop. "What is it? Did Pedro reinjure his leg?"

"It's not Pedro." His eyes had a haunted look when they met hers. "It's your father."

"No," she whispered. Her knees gave out in a blink.

Quint caught her before she crumpled to the ground.

She looked up at him through watery eyes. "Please, not my dad."

* * *

"Pedro said to tell you the helicopter's ready," Quint told Angélica as he climbed the top step leading up to the Dawn Temple. He looked over at Fernando, who stood frowning out at the surrounding jungle. "It's time to go."

The sun had crested the horizon less than an hour ago, but the day already felt old. It was hard to believe that a few hours ago, he'd been chasing after Juan up these very steps, dreading going inside.

Angélica kneeled over her father, adjusting his bandages,

the same as she'd been doing when Quint had left her ten minutes ago.

"Pedro's waiting for us," he said, touching her back.

Angélica stood, wiping her eyes. She cleared her throat, her chin quivering slightly as she focused on Fernando and then Quint. "Let's load him up."

Quint grabbed one end of the makeshift stretcher as Fernando picked up the other end. He'd carried too many people around this way in the last two weeks. The sooner they all got out of here, the better. The truth about Dr. Hughes didn't matter anymore. He just wanted to get Angélica to a safe place.

Juan lay motionless the whole way to the helicopter, his leg wrapped tight and secured with two boards they'd found inside the temple. Quint winced inwardly remembering the sight. He'd seen broken limbs before but never where the bone actually tore through the flesh.

Immediately upon seeing her father lying by the wheelbarrow, Angélica had jumped into action, cutting off Juan's pant leg, trying to stop the blood flow with Quint's shirt while she assessed the damage. It wasn't until she'd stabilized Juan's leg and slowed the blood pouring out from the ugly gash on the side of his head that she'd taken a moment to catch her breath.

With Pedro's help, they hoisted Juan up into the belly of the helicopter. Angélica climbed in beside her father, checking his bandages again.

Keeping his head low under the whirling blades, Quint turned and jogged over to where Steel waited with his bag in hand, looking red-eyed and green around the gills.

"Is he ready to go?" he hollered above the chop of the blades.

Quint nodded. The arrogant turd insisted upon being flown out of here with Juan, claiming the risks were too high now. Quint hoped the sight of Juan's bloody bandages made Steel sick as a dog all of the way to Cancun.

Steel hoisted his pack. He shot Quint a parting glare before making his way to the chopper. If Quint never saw the son of a bitch again, it would be too soon.

Fernando jogged toward Quint, openly glowering at Steel as they passed. Quint had overheard Angélica's foreman speaking to her in Spanish earlier, asking if he could strangle Steel. She'd patted his arm, telling Fernando that it was okay, Jared could have the other seat, because she wasn't going with her father. Pedro would take care of him.

What Angélica didn't realize was that if she were staying here, Quint wasn't leaving either. Fernando could take his spot in the back with Juan if she wanted to evacuate as many as the helicopter would carry.

About the same time Fernando reached Quint's side, Angélica hopped to the ground. She directed her ex to the front seat. Steel grabbed her as she started to walk away, pulling her into an awkward embrace.

Quint took a step toward them, bristling, but Fernando's hand on his shoulder kept him in line. "She'll handle it," Fernando shouted over the commotion.

Angélica shoved away from her ex, delivering a lightning fast blow to his stomach that doubled Steel over. "Get your ass on that helicopter," Quint heard her yell.

Hot damn, Quint thought. He was lucky she hadn't laid him out last night in his tent. Then he remembered her shoving him down on the floor, straddling him. On second thought, he was glad she had.

"Told you so," Fernando said, letting go of him.

Angélica scuttled under the blades toward them. Her yellow T-shirt was streaked with blood. She scowled at Quint as she drew near. "Where's your bag, Parker?"

"I'm not leaving," he yelled back.

Her stare nearly left blisters.

He crossed his arms over his chest. "If you stay, I stay."

Turning to Fernando, she yelled, "Go get Parker's bag."

Fernando glanced from Quint to her and back again, and

then he jogged off toward the tents

When Fernando disappeared around the side of a tent, Quint turned back to the face off with Angélica. "I mean it, woman. I'm not leaving without you."

Her face darkened. "I am in charge of everyone's welfare, damn it, including yours."

Pedro limped up behind her. "I need to get this bird in the air," he hollered.

"We're waiting for Fernando to grab Parker's bag, and then he'll be flying out with you." She squinted at Quint, daring him to defy her.

He'd take that dare in a heartbeat if it meant keeping her safe. "Your father told me not to leave your side." While this situation wasn't exactly what Juan had been thinking when he'd said that, Quint was pretty sure it still applied.

"Since when do you take orders from him?"

"Quint's not going," Pedro said, grabbing Angélica's arm and pointing toward the copter. "Look. Fernando is."

While they watched, Fernando climbed up into the belly of the helicopter, hat and bag in hand.

Angélica threw up her arms, her lips moving in what Quint figured was a litany of swear words that used him as the main theme.

Pedro held his hand out. "Parker, always a pleasure." Quint shook it, and then Pedro pulled him into a rough hug, telling him, "Take care of our girl. Juan and I are counting on you." When he stepped back, Quint gave him two thumbs up.

Pedro put his arm around Angélica and walked her a few feet toward the helicopter. He leaned down and said something in her ear. She glanced back at Quint, shaking her head. Pedro laughed and kissed her on the forehead, squeezing her hand before returning to his ride.

While the helicopter lifted slowly into the air, Steel stared down at them, his face as hard and cold as his name. Quint resisted the urge to flip him off.

Within seconds, the whirring blades disappeared over the

treetops. As silence spread across the ruins, dust settled around him, sticking to the sweat coating his skin.

His focus lowered to Angélica, who was still standing with her back to him as she stared out over the treetops. She brushed at her eyes, and then turned toward him, looking tired and frail. Her watery gaze pulled at him. He stepped toward her.

She held up her hand, keeping him at bay. "I'll be okay, just give me a moment."

He caught her hand and tugged her into his arms anyway. "Stop being so damned tough." He stroked her back as she sniffed against him. "He's going to be fine. He's tough as nails."

Nodding, she took a deep breath and then stepped back, straightening her shoulders. "You're right. Just seeing him like that scared the hell out of me at first."

"Me, too." He gave her some space and a few more moments to pull herself up by her bootstraps. "Now what?"

She blew out a sigh and then wiped the worry from her face with both hands. "Now we're back to sex, lies, and complications."

"Come again?"

"Last night after we had sex and I found out you'd lied to me—"

"Partially lied," he clarified, "and only by omission."

"You said you hadn't told me the whole truth about your search for Dr. Hughes because it was complicated."

"It was. It still is."

"Okay, Parker, I've calmed down and returned crazy to the closet." She threw his words from last night back at him. "I'm ready to hear your explanation."

"Maybe we should get naked again first," he joked, trying to lighten her mood before they dug into the mess.

Her hard stare didn't crack even a little. "Nice try, but I don't think you're going to want your twig and berries hanging out when I hear the truth."

"*My twig*? Come on," he growled. "For every negative thing you say, you need to say something positive or my self-esteem is going to go jump in a *cenote*."

That made the corners of her mouth twitch. "I'll tell you what, Parker. You answer all of my questions without any more lies, and I'll give you something nice and positive all wrapped up in a pretty bow."

"I prefer my pretty bows to be black and manly with skulls on them." He held out his hand. "Deal."

Her gaze wary, she took it. "No lies?"

He sobered. "No more lies, Angélica. Ask away."

"Is there really an article you're going to write, or was that part of the lie?" She pulled her hand back.

"That's for real. I called in a favor from an old friend who works for the magazine in order to line up this job."

She chewed on her lower lip for a moment. "Why do you have all of that information on Jared? You're not some kind of stalker are you?"

"No."

Her eyes narrowed. "Do you have a thing for him?"

Yep, he hated the jerk's guts. "What kind of a thing?"

"You know, a thing-thing." She wiggled her eyebrows.

He laughed so loud that he scared a pair of jays out of a nearby tree. "No, definitely not."

"Okay, I was thinking how horrible it would be if you had sex with me to get closer to him."

"No, Angélica." He ran his knuckles down her soft cheek. "I had sex with you because I have a major 'thing-thing' for *you*, which has absolutely nothing to do with your ex-husband."

"Good." She snorted. "That would be pretty mortifying otherwise."

"You have nothing to worry about on that front, especially after last night."

"What does that mean?"

He'd promised no more lies. "It means I want to be

'wowed' by you again."

"Oh." Her cheeks warmed. "Why do you have that info on Jared?"

He went along with her change of subject. "It all originally belonged to Mrs. Hughes. On her death bed, she told her son, Jeff, that his father had been murdered down here and asked him to seek justice. She said she had pieces of the puzzle tucked away in her house for safekeeping."

"She'd never mentioned anything about a murder theory until then?"

"Not a word. After her funeral, Jeff started going through his mom's house, finding boxes of articles and university correspondence regarding his dad, the dig site, and Steel, including photos of your ex tucked away in the attic. At the time, he couldn't find an explanation for why his mom had been so interested in Steel—if he had information that could help or if he was a suspect. All Jeff could figure out was that it had something to do with Dr. Hughes. So he called me to find out what I remembered about Steel and working with his dad down here, asking if I'd go through the documents. When I couldn't come up with any answers, he decided to take a trip down here. But I convinced Jeff to let me come in his place."

"Why would you do that?"

"Jeff has been one of my best friends since we were kids. His parents were good to me, and Dr. Hughes was like an uncle. I owe them for helping me through some tough times when I was a teenager. On top of that, Jeff has a brand new baby. I knew this place from working here years ago and figured I could pull some strings to make my visit down here seem more legit."

"Is that when you contacted my father?"

Quint nodded. "I found his name on one of the old articles about this site. When I looked him up, I found out that he worked at the same university as Steel. So I called the university, playing the photojournalist angle, and requested more information on this site. They gave me his name.

Nobody made any mention of a Dr. Angélica García when I began lining up the itinerary for this trip, not even your father. I thought he was the Dr. García in charge."

"Not quite."

"I was surprised as hell when you walked out of the mess tent and your father introduced you."

"And you didn't mention the Dr. Hughes angle then because you thought I'd throw you off my dig site."

"You were spitting fire that morning. I didn't want to get burned."

She blew out a breath. "Yeah, well I was having a bad day thanks to that damned curse."

"And then I arrived."

"And then you arrived all tall, dark, and nosey with an incriminating camera in tow."

He chuckled.

"What about the engagement photo?"

"It was part of Mrs. Hughes' collection. I brought it along because …" he hesitated. *The truth.* "Okay, this is going to sound stupid, but I brought it because I liked to look at your picture."

"Shut up."

"I told you it would sound dumb, but I said I wouldn't lie anymore."

She lifted her chin. "If you knew who I was based on my engagement picture, how could you not realize I was an archaeologist?"

"First of all, I'm a lousy detective. Second, I wasn't investigating you."

"Did you know we were divorced?"

"Yes. I had read somewhere that Steel was no longer married."

"And you didn't put together that my last name is the same as my father's?"

"García isn't exactly a unique last name, especially the closer you get to the Mexican border."

She seemed to weigh that and then nodded. "Why was Mrs. Hughes so focused on Jared?"

"I think she believed he was responsible for her husband's disappearance. Jeff thinks she was working on proving it when she died."

Her forehead crinkled. "You realize that if she was right, it would mean I was married to a murderer."

"Yes, it would."

She grimaced and then seemed to shake it off. "What was in all of those Express packages you kept getting?"

"Jeff keeps finding more info hidden away. Recently, he sent stuff like Steel's old high school yearbook and Mrs. Hughes' private journal, which explains more about her reasoning for believing her husband was murdered."

"I thought someone said Dr. Hughes died in a plane crash."

"Maybe he did, but Mrs. Hughes didn't believe it. In fact, she doubted it so much that she spent the next several years searching for a different answer."

Angélica blew out a breath, shaking her head. "Damn."

"I told you it was complicated."

She stared over at the Temple of the Water Witch for a long moment. When she turned back to him, she asked, "Will you be okay on your own for the day? I need to think about this. Let it soak in."

He frowned. Juan had told Quint she'd need time and space, but he wasn't comfortable with the idea of her being alone, not after what had happened to her dad this morning. "Working alone is dangerous."

"I know. There are several machetes in the supply tent, along with some other makeshift weapons. I suggest you stock up. You and I need to be on alert at all times now."

"I don't like this."

"That's why I wanted you to leave."

"I mean I don't like you being alone. I knew what I was signing up for by not getting on that helicopter, so don't worry about me."

"Pedro gave me his flare gun. I also have one of the machetes and a camp knife."

"Don't you think we should seriously consider collecting our things and getting out of here? We can contact the *federales* for help when we reach the village."

"No." Her voice grew louder with anger. "I'm pissed as hell at whoever is fucking with me, and I'm not going to let them win. They shouldn't have hurt my father."

Quint gaped at her. "Who do you think you are? Jason Bourne? What if there is more than one of them?"

"There isn't. They would have come at us harder and faster if so."

"Still …"

She jutted her chin. "Trust me, Parker. I can take care of myself."

"How? You weigh like a buck twenty-five soaking wet."

"You're shortchanging me. I'm heavier than that."

"Not by much. What if someone sneaks up on you?"

"I'll be listening for them. Besides, Pedro has taught me a few moves over the years."

"Like what?" Hitting below the belt wasn't going to save her with someone as brutal as whoever had attacked Juan.

She held out her arm. "Grab me."

He did.

In a flash she took hold of him, twirled, wrenched his arm around his back, kicked the back of his knees, and pinned him face down on the dirt while she straddled his back.

"Like this, for example," she said, settling onto his lower back. "Here we are again with me on top of you, back in the saddle. Sort of like last night, huh, Parker?"

He spit dust out, turning his head so he could see her with one eye. "If this is supposed to be my package of nice positivity, you forgot the pretty bow."

"You want your bow?" At his nod, she leaned down next to his ear. "You were right, Parker. The truth was more complicated." The warmth of her breath on his skin heated him from the outside in. "And as for your self-esteem, you're not such a bad guy … when you're not lying to me."

Chapter Twenty-Two

Moan: A mythical bird (sometimes identified as an owl) associated with death.

The dig site felt like a ghost town at high noon. All that was missing was a creaky shutter and a lone dust devil.

Actually it was a ghost town, Angélica thought as she swung into the dark, empty mess tent for a lunchtime refill.

Grabbing one of the vegetarian *panuchos* from the cooler, she filled her water bottle and headed back out into the hot sunshine to find Quint. That damned block in the Temple of the Water Witch wasn't coming out no matter how hard she tugged. She needed his help to pull it free. The sooner she got through that wall, the sooner she could find the shell and then go check on her father.

Angélica had faith that Pedro was taking good care of her dad, but she wanted to see him up and laughing again with her own eyes. That would ease one of the aches in her heart.

The other ache might be tougher to alleviate since it involved a certain hazel-eyed troublemaker who lived a long way away, traveled for a living, and didn't have much good to say about spending time in the Yucatán jungle.

She'd spent a lot of time this morning thinking about Quint and not only about why he'd hidden the truth from her. Her explosive rage to his admission last night welled from feelings that went way deeper than a stranger betraying her trust. She liked him. She really, really liked him, and she wanted to keep liking him up close and personal for however long this thing between them played out. But their worlds didn't mesh.

Long ago, while going through her divorce from Jared, she had accepted that she'd never have the dream life her parents had been lucky enough to experience—a mutual career, a shared dig site, *and* a love-filled marriage. She'd decided over the lonely years since then that she'd be willing to settle for one of those three with someone who made her smile every day, like her dad had her mom. But she didn't want to get mired in a long distance relationship. They required too much trust. On top of that, the goodbyes would make the lonely pains sharper, the pining worse.

When she'd grown tired of spinning her wheels on why she needed to just have fun with Quint for now and not make any long-term plans, she'd focused on his explanation about Mrs. Hughes. By the time her stomach won the battle of wills and food had lured her out of the temple, she'd come to one solid conclusion—she needed to read through the information Quint had in his tent about Jared. Her ex-husband had been all sorts of an asshole over the years, but she had trouble believing he was a murdering one.

She stopped outside of Quint's tent, listening. "Parker?" When he didn't reply, she unzipped the tent flap. "Hello?"

Inside, Rover lay on top of Quint's cot. He looked over at her without raising his snout from a tin plate littered with the shredded remains of a tortilla.

She squatted in front of the little javelina. "What's wrong, sweetie?" She took a closer look at the plate of food, noticing the way he'd chewed on the bits of food but not eaten them. "Are you feeling sick today?"

He let out a quiet snort and nuzzled her hand. His skin felt warm but not hot. His stomach wasn't swollen any more than usual. As she scratched behind his ears he whined, and then flipped over onto his side and flopped his head down on the cot. Eeyore had nothing on the poor guy.

She rubbed his belly. "If I didn't know better, I'd think you were sad."

He sighed, blinking several times as he looked at her.

She smiled and scratched under his snout. "As soon as I find that shell, everything will turn around, I promise."

Heading back out into the sunshine, she zipped the mesh flap closed and frowned over at the Dawn Temple.

"Where are you, Parker?"

* * *

There was something important in the Dawn Temple.

Something to do with that head variants glyph.

Juan had felt it, and now Quint's gut rallied behind that theory, too.

After Angélica had left him to his own devices earlier this morning, he'd returned—machete in hand. Hours later, between the wheelbarrow and a whole lot of sweat, he'd cleared a path through the rubble over to the wall. There was one barrier left, and one way or another he'd get past it. When he made it back to civilization he planned to tell Juan about what they'd found—together.

He pulled on the huge chunk of limestone that leaned against the block with the head variants glyph on it. The back of the rock lifted slightly, then slipped out of his grip and fell back into the shallow hole between several other large pieces of the ceiling.

Damn it! If he could just get a solid grip on the thing.

The sound of footfalls on the stone floor behind him made him reach for the machete.

"What are you doing in here?" Angélica asked.

He spun around, the machete half-raised, and tripped over a large stone on the floor behind him. He flat-handed the wall while catching himself, making his hand sting like a son of a bitch. "You scared the shit out of me, woman."

She looked down at his bared chest. "Apparently, I scared the shirt off of you, as well."

"It's freaking hot." He shook the pain from his hand.

"I noticed." The heat in her eyes when her gaze returned north made him wonder if she were referring to something more than the temperature. "You feeling jumpy, Parker?"

"This place gives me the creeps." His ego wasn't too big to admit it either.

"Then why are you in here?"

"Would you believe me if I said I was finishing what your father started?"

She nodded.

Well, that was something. Maybe Juan was right about giving her space and time to calm down and understand the whole search for Dr. Hughes secret. He pointed at the glyph. "See that block with the head variants on it?"

She made her way over the remaining pile, joining him. "You mean this?" She shined her flashlight on it. "The Sun god and Venus in the morning." At his nod, she asked, "What about it?"

"It's the exact match of the drawing in the back of Dr. Hughes' journal."

"How can you be sure?"

"Your dad told me so. He dragged me in here this morning to show it to me right before ..." Quint exhaled loudly, "you know."

"Yeah, I know. Did Dad say why he thought it was worth bringing you in here?"

"He had a notion that Dr. Hughes might have hidden something in this room, something important to him, and it may be behind this loose block the glyph is on. That's why Dr. Hughes drew it in the back of his journal."

"Why didn't he mention anything to me?" she said, more to herself than him.

Quint answered anyway. "I think he knew you had your mind on that shell."

"Still …"

"And he was protecting me. He didn't want to tell you I was looking for Dr. Hughes."

She shot him a smirk. "A partner in crime. He must like you if he's joining in your shenanigans."

"We had a deal."

"What deal?"

"It was a guy thing." When she stared, waiting, he added, "It involved freezing our balls off together."

"Male bonding with my father, Parker? Was this another attempt to get information about Dr. Hughes?"

"Not really." He shrugged. "I like your dad. He makes me laugh."

"Yeah." Her smile had a hint of sadness. "Me, too."

He squeezed her shoulder. "You'll see him again soon." Before he did something stupid like hug her, which would probably land him face down in the dirt again with her sitting sidesaddle on him this time, he squatted down and grabbed the huge stone. "If I can get this damned, over-grown pebble out of the way, we can see if your dad was right." He grunted as he lifted. His arms started shaking and then his grip slipped and the rock crashed back against the others. "Damn it."

"You're scratching the hell out of your skin." She stepped over and grabbed his sweat-soaked T-shirt, tossing it at him. "Put that on and I'll make you a deal."

He shook the shirt, making sure there were no critters on it, and slipped the wet cotton over his head. "I'm all ears," he said as he pulled it down over his stomach.

"I need your help in the Temple of the Water Witch. I'll help you move this chunk of ceiling if you help me get that block out of the wall."

"Okay. Let's get to work." He bent down, adjusting his

grip on the rock to make room for her.

She joined him, sliding in next to him, placing her hands under the backside of it. Sweat dotted her brow. "Ready."

He could smell her shampoo. The sweet citrus scent spurred flashes of her all naked and fresh from the shower, hot and ready for a whole different reason.

Shaking off the memory, he focused on the rock in his arms. "On the count of three then." He adjusted his grip once more. "One, two, three!"

The rock rose out of its bed and hovered on the edge of the stone in front of it.

Crap! His grip was slipping.

Angélica grunted, seeming to double her effort. Finally, the damned rock rolled free, taking Angélica with it.

She stumbled into him. He staggered backward, his heel catching on a rock, and fell, landing flat on his back on the chamber floor. She came down on top of him, elbows first, knocking the wind out of him.

It took him a second to catch his breath. With it came pain throbbing in his right butt cheek thanks to a small rock he'd landed on.

"Are you okay?" Angélica pushed up on her arms, her forehead wrinkled in concern.

"I think so." He dug the stone out from under him and tossed it aside. "But you were right. You do weigh more than a buck twenty-five."

Her gaze narrowed.

"And I think your elbow cracked one of my ribs."

"Keep talking about my weight, and I'm sure it will."

He grinned. "I'm just messing with you."

Her eyes lowered to his mouth, then her lips were brushing over his, slow and sexy, making his head float clear up to the ceiling. When her tongue touched his, his aches and pains slipped from his mind.

He groaned into her mouth, his body tightening as she moved over him, lighting fires all over the place. His hands spanned her hips and then slid down over her back pockets, squeezing the soft firm flesh under the cotton. God, she was intoxicating, making him crave more and more.

"Quint?" she nuzzled his neck, her hips teasing.

"Hmmmm?"

She looked down at him, her lids half-lowered. "I'm just messing with you," she whispered. She kissed him once more, hard, and then pulled away, standing over him.

He frowned up at her. "That was just sadistic."

"That'll teach you to talk shit about my weight." She held out her hand. "Come on; let's see what's behind that glyph."

He took her hand, then rubbed his sore right cheek after he made it back on his feet.

Angélica stepped back over to the glyph, squatting down and wiggling the block out several inches. He limped over to her, still working out a few kinks.

She looked up at him as he kneeled next to her, excitement lighting her eyes. "It's almost free."

"Let's get it out of there then." He grabbed it by the bottom corners and helped her pull the block out the rest of the way. Together they set it down carefully on the temple floor.

She shined her flashlight into the hole.

"Do you see anything?"

"It looks empty. Here, hold this." She handed him the light and then reached into the hole.

"Do you think that's wise? What if you touch something ..." he grimaced, "something alive?"

She glanced down at his pants, her smile quick to surface. "I've touched something much more dangerous and very alive in the last twenty-four hours. I'm not too worried about a hole in a wall."

"You have a sassy mouth, Dr. García."

"Maybe so." She shifted so she could reach deeper. "But you seem to like it."

Like? That didn't touch the truth. It was the star of many of his fantasies.

"What's this?" She frowned, leaning her head against the wall as she shoved her arm in up to her shoulder. "I think there's something way back here."

Juan had been spot on after all. "What is it?"

"It's a …" She gasped, her eyes opening wide. "Oh, God!" she cried. "It's got me! It's got me!" She struggled to pull her arm free.

Quint didn't think, he acted, scrambling behind her, tugging her backwards. She fell into him with little resistance sending him flying back into a jagged rock. Pain shot through his shoulder, rendering him immobile for a drumroll of heartbeats.

Angélica turned in his arms, her laughter filling the chamber.

He slowly sat upright. "You are an evil woman." Rolling his shoulder around to try and get blood to his bruised muscles, he gave her the stink eye. "I hope you're happy. I think I'm bleeding."

Her laughter dried up. "Are you really? Let me see." She grabbed his arm, gently turning him around. "I'm sorry, Quint. I didn't mean for you to get hurt, but I couldn't resist. Dad played that trick on Pedro two years ago in the Owl Temple, and Pedro still curses him in between laughs."

"I'll accept your apology only after you kiss me better." Quint held still while she lifted his shirt and inspected his back. "Any blood?" Something was sure burning in the middle near his upper spine.

She ran her hands over his skin and then poked him in the sore spot with her fingertip.

"Ow!" He aimed a glare at her over his shoulder. "What did you do that for?"

"It's a bruise."

"No shit. Is it bad? How big is it?"

She dropped his shirt and scooted around him, holding up her pinkie in front of his face. "The size of my fingertip." A small grin resurfaced. "Good news. It looks like you'll live."

"No thanks to you, Dr. Jekyll." He stretched his shoulder some more.

"Yeah, yeah, you big baby. Now go over there, stick your arm into that hole, and pull out whatever it is that's back there. I can brush my fingers over it, but it's out of my reach."

Quint did a double take. Was she serious? She stared back at him, nudging her head toward the hole. "Hurry up, Parker. We don't have all day."

"Okay, boss lady. But you were supposed to kiss my shoulder better," he reminded her.

"I kissed you less than ten minutes ago." She followed, kneeling next to him. "How many kisses do you need in one sitting?"

"I don't know." He shoved his arm deep into the wall, grasping what felt like a small, hard box. The top was smooth to the touch. "We should spend a few hours figuring that out some night."

He drew the box out carefully, wincing when he lightly bumped it on the wall before he cleared the hole.

Angélica shined the flashlight on it, her eyes widening. "What the ... ?"

Quint was having trouble believing it himself. "You're kidding me."

She took the rectangular plastic box from him, flipping it over, reading the word on the bottom. "Tupperware?"

He laughed, shaking his head. "Well, Dr. García, you think they'll use radiocarbon dating on this piece?"

* * *

Angélica led the way into the Temple of the Water Witch in the late afternoon sunshine.

After they'd opened the Tupperware and taken stock of its contents, or more like scratched their heads about them, they'd headed back to the mess tent so Quint could get a bite to eat while they played Sherlock and Watson a while longer.

Before following her to fulfill his end of the deal, Quint had run back to his tent to grab a clean shirt and the two short two-by-fours he'd picked up behind the Dawn Temple.

He'd paused outside the entrance to the Water Witch, cursing at temples in general, and then joined her inside.

"I still don't know what to make of those photos." Angélica said as she climbed down the second ladder on the way to the sub chamber.

For the life of her, she couldn't figure out why Dr. Hughes would store two Polaroids and an article in a piece of Tupperware in the temple wall.

"It must have something to do with the Dawn Temple, maybe a clue."

She waited for him to climb down the ladder. "A clue to what?"

He waved off her offer to take the two boards from him. "I don't know. Something else he hid in there."

Had Dr. Hughes found some relic worth hiding? If so, hide it from whom?

"They're standing in front of the temple in the first picture," Quint said, stepping off the bottom rung. "And the second one shows part of the temple's blueprint."

"What about the article?"

"I have no idea how that ties in. You're sure you've never heard of the woman in it?"

"Positive. If this Dr. Sutcliffe worked at the same university as Dr. Hughes, maybe he had a thing for her."

"Maybe, but I don't think so. He seemed very taken with Mrs. Hughes whenever I was around them. My mom and dad were having some problems when I first met Jeff. I remember wishing my parents were more like them—nice to each other, even doting at times."

Angélica paused beside the chamber's outer wall and looked back at him. "You said Jared went to the same college where Dr. Hughes taught."

"Yeah, he was a grad student there."

"Do you think he's somehow linked to this stuff Dr. Hughes hid away?"

"Possibly. He is in that one photo." Quint rubbed his hand over his stubble-covered jaw, making a scratchy sound. "The only thing I am certain of is that your ex-husband is not to be trusted, especially around you."

She smirked up at him at that last part.

"What? I'm not saying that just because I like it when you kiss me." He winked. "Not entirely anyway."

"You're such a flirt." She dropped onto her stomach and slid through the hole at the base of the outer wall.

"I'm not flirting," he said after he shoved the boards through the hole and squeezed in after them, taking the hand she offered. "I'm being honest."

She watched him dust off his clothes, warming to this honesty policy a little too much for her heart's health.

"I'd like to take another look at the stuff you have from Mrs. Hughes," she said. "Out of curiosity."

Quint nodded, looking over at the loose block. "Anytime, boss lady."

"Thanks. Now come play tug-o-war with me." She crossed the room, picked up the rope, and wrapped it around her hand. "Cross your fingers the shell is on the other side."

Quint stepped in front of her, dropping the boards next to the loosened block. "What if it's not?"

"Let's not go there."

He took up the rope, getting a grip on it.

"On three then, ready?" She grasped the rope tightly in her hands as she planted her feet on the chamber floor.

Quint nodded.

On the count of three, she dug her feet in and pulled. In front of her, Quint's arms glistened in the lamplight as his triceps bulged. The block scraped slowly across the chiseled-out floor.

Bending his knees, he put his back into it, grunting.

Her feet began to slide out from under her. Then the rope went lax in her hand and she reeled into the wall behind her.

As the dust settled, she frowned down at where Quint was lying completely still within three feet of the wall with the rope wrapped around his hand as he stared up at the blocks towering over him. Small pebble-like pieces of limestone sprinkled down around him.

A rumbling sound started low and grew louder.

Angélica took a step toward him. "Quint, move!"

"Get back!" he ordered without looking at her.

As she watched, her hand covering her mouth in alarm, he rolled onto all fours and grabbed the two short boards. Diving for the weakened wall, he shoved the boards into the spot where the block had been, pounding one under the other to jack it up.

The room fell silent, only the dust daring to move.

"Quint?" she whispered, afraid to move.

"Damn." Wiping his mouth he pushed to his feet, his hair covered with a coat of dust. "That was close."

"Get away from it," she hissed, motioning him her way.

"It's fine. Those support boards should hold it for a while until we get something stronger. It was just off balance when we pulled out the block."

Tiptoeing over to the wall, she frowned at a new crack in one of the stones at eyelevel. "You sure it's safe?"

He chuckled. "Safe is a term I like to use loosely."

Flashlight in hand, she kneeled in front of the hole. "You've been hanging around my father too long." She patted the block they'd hauled out. "Can you move this thing out of the way?"

"Sure." Quint tugged on the rope and dragged the rock several feet away from the wall. "I don't know how we're going to haul out the one that was next to it without bringing the whole wall down." He returned to her side.

She lowered onto her back. "We're not taking out any more blocks."

He caught her foot as she started to wiggle into the hole in the wall. "What do you think you're doing?"

"Finding out what's on the other side."

"Maybe we should look from this side until we secure the wall more."

"No way." She shook off his hold. "I've waited too long to see this."

"Are you crazy? You bump that board and you'll bring this whole wall down on you."

"I'll be fine. You might want to step back though."

"You can't fit through there. It's too narrow."

She looked overhead at the hole. It was about an inch wider than her shoulders, boards not included. "I'll fit."

At least she hoped she would. If the wall fell, it would take Quint days to dig her out. That was if the weight of the blocks didn't kill her outright.

As she slid her head under the wall, she pulled her arms in tight against her torso, scraping her left shoulder on the block opposite the board in order to avoid bumping the piece of wood. Her heart banged in her chest like a bell ringer stuck inside a buried coffin. A fresh dew of sweat slicked her from head to toe.

Inching along she squeezed her elbows through and then twisted at the waist to fit through the opening. When her hip bumped the wood, her pants pocket catching on the corner, she stopped, fighting the urge to flee at all costs.

"Angélica." Quint's timbre was higher than usual.

The wall didn't move.

Whew! She took a breath to steady her muscles, then carefully freed her pants. "It's okay. I got this."

His curses followed her the rest of the way through the hole. As soon as she was in the clear, she scurried away from the wall. Sweat poured down her face.

Quint peered in at her. "You're fucking insane, do you know that?"

She shielded her eyes from the flashlight beam he had

pointed at her face. "Maybe so, but you like me anyway."

"I like you a whole lot better when you're naked in my tent than when you're trying to get yourself killed in a godforsaken temple."

"What's with all of the crying today, Parker?" She shined her light around the room. Cobwebs covered the chamber from wall to wall. "You start your period this morning?"

He laughed. "Oh, the things I'm going to do to you later, woman. We'll see who's crying when I'm done."

Climbing to her feet, she crept across the stone floor. "Promises, promises."

The cobwebs crackled as she brushed them out of her way, sticking to her arms, neck, and face.

Something crawled across her scalp.

Cringing, she shook out her hair.

"Well?" Quint's light shined around her ankles. He scooted his head through a bit further "What do you see?"

"A burial chamber."

"How can you tell?"

She shined her flashlight on the only object in the room— a bench of stone set against the wall directly in front of her. "That's the equivalent of a casket."

She approached the tomb. It was covered with a thick layer of dust—a millennium's worth, she thought, wanting to jump for joy. She leaned over and blew off the top slab. Dust flew up her nose and stuck to her eyelashes.

After coughing and sputtering, she giggled. "That was smart, bonehead," she said to herself.

"That's supposed to be my line," the peanut gallery chimed in from the hole in the wall.

"Be careful, funny man."

There was still too much dust on top of the slab to see it clearly. She started to stretch the hem of her shirt, and then took it completely off, using it to wipe off the top of the stone slab.

"Nice." Quint whistled, peering through at her. "Is this

show for free? I left my dollar bills back in my other pants."

"Don't make me hurt you later." What was that carved into the stone?

"What's with you mixing my pain with your pleasure?"

"What can I say?" She angled her flashlight, trying to use shadow relief to figure out the marking. "You make me want to do wicked things to you."

"Okay, but can I be face up when you straddle me this time?"

She grinned, looking down at him. "Will you push my tools through?"

"I like the view from here." His beam spotlighted her bra. "I'll make you a trade—your tools for your bra."

"Nice try, Parker." She shook the dust from her shirt over his head, chuckling as he cursed and slid out of sight.

Her shirt was back on when her leather pouch came sliding across the floor. She scooped it up and pulled out a small paintbrush. The dust swept away easily and an image began to take shape.

"Yes," she whispered, going up on her tiptoes.

"What is it?"

She brushed away more of the dirt. "A *moan*."

"A what?"

"A *moan*. It's a mythical bird the Maya associated with death. This king had a kind of twisted fascination with it. He had it carved all over the place in the Sunset Temple."

"First a curse, now a death symbol. Didn't these people have anything better to do with their time?"

Dropping down on one knee, Angélica tried to peer under the lip of the stone coffin. Grasshoppers bounced around inside her stomach. She was close. She could feel it.

"This slab has to go." She shoved against the lid. "Jesus. I can't even budge it."

"Hold on," Quint said. A moment later he shoved a piece of rebar through. "Try this."

"Thanks." Sweat dripping from nerves as much as the

heat, she carefully worked the bar, shoving again and again until she had a good eight inches at the widest part of the gap. Setting the bar on top of the slab, she picked up her flashlight.

This was it.

It was all she had worked for since watching her mother take her last breath.

With her pulse chasing rabbits around a racetrack, she shined the light on the long-dead king, focusing on his neck. The jade necklace was there, but there was no shell on it. She looked from corner to corner inside the stone coffin, studying the king and jade trinkets littered throughout the grave. The longer she searched, the more her chest filled with lead.

"Well?" Quint's voice was tinged with expectancy.

"I'm fucked."

The shell wasn't there.

Chapter Twenty-Three
Yum Cimil: The Lord of Death.

That evening, they ate supper in Quint's tent since it was just the two of them. Cold tortillas, freeze-dried papaya, and beef jerky by lantern light wasn't Quint's idea of a romantic first dinner date, especially with Rover snorting at their feet as he practically inhaled the scraps they gave him, but it got the job done. Angélica sat on his cot in a gloomy daze, her mood dark since not finding the shell.

"What are you going to do now?" Quint asked, collecting her empty plate and stacking it on the desk along with his.

"Take a shower," Angélica stared at the last slice of papaya in her fingers. "I really stink."

"It was pretty hot and dusty in that little room."

"I mean I stink as an archaeologist."

"You're tired. Don't be too hard on yourself tonight."

She took a bite of papaya, her gaze zeroing in on him. "Don't you get it? I have no idea where to look next, and if I don't find the shell, I have nothing."

"You have your father." Quint pulled out his desk chair and straddled it, resting his forearms on the back rest. "And you have me."

"Yeah, but you're only temporary."

Oof! She wasn't pulling her punches tonight. He raised his brows. "Says who?"

"You."

"When did I say anything along those lines?"

She frowned. "You don't have to say anything, Quint. You're here to write an article and have been nice enough to stay and help me. I know what that means."

"Really? Maybe you should fill me in."

"When I walk away from here, you walk away, too. Only you'll be heading in a different direction."

"Who's to say I won't follow you and see where you're going?"

"This jungle."

"The jungle speaks?"

"No, it makes you miserable."

True. He scratched the back of his neck, thinking about the pests here. "If only there were fewer bugs. And snakes. And it wasn't so hot and muggy."

"Not to mention those damned tombs," she quoted him in a fake masculine voice.

"And those."

"See? You hate it down here. When we leave this site, you won't be coming back ever again if you can help it. Whereas if I can figure out how to save my ass, I'll be back in about six to eight months, weather allowing, for another season of bugs, snakes, and heat."

She had a good point, but he wasn't ready to walk away from her, even if it meant dealing with this hellhole and all of its vermin.

"And there's your job to consider, of course."

He rested his chin on his forearms. "What about my job?" He had a feeling he knew the road she was headed down. It was the same road that always ended where the skid marks went off the edge of the cliff—he traveled too much.

"It's dangerous."

That caught him by surprise. "How is it dangerous?"

"You travel all over the world to places far from civilization and put your life at risk."

"My life at risk? Where did you get that idea?"

She picked up a machete and held it between them. "I don't know—maybe because we're sleeping next to this in the middle of a dark jungle with nobody around for miles."

This was her doing, not his. He'd rather be holed up with her in a lush hotel right now with the only potential visitor being a staff member bringing room service.

"Yeah, but this trip is different from normal."

"Because you're looking for clues to Dr. Hughes' disappearance?"

"No, because you're here. If it wasn't for you being so stubborn about leaving, I'd have been gone by now."

"Without solving the Dr. Hughes' mystery?"

"*That* is not worth risking my life for."

"Oh." She stared at him, little vertical lines forming between her eyes. "I see."

"Do you?" Because if she really did, she needed to remove him from the fucking *Temporary* category.

"Yeah, I think I do."

"Let me know if you need me to carve it on some Maya glyph to help get it through your hard head, boss lady."

Her gaze narrowed. "So do you make a practice of sharing a tent with women you meet while on the road?"

"Nope. The last girl I shared a tent with was my sister, Violet, back when she still wore pigtails and my sleepwear had bulldozers all over it."

"You know what I mean, Parker."

"If you're asking me whether I make a habit of sleeping with women I meet while doing my job, the answer is no. You, Dr. Angélica García, are a rare exception to a rule I've had for many years about not mixing work with pleasure."

She leaned forward, resting her elbows on her knees, her

gaze hooded. "Okay, since we're being honest with each other about this, here's the thing—I'm not sure I'm up to trying a long distance relationship right now."

If she wasn't sure, that left a chance that she was up to it; she just didn't know it yet. But with her in a black mood tonight, he decided to let everything lie for now. "How about we finish up what needs to be done here and see where we land when it's over."

"Okay." She yawned, covering it. The skin under her eyes looked extra dark in the lantern light. "By the way, thanks for not making a big deal about last night."

Did she mean sex or the fight afterward? Both had left him reeling. "Define a big deal?"

"You know, wanting to talk about it."

He still didn't know what she meant. "I figured we'd save that discussion for later when I'm trying to get you to have sex with me again."

"You think words will do the trick?"

"Probably not. In my experience with you, words are shushed during sex."

Her smile came out for the first time since she'd wiggled out of that secret tomb empty-handed. "That was a rare exception to a rule I've had for many years about always mixing *words* with pleasure," she volleyed his earlier line back at him.

Her wit was going to keep him on his toes, especially if she liked to joust with him during sex. He wasn't sure he could handle multitasking when she was naked.

He watched her blink in slow motion, her eyelids drooping. "When did you get to sleep last night?"

"I didn't. I kept María company until she left this morning."

"You need to get some sleep."

"I need to go back in that temple and find the shell."

"You're practically dead on your feet."

"Some coffee will perk me right up."

He stood, holding out his hand to her. "Come on."

"Where are we going?" She let him pull her to her feet.

"The showers."

"I'm not having sex with you in the shower, Parker. Not when a thug is roaming around in the jungle at night."

"I wasn't even thinking about shower sex."

"Sorry." She grimaced. "I was."

Now that she'd raised the subject, so was he. "We both need to clean up and we're not doing it alone."

He grabbed some clean clothes, his towel, and one of the machetes, and then led her outside. "I'll stand guard while you shower and you can do the same for me."

"That makes sense." She stepped into her tent and then returned with her tank top from last night, a pair of underwear, and a towel.

He waited while she zipped her tent closed. "So you won't have shower sex while a possible killer is prowling around, huh?"

She walked beside him. "Of course not. That'd be like a scene from one of those teenager horror flicks. We'd be slaughtered in the midst of getting all hot and heavy."

"What about when no killers or thugs are roaming?"

She bumped into him on purpose, playful, knocking him off course. "That depends."

"On what?"

"The shower, of course."

He chuckled and looped his arm around her shoulders.

They walked the rest of the way in silence, listening in the darkness. The nightly serenade of the jungle drowned out most other sounds.

While she showered, he kept watch with the machete in hand. She did the same for him, only she cheated and peeked while he was in the middle of rinsing.

"No fair!" He blocked her view with his hand. "You made me promise not to peek."

"That's what you get for making rash promises."

They didn't waste time drying off, taking fast strides back to their tents. When she started to give him a goodnight spiel, he shook his head and moved her aside, slipping into her tent. A moment later, he stepped back outside carrying her cot.

"What are you doing?"

"You're sleeping in my tent."

"Parker, I'm tired and pissed about the shell. As much as I admire your physical attributes and your many talents while using them, sex is not happening tonight."

"Jeez, woman, you have a one-track mind." He set her cot down next to his, then tugged her inside and zipped the flap closed before the mosquitos decided to join them, too. "Angélica, I don't want to have sex with you tonight."

"Good." Then she frowned. "You don't?"

He tweaked her nose. "Don't be silly—of course, I do. But that doesn't mean I'm going to try to get you naked." He arranged their machetes and the flare gun in between the cots. "I moved you in here because it's smarter for you, me, and Rover to stay together. Three pairs of eyes and ears are better than one, and after what happened to some of your crew, I won't be able to sleep with you a tent away."

At her stubborn expression, he sighed. "Listen, boss lady, let me take care of you this once. I promise I won't tell anyone you showed any signs of weakness."

"I'm tired, not weak."

"Fine." He pointed at her cot. "Now lie down and shut your eyes. You need some rest to be able to think clearly tomorrow and figure out where the shell is."

Amazingly, she did, lying on her side facing his cot. He settled in across from her with Rover bedding down on the floor between their feet.

Her eyelids started to droop in no time. He reached across and took her hand in his, stroking the backside of it. "You want me to tell you a bedtime story?"

"Yes." She smiled, so sleepy, her eyes closing. "Tell me why Mrs. Hughes didn't believe her husband was killed in that plane crash."

"I don't know." He tried to remember, his own brain growing blurry with sleep. "It had to do with them finding something on the plane. You can read through Mrs. Hughes' notes tomorrow. It's somewhere in there."

"Okay." Angélica sank visibly into sleep, her shoulders slumping. Her breathing slowed down, became rhythmic.

Brushing a damp, auburn tendril from her face, Quint's thoughts returned to what she'd said earlier about his being temporary.

Christ, what a mess he'd gotten himself into down here. He'd come to this dig site to find a missing man and had ended up getting lost himself.

He watched her sleep, wondering how creeped out she'd be if she woke up right then and found him staring. She'd probably sock him in the nose or at the least dump him off his cot.

"Goodnight, siren," he whispered.

She sighed in her sleep, her lips looking soft and tempting. With a groan, he rolled onto his back and closed his eyes, trying not to think about the sexy woman wearing nothing more than a tank top and panties sleeping a couple of feet away.

* * *

Quint woke to a squawk-fest of jays outside his tent. He put his pillow over his head to drown out the commotion and then remembered where he was. Jackknifing up in his cot, he looked over at Angélica.

Her cot was empty.

Where was she? He tried to keep his head straight while he slipped into a pair of jeans, telling himself she was probably over in her tent working. Maybe she had to go to the bathroom and had been the cause of the jays squawking.

When she hadn't shown up by the time he'd finished

lacing up his boots, his stomach was also knotted up. Damn it, where was she?

He looked around under the cots and in the corners. Rover was gone, too. He prayed that they were out taking a morning stroll together.

When he grabbed his water bottle from where it sat on his desk he saw her note beside the Tupperware they'd pulled out of the wall in the Dawn Temple.

Sleeping Beauty—Got up early. Didn't want to wake you. Going to grab some food and head back inside the T. of the W.W. Took the camp knife, machete, and flare gun with me, so don't worry. Come and find me when you get your lazy ass up.

P.S. I took advantage of you while you slept.

In spite of her being armed and ready for any unwanted visitors, her being alone in that temple didn't settle well with him.

He read her note again.

So feisty! He missed her already.

Damn. He was going to have to get used to tent life for months on end.

And the bugs, snakes, and heat.

He tucked her note into his pocket.

And these godforsaken temples.

He headed over to the mess tent. Gulping down cold dregs of bitter coffee as he collected some food to take to her, something niggled at his brain about last night, something that he'd thought of as he was drifting off.

What had they been talking about? She'd wanted him to tell her a story about … oh, Mrs. Hughes and the plane crash. Why hadn't Mrs. Hughes believed her husband had been in the crash? That was it.

The lucky ring.

What about the ring? He took another swig of caffeine.

The ring was at the crash site and it should have been inside the liner of Dr. Hughes' luggage. That was it.

Okay, so what was the big deal about that? He closed his eyes, trying to focus on what it was about the lucky ring that had his wheels trying to spin this morning.

… Angélica's eyes drowsy … why didn't Mrs. Hughes believe her husband was in the crash … lucky ring …

Oh! Shit!

"There was a ring next to the pair of glasses in that photo," he told the empty tent. He put his coffee cup down on the counter, scooped up the food, and headed back to his tent to take a quick look at that picture again.

Once there, he shuffled through the photos from the Tupperware, finding the one with the map of the Dawn Temple.

There—the ring.

Was it Dr. Hughes'? He rushed next door and retrieved Angélica's magnifying glass. Turning on his lantern to add more light, he peered at the picture of the ring. The name of the university where Dr. Hughes had worked was carved on the outside of the thick band below the red stone. He lowered the picture, grabbing Mrs. Hughes' notebook. What had she written?

He never wore his lucky ring. He carried it in a small leather pouch that I'd sewn into the liner of his luggage.

So if he hadn't worn the ring, why was it sitting on this map next to his glasses?

Quint examined the picture again, thinking back to twenty years ago while sitting across from Dr. Hughes on the ground as the older man taught him how to read a grid.

Wait a second. Dr. Hughes' glasses had square wire rims, not round like these in the photo. If they weren't Dr. Hughes' glasses, whose were they? And if the glasses didn't belong to Dr. Hughes, maybe the ring didn't either.

Quint raised the magnifying glass again. He couldn't see anything distinctive about the outside of the band. Only the typical ... he caught a glimpse of something lower on the band under the year.

"What's this?" The initials *N.A.S.* were barely discernable.

Did this ring belong to Steel? The last initial was the same. Maybe it was his father's, a family heirloom. Another examination of the ring made him realize it looked more like a woman's class ring. Maybe Steel's mother had gone to college there, too.

Those initials seemed familiar though. Why? His gaze drifted to the picture of the woman in the article Dr. Hughes had stored for two decades.

Her name was printed in bold type under the fuzzy image. "Norah Ann Sutcliffe," he read aloud. *N.A. S.*

"Son of a bitch." He scanned the article again.

The body of Dr. Norah Ann Sutcliffe was found at the bottom of Schrock Lake three months after her reported disappearance. Dr. Sutcliffe was a well-respected Associate Professor in Anthropology at the University of ...

He skipped over her accreditations.

According to authorities, she must have hit her head when her car plunged into the water, knocking her unconscious. It is believed she then drowned in the frigid water ...

He flipped to the second page and skimmed the end.

... saying black ice on the road is most likely the cause of the accident. Funeral arrangements ...

Quint held the magnifying glass over the black and white newspaper photo. She had her arms crossed in front of her. It looked like she was wearing a ring on her right ring finger, but the image was too fuzzy to be sure.

Why would Dr. Sutcliffe's ring have been down here? And

the year Dr. Hughes had written in pen on the bottom of the photo was a year later than the date on the newspaper article. Quint rubbed the back of his neck, feeling the beginning of a tension headache.

If the article was linked to the ring photo, then what was the significance of the other picture? The one with Dr. Hughes and Steel standing in front of the Dawn Temple?

He picked it up and studied it, searching for something out of place in the background. The Dawn Temple looked different but most likely due to twenty years of the jungle around it aging and the restoration work Juan and Marianne García had done.

In the foreground, Dr. Hughes stood next to Steel, who clutched what looked like a map, holding his hand over it as if explaining something about it to Dr. Hughes.

Quint picked up the magnifying glass, moving closer to the light. Then he saw it—the ring—on Steel's pinky finger.

"I'll be damned."

Something nudged his calf. He glanced down at Rover and realized he hadn't zipped his tent flap closed in his hurry to get the magnifying glass. He reached down and scratched Rover under his snout, worrying about Angélica again. She had her arsenal, but he'd feel better after he went and checked on her.

He looked back down at the picture of Dr. Hughes and Steel in front of the Dawn Temple. But first he needed to figure out something he was close to grasping with this whole Dr. Hughes business. He peered through the magnifying glass again. What was Steel doing with that ring?

He lowered the photo to his desk. Where had Dr. Hughes gotten the article? Had he asked his wife to mail it down to the site? Why was it worth stuffing it into a piece of Tupperware, hiding it away in a temple wall?

Dr. Hughes must have been suspicious of Steel. He must have noticed the initials on the ring and put two and two together, realizing it belonged to Dr. Sutcliffe. Did that mean he'd suspected Steel of having something to do with her death the year prior? Why else would he have that article?

Leaning back in the chair, he closed his eyes. Why was her name so familiar? Had her disappearance been a big deal in the papers back when he had been in high school? No, he'd seen her name somewhere else—but where?

He sat up straight, looking around for the blue plastic folder. When he found it, he fingered through the documents, looking for the picture Mrs. Hughes had copied from the university newspaper.

"Here we go." He pulled it out.

The article was about the new anthropology department head, and Quint had assumed that Mrs. Hughes had copied it because it had a picture of Steel in the background talking to a pretty brunette. But he hadn't paid attention to the name of the brunette before.

Now he did; sure enough, it was Dr. Sutcliffe. He peered closer. But Steel wasn't just talking; he had his hand on her lower back. The smile on Dr. Sutcliffe's face as she looked up at Steel suddenly had more depth, more meaning.

So what did he do, Dr. Hughes?

What had Dr. Hughes been thinking? That Steel had seduced Dr. Sutcliffe and then sent her into that lake to drown? But why? What was in it for Steel? Something with his career? Or had Dr. Sutcliffe seen something that would lead to her death? Learned something Steel didn't want known?

Quint banged his fists against his forehead. Somehow, instead of solving the mystery of what had happened to Dr. Hughes, he'd managed to get mixed up in the mystery of what had happened to Dr. Sutcliffe. Jesus, as detectives went, he doubted even Daffy Duck would hire him to work at Quackbusters.

It was too bad Juan wasn't around to help with this. Then again, Angélica's father would probably have him back in that damned temple digging out more rocks, especially back around that hat.

That hat!

Mrs. Hughes' words played through his mind: *a boot with his name scrawled on it (an old Navy habit) was found close by.*

Could that be Dr. Hughes' hat? If so, his initials might still be on the inside band. Did finding his hat even matter?

Maybe. He might as well go see, since he'd hit a dead end on Dr. Sutcliffe and the ring. Grabbing his flashlight and the stash of food he'd collected for his and Angélica's breakfast, he stepped out of his tent.

Rover trotted out next to him.

"Get back inside, Rover."

The javelina ignored him, heading toward the mess tent.

Quint shrugged and then zipped the mesh flap closed. It was a free country in javelina-land.

He looked across the plaza at the Dawn Temple and then over at the Temple of the Water Witch. Should he go check on Angélica first? He'd probably be busy over there working with her for a while. Just a quick look at that hat, and then he'd hop over and join her. His decision made, he headed toward the Dawn Temple.

Pausing at the steps leading up to the temple's dark mouth, he glanced around. Sweat pooled in the usual places and a few new ones thanks to thinking about trying his luck again in that goddamned chamber of terror.

Stop being such a wuss.

Cursing, he started up the steps.

* * *

Angélica rested her head against the warm wall. Her shoulders sagged, her shirt soaked. Defeat tasted like shit.

Where could that shell be? She'd been through her charts, her mom's notes, even the drawings that Esteban had done of several different temple walls. The damned thing seemed to thwart her at every turn.

And where was Quint? He should be awake by now. Then again, they were both low on sleep, playing catch up. He'd looked so relaxed when she'd left him. She'd been tempted to forget her quest for the shell for a while longer and spend the morning convincing him to follow her back to her house in Cancun until his next job took him away. But time was of the essence, and she wouldn't stop worrying about her father until she was there with him.

She stood, collecting her drawings and books. She'd reached the hole in the outer wall when she remembered that she'd left the lid of the tomb open in the king's burial chamber.

"Crud." Maybe she could let it go until she returned later with Quint. Then she thought of the mouse she'd shooed away when she'd arrived early this morning.

Dragging her feet, Angélica approached *the wall*. Each time she had to go through that hole, it looked like it had shrunk a little more.

Shoving her tool belt and water bottle through ahead of her just in case, she inched through the hole. On the other side, she wiped her face with her T-shirt and noticed how much her hands were trembling. It was funny how her courage seemed to wane as her age increased.

Leaning over the stone casket, she shined her flashlight into the darkness once again. "Where did you hide it?" she whispered, directing the beam on the jade necklace around his neck. That was where it should be, right there, damn it.

She flipped the skeleton off. "You paranoid freak."

In spite of the missing shell, she still had lots of work to do documenting this burial chamber. The Mexican government would be happy to hear that she had found the king. Maybe happy enough to overlook the tasks she hadn't accomplished and the problems with keeping her crew intact and safe this year.

Something shifted down by the feet of the skeleton. When she shined the flashlight in that direction, two tiny eyes twinkled.

"You little shit." She grabbed a paintbrush from her tool belt and leaned further into the tomb, careful not to crush anything under her palm. She tried to scare the mouse toward the opening. It cowered against the far wall.

Grabbing the lid of the tomb, Angélica braced her foot against the wall and tugged on the stone slab. It scraped open a few more inches, sliding off the back corner, making another hole big enough for the mouse to escape.

She set her light next to the skull and stood on tiptoe as she leaned over the dead king, reaching toward the foot-end of the tomb. If a skeleton hand grabbed her boob, she was going to piss her pants.

"Get out of there." She nudged the mouse with her paintbrush. It let out a squeak and shot out through the opening she'd made.

She drew her arm back. Thanks to the shadows caused by the angle of the light, she noticed a small, irregular lump under the pelvis bone. Carefully she reached down and pulled out what felt like a wad of scratchy cloth from under the skeleton. Something clicked in the cloth as she moved it away from the pelvis.

Back flat on her feet, she pulled the wad several inches toward her and smoothed it out, doing her best not to disturb the rest of the skeleton. Whatever was inside, it must have been part of a burial cache, or maybe even attached to what was left of the king's robe. Her fingers brushed over something hard under the tattered fabric. She moved the flashlight closer. It was probably a bone tangled in the cloth. She'd seen that too many times to count.

Pulling a pair of tweezers from her tool pouch, she pinched the very edge of the cloth and pulled it back.

Her breath bottled up in her chest.

Holy crap!

She scrambled out, her heart taking a turn around the Indy 500 track.

She'd found it! She'd finally found the …

Something scuffed across the floor in the outer room.

Her heart did a tailspin, screeching.

What was that? Or rather, who? She opened her mouth to say Quint's name, but then realized he would most likely call for her right off.

She strained, listening for more scuffs or crunches from the loose pebbles that littered the floor.

Or breathing.

There! She heard it again. Another scuff.

Someone was on the other side of the wall.

Glancing around for her weapon, she swore under her breath—so was her machete.

* * *

Quint carried the stone across the chamber and placed it on top of the pile of others. In his hurry to get to the hat, he wasn't wasting time with the wheelbarrow this morning and was paying for it already in his lower back.

The hat was almost within reach.

After a few back stretches, he lifted a stone about the size of a concrete cinder block and almost dropped it on his foot when he saw what had been underneath it.

A hand.

Or at least what was left of it. More like bones with some dried flesh barely holding it together.

He tossed the block aside and squatted down to get a closer look at the cracked, yellowed bones. What was a hand doing here?

More importantly, whose hand was it?

This wasn't another one of Juan's practical jokes was it?

He touched one of the finger bones, grimacing. It felt real enough.

Hauling away another large stone revealed a tattered, faded, blue shirtsleeve.

The next stone he moved exposed the shoulder joint.

Quint blinked the sweat out of his eyes. He pushed onward, his back twinging as he hefted rocks aside, uncovering the remains grunt by grunt.

The chest cavity had been flattened by one big motherfucker of a rock. The skull had a partially crushed eye socket. He used a pencil to sift through a tuft of dusty hair. His sweat dripped down into its gaping jaws.

Whoever it was must have been in this chamber for a long time. The fabric covering the body was chewed on and holey with dust permeating the weaves of the material.

When Quint rolled a large stone out of the way near the feet, he found a pair of square-rimmed wire frames. Crushed glass sprinkled the dirt and stone.

He stood there huffing in the dusty chamber, dread chilling his blood. He knew those glasses.

Lifting the wire frames by the nose bridge, he carefully placed them off to the side. Hefting two more stones to the side, he cleared the left foot, fibula, and tibia. A boot lay in pieces around the ankle, the thread seams rotted away.

When he cleared the last of the remains, his knees gave out. He leaned over the remains of the right leg, sucking in deep breaths to get rid of the lightheadedness that was making him sway.

Grabbing his flashlight, he shined the beam down at where the right foot should have been but wasn't.

Mrs. Hughes' words clanged in his thoughts:

… a boot with his name scrawled on it (an old Navy habit) was found close by on the jungle floor. Some of his foot was still in it (mostly bones). They figure an animal dragged away what was left of his body, because they couldn't find it.

Quint scrubbed his hands down his face, his heart beating a bass drum in his ears, loud and hard.

He'd found Dr. Hughes.

Until that moment, a small part of him had believed in the fantasy that Dr. Hughes had suffered from amnesia for the last two decades and was down here growing old under a different name. He'd wanted to have something good to take home to Jeff and his family, something uplifting.

Not this. Fuck, not this.

Mrs. Hughes had been right. Her husband hadn't been on that plane. Some rotten piece of shit had cut off Dr. Hughes' foot, probably years after he was dead judging by the lack of any blood remnants around the bottom of the leg, and planted it there to fool the authorities. Someone twisted and demented and desperate, and Quint had a good idea who.

And so had Mrs. Hughes.

He heard the rasp of a shoe slide across the pebble-covered floor and lunged to his feet, reaching for his machete.

Something hard slammed into the back of his skull.

A bolt of pain streaked through his head as he fell forward. The floor kissed his cheek goodnight, and the lights went out.

* * *

Angélica was starting to lose it.

There'd been nobody in the outer chamber when she'd gotten brave enough to peek out through the hole, not even the stupid mouse.

All of the stress she'd been dealing with for so long had her brain all cattywampus. At least that excuse made her feel less skittish as she clambered up the last ladder leading away from the king's tomb and jogged through the passageway toward the temple's exit. Every so often, she'd glance behind her to make sure nobody was following her.

She shot out of the temple and down the steps, one of the two shells the king had been buried with wrapped in the piece of cloth clutched in her palm. She went straight to Quint's tent, eager to share the news of her find.

His tent flap was unzipped at the bottom. Rover must be outside, probably rooting around in María's garden. She grimaced. That was not a good habit for him to get into.

"Quint," she called as she opened the flap the rest of the way, ducking inside. Nobody was home.

Where was he? The mess tent? She walked over to his desk. The photos they'd found in the Dawn Temple were there, partially wadded up. Why'd he do that to them? He wouldn't have gone back in the Dawn Temple again without her, would he?

Back outside she slowly zipped the flap closed, debating where to look next. A whisper of fear nipped at her. Had someone gotten to him while he was sleeping? No, she would have seen a sign of a struggle, a turned over cot, something. Wouldn't she?

He was fine. She needed to keep a lid on her panic for a little bit longer until they'd hiked to the village and called Pedro to come and get them. Quint was probably messing around back in the Dawn Temple again, that was all. Something to do with those pictures Dr. Hughes had left behind.

She turned around.

Jared stood there, not five feet away, wearing the same clothes he'd been wearing yesterday. Only they looked like they'd been worn for twenty-four hours in a jungle, all dirty, sweaty, and wrinkled. Very un-Jared like.

She squeaked in surprise, echoing the mouse in the king's tomb. "Jared? What are you doing here?" Where was everyone else? Was her father okay? Had the helicopter gone down?

"Hello, darling." He pulled a handgun from behind his back and pointed it at her face. "Did you miss me?"

Chapter Twenty-Four

Cimic: To die; death.

Quint opened his eyes, blinking several times to bring the world into focus.

A skull stared at him, its jaws wide in a silent scream.

He jerked back, groaning as a bolt of pain shot through his head, and quickly lay flat on the floor again.

His right cheekbone stung as he lay there in the dirt. He tried to lift his hand to touch his face only to realize his wrists were tied together behind his back. His ankles were bound, too.

Closing his eyes, he tried to remember what had happened … footfalls … someone coming up behind him … he'd reached for the machete. That was it.

There'd been only one set of footfalls, he was pretty sure. That didn't mean an accomplice wasn't hiding outside in the tunnel though.

Angélica!

Oh, Jesus! He had to find her, warn her. He struggled to free his hands. The rope dug deeper into his skin.

"Fuck!" He stared into the skull's empty eye sockets,

swallowing back a wave of panic.

He lifted his head off the floor to look around and felt something sticky on the back of his neck. It pulled on the hairs there when he moved. That couldn't be good.

His flashlight lay next to Dr. Hughes' pelvic bone, about two feet away. The beam of light lit up a piece of limestone. Was it dimmer than before? How long had he been out?

If he could find a sharp edge on one of the rocks scattered around him, maybe he could free himself before whoever had hit him returned for more batting practice.

He rolled onto his back, lying on his bound hands, maneuvering so his head was pointing toward the exit. Another shot of pain made him grit his teeth. When it eased, he pushed with his heels and inched across the floor, bumping against his flashlight as he passed. The light spun around, pointing to the entrance to the chamber. Pausing to adjust his hands, he twisted as much as he could to look in the direction of the light.

Something hung down in the chamber entryway. What in the hell? He twisted further. It was an ax handle. The blade was buried in the main support beam overhead.

Quint's blood chilled.

Dirt trickled from the ceiling, settling onto his neck and chest.

He looked up. A large section of the support beam directly above him had been hacked away, the remaining timber was ragged from the ax blade.

Another creak of splintering wood filled the room, followed by a low rumble.

A handful of grit and dust fell from the weakened ceiling, dusting his chest and the floor next to his shoulder.

"Hells bells," he whispered.

* * *

Angélica stared at the gun aimed at her chest. Jared's

steady grip gave her the chills. She lifted her chin, holding his gaze. "What do you want from me, Jared?"

He smiled, his eyes gleaming with contempt. "To start with, I'll take that shell."

"No!" She clutched the shell tightly against her stomach and took a step back.

"You didn't think I knew about your little treasure hunt, did you? You shouldn't try to hide things from your husband, darling." His hand snaked out and grabbed her arm, yanking her toward him. "What's yours is mine. Now give it to me."

She hesitated. Her mother had worked so hard for this find, putting her reputation on the line.

He pressed the cool barrel of the gun up under her chin. "Don't be stupid."

She held the shell out toward him. He snatched it from her, keeping the gun jammed under her chin. "That's my girl." He tucked the shell into his shirt pocket and buttoned the flap.

Fury balled in her chest, burning. After all she'd worked for the last three years, he thought he could just walk onto her dig site and take the spoils from her.

"Now comes the fun part." He lowered the gun, and then swung her around so her back was to him. The barrel jabbed into her upper spine. "Let's go see how your boyfriend is doing."

Quint! "What have you done, Jared?"

"You'll see soon enough." He shoved her forward, toward the Dawn Temple.

As they neared the temple steps, the bushes at the jungle's edge rustled. Rover waddled out into the morning light.

She stopped, not wanting the javelina to follow wherever Jared was leading her. But as soon as Rover saw her, he trotted over, rubbing his snout against her leg.

"Go away!" Jared kicked at the javelina, catching Rover with the toe of his boot.

Rover squealed, running a few feet away, then stopping.

"Leave him alone, Jared."

"I've had enough of that foul pig."

"He's a javelina."

"He's disgusting. Almost every time I sneaked into your tent, he was there to squeal on me."

That's how Jared had known about the shell. He'd been stealing into her tent all along, snooping through her stuff, the nosey bunghole. "So that's why you were there with Rover that one night when I came back from the shower." She glared at him. "You said you'd heard him squealing and rushed to his aid. But that wasn't it at all, was it? Rover had been protecting his territory, ratting you out."

At the sound of his name, the javelina came running back over to her.

"No, Rover. Get out of here." She nudged him away.

He brushed against her leg again, sticking close.

"Go!" She pushed him toward the jungle.

Rover turned and looked at her, tilting his head.

"Go home," she said, shooing him away with her hands.

"Stupid, disgusting pig," Jared said from behind her. She glared over at him and froze at the sight of him aiming his gun at the javelina.

"No!" She rammed into Jared as he squeezed off a shot. The explosion was deafening, then several loud squeals pierced the air.

She turned back to Rover. Fresh blood was splattered on the dry grass, but there was no javelina to be seen. The bushes at the jungle's edge shook in his wake.

Jared bellowed a victorious shout that ended in laughter.

Her eyes watered. Rage, fear, and hatred roiled in her throat.

"Oh, please," he said when he turned the barrel back on her. "Don't tell me you're going to cry over that vile pig."

"He's a fucking javelina, you prick." And the bastard was going to pay for shooting him. "You got the seashell, Jared," she spoke through clenched teeth. "What else do you want from me?"

He rubbed the barrel of the gun down the side of her face from temple to jaw, his eyes a bit too manic for comfort. "Nothing much, darling. Just your life."

* * *

Was that a gunshot?

As Quint rubbed the ropes faster against the jagged edge of the fallen block of ceiling, he could feel the binding loosening. Sweat soaked his shirt, dripping from everywhere.

If it were a gunshot, it had to have been close for him to hear it inside this limestone coffin. Fear for Angélica made him work harder on freeing his hands. He had to hurry up and get to her, help her.

The sound of someone coming down the passageway stopped him short. There was more than one person coming this time. He looked over at the entryway, his breath held.

Angélica stumbled through first, tripping over a small pile of rocks. Quint winced as he watched her fall to her knees on the floor.

She was alive! The relief flooding him was short-lived, slowed by the sight of her escort.

Steel! He was back.

Before Quint could get a word out, Steel grabbed Angélica by the hair and yanked her to her feet. Pulling a .38 Special out from behind him, he aimed it at Quint.

Oh, hell! What was he going to do with *that*?

Then realization struck him like a cannonball to the gut. Not only had Steel been responsible for Dr. Hughes' missing foot and Dr. Norah Ann Sutcliffe's so-called accident, but all of the injuries and sabotage here at the dig site over the last few weeks. He was their curse.

Damn. They had a killer on their hands, and unfortunately, Quint's were still tied.

"Hello, Parker." Steel's flashlight blinded him. "What a nasty scrape you have there. How's that lump on the back of your head?"

Quint squinted in the bright light. "I knew you'd surface again, Steel."

"Really?" Steel turned on a lantern that sat on the floor, setting his flashlight at his feet. "You think you have me all figured out, Mr. Detective? Did all of Mrs. Hughes' clippings and notes about me that you have tucked away in your tent spell it out for you?"

"No. Shit floats." Quint wondered how many times Steel had been in his tent searching through his things. It appeared somebody had been busy digging for his own treasures when everyone else had been working.

Steel smirked. "We'll see who's the funny man when I bury you two in here under tons of rock and skip on back to my alibi in Cancun."

"Jared," Angélica broke in, stepping in front of Quint. "This is between you and me. Leave Parker out of it."

Steel kept the gun held high. "Actually, darling, Parker and I have business of our own to attend to regarding our old friend, Dr. Hughes." He nodded his head toward the skeleton Quint had uncovered. "But I'll take care of you first, if you insist." He pointed the barrel at her. "Untie Parker's feet. I want him standing for this."

She knelt next to Quint's legs, her hands trembling as she tried to untie the knot. She looked up at him. He'd expected to see fear in her eyes; instead, fury burned there, blasting him back in surprise.

"I'm gonna fuck him up royally," she whispered.

Quint's chest tightened. Oh, no, what was she going to try in the sights of a loaded .38?

"What was that, darling?" Steel was squinting, practicing aiming the gun at arm's length, focusing on different parts of Angélica's body.

"She wondered why you killed Dr. Hughes," Quint lied, trying to distract Steel from pulling the trigger.

Steel closed one eye, targeting, then the other. "He got too nosey."

"Dr. Hughes knew about Norah, didn't he?"

"The old man got lucky."

Angélica freed Quint's ankles, tossing the rope aside. She stood a little stiffly, rubbing the side of her thigh as she rose. What had Steel done to her already? Kicked her? Went to town on her, too?

"Lucky, my ass," Quint said. "You were so eager to climb to the top back then that you got reckless. He saw that in you. That's why he never trusted you." That explained several decisions Dr. Hughes had made that last dig season, involving Quint oftentimes when protocol would have called for Steel.

Steel shrugged. "He's dead now, so his trust doesn't matter anymore." He pointed at Quint with the gun. "Darling, help Parker up. I have a feeling he's going to feel a little woozy when he's on his feet, so keep him standing."

She followed his order, her hands gentle on Quint while her glare sliced and diced her ex-husband.

A sharp pain pierced Quint's skull as soon as he was upright. A wave of nausea made him double over, while shooting stars filled his vision. He felt himself tipping. Angélica wrapped her arms around him, holding him upright. After several seconds his head cleared. The nausea ebbed and the pain between his eyes waned to a dull throb. He pulled out of her grip, waving off her look of concern.

She touched the back of his neck, the sticky part. Her fingers were dark red when she pulled them away. "What did you do to him, Jared?"

"You should be more concerned about what I'm going to do to you." Steel held the gun pointed toward her forehead.

They needed that .38! "Why did you kill Norah?"

Steel's focus shifted back to Quint. "For a man who should be enjoying his last few breaths in the present, you sure seem obsessed with the past."

"Did Norah know about Roy Bumm?" he asked, trying to keep the self-important jerk talking, not shooting.

The gun lowered slightly. "Ah, so you found out about Roy Bumm. I'm surprised you're clever enough to put that together."

"That wasn't it." Angélica's voice overflowed with loathing. "Knowing you, Jared, Dr. Sutcliffe had something you wanted. A certain theory, I'm betting, that would secure you a master's degree."

"Now, darling, remember your place."

Quint inched toward Angélica, who looked ready to pounce. That's when he noticed the camp knife she had partially tucked behind her, hidden from Steel's sight.

Oh, hell. She knew better than to bring a knife to a gunfight.

"Of course, it all makes sense now," she said. "You seduced her into sharing her theory with you, and then you killed her."

Quint frowned, sidetracked. "Really?"

She nodded. "Ask Jared to explain to you the relationship between the *tzolkin* and *haab* calendar cycles?" She sneered at Steel. "Better yet, have him tell you the date in our calendar system that is equivalent to 12 *Baktun*, 19 *Katun*, 2 *Tun*, 13 *Uinal*, and 19 *Kin*."

Where was she going with this? Quint turned to Steel, wondering if he were going to bite.

"Oh, that's right," Angélica taunted. "You don't know the answer to either one, do you?" Her scoff echoed off the walls. "I never understood how you could've written such a highly praised paper on the Maya calendar cycles in relation to the Long Count calendar system without even knowing how to read the representational glyphs—until now."

Steel's face contorted in fury. "You think you're so smart, don't you? Speaking and writing in Mayan, reading glyphs as if they're comic books."

"It's called education, you village idiot. You should try it sometime."

The .38 Special was back, leveled on Angélica's face.

"Norah got what was coming to her. Like you, she thought she was smarter than me." Looking mad as a hatter, Steel's smile returned, too. "Like her, you're going to pay for that mistake."

Out of the corner of his eye, Quint saw her shift her grip on the knife, getting it prepped to throw.

"You don't know what you're doing with those shells, Jared." She angled her body ever so slightly, her focus solely on her ex, holding him in place. "You need me to explain and write the papers, or you'll look like a fool."

"I'll use your mother's notes. She was always very thorough in her reports." Steel raised an eyebrow. "Any last words, darling?"

"Yeah, I have it here in my pants." She shoved her left hand into her pocket. When she pulled it back out, her middle finger stood solo. "Here," she held it out to him like a gift, "take this and go fuck yourself!"

Everything shifted into fast motion.

Quint saw Steel's eyes narrow in preparation for the gunshot.

On instinct, he dodged in front of Angélica, almost getting sliced by the knife whizzing past him.

He saw the knife make purchase in Steel's ribs right as he squeezed the trigger. The gunshot exploded in the small chamber, deafening.

Quint's left shoulder kicked back. Pain rocketed through his chest and arm, knocking him to his knees.

"No!" Angélica reached for him.

Another shot rang out.

Quint's thigh bucked. A flash of pain jammed into it like a red hot poker. Then his leg gave out and he collapsed, landing on his throbbing left shoulder.

Agony clouded his vision. He rolled onto his stomach. The floor felt so warm against his cheek.

Angélica's boot came into his line of sight.

His vision narrowed, a dark vignette edging the scene in

front of him, swelling inward.

Angélica's voice echoed as she called his name.

Before he could answer, the world faded away, taking the pain with it.

* * *

Jared clutched his side, the knife handle sticking out below his rib. He still held the gun on Quint, who lay on the floor, blood from his wounds soaking through his shirt and pants.

"You fucking prick!" Angélica glared up at him from where she crouched next to Quint.

"I wanted to do that so badly twenty years ago. It was worth the wait." He turned the gun on her. "And then there was one. What do you think? Red roses at your memorial service?" He yanked the knife out of his side, his face scrunching in pain for a moment.

Counting on Jared's weakness for blood to work in her favor, she rubbed her palm over Quint's blood. "Look, Jared." She held her hand out toward him. "Look at the wet, sticky blood."

He turned his head away, squinting at her through the corners of his eyes. "I'd rather not." He flexed his finger over the trigger. "Say goodbye to your photojournalist, darling."

A streak of movement came from the outer passageway, darting across the floor toward Jared. It took a split second for her mind to make sense of it.

Rover? Blood from his half shot off ear covered part of his head and neck. The javelina bit down hard on the back of Jared's lower leg.

Her ex-husband screeched in pain.

A gunshot boomed. The bullet whistled past her ear, ricocheting off the stone wall into the partially cut away support beam that spanned the ceiling.

Howling still, Jared fell to his knees trying to kick Rover away, but the javelina held on, jaws locked.

The howl turned into a roar. Jared turned trying to aim at his attacker. Before he could pull the trigger again, Angélica tackled him and sent him tumbling back into a pile of rocks.

His gun clattered onto the stone floor. She lunged for it, grabbing the grip. Jared latched onto it, too, his hand covering hers. He swung at her with his free hand, catching a fistful of hair and yanking it hard. She kicked him in the jaw, sending him reeling to the side. He pulled her with him as he fell, falling on top of her.

Jared tried to take the gun from her, but she managed to get her finger on the trigger. He tugged at it and she squeezed.

Another shot rang out.

The bullet hit the ceiling, ricocheting down into the pile of rocks to his left.

Jared squeezed her gun wrist. She turned her head and sank her teeth into his hand that still clutched her hair, feeling tendons crunch between her jaws.

His scream of pain was guttural. He fell back, holding his hand to his chest. "You bitch!"

She scrambled to her feet, clutching the gun tightly. "I may be a bitch." She wiped her mouth with the back of her hand, spitting his blood on the floor next to him. "But I'm a bitch with a gun. Now stand up, you worthless piece of shit."

"Angélica, darling." He held out his good hand as he rose. "You don't want to kill me. It will ruin your career, and taint your family's reputation in the archaeological field."

"You've stolen your last theory, Jared. I'm going to make sure the world knows what you've done."

His face contorted into a rage-filled mask. "I should have killed you while you were sleeping."

"That was your first mistake. Your second was hurting my father."

Jared flew toward her, but she was ready. She squeezed the trigger again while stepping out of his path. The bullet ripped into his hip. As he spun around from the force, her boot heel came down on a loose rock. Her ankle turned, and she fell hard onto her ass next to him.

A loud crack splintered through the chamber, followed by a high-pitched creaking sound. Small stones and dust rained down on the floor around them.

She looked up.

The support beam above her rumbled and dropped several inches, then sagged, creaking under the weight of the ceiling.

A scream crawled up her throat.

Groaning, Jared latched onto her boot.

She kicked free and struggled to her feet.

Jared lay on his stomach, blood spreading on the floor beneath his right hip.

Another resounding crack came from the beam above. She cringed as a shower of pebbles fell around her. The lantern lit the cloud of dust, giving the chamber an eerie glow.

She set the handgun on the floor next to Quint and crouched next to him. The rope binding his wrists was almost shredded clear through. It was loose enough to work over his wrists.

"Quint," she called, gently rolling him onto his back. She searched for a pulse in his neck. A steady beat thumped under her fingers.

A series of creaaaaks and snaps came from overhead, and then the beam above gave another inch.

God! She needed to get Quint out of there before the ceiling crashed down on both of them, but moving him would increase the bleeding. The wheelbarrow was out in the passageway. She couldn't risk going for it with the ceiling about to give.

Rover stood in the entryway, skittish as the pebbles fell around them. He snorted and backed out of the room.

Mindful of the bullet wound in Quint's shoulder, she lifted him under the arms and pulled. Her lower back strained as she lugged him across the floor.

When she neared Jared, she hesitated. She needed that

shell. Without warning, three huge stones crashed to the floor around her, one narrowly missing Quint's leg. She yelped in surprise.

Fuck the shell. She needed Quint more.

Angélica dragged him as fast as she could toward the outer passageway. Just as she reached the threshold, one of the ceiling beams crashed to the floor.

With a cry, she heaved them both into the passageway, falling back, dragging Quint on top of her.

Another low moan from the remaining support beam echoed out and down through the temple.

Silence followed, as thick as the dust in the air.

She had to get Quint all of the way out. The structural shift from the chamber collapsing could bring the passageway they were in down around them, too. Scooting out from under him, she scrambled to her feet.

Where was that wheelbarrow?

There!

She managed to load Quint into it with a lot of sweat and grunts.

As she gripped the handles, she saw a light beam moving around in the dust-filled chamber. She hesitated, her heart pounding.

Oh no. In her haste to get Quint out, she'd forgotten the gun in there with Jared.

"Angélica," her ex-husband called, his voice weak. "Don't leave me here to die."

She coughed, her throat burning. Should she try rescuing him? Could she make it in and drag him out, too, before the other beam gave way?

"I can hear you breathing out there, darling."

Was saving him worth risking her life?

She thought of the people he'd hurt, the sadness he'd caused for so many.

She cleared her throat. "I've been thinking about you and me getting back together, Jared, and I just don't think it's gonna work out."

A staccato of loud cracks reverberated from the chamber, the final timber yielding.

She stepped back, shielding Quint with her body.

"Angélica!" Jared screamed, his voice ugly with hatred and fear.

The final beam succumbed to the weight of the ceiling. A rumbling crash followed, spewing billows of dust out into the passageway.

She coughed several times, pulling her shirt up over her nose and mouth.

"*Adios*, you murdering bastard."

Grabbing the wheelbarrow handles, she rolled Quint toward the sunlight.

* * *

"Damn it, Parker. Open your eyes." Angélica's voice reached through the darkness.

Quint obeyed, blinking his way into the light. When he tried to sit up, the pain almost sucked him back down into the dark.

Angélica eased him flat again and leaned over him, the morning sunlight streaming all around her. "I didn't tell you to sit up." Dust smudged her face in between the lines of worry. "You've been shot twice; you need to hold still while I try to fix you."

Did she say *twice*? He remembered the stinging pain in his leg. That must have been the second bullet.

"Where's Steel?" As soon as he could stand, Quint wanted to beat the hell out of that dickless wonder for using him as target practice.

"He's dead." She spoke like a robot while she inspected his wounds. "The ceiling caved in on him before I could get him out."

He caught her wrist with his good arm. "Are you okay?"

"I'll let you know after I finish tending to you."

She gently tucked his hand beside him and then pulled his shirt away from his shoulder wound. Sticking her fingers in the cotton's blood-covered bullet hole, she ripped the shirt apart.

"I've always wanted a woman to tear my clothes off."

"Next time I'll use my teeth," she shot back, her lips turning downward as she focused on his injury.

When she lifted him enough to get a look at the back of his shoulder, a stab of pain lanced through it. He stiffened, lock-jawed until it subsided. She ran her hand over his skin, her touch feather-light.

"Fuck." She sat back on her heels, wiping away the sweat from her forehead with her arm. Her hands were trembling, smeared with his blood. "The bullet is lodged in your shoulder."

"It's a one-of-a-kind souvenir," he tried to joke. "You think I'll have any trouble getting through customs?"

She didn't laugh.

Moving down to his thigh, she carefully pulled his pant leg away from his wound.

"Angélica."

She shook her head, sniffing. "This one went clear through. I think it's too far to the side to have hit the femoral artery, but you're still losing a lot of blood."

"Boss lady," he tried again to get her attention.

She moved back up to his shoulder. "Maybe if I ..." She reached toward his wound.

"Don't touch it."

She froze, hands in mid-air, and finally looked into his eyes. "But I could—"

"No." With his right hand, he touched her cheek. "You're going to have to go get help."

"I can't leave you here like this."

She needed to work on her bedside manner. The way she kept wringing the front of her T-shirt wasn't helping him feel all sunshine and lollipops.

"You're not dragging me down those steps."

Rover waddled up, gently nudging Quint's non-injured shoulder, dropping onto his side next to him. He huffed in the morning heat.

"Look, Rover's here to keep me company while you're gone." Quint noticed the blood darkening his fur. "What happened to him?"

"Jared shot him." She wiped her hands off on her thighs. "Going to get help for you means running to the village and back since Teodoro took his bike with him. That will take an hour or two. It's too long. There must be some other way."

"We're out here in the boonies. It's the only way."

Her eyes filled with tears. "You don't understand, Quint. You're losing too much blood. I don't know if you'll last another hour, let alone the additional time it will take to get you to a hospital. We went through this with my mom and it didn't end well. There has to be another way!"

Short of teleportation, he was up shit creek and they both knew it. But he'd be damned if he'd take his last breath while watching her cry. He searched for something to lighten the moment.

"Never in my wildest dreams did I figure I'd go out while lying on the steps of a Maya temple with a javelina at my side."

"I won't let you die, damn it."

He wiped a tear off her cheek. "Boss lady, I know you're in charge of this site, but I don't think you have jurisdiction over me on that level."

"Shut up, Parker. I need to think of a way to save your ass."

"I hate this goddamned jungle."

"You've mentioned that before." She looked down the steps. "Maybe if I got the stretcher up here."

"I didn't like your ex-husband from the start."

"No shit." She chewed on her knuckles. "Teodoro may have left behind something that would slow the bleeding long enough to—"

"Your father wants you to have kids."

"Yeah, I know." She raked her fingers through her hair. "But how will I get you down the steps without—"

"He told me I need to hurry up and get you pregnant before he gets old."

"He what?" She gaped down at him.

Without thinking, he reached toward her with his left arm. A fresh flare of pain burned clear through his left shoulder. He clamped his teeth together and held his breath as he waited for it to pass.

Angélica gripped his hand. "Parker?"

A sudden chill spread through his body. He shivered and blinked several times, trying to clear away the dark fog that fringed his vision.

She brushed the hair off his forehead. "Breathe, Quint. Breathe through it."

The clouds above him spun. The pain burrowed deeper in his shoulder. He groaned. Cold sweat covered his skin. He was vaguely aware of Angélica leaning over him.

"Listen to me, Quint. Let's make a deal." She cupped his cheeks. "You keep breathing, and I'll do whatever you want when it comes to you and me—sex in the shower, a long-distance relationship, you name it. Just don't give up."

He frowned at her, gasping for breath as the pain refused to ease. "You picked a hell of a time," he rasped, "to take me off the 'temporary' list."

Her lips moved, but a loud ringing filled his ears, drowning out whatever she was saying. He squeezed his eyes shut, trying to focus on his breathing. The throbbing in his shoulder pounded harder. A wave of heat crashed over his body, feeling like someone had thrown gas on him and lit him on fire. Above the shrill clanging in his head, he heard a bass-like thumping noise growing steadily louder.

He struggled to open his eyes and sit up, but a fresh knock-out punch of pain put him down for the count.

Everything stopped.

Chapter Twenty-Five
Cuxta: To live; life.

Three weeks later …

Angélica lay back on her towel on the warm sand, staring up at the bright full moon, listening to the waves tumbling onto the shore. A cool, Caribbean breeze brushed across her face. She closed her eyes, breathing deeply as the sound of her father's laughter echoed down from her beach house.

Damn. She'd come so close to losing everything.

"Is anybody sitting here?" Quint asked from above her.

She opened her eyes. He stood over her, gripping two Coronas in his right hand. "If one of those is for me," she sat upright, "then you are."

"A moonlit beach, a sexy siren, and a cold beer. Shit, I must be dreaming." He held the bottles out toward her. "Can you hold these for a second while I make my way down there?"

She stuck them in the sand and rose to her knees to help him, careful not to bump the sling cradling his left arm and shoulder as she helped him down onto the sand beside her. He grunted as he straightened his bare, long legs out in front of him. The white bandage wrapped around his thigh glowed against his tanned skin in the moonlight.

"You okay?" She handed him his beer, purposely brushing her fingers over the back of his hand before pulling away.

He chuckled, the shadows making him look even more rugged. "Now I am."

"Did you get bored with Dad and Pedro's anecdotes?"

"Actually, your father told me to get my ass down here so that he could talk about us behind our backs."

She snorted, watching the white caps roll in. "Why am I not surprised?" She hated to ruin the lighthearted banter they'd shared all evening, but there was something bugging her. "Did you talk to your editor?"

"She gave me another month, but only if I include an additional article on what happened to Dr. Hughes."

Tipping the beer bottle to her lips, Angélica weighed his words, considering what effect that story could have on the dig site's future.

"I told her I'd have to talk to the head archaeologist first," Quint said. "That I'd write it only if I had her approval."

She turned to find him watching her, half of his face shaded.

"If you don't want me to write it, I won't."

She scooted close to him so her shoulder touched his. "Thank you for that." She took another sip, savoring it along with the happiness swirling inside of her at his honesty. "But I think the publicity could benefit the site. Hell, maybe it will even help to guarantee it a place in the history books, along with my mom's name."

"I'll let you read what I write before sending it out."

"No need." She looked out at the surf. "I trust you."

He was silent for several heartbeats. Then she felt his lips feather across her cheekbone, hovering near her ear. Tingles of electricity spread from her neck south. "Thanks, boss lady."

She couldn't keep from smiling, knowing she'd be feeling those lips all over her skin later when they were alone in her bed once again.

"How was your crew last week?" Quint asked.

"Happy." She pulled her knees to her chest and wrapped her arms around them. "They worked hard to help close up shop for the rainy season. I couldn't have done it without them." She rested her chin on her kneecaps. "Esteban wanted me to tell you how much he appreciates the jade Quetzalcoatl statue. He carries it in his front pocket inside his sandwich bag along with his rosary beads."

"The guy I bought it from swears it's supposed to bring good luck to its owner." He bounced his bottle off his thigh below the wrap. "Does Esteban still believe in the curse?"

"Only after the sun goes down. He shared a tent with Fernando all week, much to Fernando's chagrin."

"What about you?"

She glanced at him. "What about me?"

"Do you still think the curse was a bunch of hogwash?"

She thought about the so-called curse glyph, repeating it aloud, "*Yum Cimil, the Lord of Death, rode in on the wind with a traveler.*" That big windstorm had hit right before Quint had showed up, and Jared had been right on his heels. Quint was a traveler; Jared was a murderer, a Lord of Death by some accounts.

No, it couldn't be ... or could it?

The skeptic in her kept shaking her head.

Yet here she sat with the traveler, worrying about when the wind would take him away and where it would blow him next.

"Beware the evil wind," Quint said, with a crackly Vincent Price laugh.

"You know what, Parker?" She drew a heart in the sand, punching an arrow through it. "Between you and me, when I think back to all that happened over the last month, I believe I've changed my mind. It was a curse."

He chuckled. "I must be drunk on moonlight. Did you just say you believe the curse was real?"

"I did and I do. Dad was right, but don't tell him I said that or I'll poke you in your sore shoulder."

"What changed your mind?"

"Look what the wind blew in."

He cocked his head to the side. "Come again?"

"You. The wind blew you in. You're the traveler."

"So, I'm the one who brought the Lord of Death?"

"In a way, sure. Jared upped his game after you arrived, doing everything he could to get rid of you."

"Including filling me with bullet holes."

"It was only two, you big baby."

"And giving me a concussion."

"Only a mild one. The doctor said you have an *amazingly* thick skull."

"All the better to protect my big brain," he joked.

"I would have chosen a totally different adjective than *amazingly*." She dodged his pinches, laughing.

When she stilled, he scooped up a handful of sand and let it slip through his fingers. "Speaking of the Lord of Death, did you find the other shell?"

"The *federales* gave it to me after I identified Jared's body." An echo of Jared's final scream played through her head, spurring a grimace. It had haunted her nightmares off and on for the last three weeks. She kept waiting for the memory to fade. Maybe with more time, more memory building with Quint.

"Thanks again for saving my life, Angélica."

"I told you before; you should thank Dad, not me. He's the one who sent Pedro back to the site with the helicopter. Jared should've been more careful when he attacked him. He shouldn't have let Dad see him first." She leaned into his warmth, the smell of his cologne made her heady. "All I can figure out is that Jared hadn't planned on you coming up the passageway so quickly to see what was going on." She rested her head on his shoulder. "He probably would've killed Dad if you hadn't showed up. Murdered him just like Dr. Hughes and in the same temple, too."

Quint twirled a tendril of her hair around his finger. "Your father told me that he'd been watching your ex for several days prior to the attack, but he hadn't been able to pinpoint what it was about Steel that had him sniffing the air."

"I keep thinking about Dr. Hughes. All of this time, he was right under my nose."

"That explains why Steel kept such a close eye on your progress, making sure he was placed in charge of Juan's funding." Quint's fingers trailed down over her shoulder, his touch mesmerizing her.

She put her bottle down on the ground, fighting the urge to tackle Quint and take advantage of him right there on the beach.

"The *federales* found a camp in the jungle about a half-mile from the site." Her voice sounded huskier than usual to her. "There was an airline ticket dated three weeks prior to the morning we saw him arrive during breakfast. He must have been spying on us during that time and overheard the men talking about the curse. That was all he needed to work on getting rid of my crew." She sighed in disgust. "And I was too naïve to think he had anything to do with what was happening."

"Why should you have suspected him? You'd been married to him and not witnessed anything odd."

"I knew he was an asshole."

Quint chuckled, lying back. He wadded up her beach sarong and used it for a pillow. "I think that was included on Steel's birth certificate."

"You mean Roy Bumm's birth certificate." She turned onto her side and lay next to him, settling partway onto his chest. Careful of his thigh wound, she draped one leg over his, wanting more skin on skin contact, and began unbuttoning his shirt. "I still can't believe I was married to a man who wasn't who he said he was."

"You were married to a psychopath, Angélica. You're lucky to still be alive." Quint glanced down at her fingers. "I keep thinking about how Mrs. Hughes had figured out Steel was Roy Bumm. Too bad she didn't get the proof she needed before she died."

"What kind of a teenager kills his best friend and steals his identity?" She finished unbuttoning his shirt, loving the feel of his chest and stomach under her palm. "That's just twisted."

"It gets worse. When I called Jeff this afternoon, he told me that Steel's—I mean Roy Bumm's—parents were killed when Roy was twelve. Their house caught fire while they were asleep. The police report says he was running around the front yard in his underwear screaming obscenities at the burning house when the cops arrived at the scene, laughing uncontrollably in between calling his father all kinds of names."

She frowned, stunned. "He told me his parents died in a yachting accident."

"He lived a life of lies."

"You think he killed his own parents?"

"I don't know." He stroked her cheek, his touch more of a caress. "I'm just glad he didn't hurt you."

"You weren't supposed to jump in front of me like that. If that bullet had gone a few inches lower …" She shuddered.

"It didn't."

She crawled on top of him, mindful of his injuries. The heat of his skin soaked through her tankini top. "I didn't want you to risk your life for me."

"I couldn't help myself."

"Because you rescue damsels in distress."

"Because you'd lured me in, siren." He cupped the back of her head, pulling her down to his mouth. His kiss was soft, tender. "I'd crash into the rocks anytime for you."

She moved against him, luring him again. "I missed you last week, Parker. So did Rover."

"How's his ear?"

"It's fine. He's a hero now, you know. Everyone gave him a lot of extra attention for helping save the day. He probably put on five pounds thanks to all of the handouts the guys gave him, not to mention the extra veggie-filled *panuchos* and *gordas* María kept making for her 'favorite *jabalí*.'"

"Are you going to bring him here during the off season?"

"I haven't decided. I want to see if he can be de-scented and neutered. Some locals keep javelinas as pets according to Teodoro." She trailed kisses down Quint's neck, tasting the salt from the ocean air on his skin. "For now, Teodoro is going to keep him at the site. He says he's going to train him to be a 'watch-dog' so he can help guard against any looters."

"I miss that little javelina."

"We can go visit him whenever you're down here." She hesitated, her breath bouncing off his skin. "Unless you've changed your mind about our deal."

He said nothing.

She swallowed the nervous flutter in her throat. "Pedro said he'd take you anywhere anytime, that he owes you for all you've done for Dad and me." She was babbling and she knew it, afraid of what his silence about their deal meant. "We're kind of Pedro's family, you know. I mean, he has a mom, but he spends most of his time with us."

"Angélica." He towed her up so they were eye to eye. "I'm not temporary."

"You say that, but you're going to leave someday soon."

"Just for a week or so at a time."

"You hate it down here, remember?"

His good hand trailed down over her backside, squeezing through her swim shorts. "But I like it right here with you."

She took a deep breath and gave him the news she'd learned earlier today. "I've been asked to take a new position down here. I can continue to work my dig site part of the time. The rest of the year, I'd divide my time between other sites, helping to prep them for the public."

"Did you take it?"

"Not yet."

"Why not?"

"You hate the jungle."

His eyelids lowered. She felt his sigh under her as much as heard it. "Leave my dislike for jungle living out of this."

"There's more. When I told them I need to think about taking the position, they upped the ante."

He waited, his face unreadable in the moonlight.

"They told me I could have Dad join me at any of the sites, working with me. They think a father-daughter archaeology team will be a great marketing tool to draw in more tourists."

"You need to take the job, Angélica."

"But we'd be spending more time in the jungle."

"With all of those snakes and bugs," he said, tracing her face, circling around her mouth.

"And the heat."

"Hmmm." His hand traveled south, down along her ribs, his fingers finding her curves. "Do you promise to share your tent with me whenever I'm down here with you?"

"Of course, but I'm a little messy."

"I'll hire a tent maid." His hand slipped inside her swim shorts, spanning her bare hip. "And share your bed?"

She moved against him, reveling in his body's quick response. "I wouldn't want you anywhere else, Parker." She kissed him to show how much she meant that.

"You need to take that new position, Angélica."

"You're sure?"

"I'll start buying bug repellent by the case."

Oh, hell. She could feel herself falling for him, her heart rolling around in a field of flowers, chasing after the butterflies in her stomach. What if he grew tired of the jungle ... no, she had to stop letting worry block out the sun.

She nuzzled his Adam's apple. "I thought maybe you could stay down here more often, writing articles about the different sites where we're working. I could help you translate them into Spanish to reach a wider market."

"I like that idea. That reminds me," he adjusted so she could press closer. "What was the thing you rattled off in the Dawn Temple about calendar cycles when your ex was about to shoot you?"

She thought back for a moment. "You mean 12 *Baktun*, 19 *Katun*, 2 *Tun*, 13 *Uinal*, and 19 *Kin*?"

"Yeah."

"It's the Maya Long Count calendar date for the day he and I got married."

"You're such a clever girl." He tugged one of her tankini straps down, giving him more access.

It wasn't enough. She shrugged off the other strap, shoving her top down to her midriff, and then settled back down on him. Skin on skin. That was much better.

"Angélica," he said in a low, velvety tone.

"Hmm?"

"Have I told you it turns me on when you speak Mayan?"

Her smile was set on high beam. "You said it several times last night when I was having my wicked way with you, telling you in Mayan what all I wanted to do to you."

"Mmmm, you were very wicked with that sassy mouth of yours." He kissed said sassy part, making her body hum.

"Parker?"

"Yes, boss lady?"

"How do you feel about sex on the beach?"

"I'm going to need you to help get these shorts off."

She unbuttoned them.

"Angélica!" She froze at the sound of her father's voice.

Quint covered her lips. "She's a little busy," he called back.

"Right. I'm sure she's in the middle of showing you something again."

Oh, dear Lord. Angélica shook her head in resignation.

"When she gets done whispering in your mouth," Juan

continued, "can you tell her that I used the water in her fish tank to put out the fire Pedro started in the kitchen, and now I can find only one of her goldfish."

Quint hesitated, staring up at her with his mouth half open. "Is he serious?"

She giggled as the screen door slammed shut. "Welcome to the family." She kissed him hard and blistering, the way that always made him groan and get all handy with her. "I really like those goldfish," she unzipped his fly, "so hurry up and finish what you started."

He did.

And then some.

El Fin … for now

For a chance to win a fun prize in a weekly drawing, head over to my website and show me your amateur sleuth skills at *Angélica's Dig Site Challenge*.

Here is the password and link to the Challenge page:
Password: Rover
Link: http://www.anncharles.com/?page_id=1785

Five Questions and Answers from Ann

Is it correct to say "Maya" or "Mayan"?
Because this question was asked in the feedback from my awesome crew of beta readers, I am addressing it here at the end of the book as well as the beginning.

There are various schools of thought on this. I chose to follow this one: The adjective "Mayan" is used in reference to the language or languages; "Maya" is used as a noun or adjective when referring to people, places, culture, etc., whether singular or plural.

(Source: http://archaeology.about.com/od/mameterms/a/Maya-or-Mayan.htm)

What's a javelina (aka Peccary)?
A javelina (pronounced *hah-vuh-lee-nuh*) or peccary (***pek***-*uh-ree*) is a medium-sized animal that strongly resembles a pig. While it has a snout and eyes that are small relative to its head, its stomach is more complex than a pig's. Javelinas are omnivores. They will eat small animals but prefer roots, grasses, seeds, fruit, and cacti—particularly prickly pear. They have scent glands that make them smell a little like skunks, which is why they are sometimes called "skunk-pigs."

(Source: http://en.wikipedia.org/wiki/Peccary; http://library.sandiegozoo.org/factsheets/chacoan_peccary/peccary.htm)

If you want to see some cute baby javelina pictures to have a better idea what Rover looks like, search for "baby javelina" on the internet and check out the images.

What's a *cenote*?

A *cenote* (pronounced *suh-**noh**-tee*) is a natural pit or sinkhole resulting from the collapse of limestone bedrock that exposes groundwater underneath. Especially associated with the Yucatán Peninsula of Mexico, *cenotes* were sometimes used by the ancient Maya for sacrificial offerings. *Cenote* water is often very clear, as the water comes from rain water filtering slowly through the ground.

(Source: http://en.wikipedia.org/wiki/Cenote)

Is the dig site in this story a real place?

Angélica's dig site and the temples on it are all fictional products of my imagination. I did a lot of reading and studying of actual Maya dig sites on the Yucatán Peninsula, including Chichen Itza, Tulum, and Coba, especially those in the Mexican states of Quintana Roo and Yucatán. Here is a website with some great pictures of the temples and a map showing several of the Maya sites:

http://mexpeditions.travel/archaeology-maya-world.html

What characters in this book have had cameos in my other stories?

Quint Parker—Quint is the older brother of Violet Parker (the heroine in the Deadwood Mystery Series). He is mentioned off and on in different books in that series, and he made an appearance in *Deadwood Shorts: Boot Points*.

Dr. Juan García—Juan is the head archaeologist who is working on the dig site in one of Ruby Martino-Ford's mines in *The Great Jackalope Stampede* (the third book in the Jackrabbit Junction Mystery Series).

Angélica García—Angélica is briefly talked about by Juan in *The Great Jackalope Stampede*. She acts as a source of information for him.

Connect with Me Online

Facebook (Personal Page):
http://www.facebook.com/ann.charles.author

Facebook (Author Page):
http://www.facebook.com/pages/Ann-
Charles/37302789804?ref=share

Twitter (as Ann W. Charles):
http://twitter.com/AnnWCharles

Ann Charles Website: http://www.anncharles.com

About the Author

Ann Charles is an award-winning author who writes mysteries that are splashed with humor and romance and whatever else she feels like throwing into the mix. When she is not dabbling in fiction, arm-wrestling with her children, attempting to seduce her husband, or arguing with her sassy cat, she is daydreaming of lounging poolside at a fancy resort with a blended margarita in one hand and a great book in the other.